ONLY US

Panther took Shanndel into a grove of cottonwood trees where there was a private glen beside a slowly flowing stream. Gently he placed her on the ground where the grass was thick and soft, and wildflowers grew thick.

"I want you now," Panther said huskily, his hand trembling as he slowly traced her facial features with a forefinger. "Say you want me. Say you love me."

Trembling, caught by a sudden, sweet desire, Shanndel looked into his smoldering dark eyes. "I want you desperately," she whispered, her heart thudding so hard she was breathless.

He reached for one of her hands. He drew her fingers to his lips and kissed them lightly, his tongue flicking.

"There is only now," Panther said huskily. "There is only us."

"Yes, yes—"

Savage Joy

Cassie Edwards

LEISURE BOOKS   NEW YORK CITY

A LEISURE BOOK®

February 1999

Published by
Dorchester Publishing Co., Inc.
276 Fifth Avenue
New York, NY 10001

ISBN 0-8439-4480-3

A very special dedication for *Savage Joy* goes to my Leisure editor, Alicia Condon, a sweet person who cares for her authors, who is *always* there for advice, guidance, and friendship. Alicia's sweet, soft laughter is so welcome on a day that might otherwise be frenzied with work!

Alicia, you are truly, deeply appreciated!

Always,
Cassie Edwards

Savage Joy is, in part, dedicated to the following people: Charles Roy and Nancy Christner; Ray and Myra Boles; Bill and Mary Kent; Betty Jarrell, Viola Fink, Fern Furry, Betty Barger, Mollijean (Brinkley) Frazier, Ben J. Brinkley, Bill and Grady Ewell, Nadine (Seibert) Wintizer and Jim, and my dear parents Virgil and Mary Kathryn Cline.

Also, in memory of Virginia Griffith.

Also, *Savage Joy* is dedicated to the following Harrisburg, Illinois, childhood friends: Eugenia Gollier, Dorothy Stilley, Jean Keltner, Sally Russler, Myra Burnam, Joyce Dunn, Nancy Fulkerson, Janeen Jones, Shirley Josey, June Partain, Carol Richmond, Marjorie Zimmer, Carolyn Wilson, Martha Armistead, Betty Butner (and Eddie), and Regina McCormick.

Love,
Cassie Edwards

SPIRITUAL LOVE

I feel as though we met before,
Seeking to know you more and more.
I open my heart and soul to you,
As if it is something I always do.
You teach me things I long to know,
I can feel your spirit embrace my soul.
I don't know you, you don't know me,
Yet we're drawn together so willfully.
Is there something hidden in the past,
That makes this love of ours grow fast?
Two different worlds from which we come,
Yet sharing our heart as if we are one.
My life has changed since we first met,
A love that I could never forget.
Across the miles a distance away,
I'm thinking of you throughout the day.
Then as nightfall darkens the sky,
My spirit will begin to fly.
Sending you a tender kiss,
To let you know how much you're missed.
I love you, my friend, for who you are,
As if you really aren't so far.
I hope our love will always be,
Just enough for you and me.
And as the path of life unfolds,
Your spirit warms away the cold.
You light a fire deep in me,
As if it is our destiny.
You are so thoughtful in all you do,
It's no wonder that I'm falling for you.
Your loving ways, they touch me, too,
Being with you I'd never be blue.
So, my friend, this poem's for you,
For I will forever be thinking of you.

By
Jacqueline Lee Holst
Poet and friend

Savage Joy

Chapter One

Upper New York State
April, the Rain Moon—1847

Light rain had fallen during the night, and the morning
air was sweet and fresh and redolent of rich, moist earth
and the fragrance of new spring growth. Wide, expan-
sive meadows with long, waving grass were jeweled
with myriad wildflowers. Here and there stood little
copses and clusters of plum trees, gooseberries, and
wild currants, which in a few months would be loaded
down with fruit. In the distance *poi-ithakis*, passenger
pigeons, flew in a vast, undulating flock, dipping and
rising as they traveled north from their winter's migra-
tion.

   Among the widely separated oaks and elms and hickories stood two braves of ten winters. They were of the

Kispokotha, the Shawnee, and they were hunting small forest creatures with their newly crafted bows and arrows. An unseen squirrel overhead suddenly barked angrily, startling the two small braves.

When they looked upward and saw the cause of the squirrel's outburst, they smiled and admiringly watched a pair of red-tailed hawks soaring overhead in the sky like beautiful, moving clouds.

Knowing they were always under the protection of *Moneto*, the Supreme Being of all things who ruled the *Yalakuquaku-migigi*, the universe, they walked onward. The fear that had come with being startled was gone as quickly as it had come.

Panther, the son of the powerful Shawnee chief Red Thunder, was the first to break the silence. He held his bow at his side and smiled over at Cloud, his best friend from the time they could talk and laugh together.

"This one is yours," he whispered as the bushy-tailed squirrel hopped to the ground only a few feet from them. "My friend, you will have the first kill of the day."

Cloud didn't have time to notch his arrow onto his bowstring before the squirrel scampered away into the thicket. "My first kill today will have to be some other small creature, Panther, for this squirrel is more cunning than both of us." He laughed softly and slid his arrow back into the otter-skin quiver at his back. "It seems the squirrel is acquainted with the weapons of the Shawnee, for when it saw my arrow drawn from my quiver it fled."

Panther shrugged. "There will be more," he said, walking onward with Cloud at his side. "We have just

14

begun our hunt today. The sun has many hours left in the sky.

"It is my deep desire to grow into a man quickly so that I can join the true hunt with the warriors of our village and bring home not only the meat of small creatures and fleet-footed deer, but also pelts from the most powerful and feared animal of the forest, the bear," Panther then said, recalling his father's tale of how he had battled a bear with no weapon but a knife and had come from the battle the winner.

Even today Panther's father wore the proof of that victorious battle, a prized necklace of down-curved bear claws, separated by silver cylinders, hung around his neck.

It made Panther smile to recall himself as a child, clinging to his father's powerful neck as his father strove to implant the proud history of the Shawnee tribe in the mind of his son. Ah, how Panther had enjoyed running his tiny fingers over the smooth finish of the bear claws of his father's necklace as he talked to him. It was then that Panther had dreamed of wearing the same sort of necklace around his own neck when he was a grown man who could hunt as well as any of the other warriors. A man who could boast of such a bear kill and wear the prize around his neck was a man both feared and respected by his peers.

But for now it was enough for Panther to wear about his neck his medicine bag, or *mystery*. The *mystery bag*, made of otter skin and ornamented with ermine, was the key to all Shawnee life and character. Inside Panther's bag were many prized possessions. A rabbit's paw was his favorite, for it was the paw from his very first kill. The pelt was now a part of the robe his mother wore around her delicate shoulders.

A lad with large, expressive eyes, Panther was already well built for his age. He was keen in his senses and swift in his reflexes. He was strong and erect in posture, excelling in sports, games, and hunting. Today he, like his friend, wore leggings of buckskin decorated with painted porcupine quills, ribbons, and beads. Their chests were bare, but on their feet they wore low-cut sturdy buckskin moccasins, and around their long, flowing hair each wore a beaded headband, tied and knotted at the back.

"Spring is my favorite time of the year to hunt," Cloud said, interrupting Panther's deep thoughts. He inhaled a deep breath of fragrant air. "I, too, wish to down a bear one day, but not so much for the claws to make a necklace as for the pelt, which I will give to my ailing grandmother. Too often I see her sitting beside the fire and she is still not warm enough. I fear her time on this earth grows shorter each day."

"Your sympathy for her is good," Panther said as he brushed aside the low-hanging branch of an ancient elm tree, revealing a river a short distance away, its ripples shining like millions of diamonds beneath the brightness of the sun. "You will be rewarded twofold in the hereafter because of your goodness here on earth."

"You are as good, my friend," Cloud said, his eyes catching a movement ahead through the trees. His insides tightened when he saw a boat rocking at the very edge of the river as waves splashed against its sides, a rope from a tree keeping it from floating away.

"A boat, Panther," Cloud said, his eyes narrowing.

"Look. Do you see it? It is one of the white man's strange river craft called a keelboat. I would like to take a closer look."

His eyes shifted and narrowed when he saw the muted orange glow of a campfire. "I see a campfire some distance from the moored boat," he whispered harshly. "The white-eyes who are traveling in this boat have surely stopped to eat."

Panther's nose twitched. "*Nyoh*, yes, they are near, for I smell the aroma of white man's coffee," he whispered. "*Nyoh*, let us go and take a look at their boat. But we must be careful not to make any noise. If they catch us, who is to say what our fate will be?"

He slid his bow over his left shoulder and held it there as he walked stealthily onward through the thick brush.

Before they got far they saw something that made them both grow cold with disgust.

"Cloud, do you see? The white-eyes are surveyors," Panther hissed as he stared at many stakes in the ground. "The stakes planted in the ground are the first seed of another white man's settlement."

"I wish I were a man ten times as strong as I am now," Cloud said bitterly. "I would rid the land of *all* white-eyes!"

Panther was just as bitter, but did not voice his feelings to his friend. It was bad enough to recall what his father and his grandfather before him had said about the onslaught of white people in the area that was once occupied solely by the red man. His father and grandfather had said that life under white tyranny would be a life without honor, dignity, or self-respect, to which death itself was infinitely preferable.

"All white-eyes are *sholees*, vultures!" Cloud said venomously. "Let us make it hard on those who have wrongly come to our people's land today! Let us go and overturn their river craft. Better yet, let us loose it so that it will float downriver with their supplies. They will be too busy going after it to think of the stakes they leave behind. While they are gone we shall uproot the seeds they planted on our soil and throw them so far away they can never find them."

"We have been taught not to interfere in anything the white men do, for our deeds will come back to our village and bring harm to our people," Panther said sadly. He sighed as he stopped and stared first at the keelboat, and then at the campfire from which came much boisterous laughter.

"Let us at least go ahead and look inside the white-eyes' river craft," Cloud insisted. "Most boats are loaded with many tempting items rarely seen by the red man, especially young braves such as you and me. What can it hurt, Panther? Let us take one look and *then* return to our hunt. We can never forget the importance of the hunt. We Shawnee are hunters by tradition!"

Panther kneaded his brow as he gazed at the boat with a longing he could not deny. "*Nyoh*, let us go ahead and take one quick look and then hurry away from here," he said.

His heart pounded with the excitement of seeing new things, and from the danger of possibly being discovered.

The thrilling combination made Panther feel

strangely alive inside, urging his moccasined feet onward until he came to the banks of the river where the boat swayed and rocked in the waves.

"We must hurry," Panther whispered as he looked over his shoulder at the glow of the campfire through the trees. Then he stepped into the water and made his way toward the boat. The river bed was gravelly and its waters were sparkling clear. In the deepest parts could be seen *sharla*, trout.

When they came up to the side of the keelboat, their eyes widened with wonder. Never had they seen so many strange-looking tools and food supplies. Even the pelts that lay stacked at one end seemed finer than any that Panther had ever seen.

Cloud lifted the corner of one of the pelts. His eyes widened even more when he saw a large jug of what he knew was white man's firewater. He had spied on white men sitting beside campfires many times and had watched how they drank from this type of jug and soon began to behave strangely.

"Is that firewater?" Panther asked, staring at the jug.

"I have heard it called by the strange name 'rum,' " Cloud whispered back, a mischievous gleam in his eyes. "I would like to taste it, Panther, to see if the tales I have heard of it are true." His eyes now begged Panther. "Let us steal it. Surely the white men will only believe they lost it by mistake. They would never suspect that two young braves took it."

"My father and yours have taught us the evil of firewater," Panther said, yet he was unable to stop the racing of his heart at the mere thought of stealing the firewater from the white men, let alone taking a taste from the jug.

"Just this once, Panther," Cloud said, his hand inching toward the jug. "See how easy it would be to take it?" His fingers trembled as he placed them around the coldness of the jug. "All I have to do now is to take it from the boat and it is ours."

Panther again gazed over his shoulder toward the campfire, his ears picking up the men's laughter.

The sound took him back to a time when white men came to his village and poked fun at his father and the warriors who stood square-shouldered and proud at their chief's side.

Since then, Panther had grown to hate the laugh of the evil white men. His hate had grown through the years; he had found few white men who deserved to be called "friend" among the many who trespassed on the land of the Shawnee.

"*Nyoh*, we will take it," Panther blurted out. "If it is left for the white-eyes, they will drink it, and who is to say what they might do when their minds are clouded with the firewater? The white-eyes are too close to our village. They might come and defile some of our women!"

His face twisted with hate, Cloud grabbed up the jug, and soon he and Panther were far from the white men's boat and camping place. They sat down comfortably beneath a grand old oak tree. Panther watched guardedly as Cloud yanked the cork from the jug.

"I am not sure if we should . . ." Panther began, now hesitant to do something he knew his father would abhor. Yet what could only one taste matter? he reassured himself. Surely that could do no harm!

"You first," Cloud said, holding the jug out for Panther.

Panther placed a hand up between himself and the jug. "*Neh, you* drink first," he said thickly, again troubled by what they were doing. He didn't make it a practice to do wrong behind his beloved father's back. He truly hated starting now. "I might not even take that first drink. It is wrong, Cloud. So very wrong, what we have done, and are about to do."

"It was good to take the firewater. The white men would have caused trouble for our people if they had consumed it," Cloud said stubbornly. "And I *must* have a taste. I have heard so much about the firewater. I *must* see if it burns the belly as most say it does."

"And if it does?" Panther said, arching an eyebrow. "Once the burn is there, my friend, how will you remove it if you wish it removed?"

"It will go away," Cloud said, shrugging.

Panther scarcely breathed as he watched Cloud take that first sip of firewater. He flinched when Cloud yanked the jug from his lips and began to gag and choke, his eyes wide and watery.

"Is it that horrible?" Panther asked softly, disbelieving when Cloud ignored his question and quickly took his second sip, and then another and another.

"Cloud, you are drinking too much firewater," Panther said, trying to take the jug from his friend.

Cloud held onto the jug tightly and took another long swallow, then rested the jug on his lap as the alcohol seemed to spread and burn in the pit of his belly.

A strange look came into his eyes as euphoria spread along with the warmth through his entire being. Suddenly he felt as though he had no care in the world, as though the firewater had erased it from his brain. The feeling of well-being was wonderful. He felt as though he were flying among the clouds with the beautiful eagles!

He took another drink, then finally handed the jug to Panther. "It is now your time to taste the wonders of the firewater," he said, his words slurred. He was having trouble focusing his eyes on his friend. "It is something more pleasant than bad," he said, hiccoughing and then laughing.

"You have changed to someone different from who you normally are," Panther said warily as he gazed at Cloud, and then at the jug. "I doubt I should drink. If it changes someone so much, I—"

"Drink!" Cloud said, placing his hands around the jug and forcing it to Panther's lips. "You may never have the opportunity again to taste firewater. See that it is not bad as everyone says. I enjoy it very much."

Panther took a slow sip, then shoved the jug away as the fire burned down his throat into his belly.

"*Neh*," he said, not allowing Cloud to put the jug back to his lips. He wiped at his mouth with his free hand. "I want no more of that stuff. I see nothing good in the taste. It *is* firewater. It burns all the way down to my belly. Surely an evil spirit is tucked away in the fiery liquid."

"It is a spirit that I enjoy very much," Cloud said, chuckling. He took another long drink from the jug, then winced when he dropped the jug and broke it.

"Good. Now you can drink no more," Panther said, getting to his feet. "Come, friend. You must walk off the effects of the fiery liquid. We will then return home. Now that you have drunk so much firewater, there is no use in hunting."

"*Neh*!" Cloud said, stumbling to his feet. "I still hunt! I will take home food even if you do not."

"Cloud, no—" Panther said as Cloud clumsily nocked an arrow on his bowstring, pulled back the bow, and started to release it. He was not shooting at anything in particular, just proving to his friend that he still had the ability to shoot.

Waves of panic swept through Panther when Cloud's hand slipped from the bow and sent the extremely sharp flint arrowhead into a wild flip backwards.

Panther gasped with horror when the arrow entered Cloud's left eye.

Stunned by the sight of the arrow lodged in his friend's eye, Panther stood frozen, unable to move.

But Cloud's loud cries of pain as he fell on his back on the ground, his hands trembling as they clawed at the lodged arrow, brought Panther quickly back to his senses.

Panther fell to his knees beside Cloud. "*Oui-shi-cat-to-oui*, be strong, my friend," he cried. "I dare not remove the arrow. We must return home so that our medicine man prophet can remove it. Two Spirits has the skills required. Please come, Cloud. Please get to your feet so we can go home and get help."

Blood streaming from his eye, his body racked with deep sobs of pain, Cloud allowed Panther to help him to his feet.

23

Staggering, Cloud's arm around Panther's neck, they struggled through the thick brush, and then through the forest, until finally their village came into sight through a break in the trees.

"We will soon be there," Panther said reassuringly. He held his friend close to his side.

As Cloud took each step, crying out with more pain, the pain reached clean inside Panther's heart as though it were his own.

"Cloud, you will soon be all right," Panther said, sobbing. "We have just a little farther to go and you will be in Two Spirits' care. He will know what to do."

"It hurts so," Cloud sobbed, the blood still spilling from the wound around the lodged arrow. His bare chest was now crimson.

"*Nyoh*, I know the pain must be more than anyone can imagine," Panther said, swallowing hard. "But you have been *oui-shi-cat-to-oui*, strong. You have been more brave than anyone I have ever known."

"Was my accident because of the firewater?"

"*Nyoh*, I would say *entirely* because of it."

"But it made me feel good."

"It altered your brain. It slowed your hand and dulled your eye. That is good for no one."

"But I crave more even now."

"*Nyoh*, it is said that is how firewater works. You want more and more."

"If I had more, surely I would not feel as much pain."

"Perhaps *more* pain, my friend."

"Please, Panther," Cloud sobbed. "Please help me, Panther. I . . . hurt . . . so bad."

"Soon the pain will lessen," Panther promised. "Two Spirits will take it away."

Panther continued to walk toward the village, but Cloud's footsteps were slowing. A faint bluish haze of smoke from cook fires filled the air. Panther heard the pleasant sounds of children squealing in play, dogs barking, horses nickering in their pole corrals beyond the village limits.

He was glad when he reached the village where a series of avenues radiated outward from a central clearing. In the center stood the largest, sturdiest building, the people's *msi-kah-mi-qui*, council house.

Narrower, curving avenues arced from one side of the village to the other, where the dwellings had been erected. Some were *wegiwas*, constructed of poles lashed to a framework of wood and covered with broad strips of bark; most were log cabins.

As Panther entered the village with Cloud hanging limply at his side, covered with blood, everyone stopped and stared in disbelief and made room for them to continue to Two Spirits' lodge.

Finally there, they pulled aside a heavy buffalo skin at the doorway of the *wegiwa* and stepped into a room of semidarkness, filled with the rich aroma of smoldering *kinnikinnick* from the medicine man's sacred pipe.

A fox skin draped around his lean, old shoulders, Two Spirits was sitting on his mat in his darkened dwelling, with only the coals of the cook fire illuminating the interior.

Panther was only vaguely aware of the wondrous decorations on the walls, the symbolic glyphs, geometric designs, and renderings of animals.

As soon as Two Spirits saw Cloud and his injury, he stood up and helped Cloud to his bed of thick pelts and blankets at the far side of the dwelling.

Cloud's parents came inside, gasping with horror when they saw their son, as did Panther's chieftain father, who had come to see what was the matter.

As everyone quietly watched, Two Spirits did his magic on Cloud's injury by removing the arrow and the eye as well, then packing the empty socket with buzzard down to absorb the liquid.

With Cloud resting comfortably on the medicine man's bed, his parents sitting vigil at his side, and Two Spirits chanting and shaking his rattle, Panther left the dwelling with his father.

For a moment they walked in silence through the throng of people who stood outside the medicine man's lodge, praying to *Moneto* for the young brave's quick recovery. Then Chief Red Thunder gazed with contempt down at his son.

"I do not have to ask how the accident happened," he said tightly. "I smelled the firewater on both your breath and Cloud's. But I do not know where you got it, or why you were foolish enough to drink it."

"Cloud drank much more than I," Panther said, swallowing hard. He feared looking directly into his father's eyes. "That is why he is injured and I am not."

"But that does not lessen your guilt, does it?" Red Thunder said, his voice filled with a cold, implacable anger.

"*Neh*, nothing will ever lessen my guilt over what happened today," Panther said, going to his father's log cabin and holding the entrance hide aside for him.

Panther sat down with his father on a large, soft buffalo hide stretched over a mat of cedar boughs before a fireplace where a large fire, built of tented logs, burned brightly.

Panther stiffly bent his legs and crossed them at his ankles, his eyes burning with the need to weep every time he thought of his friend who now had only one eye.

Under the glow of the fire and the large, brass-bellied hurricane lamps hanging around the vast room, Panther awaited his father's fury.

As his father silently packed the bowl of his calumet pipe with tobacco and lighted it with a glowing stick from the fire, Panther gazed at the pipe in admiration. It was about three feet long, its hickory stem painted and decorated with geometric figures and hung with strands of dyed rawhide. Its hard, red-clay bowl was also carved with geometric symbols and figures of animals.

And when his father still said nothing, only smoked and stared into the flames of the fire, Panther tried to hold back his fear by focusing on other things, how the windows were covered with *pahkapoomis*, thinly stretched rabbit skins, tanned and neatly sewn together. Bear grease had been rubbed into the skins until they had become translucent, allowing light to enter but warding off drafts.

Panther's mother, who was out digging roots for tomorrow's cook pot, had hung a stew pot over the flames of the fire; its contents were always warmly and gladly shared. The log cabin still smelled of his mother's presence.

27

Wishing his father would say something to get this over with, Panther gazed over at him. He stiffened when he saw that his father was staring into the fire unseeingly as he smoked his pipe, his long, glossy black hair falling over his wide, bare shoulders.

When he saw the fire's glow reflected on his father's necklace of bear claws, Panther looked quickly away. The necklace symbolized bravery, whereas Panther was feeling quite cowardly at this moment. He now realized that stealing the firewater was almost as bad as drinking it, even though he, himself, had only taken one deep swallow. He now knew that he should have taken the jug from Cloud and broken it before Cloud had consumed so much. Had he done this, Cloud would still have both eyes.

"I was wrong, Father," Panther blurted out as he looked over at him again. "*We* were wrong. Cloud and I came across several white-eyes camping beside the river. They had planted stakes for a new settlement. They had left their boat untended. Cloud and I went to it. We found firewater. We stole it. But I only tasted it. Cloud consumed much of it. It dulled his senses. When he drew back the bowstring, the arrow . . . the arrow . . . it flipped backwards instead of flying forward."

Red Thunder sat in stony silence, his lips tight on the stem of the pipe, sucking, his eyes staring unseeingly into the fire.

Then he slipped the pipe from his mouth and turned toward Panther. "First, Panther, stealing *anything* is beneath you," he said, scorn heavy in his voice. His eyes smoldered with controlled fury. "From your early child-

28

hood I taught you that deceitfulness of any kind is a crime, even if those you deceive are men both you and I abhor. But, my son, I do not condemn you for what you and Cloud did today. It is the curiosity of children that sent you to the boat to steal from it. For too long you have heard about firewater. As a child, I myself tasted it. But like you, my son, I did not enjoy the taste. Because Cloud did, he suffers now from it. It is a lesson that he will never forget. I doubt that he will ever drink firewater again.''

Panther recalled how Cloud still wished to drink it even only moments after his accident, but he said nothing to his father. It was with much relief that he realized his father would treat him gently; he could have put all sort of punishments on him for what he had done.

''*Ouisah*, good. You and Cloud learned a harsh lesson today,'' Red Thunder said. ''You learned that firewater can be the ruination of those who drink it. White fire is a fatal poison among the tribes. Even the white government now suppresses the trade in liquor. Panther, you will one day be chief of our Shawnee people. From now on you must think before you act, or you will never be the sort of *psai-wi-ne-noth-tu*, great warrior chief, our people can depend on.''

Hanging his head, Panther nodded. ''Father, *qui-sah-ki-te-hi*, your heart is full of understanding and I vow to you that I will never touch firewater again,'' he murmured. ''I vow to you to be the sort of man you wish me to be.''

''That *you* wish to be,'' Red Thunder said. He placed a gentle hand on Panther's shoulder. ''You should aspire to goodness for yourself, not because it is someone else's desire. Remember that, my son. You must want it. You!''

"I *do* wish to be the best that I can be," Panther said, raising his eyes to look directly into his father's.

Smiling, Red Thunder laid his pipe down on a stone, then reached out and drew Panther into his arms. "I believe your words are sincerely spoken from the heart," he said softly. "There will be no punishment for you for what happened today. But as for Cloud? He does not get off that easily. His whole life he will be forced to live with only one eye; it is a punishment from which he will never be able to escape."

"I wish it were not so, but what you say is true," Panther said softly. "I shall be there for him always, Father. I shall be Cloud's other eye. I will never allow anything bad to happen to him again."

Red Thunder nodded proudly and hugged his son again, but grew quiet and somber while Panther told him more about the white men and the stakes they had planted on the soil of the Shawnee.

"One day we will have to leave our precious land behind us and seek a new home away from the white men who multiply along Shawnee land each day the sun rises," he said, lowering his arms from around his son. His face was set in grim lines. His broad chest expanded as he inhaled deeply.

"But, Father, will not it be the same everywhere we go?" Panther asked. "The red man is outnumbered now by whites. The whites are like flies . . . they multiply faster than an eye blink!"

"*Nyoh*, that is so, but nevertheless, we *will* find a

way to make the lives of our people safe."

"It will be my life's goal to see that it is so," Panther said, in the voice of a young man already aged in his heart and mind.

Chapter Two

Twenty Years Later—1867

The afternoon harvest sun flared through a coppery haze across the rolling hills of southern Illinois. The land was covered with a luxuriant growth of timber, whose leaves had already turned the brilliant reds and yellows of autumn.

A golden blanket of fine prairie grass stretched out on both sides of the slow-moving procession of Shawnee Indians. They were on their way to Oklahoma to join others of their tribe who had traveled there before them.

Leaving warring behind, the Shawnee were an unhappy people who were ready to plant solid roots where no one would bother them again. Chief Panther was leading them to their new homeland. He was taking his people away from the tyrannical, poisonous snake Iroquois, the Shawnee's avowed worst enemy, and the evil white people who lied and cheated the red man of his land.

The Shawnee wanted nothing more now than to live in peace among their brethren, especially since the last attack by the Iroquois under the leadership of the war-hungry Chief Iron Nose killed and maimed many of their people. Among the dead was Panther's beloved young wife, *Matchsquathi-Kisathoi*, Little Sun, named so by her parents because she was one who smiled much.

Also killed that day was the child that Little Sun carried within her womb, as well as Panther's beloved mother.

His father, Red Thunder, who was at one time the powerful chief of their band of Shawnee, had been left totally blind from the vicious attack.

Panther was now acting chief, and the weight of responsibility lay heavy on his shoulders.

Wearing a buckskin eye patch over the hollow socket of his left eye, Cloud rode proudly beside Panther. Yet on his face he wore a frown, for he knew, as did his chieftain friend, that with the leaves on the trees now turning crimson and yellow, it was time to choose a resting place for their people where they could be sheltered from the raw winds of winter.

If they did not stop soon, they might lose too many of the elderly, who were even now fighting to stay alive on the long march.

"Soon we will stop?" Cloud asked as he sidled his white steed closer to Panther's sleek, coal black stallion.

As he waited for his friend to answer, Cloud gazed admiringly at Panther. He had grown into a man who emanated strength. With an athletic frame, he was lean and solidly muscled and held himself erect. He was noble in appearance; strength and courage were evident in his midnight dark eyes.

Dressed like Cloud, Panther wore tanned doeskin leather leggings with a fringe running down each outseam, and a similarly fringed blouse of the same material belted at the waist, covering him halfway to the knees. Around each upper arm and his right wrist he wore a band of beaten silver. His leggings were tucked into calf-high elk-hide moccasins crisscrossed with rawhide thong lacings and were intricately decorated with tiny colorful beads and dyed porcupine quills.

But Panther alone wore the symbol of a warrior's prowess, the prized ornamentation that he had so longed for as a child—a necklace of forty upturned, enormous, yellow-striped grizzly bear claws. They could neither be traded for, nor purchased. They could be obtained in only one way—by taking down a bear with one's own strength and cunning.

A leader, a great chief despite his youth, Panther wore the emblem of his rank in his sleek, long, black hair—a single white-tipped eagle feather affixed at the quill to a brass medallion and attached just over his left ear, with the tip trailing downward over his shoulder. It was a symbol of rank that Cloud knew that his best friend wore with much pride.

Nyoh, his friend was as strong as a bear and canny as a wolf!

"Do we stop soon?" Panther said, repeating his

friend's question. He cast a look back at his father, whose shoulders were slumped with weariness from riding his steed too many miles today.

He then gazed at the other people, who looked hopeful that their travel was over, at least for now.

Touched deeply by his people's plight, Panther looked quickly away and gazed out at the land around them. It was as though the hand of *Moneto*, the Shawnee's Great Spirit, had placed the river and the wildlife there just for the Shawnee's long *augustuskes*, their winter away from their homeland.

He looked at the river. He had only yesterday questioned a traveler about it. He had been told that it was the Maple Fork River, the name acquired because it forked through a vast forest of maple trees.

Panther looked elsewhere and saw a large grove of birch trees. Many of them had been stripped of bark, perhaps by some red man who was there before Panther and his people. The bark had probably been used for either making a canoe or a lodge.

Something else grew along portions of the riverbank. Panther looked with much admiration at a shrub called *shepperdia*. It was the most beautiful bush on the wild prairie. It formed a striking contrast to the rest of the green foliage. The blue appearance of its leaves could be distinguished for miles.

Panther looked forward to spring when the fruit from this plant would hang in great clusters from every limb. They would be about the size of ordinary currants, yet would taste like grapes.

He looked elsewhere as he slowly nodded and drew a tight rein. "*Nyoh*, Cloud, this place you see before you will be our winter home," he pronounced. His gaze lingered for a moment longer on Cloud, whose reason was often clouded by his addiction to the white man's firewater.

It saddened Panther that his friend sought firewater to drown his worries, now that the Shawnee had lost so much.

Panther tried hard to understand his friend, who was troubled by life in general. He discouraged Cloud from drinking whenever he thought he might be able to break through that wall that rose between them when it came to discussions of firewater.

"My friend, do *you* see this place as right for our people?" Panther asked, trying hard to bring Cloud into the decision making so that he would feel more important. Perhaps if he found other ways of gaining satisfaction, he would not turn to firewater.

Cloud beamed when he heard Panther asking his opinion instead of consulting his father. His chest filled with pride to know that Panther thought so much of him. It meant everything to Cloud that Panther could still care so much for his longtime friend.

"*Nyoh*, it is a good place for us to stop for the *augustuskes*," Cloud said, nodding. "We passed by a trading post only a mile downriver. And our scout has returned with news about the town we now see so close. It is called Harrisburg. Both places can provide supplies for our people during the long, cold days ahead of us."

Panther's gaze moved past Cloud to the settlement of Harrisburg. He longed to find friendship there instead of the usual prejudice. He hoped that if there was prejudice, it would not run so deep that his people would not be allowed to remain so close to the town.

Panther then looked over his shoulder at the land his people had just traveled through. The thing he feared most was that Chief Iron Nose might be on that same trail. The Iroquois chief, who was the same age as Panther's father, and who was still powerful and muscled at the age of fifty winters, had cause to seek out Panther and his warriors. After Panther had led his people far from the Iroquois encampment, he and many of his *psai-wi-ne-noth-tu*, his great warriors, had backtracked and avenged the deaths of their loved ones.

Now many of the Iroquois people were mourning, for although Panther loathed warring and causing injury to any people, this time he could not rest until he made those who had killed so needlessly pay for their ugly deeds.

It had been easier for Panther to take up his weapons and use them against the Iroquois because of the loss of his wife and unborn child!

Now that the deed was done and behind him, Panther hoped that Iron Nose would let things rest, for now they were even, with their own separate futures to deal with.

Panther wheeled his horse around and faced his people. "My people, we will travel no more until spring comes with its sunshine and warm nights," he said. He smiled at his father when he saw the joy this news brought to his face, how his lips quivered into a grateful smile. "I have studied the land as we traveled it and have seen plenty of game for the bellies of your children. The woodlands are rich in nuts and fruits and berries. The river will give us much fresh water for bathing and cooking. The trees will give us much firewood for our fires and for building our lodges.''

He looked over his shoulder again toward Harrisburg, then looked at his people. "My people, we will build *wegiwas*, temporary shelters, until we are assured that we can stay here," he said, his voice wary. "As you get settled in, Cloud and I will travel to yonder town called Harrisburg and speak with the man in authority there. It is my hope that I will return with good news that will give you cause to build lodges that are more permanent so that the winter winds will be locked outside.''

Red Thunder nudged his horse's flanks with his moccasined heels and rode up to Panther's left side while Cloud remained at Panther's right. "My son, I wish to go with you to speak with the white man," he said, reaching a trembling hand to Panther's face and resting it on his cheek. "My son, this father might be blind, but he is not ignorant in the ways of speaking one's mind to white men.''

"Father, you know that when I look at you I do not see a blind man, but one who is a man among men, a *leader*," Panther said thickly. "I see a man whose heart is lonely for his wife, yet filled with much love for those he still has around him. I would never do anything to make you feel anything less than that proud, courageous man I have always known. I did not mean to leave you out. I just failed to speak your name. Do come. Ride at my side. I am proud that it is *you* I can call my father.''

As his father's hand wandered slowly over his face, Panther waited, knowing that his father's pride in him showed every time he spoke with him, or touched him gently on the shoulder or cheek. Touching was now more important to Red Thunder than seeing; his fingers had become his eyes.

"Let us go," Red Thunder said, slowly dropping his hand away.

"*Nyoh*, let us go," Panther said, swallowing hard as he watched his father ride away, his lean shoulders wrapped in a bright-hued blanket.

Putting his heels to his horse, Panther rode after him and proudly took his place at his father's side, while Cloud rode up and took his place on the opposite side.

Always concerned about his people, Panther looked over his shoulder. He was proud to see that hasty shelters were already being erected. By the time the moon changed places with the sun in the sky, family groups would be clustered about the evening cook fires, bundled well in their blankets.

Content that all was well with his people for now, Panther concentrated on what lay before him . . . the dreadful first moments of meeting face to face with yet another white man in authority. He had no love for any of them, only a deep-seated hatred that grew with each new acquaintance.

Chapter Three

Dressed in a leather riding skirt and blouse, with shiny leather boots snug on her feet, Shanndel Lynn Burton edged her horse deeper into the shadows of a huge growth of cottonwoods as she watched the three Indians ride away from the others in the direction of Harrisburg.

She had seen the full band of Indians on the trail earlier while she was horseback riding. Curious about them because she was herself part Indian, she had followed them, staying far enough back that they would not detect her presence.

Before the three Indians had left the others, Shanndel had hidden among cottonwoods so she could watch them. She had especially watched the one who seemed to be the leader of the small band.

She wasn't sure if she was attracted to the handsome warrior because she was part Indian herself, or because he seemed different from the others. He held himself so tall, so straight, and seemed so authoritative.

Certainly he was the most handsome man she had ever seen in her life.

As she had continued to watch, Shanndel had grown to realize that this Indian's position was above the others, for when he spoke, all listened. Even the elders looked upon him with awe and respect.

When the handsome warrior rode off with two others, Shanndel watched until they were lost to sight among the tall, white birches.

She wanted to follow them and observe them some more, but she had been away from home for too long, and she did not want to worry her father, whose health was not good. Lately he had suffered from a constant wheezing that worried her. So Shanndel Lynn decided not to follow the three Indians, but to hurry on home.

Once she had let her parents see that she was all right, she would leave again and go into Harrisburg to find the three Indians. She could pretend to be shopping on the town's square, but she would really be watching for the warrior who had touched something deep inside that part of her that was Indian. Her Iroquois heritage had been lost to her when her Iroquois mother had chosen to live the life of a white person with her white husband.

"I wonder what tribe they are from," Shanndel Lynn whispered as she wheeled her horse around and rode from the cover of trees. She hoped her presence wouldn't startle the small group of Indians. She would have to pass by them to get to her home or else make a wide circle around them, and she did not want to take the time to do that. She wanted to waste no time getting home and then on to Harrisburg. She could hardly wait to see the handsome Indian again.

And she must find a way to discover why the Indians were there. It was obvious they planned to stay awhile because some of them were already building *wegiwas*.

"If their plans are to get Sheriff Braddock's permission, I'd not want to be there in his office to see his response," Shanndel Lynn whispered as she rode on past the Shawnee encampment, her long, sleek, black hair lifting from her shoulders and flying like wings in the wind behind her.

She knew how Sheriff Braddock felt about anyone whose skin differed from his. He had revealed his nasty prejudices too often in her and her mother's presence. He only tolerated them because Shanndel Lynn's father was a rich landowner. Her father's huge tobacco plantation lay just on the outskirts of Harrisburg to the west. Edward Burton, her father, owned acres and acres of tobacco plants.

Before her father had bought and developed his land, the neighboring town of Galatia had been the leading dealer of tobacco in the area. It had been the center of the tobacco industry in southern Illinois. Each year one and one-half million pounds were prepared for market there.

But after her father's business was established, he had become the leader. He had two huge tobacco barns. Millions of pounds of tobacco were handled in those barns each year. A great amount was hauled to Shawneetown in huge wagons and shipped to New Orleans down the Ohio River.

Shanndel's father had discovered long ago that Saline County was the ideal location to raise tobacco because of its mild climate in the spring and fall, along with the fact that the soil was very fertile.

Harrisburg had fit well enough into her father's plans once it was established as a town. It had been selected as a site for a new town in 1852 and was made the county seat. Four men had bought five acres each for the town site—John Pankey, John Cain, James Yandall, and James Harris.

The twenty acres had been surveyed by the county surveyor, and two streets were mapped out, Main Street and Poplar Street.

The city had been populated quickly and had grown into a place where people could proudly raise their children.

Her father now employed fifty people during the handling season. He owned the only cigar factory in the area. His employees made five-cent cigars that were sold at the stores under the brand name of Holy Terror.

Shanndel rode onward and soon caught sight of her home in the distance, the tall pillars gracing the front like sentinels keeping watch on the riches inside. She could picture her mother waiting there for her. Grace, named by her white husband for her graciousness, was a full-blooded Iroquois whose Indian given name was Dancing Sky.

Shanndel looked more Indian than white, yet she was tall and statuesque like her father.

Her hair was coal black and worn long and loose to her waist. Her face was a smooth, beautiful copper color. With her high cheekbones and large, expressive, bold brown eyes, and beautifully shaped, ripe-red lips, her features were ravishing.

But beauty was not her only gift. Shanndel was very intelligent and knew the cigar business as well as her father. As she was the only child born to her mother and father, he planned for her to take over the business when he retired.

"But not too soon, I hope," she whispered as she rode down the long, white gravel lane toward her home.

Although she did what she could to help her father because it pleased him, even making dreaded speeches about the cigar industry, it was not Shanndel's dream to make tobacco her life. Deep inside her heart she wanted to have children and to live her life with a wonderful husband, not work like a man among stinking cigars.

She was just beginning to believe that the cigars her father smoked from morning to night were the cause of his lung problems. But when she dared mention her suspicions to him, his scowling look made her grow quiet. Cigars were his life. The cigar industry had made him the wealthiest man in Saline County.

As she slid from the saddle and looped her reins around a hitching rail, her mind again wandered to the Indians she had seen making camp beside the Maple Fork River. Since she was a child, she had never seen a full band of Indians this close to Harrisburg.

The handsome warrior crowded all thoughts of anything else from her mind today. She *would* find a way to meet him, face to face. If she could get to Harrisburg before he left, it would be easy to mingle among the people on the square and "accidentally" bump into him. It was exciting to think of meeting him. . . .

"Shanndel Lynn, what has taken you so long?"

Her father's loud, authoritative voice drew Shanndel out of her thoughts. She looked up at him as he stood on the wide porch in his expensive suit and boots. His blond hair was parted in the middle and hung down to the top of his stiffly starched white collar. His hands were on his hips, and his blue eyes narrowed as he looked accusingly down at her.

"Father, I—" Shanndel stopped before making the mistake of saying that seeing Indians had delayed her. She knew that it was best not to mention them to her father. They were camping much too close to her father's property. Although he had married an Indian and his daughter looked more Indian than white, he didn't trust Indians. Some years ago, when Shanndel had been only five, there had been Indian settlements in Saline County. Both the Piankashaws and the Shawnee had made their homes there. The Piankashaws had been part of a tribe called the Miamis, which had originated from the Algonquin family of the North Atlantic area.

The Shawnee had also originated from the Algonquin, but came from the central Atlantic area.

While both tribes had been in the area, large quantities of tobacco disappeared from her father's fields. Her father had blamed the Indians, yet he had tried to be peaceful in his deliberations with the tribes about the problem. But the chiefs had become insulted and from that point on had caused trouble for Shanndel's father whenever possible.

That led to her father joining together with Sheriff

Braddock and other landowners, who then succeeded in running the Indians off the land.

Since then there had been only a scant few in the area.

Shanndel had forever since felt bad about how the Indians had been treated, for there had never been absolute proof that they had been the ones who stole the tobacco. She wondered now how her father might treat these new Indians.

"Well? What detained you?" Edward asked as Shanndel walked up the steps and stopped on the porch to give him a hug.

"Just the loveliness of the day, I suppose," Shanndel said, stepping away from her father. Feeling wicked for keeping a secret from her father, she smiled sheepishly at him. "I love autumn in Illinois, Father. It's the best time to go horseback riding."

"Yes, I love autumn, as well," Edward said, wheezing. He slipped a folded paper from his vest pocket and handed it to Shanndel, then slid his thick wallet from his back pants pocket. "And since you enjoy it so much, you won't mind going into town for some supplies. What I need is on the list." He took several green bills from his wallet and slipped them into Shanndel's hand. "This should do it. If it's not enough, get the rest on credit. I'll pay the bill the next time I go to town."

He glanced at her horse, and then the stable. "You'd best hitch your roan to the buckboard wagon," he said, wheezing again. "What I need can't be carried on a horseback."

Shanndel couldn't believe her luck. She had wanted an excuse to go into town, and now she had it. But hitching the horse to the wagon was going to take more time than she wanted to spend. The Indians had a head start on her. Surely they would have their business finished soon and would be heading back for their camp.

She ran from the porch. "I'd be glad to go for you," she said, giving her father a quick glance over her shoulder. She laughed softly. "I'll be back in a jiffy!"

She grabbed her horse's reins and hurried away from her father, almost tripping over a rock in her haste to get to the stable.

"What the hell's the hurry?" Edward shouted at her, idly scratching his brow. "You weren't in any hurry to get home and now you're so anxious to leave again?"

"It's not that I'm anxious to leave, Father," Shanndel said, nodding a hello to Danny, the fourteen-year-old stable hand. "But if I've supplies to get, I'd best get them before dark sets in, don't you think?"

"You should've thought about that while you were out there gallivanting about like you'd nothing better to do," Edward snapped back, then turned and went inside the house.

"Danny, help me get Blue Smoke hitched to the buckboard wagon," Shanndel said, handing her horse's reins to the lad. "Hurry and it'll be worth your while." She removed a crisp one-dollar bill from the money her father had given to her and slid it into the stable boy's hand. "Now hurry, Danny. I've no time to waste."

She saw the surprise that leapt into his eyes at the huge amount of money she had so generously given to him. He eyed the bill, then gave her a questioning look.

"Danny, I paid you that money for your quick help, not for you to stand there gaping at me like I'm a foreigner,'' Shanndel said, her hands on her hips as she patiently waited for him to get things ready for her. Her heart was pounding at the thought of actually seeing the Indian again. She silently prayed that he would still be in Harrisburg and that she *would* find a way to meet him.

"Ma'am, one wheel seems loose on the wagon,'' Danny said, stooping to check it.

"It's fine, Danny,'' Shanndel said, now pacing. "Just get it ready. Lord's sake, it never takes you this long.''

"Sorry, ma'am,'' Danny said, hurrying now to hitch Blue Smoke to the wagon.

"And, Danny, please quit calling me 'ma'am,' '' Shanndel said, smiling at him. "Call me Shanndel. It's less formal.''

"Yes, ma'am,'' Danny said, smiling awkwardly at her through wisps of red hair that had fallen down across his golden eyes.

Shanndel sighed, then looked toward Harrisburg as the sun lowered behind the town's tall, two-storied brick courthouse, where a part of the upper floor was used to house those convicted of a felony, while the other half was used for the Circuit Court.

The ground floor was used for the sheriff's office. She could not help believing that was where the Indians had gone. They would know that they must have permission to stay even one night near any white man's town.

"Done and ready, Shanndel,'' Danny said. He stepped back from the wagon, pride in his eyes as he slid his hand into his front breeches pocket and circled his fingers around the bill. He pulled it out and gazed at it again.

Shanndel smiled. "And, Danny, don't spend that money all in one place," she said, gently patting his cheek.

She then hurried onto the wagon and rode off, white dust flying in the wind as the wheels rolled and rattled over the long lane of loose, white gravel.

From an upper bedroom window Shanndel's mother watched her daughter. She could not help wondering what was causing her daughter's frenzied flight. It seemed that there was an anxiousness about Shanndel that had nothing to do with buying supplies for her father. Grace shrugged and returned to her knitting. She was sitting in her favorite rocker beside a slow-burning fire in her bedroom fireplace. Her dark eyes reflected the fire as her copper fingers plied the knitting needles to skillfully fashion a shawl displaying an emblem of her Iroquois people in the design. She loved her husband but missed her people, whom she had not seen since she had left them to flee her abusive first husband.

When she met Edward all those years ago, it had been so easy to leave with him, to accept the riches and love of this white man. She had been blessed, but she was ashamed that she lived a life of luxury while others of her tribe still suffered.

"I long to see them again," she whispered, tears filling her eyes. "Before I die, perhaps I shall. I wonder . . . how . . . *she* . . . is."

She forced herself not to go any further with her thoughts. She had left behind loved ones when she fled

49

the land where her evil husband lived, and she knew those goodbyes would be forever.

Yes, she knew better than to ever go back. That would mean that she would have to face the man she had fled . . . a man who was in truth still her husband. Her marriage to Edward was legitimate in everyone's eyes but hers . . . and . . . Iron Nose's!

She shuddered at the thought of the man she hated with every fiber of her being.

Chapter Four

Panther had passed through many towns during his people's long trek, and each new town made him more bitter, for he knew that upon the spot where the town now stood, at one time or another there had been redskinned people making their homes there.

Now, as he rode into the outskirts of Harrisburg with his father and Cloud, he felt especially tense and bitter when he realized that many people had stopped their fancy carriages to stare at the newcomers.

Although such reactions made Panther furious, he forced himself to ignore the insults from white men on horseback as they rode past.

He was concentrating on one goal—speaking to the man in authority in this town and securing a safe lodging for his people until spring made safe travel possible again.

Forcing himself to focus on other things besides the insults he heard, he looked at the town and saw that a substantial percentage of Harrisburg's structures were permanent buildings.

There were fine, well-built houses and business establishments of good size. Board sidewalks had been laid in front of the buildings facing the main central square so that the fine ladies of the town could pass from building to building during inclement weather and not get their flowing, long skirts muddied.

As in all white communities, the buildings around the square had signs erected, identifying them. The finest of the buildings was the large establishment that sat in the middle of the square. It was a brick building with four columns encased in plaster. Atop the building was a huge clock, with faces looking out at all four sides of the square.

The sight of many people coming and going from the fancy courthouse made Panther's insides tighten, yet he knew without a doubt that this was the place where his council must be held with the man in authority of this town. Once inside, he knew that he would find the sheriff in one of the rooms. He had learned that a sheriff was the voice of authority when there were no forts where uniformed men called "colonels" were in charge.

In the past, Panther hadn't found either of those voices of authority to his liking. More often than not, the men were bigoted and had a deep hatred for anyone whose skin was not the same color as theirs.

Nyoh, Panther dreaded facing another white man to ask *any*thing of him, for no matter whether the Indian offered peace or waged war, he was resented.

But with the winter winds and snows close at hand, his people's welfare came before Panther's pride. Warm lodges must be erected. They had brought their garden produce with them in large bags, which should last them until the next growing season, but they must hunt to build up their food supplies.

He regretted not having a permanent place where his people could plant crops next year. Once they started the long, slow march to Oklahoma again in the spring, they would have to learn how to live solely off the land until they could again build their lodges and plant gardens.

Quiet and tight-lipped, Panther rode up to a long hitching rail, slid out of his saddle, and secured his reins.

As Cloud secured his, Panther went to his father and helped him from his horse, then slid his father's cane from a sheath at the side of the horse and handed it to him.

"I hear much commotion around us," Red Thunder said, lifting his sightless eyes and trying hard to see from them as Panther led him up the steep stone steps of the courthouse. Several white men on the steps moved hurriedly aside, not so much to make room as to be sure they were not touched by the red men.

"Are there any men with red skins other than ourselves?" Red Thunder asked.

"We are the only ones," Panther said tightly. He was glad when they finally reached the top landing, which led inside the huge building. He wished to get this business behind him so that he could take his place again among his brethren instead of being an object of scorn and prejudice among the whites.

"The people here are no different from those in other places we have been," Cloud said, his one eye narrowing as he stared back at a tall gentlemen in a fancy suit with a diamond shining from the folds of his silken ascot. "They would rather red men were not here mingling among them."

Having entered such establishments countless times since they began their trek to Oklahoma, Panther had a sense of where to go to find the man in authority, but for a moment he was disoriented and in awe of what he had found just inside the building. Two spiral staircases wound up on each side of the massive entry hall. He looked up at the second floor and saw many paintings on the walls and people wandering around, studying them.

Remembering what his reasons were for being there, Panther led his father slowly down a long corridor hung with more huge paintings. He saw that railroad cars and tracks had been painted on the massive walls, reminding him that he had crossed a railroad track as he had entered the city. He surmised that railroads had played a big role in the history of this town.

Seeing a sign over a door that had a familiar word painted on it, Panther hesitated. The word "Sheriff" was like a bitter taste in his mouth, but he went on inside the sheriff's office, followed by his father and Cloud.

He paused again, his eyes going around the room. A kerosene hurricane lamp, its wick screwed high to the brightest point, shone its light across a paper-cluttered oak desk, behind which sat a paunchy, bald man who wore gold-framed glasses, and who held a cigar lazily in the corner of his mouth.

The sheriff wore dark clothing, making his badge even more prominent against this backdrop of black.

Suddenly the sheriff sensed that someone was standing there. He looked quickly up at Panther, then glanced at Red Thunder and Cloud with small, beady eyes.

"What the hell are you Injuns doin' in my office?" Sheriff Braddock demanded. He took a deep drag from his cigar, then exhaled, squinting through the smoke that spiraled upward from the cigar into his eyes.

Panther remembered that his father wanted to speak for them once they were in the sheriff's office, so he stepped back, took his father by an elbow, and brought him directly in front of the sheriff's desk. He dropped his hand from his father's elbow and stood stiffly beside him as his father spoke in a deep voice of authority.

"*Se-go-li*, greetings, white man. My people have traveled far but not far enough. Yet with winter so close, we must stop," Red Thunder said. "We are of the *Kispotkotha* tribe, known as Shawnee to white-eyes. We have left our home in the Upper New York State area, with the destination of Oklahoma in mind, where my people will then finally have a place that is theirs for always."

"And what does any of that have to do with me?" Sheriff Braddock growled. He yanked his cigar from his mouth and crushed it out in an ashtray.

"Let me introduce myself and then my son and his friend," Red Thunder said, ignoring the sheriff's insulting behavior. "I am Red Thunder, who was once chief of our band of Shawnee. My son, Panther, is now acting chief. The warrior who has come with us for this council is Cloud, a trusted friend to all Shawnee.''

"My name is Sheriff Carl Braddock,'' the sheriff said sarcastically, lighting a fresh cigar. ''And now that acquaintances are made, let me repeat. What does any of this have to do with anything? What the hell do you mean bargin' in here as though you own the place? I spit on most Injuns, don't you know?''

Panther was filled with boiling rage over the man's insulting remarks and behavior. He stepped closer to the desk. He glared down at the sheriff. "You spit on most red men?'' he said, the words bursting like pistol shots from his lips. ''I *scalp* insulting white men.''

Panther's lips curled into a slow smile when he saw how that statement wiped the smirk as well as the color from the sheriff's face.

"You know that I could have you hanged for saying that to me, don't you?'' Sheriff Braddock said. He sighed nervously as he ran a quivering finger around the collar of his shirt, loosening it around his sweating neck. ''I could take that as a threat and even place a hangman's noose around your neck myself, and who do you think would care?''

"White man, we knew that you could do anything you wished to me and my father and my friend, and still we came to ask permission for our people to stay the winter alongside the Maple Fork River,'' Panther said, resting a hand on the knife sheathed at his right side. ''I have learned to expect threats and prejudice, but I have learned to ignore them, for it is my people's best interest, always, that I look out for. All we need is your permission to stay the winter and then we will be on our way again. We will leave and stay among our people unless supplies are needed during the long winter months ahead. If we do need supplies, we will try to get what we need at the trading post so that my people will not have to suffer such indignities as my father, my friend, and I have suffered today at the hands of you and your townspeople.''

Sheriff Braddock scowled up at Panther. He grabbed his cigar from his mouth and held it tightly between two fingers. "I wish I *did* have the authority to tell you where to go," he spat out viciously. "But as it stands, red-skins, I no longer have the authority to tell you one way or another whether you can stay. Since my last confrontation with your kind, when some red-skins were killed before they fled the area, the United States Congress has prohibited individuals from dealing with Indians in our area in *any* matter except killin' one, should one rightfully deserve it.''

''So you are saying that you have no authority to tell us to move onward?" Panther said, slowly smiling.

''What I'm saying is that I'll wire ahead to Washington and see whether or not you can stay the entire winter," Sheriff Braddock said dryly. "Until then, yes, I have no choice but to allow you to stay. I warn you, listen to me when I say not to cause any trouble, for if you do, I *will* at that point have the authority to either jail you . . . or hang the guilty party.''

Sheriff Braddock took a deep drag from his cigar, then laid it aside and continued talking. "You see, many years ago there were Shawnee living in the area," he said. "Things became confused between the white set-

57

tlers and the Shawnee. Many whites lost great portions of land through overlapping land claims. Then there was the theft of tobacco in the area. Now no one in these parts trusts anyone whose skin is red.''

Panther wanted to tell the sheriff to pull back the husks from his eyes and see things as they truly were, that it was the greed of whites that overcame their common sense and caused all the trouble between red- and white-skinned people.

But instead, his eyes narrowed dangerously, Panther said, ''There will be no trouble from my people. *Maneto*, the Shawnee's Great Spirit, made the world and placed the Shawnee on it to be good, not evil.''

''Yeah, and I saw all of the stars drop from the sky last night,'' Sheriff Braddock said sarcastically. He waved a hand toward Panther. ''Get on outta here. Keep your noses clean.''

Dispirited and humiliated, Panther led his father from the building and helped him onto his horse. Just as he was about to mount his own black steed, a shriek from a woman a few yards away on the street drew his attention.

He turned and stared at a woman as she climbed from her wagon, which seemed to have lost a wheel. Her back was to Panther, but much about her was familiar. The long, sleek black hair, her tallness, the way she carried herself, so proud, so sure. . . .

His breath was stolen away when she turned enough for him to see her face, especially the color. She was copper skinned and she looked enough like his dearly departed wife that it made him dizzy . . . the delicacy of

58

her features, the chin so straight and determined, the large, expressive eyes!

For a moment he was consumed by memories . . . of the first time he had held Little Sun in his arms; of the first time they had made love; of the very moment she had told him that she was with child!

"Little Sun?" he whispered, his throat dry. His heart pounded hard as he walked toward the woman, then stopped when she turned and stared into his eyes. He felt as though Little Sun were alive again, her eyes speaking volumes to him of how she adored him.

"Panther! What are you doing?"

Panther's father's voice broke into Panther's consciousness, making him suddenly aware of what he *was* doing. He felt foolish for having mistaken someone for his wife when he had buried her many sunrises ago and had gone through a great time of mourning her.

Shanndel Lynn could not believe it, but she had gotten to town soon enough to see the handsome Indian. How strangely he was looking at her now, as though he knew her!

When he turned quickly and began to mount his horse, Shanndel wanted to go after him, but the one-eyed man was staring at her in a way that unnerved her. She decided to stay her ground and tend to the wagon wheel so that she could get her supplies and return home before she needlessly worried her father again.

But that brief moment, when she was under the spell of the handsome Indian, would stay with her forever!

"Cloud, did you see her?" Panther asked as he rode off with his father toward the edge of town. "Did she not resemble my Little Sun so much that it might even be she, reincarnated?''

"It was not Little Sun," Cloud assured him. "It is only that you wish so hard for your wife, for a moment you were lost in that woman's loveliness."

"She *was* a beautiful woman," Panther said. He looked over his shoulder, sad that he was riding down another street now so that he was unable to take another look at the woman.

"I do not understand something," Cloud said, kneading his chin thoughtfully. "We all know how red-skins are not accepted in white communities, yet there is a red-skinned woman riding along the streets of the town as though she is perfectly at home."

"This woman you both speak of was perhaps just imagination . . . a vision?" Red Thunder said softly.

"*Neh*, she was no vision. She was real enough," Panther said softly. "And I will find a way to see her again and know her."

"If she *is* real, and she is a part of this community, my son, do you not know that she, too, will be prejudiced against you?" Red Thunder said. "If she is dressed like the whites, she surely lives among them as though one with them."

"When she looked at me I saw no prejudice in her eyes," Panther said as he rode on away from the town toward the river. "In her eyes I saw only the curiosity of a woman who is interested in a man."

"Too much imagination, my son," Red Thunder said, tsk-tsking. "You were born with too much imagination."

"Perhaps, but not when it comes to women and the

messages they send with their eyes,'' Panther said, glad to be at the campsite now so that he could busy himself and for the moment get the woman off his mind. His first concern must be his people's welfare. But he knew that no matter how hard he worked, his heart would not be peaceful until he talked to the woman and discovered her role on this earth.

Was she married?

Did she have children?

Why was she there amidst a community of whites when he knew that most red-skins had been forced from this land long ago?

Many cook fires were burning high. The smell of meat was spreading across the land like some wonderful elixir in the gathering twilight. Panther was glad to see that all of the people's *wegiwas* were built, but soon, when they were rested from the long journey, they must build something more substantial, for no matter what Washington said, he was not going to budge from this land until spring.

And he would take advantage of this time on Illinois land to make the acquaintance of the woman who resembled his late wife so much that her image reached into his heart like some soft, sweet song!

Chapter Five

Breathless from her rush back home, and dirty from getting the wheel back on the wagon, Shanndel hurried toward the parlor, where she expected to find her parents. They spent much time there. It was a huge room filled with exquisite furnishings and art, and with fine walls and ceilings of the most modern architectural design.

Shanndel knew by the smells emanating from the kitchen that dinner tonight on the great dining table had been a magnificent array of foods shipped in from the East or all the way from Europe. The place settings on the table had been of the finest china, crystal, and silver.

Polite and formally clad servants were always on hand to move among guests when her father felt the need to entertain. They would pass around dainty cups filled with wonderfully aromatic coffee, and sweets that would delight a queen.

Shanndel's mother rarely initiated such a dinner party, only agreeing to her husband's whims to please him.

Shanndel stopped just inside the parlor door. She gulped in a deep breath as her father looked up at her from his evening paper, wearing the scowl he gave when she had done something that displeased him. She knew she could expect his usual scolding.

"Where in damnation have you been?" Edward shouted, wheezing and red-faced as he slammed the paper on the table beside him. "Twice today, Shanndel Lynn, you have taken your damn time coming home."

Although she'd expected her father to be annoyed by her late arrival, Shanndel was never really ready for his explosions.

Her lips parted in disbelief. She clutched at her riding skirt and held it out away from her. "Father, don't you see how filthy I am?" she said. "Aren't you concerned why?"

As her father's blue eyes swept slowly over her, Shanndel looked to her mother for moral support. Grace sat, looking beautiful and petite in a lovely blue silk dress, before the massive brick fireplace, her hands busy with her knitting. It was obvious she hoped to avoid Shanndel's quiet pleading.

Shanndel understood. Her mother had learned long ago not to involve herself when Shanndel was being scolded by her father for one thing or another.

Shanndel knew that it was not so much that her

mother was afraid of her husband. It was because of her upbringing among her Iroquois people. Respect for a husband had been taught to her by her Iroquois mother long ago.

Except for Shanndel's mother being so obviously Indian, with her dark skin and hair, it would be hard for anyone to think that she had been raised in an Indian village. Since she had left that life behind her long ago and had married her white husband, she had become white in every manner.

Her mother even knew the tobacco trade as well as her husband, but she never interfered in decisions about the business. She appeared to be content being a woman, doing things that were purely feminine in nature.

And having so many servants, and even a personal maid who saw to her every need, her mother enjoyed things rich women enjoyed—sewing, reading, drinking tea. . . .

"You are rather a mess," Edward said, his tone softening as he pushed his chair back from the table. He stood up and started to go to Shanndel, then stopped. "But that's nothing unusual for you. You love the outdoors so much and are always finding some way to get into one scrape or another. Why would I ask what happened this time, Shanndel? Heaven forbid my even knowing now."

Shanndel felt a slow burn inside at her father's nonchalance. She had taken a beating today, not only because she'd lost a wagon wheel, but becaused she had been snubbed by the townsfolk when she so desperately needed someone to help her.

A breed.

Too many labeled her a "breed" and treated her like someone who had the plague.

Her anger raged when she watched her father take his watch from his inside coat pocket and impatiently study the time.

"Grace, lay your knitting aside now," he said, slipping the watch back into his pocket. "It will soon be time for the opera to begin at the new opera house that Valentine Rathbone built on the north side of the square. We must be on our way."

He slowly slid his eyes over to Shanndel again. "Shanndel shan't be going with us tonight," he said smoothly. "She'll be spending some time in her bath."

Shanndel couldn't believe it when her mother and father walked past her. She knew that her mother cared about what had happened to her but again, as in so many things, did not interfere.

But Shanndel didn't think that her father cared. His annoyance over her being late was only because she had delayed their departure to the opera.

"Father, I could've been killed today because of that damn rickety wagon you force upon me when I am sent into town for your supplies," she blurted out, causing them to stop.

"Oh, Shanndel, my dear, do tell us what happened," Grace said, her silk skirt rustling around her legs as she went to Shanndel and took her hands into hers. "Tell us. We shall take the time to listen."

"Thank you, Mother," Shanndel said, slowly slipping her hands free. She went to her father and gazed up at him, his six foot four height hardly towering over hers, since her own height almost reached six feet on the measuring stick.

"Father, just as I got to the square today, a wheel fell from the wagon," she said, her eyes sparkling as she recalled something else about the moment she had arrived at the square.

Seeing the handsome Indian had for a moment taken the sting off her embarrassing dilemma of having lost a wheel. She would never forget how their eyes had met and held, and how she had felt something drawing them together as though they had known each other in another life.

But she was glad that he hadn't delayed his departure from town, or he would have seen her embarrassment when she had asked for help and no one had cared enough about her welfare to give her assistance.

She wouldn't have wanted the Indian to see that she was treated as a "breed." But if he had seen how people hesitated to go to her rescue, she knew that he would have helped her get the wheel back on the wagon himself.

"I told Danny to get that wheel replaced," Edward said, wheezing and grabbing at his throat and at the same time nervously checking his watch. "I guess the young man has been lax in his duties again."

"Father, don't blame Danny," Shanndel said, sighing heavily. "You should have replaced that wagon long ago. Aren't you even the least bit ashamed to take it into town?"

"That wagon goes back a long way in our family," Edward said, reaching out a hand for his wife, who dutifully went to him and took it. "It was my great-grandfather's in Kentucky. It's seen many a tobacco leaf, daughter. *Many* a tobacco leaf."

Again he gazed at her filthy attire. "As for your clothes, did you soil them while seeing to the wheel?" he asked guardedly. "If so, does that mean that no one offered you a hand? They let you do it alone?"

"Almost alone," Shanndel said, raking her fingers through her thick black hair to draw it farther back from her face. "A couple of gentlemen finally took mercy on this lady in distress. Otherwise, it was as before, Father. I'm treated with much prejudice. It doesn't even matter that my father is the wealthiest landowner in Saline County. All that people see when they look at me is the color of my skin, not the fact that I was raised among them."

She shivered visibly. "I am so grateful that I have turned eighteen and graduated from high school," she said solemnly. "Things were no better for me while I attended school. Only a few classmates looked past who my ancestors are. Thank God for those few."

"But, Shanndel, many men have come calling," Grace said softly. "They see you as you are . . . so beautiful and sweet."

"Mother, they see dollar signs when they see me, that's all," Shanndel said, recalling times when she had been at a dance, or at the theater with a gentleman, and how embarrassed the men would become when people would gawk at her skin color.

After a while men stopped calling, despite the lure of winning the Burton fortune.

"Grace, we *must* leave," Edward said, sweeping an arm around his wife's tiny waist.

"The supplies, Father," Shanndel said, following her parents to the grand entrance foyer and then to the door. "I did get them for you. They are still in the wagon."

"I'll have Danny see to them," Edward said, reaching for a high-top hat on a hat tree and slamming it onto his head. He lifted a shawl from a peg on the wall and gently placed it around his wife's petite shoulders. "Just you run on to your room. A bath is waiting."

He frowned down at her. "And so is your supper," he said. "Your mother and I ate without you. Your soufflé is being kept warm in the oven."

Shanndel nodded. "Have fun at the opera," she said, actually glad they were leaving. Their absence would give her a reprieve from her father, whose tongue seemed to get more bitter each time he had cause to scold her. Blaming his bad temper on his worsening health, she tried to accept his ill treatment of her.

Her shoulders slumped, and ignoring the hungry growling of her stomach, Shanndel took the steps slowly, one at a time, instead of her usual spirited two at a time when she was in a hurry. She suddenly wished that her mother had not left after all. She longed to tell her about having seen the Indian encampment today. She longed to tell her mother about having seen the one Indian warrior in particular, and how tall and noble he was, and, oh, how so wonderfully handsome!

Yet maybe it was best not to share this with her mother. Her mother would probably say that Shanndel must fight such attraction to an Indian.

She would tell Shanndel the hardships and sadness of living the life of an Indian.

She would tell Shanndel that she doubted that any

full-blooded Indian warrior would consider falling in love with a woman who was a "breed," for the word "breed" was hated in both white and red communities.

Her mother would also remind Shanndel that her father was planning on her inheriting the business.

Shanndel went to her room, and just as her father had said, a copper bathtub with steaming water and perfumed bath salts awaited her, as did a change of clothes arranged neatly on the pink crocheted bedspread on her handcrafted pine bed with its loon carvings gracing the four posts. Pretty shoes and black stockings also awaited her beside the bed, as did a fresh bouquet of autumn flowers arranged in a vase on the dressing table.

Although the water was tempting, as was the thought of the food awaiting her downstairs in the oven, she was suddenly captivated by a still more satisfying idea. She had just thought of a way to meet the Indian without him having to know about her mixed heritage.

Her fingers trembling with anticipation, Shanndel lit a kerosene lamp and left her room. She went to the stairs at the far end of the corridor and held the lamp high as she made her way up the steep steps to the attic.

Once there, she searched until she finally found a trunk that belonged to her mother. Her eyes wide, her pulse racing, Shanndel placed the lamp on the floor and slowly lifted the lid of the trunk.

Her eyes brightened when she saw her mother's beautiful Indian dresses folded neatly in piles.

"As beautiful as I remember them," she whispered, recalling the one time long ago when her mother had taken her to the attic and showed her this part of her heritage.

She lifted a dress into her arms. She held it closer to the lamplight and sighed when she saw how beautiful it was. The beads on the bodice were so intricately designed. And the doeskin fabric of the dress was so wonderfully soft.

Her heart racing, Shanndel slipped out of her riding skirt and blouse and drew the dress carefully over her head.

She carried the lamp to the other side of the attic and held it out to one side as she stood before a full-length mirror and looked at herself. She sighed when she saw how the dress erased all signs of her being white.

She *was* Indian.

Through and through!

When the Indian warrior saw her again wearing this dress, he would have no cause to think she was a breed!

Excited, she went through the trunk again until she found moccasins. She hugged them to her bosom, then gasped when she saw a beautifully beaded shoulder purse in the trunk. She took it out and was amazed at how exquisite it was. Yet she knew she shouldn't be surprised. Her mother was quite talented at sewing; surely she had made the purse.

Shanndel took the beautiful things and hurried back to her room. She hid them all beneath her bed until the time was right to wear them.

Starry-eyed, she slid down into the warm bath water. She was hardly able to wait until she could put on the Indian dress and find a way to meet the handsome warrior.

*   *   *

His people were asleep in their lodges but Panther could not keep his eyes closed. He couldn't get the woman he had seen in Harrisburg off his mind. He *had* to find a way to find her again and delve into the mystery of who she was and why she so resembled his late wife.

"I must place this behind me," he argued with himself. He threw off his blanket inside the *wegiwa* that he had quickly assembled after eating his evening meal.

He crawled from the small dwelling and looked toward Cloud's *wegiwa*. Having the need to talk, he went and leaned down just inside Cloud's small temporary lodge to awaken his friend, but stopped, eyes wide, when he found no one there.

"Where can he be?" Panther whispered, straightening his back to look around him.

All was quiet except for the snapping and popping of the outdoor fires and an occasional cry from a distant loon on the water.

And then he heard a sound that was disgustingly familiar to him, the sound that came with too much consumption of white man's firewater. A hiccough, and he knew who had made it—his best friend in the world, a man lost to the evil of firewater.

Following the sound, Panther sighed heavily when he found Cloud sitting on the ground beneath a tree, leaning against its trunk. The spill of the moon revealed the jug resting on his lap and the lethargic sluggishness of Cloud's one eye as he gazed up at Panther.

"My friend, you found me," Cloud said, his words slurred. "You should be asleep. Then you would not know that I stole another jug of firewater from a passing stranger a few days ago."

Disappointed, and feeling strangely empty, Panther sat down beside Cloud. He turned his eyes away when Cloud lifted the jug to his lips and took several deep swallows.

"I still cannot understand how you can drink firewater after what happened to you," Panther said thickly, turning to look at Cloud again. "Because of that experience you are without one of your eyes. Do you wish to have another such accident and be totally sightless like my father?"

"That was many winters ago when I was young and careless," Cloud said, hiccoughing again. "I am older now and careful."

"*Nyoh*, you are older but no wiser about what you should and should not put into your body," Panther argued as he gazed up at the sky sprinkled with stars. He gestured with a hand toward the heavens. "Cloud, *Moneto* dispenses his blessings and favors to those who earn his good will, just as he brings unspeakable sorrow to those whose conduct merits his displeasure. You must listen to *Moneto*."

"I know that I have developed a fondness for firewater and I go to great lengths to satisfy my cravings for it," Cloud said, clumsily slipping an arm around Panther's shoulders. "My friend, join me. You will become more mellow and humorous. Do you not wish to laugh more? To be more carefree? Firewater does that for me. It could do the same for you."

He lifted his arm away from Panther, placed the jug to his lips again, and hurriedly gulped several more swallows.

"You are more addicted to the fiery liquid than I

thought," Panther said with disgust, rising quickly to his feet. He glowered down at his friend. "I know now that you will go to any lengths to satisfy your thirst for the evil drink. If a trader leaves a jug or bottle or flask of whiskey unattended in your presence, you go after it with the determination of a bee after nectar. I imagine you have a hidden hoard somewhere."

Cloud lowered the jug. He looked up at Panther and chuckled at his remark. "Talk against the firewater all you want, my friend, but it is a refuge from a world grown much too complex and greedy for this red man," he said sullenly.

"Firewater fogs the reason of anyone who drinks it and results in things being said, fights being started, lands being sold, and treaties being made that should never have occurred," Panther said, placing a gentle hand on Cloud's bare shoulder. "If that is the world you wish to belong to, my friend, so be it. I am sorely tired of debating it with you."

Cloud nodded. "Go to bed alone, my friend," he said, chuckling. "At least I have my firewater."

Shaking his head with disappointment, Panther left Cloud to his world of disillusionment. When he heard the snapping of a twig at his left side, he jumped, for he knew that he should never be off guard, especially in the dark, for Iron Nose could be out there somewhere awaiting the opportunity to ambush him.

When he saw that it was only a deer browsing among the trees, he sighed with relief and went on to his small lodge and tried to sleep but again found it impossible. His mind was filled with a jumbled montage of images . . . his wife . . . the *woman* . . . and then again his wife!

*   *   *

Alone, Chief Iron Nose rode onward. He knew that he couldn't be far behind Panther and his people. And when he found them, he would first kill Panther's father, and then he would enjoy killing Panther slowly, making sure he inflicted much pain on him before the Shawnee dog inhaled his last breath of life.

Iron Nose had chosen to travel alone so that the warriors who usually accompanied him on his missions could stay behind at his village and help rebuild his people's homes so that their lives could start anew after Panther's warriors' attack. Iron Nose had not been able to leave right away to avenge those deaths, for many burials had to be seen to.

Now he was accountable only to himself. Back at his village he had appointed a sub-chief in his absence. If Iron Nose died, his people would not suffer. And he had chosen well. His people were under a chief who would lead them into a blessed future as well as he could himself. His very own sister, Princess Bright Star, would be their chief!

Smiling, he rode onward, his eyes ever scanning the land for signs of the enemy snake Shawnee!

Chapter Six

Panther gave a start when a young brave gently shook his shoulder and awakened him. He gazed up at Little Bear, the lad who often slept in Panther's father's lodge in case he needed something in the night. When Little Bear started talking excitedly in the Shawnee tongue, his brown eyes large and wide with worry, Panther's insides grew cold, for he knew that something was wrong with his father.

"Your father," Little Bear said. "Come. He asks for you. He slept little last night. Coughing disturbed his sleep."

Little Bear needed to say no more. Panther tossed aside his blanket, slid his feet into moccasins, and in his breechclout left the small dwelling with the young brave. When they came to Panther's father's *wegiwa*, Little Bear didn't enter with Panther. He busied himself stoking the fire just outside the entrance, adding more logs to the smoldering coals.

The morning light coming through the small doorway and cracks between the twigs and leaves that had been used to make the *wegiwa* was faint, yet enough for Panther to see how lethargic his father was. He lay listlessly on his pallet of furs, a blanket drawn over him. Something seemed to tighten around Panther's heart when his father went into a bout of coughing that left him red-faced and breathless.

Settling down on the earthen floor beside his father, Panther reached a hand to Red Thunder's brow. He was relieved to find that the flesh was cool, which meant that his father did not have a fever.

"Father, Little Bear came for me," Panther said softly, drawing his hand away. "He told me how little you slept last night. The cough. Do you feel threatened by it?"

Red Thunder smiled up at Panther. "My son, it is only an irritation in my throat," he said hoarsely. He reached a hand over and patted Panther's bare knee. "I told Little Bear not to worry you needlessly. This old man has many years left in him. A mere cough will not down him."

"You do not take things such as a cough seriously enough," Panther quietly scolded. "You know, as well as I, that the journey has weakened many of our people. It has taken its toll on you, too. What can I do for you this morning, Father, to make you more comfortable?"

"My tin of hot chocolate powder is empty, Panther," Red Thunder said. "The trading post is not far from where we have stopped for the long winter's rest. Check over all of our supplies and go there and stock up for the weeks ahead. While there, see if they have chocolate powder. That is what would make the annoyance in my throat go away.''

Panther's eyes twinkled. ''If that is what your heart desires this morning, my father, then this son will make sure you will have hot chocolate by the time you eat your noon meal.''

''But what if they do not sell chocolate powder at the trading post?'' Red Thunder asked.

''Then I will travel into the town of Harrisburg and find a store that stocks it,'' Panther said. The thought of the woman he had seen there yesterday leaped into his mind as quickly as the mention of Harrisburg crossed his lips. ''I have not yet had trouble finding chocolate powder in white people's establishments, for it seems they find joy in drinking it the same as you.''

''And *you*,'' Red Thunder said, chuckling. ''Before I was blinded I saw the pleasure this drink brings to your eyes as you joined your father for a cup.''

''*Nyoh*, I do enjoy the delicious brown liquid,'' Panther said, smiling. ''It gives my stomach a much better feeling of satisfaction than does that drink whites call coffee.''

''Do not go to the trading post or Harrisburg alone,'' Red Thunder urged, his voice filled with warning. ''We are new in these parts. Who is to say when someone of the white community might decide to eliminate redskins from their domain? After witnessing the sheriff's prejudiced attitude toward us yesterday, I feel it is best to travel in numbers, not alone.''

''I shall go to Cloud's dwelling and ask him to go

with me," Panther said. He recalled how he had left Cloud the previous evening. Not only was Cloud taking chances with his life by drinking firewater in great quantities, he risked much more by drinking alone. It would be easy for someone to come up behind him and strangle or stab him.

And Panther was not thinking only of white people doing the dirty deed. There was always Iron Nose to consider. If Iron Nose still desired vengeance after Panther's raid on his village, he would not rest until it was achieved.

"I shall try to sleep some more before my morning meal," Red Thunder said, turning on his side away from Panther.

Panther sat there a moment longer and flinched as his father coughed again, this time low and deep and strange-sounding.

Remembering other times when his father had been seized by bouts of coughing on the trail, and having seen how the hot chocolate had helped soothe his throat, Panther left the lodge in a hurry.

He nodded a thank you to Little Bear, who sat dutifully beside the entrance of Panther's father's lodge, within earshot should Red Thunder need him.

As Panther made his way toward Cloud's dwelling, he looked around at the activity of his people. Good smells were wafting from the cook fires as the women busied themselves making breakfast out of their supplies while children already romped and played with each other and their pet dogs.

Warriors were already going out with their firearms and bows and arrows for the morning hunt, while the elderly sat around in small clusters, sharing talk and smokes.

Everyone seemed content enough even though their world had been torn asunder by the move from their homeland. Although whites and Iroquois alike had tried to wipe the hope from the eyes of the Shawnee people, none had yet succeeded.

Panther stopped just outside Cloud's lodge. He was almost afraid to see the condition of his friend today. Panther knew how much firewater Cloud must have consumed the previous night for his words to have been so slurred, and his eye to be so bloodshot.

It ate away at Panther's heart to know that no words, no embarrassment, *nothing* seemed to reach inside Cloud's heart. He refused to admit the harm he was doing, not only to his body by putting firewater in it, but also to his people, for Cloud was a warrior needed by all for emergencies such as attacks from enemies. Panther doubted that Cloud could shoot any more accurately now than that day he had shot out his own eye.

Stiffly, Panther bent down and crawled inside Cloud's makeshift dwelling. He wasn't surprised to see Cloud lying on his blankets holding his head, groaning. He had seen this many times, how firewater affected his friend the next day.

"And so today you are incapacitated because of what you drank last night," Panther said disgustedly. He sat down on a woven mat beside his friend's blanket bed. "Cloud, when will you tire of such mornings as this? Would you not rather wake up feeling eager and alive instead of reeling from a night of wrongdoing? I should trade for many mirrors and give them to you so that each day you can look at yourself and be reminded of what firewater has done to you. You are one-eyed, Cloud. Do you wish to also lose the other? It could happen. Your hands tremble often from the firewater. One day, as you affix your arrow to your bow, again you could have such an accident as you did when we were young braves."

"Leave me in peace," Cloud groaned. "Do you not understand anything? I drink because of my lost eye! It makes me forget how ugly I am without two eyes. Yesterday, when we were in the town of Harrisburg, I saw many *u-le-thi-e-qui-wa*, beautiful women . . . *white* women. They gawked much longer at me than at you because of my eye patch! They knew no eye was there. No woman will ever have me. All women look at me with disgust!"

"Then drink and drink until you *do* shoot out your other eye and then you will not see the women look at you with disfavor," Panther growled. "You will see nothing, my friend. Your reflection in the water will go away, but not the cowardice that goes with drinking firewater!"

Feeling ashamed for having talked to his friend in such a manner, Panther fled Cloud's lodge. He almost went back inside when he heard Cloud weeping.

He wanted to go and hold his friend in his arms and soothe his woes, yet he knew that Cloud much preferred firewater to a friend's comforting arms, so he went to the makeshift corral made of ropes tied from tree to tree and readied his horse for travel.

He recalled his father's words about not traveling alone, yet he felt the need to be alone today. He had much on his mind: a troubled friend who ignored his advice; a father whose health seemed to be failing much too quickly now that he had left behind the world he had always known, and a woman who haunted his every breathing moment.

He lifted his eyes to the heavens. "*Moneto*, scarcely ever do I ask for anything but what is good for my people," he whispered. "But today I ask something for myself. Please cross my path with the woman's again. Let me uncover the mystery of who she is."

A fluttering of the birch tree's leaves overhead made Panther smile, for he knew that his words to the Great Spirit had not been ignored as trivial.

Moneto knew of the hurt that had come with the death of Panther's wife. Panther even believed that *Moneto*, with his powerful ways, had purposely placed the woman in his path yesterday.

Today he would see her again!

With a cloudless blue sky above, and the wonderful fragrance of autumn all around him, Panther mounted his black steed and rode from the Shawnee encampment in search of the trading post he had seen earlier. He knew that all he had to do was follow the river and he would soon be there. The trading post had been built on the river where the trappers' boats could easily reach it.

He recalled the many pelts he had seen in those boats and longed to go on the hunt for such animals himself. After he saw to it that his people were settled in for the winter, he would form a large hunting party and make sure there were enough pelts and meat to last through the icy days of winter.

81

Panther's spine stiffened when he heard horses approaching from behind. Although he knew that it could be warriors coming from his encampment to join him for the trek to the trading post, he doubted that it was. Everyone had seen him leave. They would have joined him back at the encampment.

Resting a hand on the rifle sheathed at the right side of his horse, Panther wheeled his steed around and waited for these men who were now coming into sight through a break in the trees.

His eyes narrowed when he recognized the sheriff. He suddenly felt vulnerable and recalled his father's warning not to travel alone. If this sheriff chose to eliminate him, he had the perfect opportunity now. Panther could get off only one shot from his rifle before the white men shot him from his horse.

His jaw stiff, his shoulders squared, Panther waited until Sheriff Braddock reined in beside him. The other white men kept a short distance away, their eyes unfriendly.

"Chief, I've received a wire from Washington," Sheriff Braddock said, edging his horse closer to Panther's. "I went to your encampment. I was told that your father was not feeling well enough for a council with me. I was told that you were headed for the trading post. I decided to follow you and give you the news directly."

Panther was impatiently waiting to hear what the response from Washington was, but he was too proud to interrupt the man and tell him to get to the point. Panther feared the worst; he had learned to expect it.

"President Johnson has given you permission to stay

near Harrisburg for the winter,'' Sheriff Braddock continued. ''But when spring arrives you must move onward.''

A keen relief flooded Panther, for he had already decided that he would not move his people onward, even if he did not receive word that they could stay. He knew the white men could not force them to move, short of killing all of the Shawnee, and he knew that the President of this country did not want such bloodshed on his hands. He had already been involved in too much scandal since President Lincoln's assassination.

''When the buds appear on the trees and ice cracks in the river, I will lead my people onward from this land to that which awaits us in Oklahoma,'' Panther said.

Just as he started to turn his horse around, he was stopped by the cold warning in the sheriff's voice.

''Since you don't have any knowledge of how civilized people behave, Panther, I'll ignore the fact that you didn't thank me for my trouble,'' Sheriff Braddock said, his eyes locking with Panther's as Panther gazed icily back at him. ''And, remember this, Chief, if any of your people cause trouble in the white community, even if it is forty degrees below zero, you will have to move onward.''

Panther still said nothing. His eyes lingered on the sheriff's, enjoying the other man's uneasiness at Panther's silence. He smiled when the sheriff suddenly wheeled his horse around and rode off, his men following him.

Sighing, his spirits low as he tried not to think of all the things the whites had taken from the red man, Panther turned his horse back in the direction of the trading post. If he lingered too long on the subject of what the white men had done to his people, his heart would break.

Forcing himself to think of the future, he sank his heels into the flanks of his horse and traveled onward in a hard gallop across the open plain.

Shanndel had hardly slept at all the previous night. The dress, shoulder purse, and moccasins hidden beneath her bed were the cause of her insomnia.

Finally, as the sun was rising in its full splendor over the horizon, she had leapt from her bed and carefully slid the Indian attire into a travel bag, then dressed in her usual riding gear and left the house before anyone else was stirring.

After she had left the outskirts of Harrisburg behind, Shanndel had stopped and exchanged her riding clothes for her mother's lovely buckskin dress.

When she had exchanged her boots for the butter-soft moccasins, she wished that she would never have to wear boots again. The moccasins were like heaven on her feet. The dress was like soft rose petals against her skin.

And oh, the lovely purse! It thrilled her to slide a few coins inside it so that if she were near the trading post she could go there and pretend that she was a full-blooded Indian who had come to do her trading. Although Indians were very scarce in these parts, there were some who came through the area from time to time, such as those who were now making camp close to her father's property.

She smiled at the possibility of many Indians returning to the area and stubbornly taking back the land that was theirs!

She loved the change these clothes made in her, as though she had met head on with her Iroquois heritage. When she'd arrived at the encampment where she had seen the handsome Indian, she'd hidden among the thick cottonwoods. He had left shortly after on his horse, and she had become breathless with excitement as she followed him. She knew that he was headed in the direction of the trading post. It would be so easy to mingle with the people there, and let him discover her. When he saw her dressed in such a way, surely his first thought would be that she was a full-blooded Indian.

Her plan had almost gone awry when Sheriff Braddock and his men stopped the Indian. She had stayed hidden, yet close enough to hear their conversation. She had not only discovered that his name was Panther and that he was a chief, but that he and his people had been given permission to stay the winter. That made her need to meet him not so desperate. Perhaps she should take her time and plan a more perfect meeting.

Yet she had not been able to keep herself from following him again when he had continued on his way, alone.

She was now only a few yards behind him. She could so easily overtake him and let herself be known to him. But a part of her held back. She was afraid.

She had never been so bold with a man; there had never been a man who made her wish to do anything so daring.

What if her father discovered her gone and came after her?

The sudden appearance of a doe leaping out from behind some bushes startled her horse into rearing. Shanndel screamed and clutched her reins with wild desperation.

Just as her horse settled down, she realized that she was no longer alone. Her scream had frightened the deer away and at the same time alerted Panther that he was not alone.

As he rode out into the open, his eyes locked instantly with Shanndel Lynn's. Everything within Shanndel grew warm with passion, for up this close she could see Panther's perfect features. He was so handsome it took her breath away.

Panther was also breathless, for up this close it was even more clear how much this woman resembled his late wife. His Little Sun had been just as radiant in her loveliness as this woman.

"Who are you?" he blurted out, his eyes taking in her Indian attire with surprise. When he had seen her yesterday, she wore the clothes that white women wore when they rode horses. "What is your name? Where have you come from?"

Panther swallowed hard and reached a trembling hand out toward her. "Surely you are not real," he said thickly. "Surely you are but a vision born from my longing to see my wife again. . . ."

Shanndel's eyes widened as her lips parted in a slight gasp.

Chapter Seven

"Wife?" Shanndel finally managed to say. Suddenly she recalled that the first time he had seen her, he had called her by someone else's name. It made her heart sink to know now that he'd been attracted to her only because he'd mistaken her for someone else.

"*Nyoh*, you look so much like her you could be my Little Sun," Panther said, trying desperately to find a flaw in this woman's features that would make her less beautiful than his Little Sun.

But no matter how hard he looked, he saw nothing about her that was not lovely. He knew that she was not his wife, yet being with her, seeing the resemblance, made him feel as though he were with Little Sun again.

That caused mixed feelings within him. The longing to hold Little Sun again was so deep that it cut into the very core of his being. Yet that other part of him that needed a woman ached with desires he had ignored since the burial rites of his wife.

Yet he had to fight this want . . . this need. How could he ever love a woman who resembled his wife so much and not think of Little Sun while with her? He doubted he could ever get past comparing them.

"Panther, I . . . I . . . am no man's wife and never have been, and . . . and there is only one of me," Shanndel said softly, her voice breaking as she stood there under the spell of this man who had suddenly entered her life, yet who belonged to someone else, heart and soul.

Yet where was this other woman? How could he mistake Shanndel for her? Could it be that . . . she . . . was dead?

Yes, surely his wife was dead or he would be with her now. And seeing someone who resembled her would not have disturbed him so deeply if she were not gone from his life forever.

"Panther?" he said, lifting an eyebrow. "You know that I am called by the name Panther? How?" The sound of his name on her lips had shaken him from his continued marveling at her likeness to Little Sun. Did she know him somehow?

Or worse yet, was she traveling with someone who knew him?

A warning grabbed at his insides.

Could she be a part of Iron Nose's search party?

Had the Iroquois warriors brought along wives to warm their blankets at night on their long search for the Shawnee?

His wife had been from an Iroquois band, but she

had not known Iron Nose. Chances were that she would not have known this woman either. She had certainly never mentioned someone who resembled her so much they could have been born of the same womb! Had Little Sun known of such a woman, she would have been as intrigued as Panther and would have pointed her out to him.

No. None of this made any sense, yet this woman *did* know his name, and he had to know how!

Shanndel suddenly felt trapped. Unknowingly she had spoken his name. How could she tell him that she had been watching him since his arrival and that she had heard Sheriff Braddock address him by that name?

No matter how she would try to explain this to him, she would look brazenly forward.

Everything seemed to be going wrong, and she had wanted their first meeting to be nothing but wonderful and sweet.

"Words do not come to you?" Panther said, his eyes searching hers. "You do not answer my question about how you know me? Then let me ask you this. What tribe are you a part of? What is your name?"

Shanndel's insides tightened, for the situation was worsening by the minute. All the while she had planned to meet him face to face, she had not looked ahead enough to know that he would be full of questions, especially about her tribe, and where she made her camp. All she'd been able to think of was meeting him . . . knowing him.

"My n-name?" Shanndel said, hating it when she stammered instead of speaking straight out as she normally did. She had given many speeches before throngs of men about the tobacco industry and not once had her voice quavered.

But now? Speaking before this one man made her more nervous than she would have ever thought possible.

"Yes, I want to know your name and the name of your tribe," Panther said, his eyes narrowing, for it seemed that even such a simple question as that made her hesitate. Telling someone one's name was the simplest task of all. Unless one had something to hide!

"Rain Singing," Shanndel blurted out. She was relieved when he seemed satisfied with her answer. This was the very first time she had spoken her Indian given name to anyone but her mother. Grace had secretly, away from the presence of her father, given it to her when Shanndel was old enough to be told about her Iroquois heritage.

Now she was thankful that her mother had given her an Indian name. It would make her seem more Indian to this handsome chief.

Panther pondered the name carefully. He did not recognize it.

"I am of the Shawnee tribe," he said, watching for her reaction. He was pleased when he saw no reaction in her beautiful brown eyes. Surely if she was part of Iron Nose's band she would be terrified to hear that he was Shawnee and to know that she was alone in the presence of an avowed enemy.

"You still have not told me *your* tribe," he said guardedly.

"My tribe?" Shanndel said, in her mind's eye seeing

herself with her mother during those secret hours when she'd learned the tales of her people.

Her mother had even taught Shanndel some of the Iroquois language.

Shanndel would be proud to finally admit her heritage to someone besides her mother!

She lifted her chin proudly. "I am Iroquois," she said, flinching when she saw how he stiffened, and his eyes lit with a sudden fire.

Her hands tightened about her reins. She was ready to take flight should he reach out to grab her, for she suddenly felt threatened by his presence.

And she realized that it was because she had admitted to being Iroquois!

A warning flashed through her mind when she recalled something else of her mother's teachings. She vaguely remembered now that her mother had talked of the Shawnee as her people's enemy. Oh, why couldn't she have remembered it earlier and kept that fact to herself?

Hearing her speak the name Iroquois, Panther was filled with many emotions. It made him recall his first meeting with Little Sun, when they knew they belonged to enemy tribes.

Their relationship as enemies had quickly changed when Little Sun said in her soft, sweet voice that she was no one's enemy and that she had always wanted to know him!

He had quickly agreed to their next meeting, and then the next and next until their love was so strong that no one could have drawn them apart.

He knew that he should be no less unbiased now. But

he must know whether he was in the presence of an enemy, whether Iron Nose was near.

He knew how to test this woman to learn the truth he needed. "Where is Chief Iron Nose?" he blurted out, awaiting her reaction.

"I know no one by that name," Shanndel said, unhappy at being forced to lie. But it was a necessary lie, for she could tell by the way he said Iron Nose's name in a low hiss that Iron Nose was a man he hated with all of his being.

"Then tell me where you make camp," Panther insisted. He looked past her, searching through the break in the trees for others of her tribe who might be hiding there, perhaps ready to ambush him should she give the signal.

"You must have a camp somewhere," he said. "I saw you yesterday in Harrisburg."

His eyes skimmed quickly over her, and then he met her gaze. "You were dressed differently yesterday," he said guardedly. "I suppose it is easier to do your trading wearing the clothes of the white people."

"Where . . . do . . . I make camp?" Shanndel stammered, ignoring his remark about her clothes.

Again she felt trapped. If she told him that she was no part of any camp, that she lived in a huge, pillared house, that might be worse than telling him that she knew of the Indian chief named Iron Nose.

Either way, she had lost this game of cat and mouse. She doubted now that they would ever get to know each other.

Everything seemed suddenly against her. She had no choice but to flee.

With a sob lodged in her throat, Shanndel started to ride away, but she hesitated. There was something she must say first.

"Panther, neither I, nor anyone I know, is a threat to you and your people," she said. "And I promise that I do not know Chief Iron Nose. If he is a threat to you and your people, I am not a part of that threat."

With that, Shanndel wheeled her horse around and rode away from him.

She knew the moment when things had gone sour between herself and Panther. It had been when she had told him that she was of Iroquois descent. Surely sometime in his past he had had bad dealings with the Iroquois and Chief Iron Nose.

Oh, if only she had known, if only she had remembered what her mother had told her about the Iroquois being the Shawnee's worst enemy, she would have lied and told him that she was Shawnee! She would have done anything to have gotten to know him.

But now it was too late, she despaired to herself as tears filled her eyes. She had already said the word that had poisoned him against her. She couldn't take it back.

Downhearted, she rode on toward home. On the way she would stop only long enough to change back into her riding habit so that her parents would never guess what she had done early this morning while they still slept.

Panther watched her riding away, even more puzzled about her than before. He hoped that what she said was true. If so, she had nothing to do with Iron Nose. Yet why did she refuse to tell him where she made camp?

A part of him wanted to go after her, to see where

she went, yet good sense told him to let her go and forget her. Obviously they were not destined to know each other any better or their first meeting would not have been filled with such distrust and questioning.

Nyoh, at least for now, he would put her from his mind and go on his way. He must get his father's chocolate powder to soothe his throat.

Nyoh, he must forget everything but the welfare of his people, especially his ailing father. They were the reason he was on this earth. His true destiny was leading his people to a new land where they could be at peace, at long last, in their hearts and souls.

Yet, no matter how hard he might try, he knew that he would never be able to put this woman called Rain Singing from his mind. He would have to fight against the urge to search for her camp. He must remember that she was Iroquois. He had known only one Iroquois who could be trusted and that was his wife! And she had been slain in a raid by the man he least trusted. Iron Nose!

"I cannot let this Rain Singing change anything in my life," he whispered. "I must forget her!"

Having changed into her riding habit and arrived home before her parents went to the breakfast table, Shanndel tried to sneak to her room. She would fake illness when her mother came to ask her to come downstairs for the morning meal.

But Shanndel had gotten only halfway up the huge, winding staircase when both her mother and father appeared on the landing above her.

"Shanndel, where have you been?" Grace asked, her

eyes taking in Shanndel's flushed cheeks and eyes that were red from crying.

She noticed Shanndel's wrinkled skirt and blouse, not knowing they were wrinkled from having been stuffed into the travel bag while she pretended to be a full-blooded Indian.

"Shanndel, have you been horseback riding already?" Grace asked. "Did Blue Smoke throw you? You look distraught. Your clothes are mussed."

Shanndel was glad that she had left the travel bag filled with the Indian attire hidden beneath a scattering of straw at the back of the stable or that would have given her morning's venture away, for her mother would have asked what was inside it.

She stopped and glanced from her mother to her father, then smiled weakly. "Yes, I went riding," she murmured. "You know that time is drawing nigh when I'll not be able to ride at all. Soon it will be too cold."

She absently wiped a tear from the corner of her eye. "But I guess I was wrong about this morning's air," she said softly. "It was somewhat bitter as I rode Blue Smoke this morning. It made tears come to my eyes."

"But your clothes?" her father asked. "They are wrinkled. Were you thrown?"

Shanndel's insides tightened. Lies and more lies were becoming necessary this morning, whereas she scarcely recalled ever having the need to lie about anything before.

But there was no doubting her life had changed the very moment she first saw Panther. She had been so quickly attracted to him she could not fight it.

But now she knew that she must. Only a few more

lies and she would be able to live life as normally as she had before having met Panther.

"I . . . I . . . stopped to let Blue Smoke have a rest," she said, looking sheepishly from her mother to her father to see if they believed her. "I tripped. I rolled down an incline. I just barely missed falling into the river."

"Thank goodness you didn't," Grace said, going to Shanndel and gently slipping an arm around her waist. "Come on, darling. Let me help you up the stairs to your room. What you need is a warm soaking before breakfast."

"Mother, please quit fussing over me so much," Shanndel said, but she secretly welcomed the comfort of her mother's arms around her waist. "I'm fine. All I need is a change of clothes. Then I'll join you and Father at the breakfast table."

Grace stepped away from her and questioned her silently with her eyes.

Shanndel felt uneasy, for it seemed as though her mother sensed that what she'd said this morning was not absolutely true.

Did it show in her eyes that she had been hurt deeply by a man for the very first time in her life?

Her eyes wavered as she gazed back at her mother, and then she ran up the stairs and into her room, welcoming the seclusion it offered her.

She waited for her mother and father to come to her and question her further about her strange behavior, and was relieved when they didn't.

She slowly closed her door and leaned against it, feeling hollow with regret that she had not handled her meeting with Panther more cleverly.

Going to the window, she peered into the distance. She longed to be at the trading post, getting to know him as she had originally planned. Because of her bungling today, she doubted she would ever get a second chance to make things right between her and the most intriguing man she had ever met.

She felt cheated.

Chapter Eight

Panther had found the chocolate powder at the trading post, and his father was even now sipping a cup inside his small dwelling. Meanwhile, Panther sat alone beside a fire outside his own lodge. He was thinking through things that troubled him.

Could he trust the word of Sheriff Braddock enough to tell his people to go ahead and build their permanent lodges for the winter?

Or should he wait awhile longer to see if the sheriff was going to cause his people so much trouble that they would be better off chancing the bitter winds of winter and moving onward?

He had seen the hatred in the eyes of the men who came with the sheriff to deliver the message from the President.

He knew, from his conversation with the sheriff,

how *he* felt about all men whose skin was red.

He knew that this sheriff had seen other Shawnee being forced from the area some time ago.

Many of Panther's people were tired, especially the elderly. Building log lodges would tire them out even more. Yet waiting longer to build their winter homes was risky.

Even so, he felt more comfortable waiting awhile longer. Though he had earlier told himself that nothing anyone said or did would make them leave, he had known that the whites had the power to take everything away from him and his people.

And then there was the woman. He found it impossible to get her off his mind. He couldn't fight the way she affected him. It was more than her resemblance to his beloved wife. The woman's deep brown eyes had reached clean inside his heart, reminding him of how it was to *love* and to want a woman again!

Since his wife's death he had forced such feelings to lie dormant inside him.

Even now he was trying with every ounce of his being not to think of Rain Singing.

"Rain Singing," he whispered to himself as he gazed into the flames of his fire. "The name is as beautiful as the woman."

"My friend, my head no longer throbs as if drums were pounding inside it," Cloud said as he sat down next to Panther. "You are alone. I am alone. Why not pass the time playing cards? I have brought a deck with me. I have brought coins from my last trading with whites. Let us gamble, my friend. Let us bring some sunshine into our hearts tonight."

Panther was glad to be drawn from his troubled reverie, but a game of cards was the last thing he wanted to do at this time. He wanted to search until he found Rain Singing's campsite.

"My friend, do you not hear my offer of a pleasant pastime this night?" Cloud persisted as he leaned closer to Panther to draw his friend's attention.

Panther looked quickly over at Cloud. He was glad that his friend was not drinking firewater, and knew that if he did not agree to gamble with him tonight Cloud might seek its solace again.

And Panther longed to tell Cloud his secret, that he had met the woman of his dreams.

But he would say nothing, because he did not want to reveal the horrid truth about her—that she was Iroquois, the Shawnee's worst enemy.

"Friend, still you have not answered me," Cloud said, shuffling the cards, which he had learned to do from a party of white hunters. They had taught Cloud how to play cards while they shared their supply of firewater.

Cloud had, in turn, taught Panther how to play the game called poker. They had spent many enjoyable evenings beside the lodge fires laughing and gambling, but never once had Panther taken a drink of firewater. His fun came from playing cards, not from drinking.

"*Neh*, tonight is not the night for playing cards," Panther finally said. "Cloud, a late night ride is what I need. I must think. I must think *alone*."

Panther was not used to telling only half truths to his friend. But the ride he planned would have a purpose other than thinking. He would search until he found Rain Singing's camp. It could not be far.

"What you need, my friend, is to quit being so stubborn about firewater," Cloud said, sliding the deck of cards into a small leather pouch. "It is apparent that something is troubling you. Drink. Let the firewater free your mind of such worries. Relax tonight. Let it all leave your mind as though the worries were floating away on a butterfly's wings."

"Can you think of nothing but that worthless firewater?" Panther said, his voice harsh and edged with anger. "How can you even *think* that firewater is what I need, when you know that it is bad, not good, to partake in such drink. Cloud, I want a clear mind tonight, for I have much to work out inside it." And also inside his heart, Panther reminded himself

He gave Cloud a scolding look. "Cloud, you will learn again in a tragic way that drinking firewater harms rather than helps you," Panther said. He nodded toward Cloud's dwelling. "Go, Cloud. I have things to do . . . places to go."

"I will go with you," Cloud said, jumping to his feet and following Panther as he went to the horse corral.

Full of conflicting feelings about Cloud, Panther stopped and turned to him. He knew that if he allowed Cloud to go with him, that would keep his friend from drinking, but Panther needed to be alone. He didn't want to have to explain things about the woman to anyone just yet, especially if he would never see her again. He would only look foolish for having continued to think of her when he knew it was best not to.

"My friend, tonight must be mine alone with my

thoughts," Panther said, placing a gentle hand on Cloud's shoulder.

"Then go," Cloud said, sliding Panther's hand from his shoulder with a quivering hand. He walked away, his head hanging, his dejection plain in the sullen way he walked toward his lodge.

Panther's heart went out to Cloud. He felt his friend's dejection deep inside his soul, yet he still let him go to his lodge. Panther had to search for Rain Singing's camp alone. Should she happen into his path again, this time he would not demand answers from her. Suddenly just being with her was all that mattered!

He grabbed the reins, swung himself into the saddle, and rode into the moonlit night. He wasn't sure which direction to go first, but before the night was over he would have gone in *all* directions if that was what it took to find the woman of his desire . . . his Rain Singing.

He rode and rode, searching endlessly, yet found no other Indian camps in the vicinity. Yet he knew that at least one more camp besides his own must exist. Rain Singing was real. She was not a figment of his imagination, having materialized twice from out of nowhere.

"Where has she made her camp?" Panther whispered as he drew his horse to a halt.

He peered into the night sky for signs of campfires casting off a golden glow against the black backdrop of the night. All he saw was the glow sent skyward from his own people's fires. Nothing more.

"I do not understand," Panther whispered, again riding in a slow lope on his black steed. Surely Rain Singing wouldn't have ridden far from her camp alone. It was never safe for an Indian woman of any tribe to travel alone, especially on land that belonged to white men. Too many white men enjoyed abducting and raping Indian women, as though women with red skin were not human but instead animals—something to use and discard at will.

He rode awhile longer in what seemed to him to be a wide circle, then saw something in the dark that he hadn't noticed before. He saw a huge field of tobacco.

He went to the outskirts of the tobacco field and drew his steed to a halt. As he clung to the reins, he gazed past the tobacco plants that stretched far and wide on each side of him and saw two huge tobacco barns.

And then past them he saw two larger dwellings. One seemed to be the home of those who owned the tobacco. The other seemed to be some sort of establishment. He wondered if it might be a sort of council house such as the Shawnee build separate from their smaller dwellings.

His gaze shifted again. He stared at the two-storied house where lamplight glowed from many of the windows. The house was so large it cast a huge shadow over the land as the moon shone high and bright behind it.

Something else grabbed his attention. He saw the silhouette of a woman standing in an upstairs window, lamplight behind her. He could tell that she was gazing from the window.

He inched his horse closer to get a better look, but not wanting to be seen, he couldn't get close enough to see any of the woman's features.

Fearing that he would be placed in a white man's jail

for trespassing on land where he had not been given permission to go, Panther could not allow himself to be caught anywhere near the white man's establishments.

And if the woman did see him, she would surely become alarmed and alert the men who lived there to the presence of a stranger lurking in the dark outside their home.

They might not stop to question him.

They might come gunning first, especially if they discovered that he was an Indian.

Panther gazed at the woman in the window one last time, then glanced at the tobacco fields, then rode away, his thoughts again on Rain Singing. The solitary figure in the window reminded him of how alone she'd been. How could any Iroquois warrior, or *any* family, allow this woman to ride and trade alone? Did those who loved her not know that she was vulnerable in every way?

If this woman were his, so beautiful she drew a man's breath away, he would watch her like a hawk and protect her with his life.

Sighing, sorely tired of thinking of things that could not be, he headed back toward his campsite.

Chapter Nine

Hardly touching her eggs and bacon at the breakfast table, Shanndel was thinking about the man she'd seen looking up at her window last night. When he had moved into the clearing, where the moonlight outlined him, she'd known who it was so near to her, yet so far.

Panther!

The handsome Shawnee chief!

At first she had been amazed that he'd sought her out and found her, then fear had grabbed at her heart when she realized that now he knew of the lies she'd told him.

If he knew she lived in a mansion, with all of the trappings of the rich, he would know that she had only been pretending to be a full-blooded Indian, while all along she was a breed with a rich white father.

"Shanndel, your mind is a million miles away," Edward said as he slid his empty plate aside. "Lord, Shanndel Lynn, you haven't been the same since that damn wheel fell off the wagon in Harrisburg. It's unusual for you to let anything like that disturb you, yet there you are, behaving like someone strange to me instead of my daughter."

Grace reached a gentle hand over to her husband and twined her fingers through his. "Darling, leave her be," she quietly urged. Her raven black hair was wound up in a fancy bun atop her head. Jewels sparkled at her throat where a necklace heavy with diamonds lay against a sleek maroon velveteen dress. "Husband, allow Shanndel her moods. You certainly know who she got them from. I've learned to live with your moods. Please learn to live with Shanndel's."

Edward gave his wife a quick glance, then smiled as their eyes met and held. Her radiant loveliness always reached inside his heart, causing it to flutter. He nodded. "Yes, my moods," he chuckled, his eyes twinkling.

Then his smile faded and he gazed over at Shanndel again. "But, Shanndel, you are not usually one to be moody," he said thickly. "Would you like to tell your mother and father about it? If there's something worrying you, it would be best to get it off your chest, wouldn't it?"

Shanndel avoided his steady stare.

Instead she looked down at her clean denim riding skirt and white blouse.

Even though she would rather go to the stable and grab up the satchel and change into the Indian attire again so that she could go to Panther, she knew it would be pointless.

She would have to find him and address him in her usual attire. She must somehow set things right with him.

But if he *did* know who she was, and he believed her a treacherous schemer, she doubted he would listen to her explanation.

"Shanndel, there you go again, your mind everywhere but here," Edward snapped. He wheezed, then slid his hand from his wife's. He slammed a fist on the table, startling Shanndel. "Damn it, Shanndel, 'fess up. Tell us what's wrong. Has someone bothered you? Is it one of our hired hands? If so, I'll see to him right away."

"Father, no," Shanndel gasped, nervously raking her fingers through her waist-length hair, which hung loose and free down her slender back. "There's nothing specifically wrong. I...I..."

"Then if there isn't anything wrong, I've plans for you today that will occupy your time and mind," Edward said. He folded his napkin and laid it beside his empty plate. "I've got too much to do today. You can help me by going and checking on the men who are making the cigars. Make sure they are doing everything properly. I've found several among the recent batches of cigars that are of poor quality. They haven't passed my inspection. Those I sell must be of the highest quality. Report back to me if you see someone not doing the job he is paid to do."

Shanndel's eyes wavered and her heart sank. "Father, I had other plans," she said softly.

"Shanndel, you know that I don't ask much of you,"

Edward grumbled. "But when I *do* need you, I expect you to be there for me."

Shanndel said nothing for a moment, again seeing the outline of the man on the horse in the moonlight, knowing without a doubt that it was Panther.

She realized however, that her father must come first, the Shawnee second. Panther could never be anything to her, especially if he knew her true identity.

"I'll be happy to assist you today, Father," she murmured.

Yes, finding Panther and trying to explain things to him must be delayed to another time.

She silently prayed that he wouldn't change his mind about staying in the area. If he moved onward with his people, he would disappear from her life forever.

After another restless night, Panther decided that he would go again and try to find the lovely Iroquois woman. He would get answers from her this time. He would ask her to point out where she made her camp. He would meet with her people and see if they knew Iron Nose and if they were connected with him in any way.

Although Rain Singing had denied knowing Iron Nose, perhaps she wasn't aware of what her own chief's plans were. If he was somehow in cahoots with Iron Nose, the peace that Panther's people had found away from the Upper New York area would again be jeopardized.

Nyoh, he would find Rain Singing today. First he would go to Harrisburg to see if by chance she might be there again for supplies.

If she was not there, he would then go to the trading post to see if she might appear *there*.

No matter what it took, he *would* find her and get answers from her. Deep down, though, he knew that his true purpose in going today was simply to be with her.

His breakfast eaten, his father settled comfortably in his bed of blankets, Panther was ready to leave his father's small lodge when he thought of something he had forgotten to say.

He sat back down beside his father's bed as Red Thunder gazed questioningly up at him. "Father, last night, while I was riding in the moonlight, I discovered a large field of tobacco," he said. "I have never seen so much tobacco in one place before. It covered a vast amount of land. Our supply is low. Should I go and make trade for some of the white man's tobacco?"

"*Nyoh*, go my son, make trade," Red Thunder said. He leaned shakily on an elbow and pointed to a large leather pouch. "Take what you find in the bag, my son, for trade. There are many beads and blankets. That should be payment enough for the amount of tobacco we will need to get us through the winter months."

"Trading things that are valuable to you is not necessary," Panther said, reaching a comforting hand to his father's hollow cheek. "There are enough coins left from the sale of my possessions before we left. I have enough coins to pay for the amount of tobacco we need."

"You are a good, thoughtful son," Red Thunder said, turning his head from Panther as he coughed.

"As I brought you sweet hot chocolate powder yesterday to please you, Father, I shall also please you today when I return with tobacco," he said, then leaned over his father and gave him a hug.

"Sleep, father," he murmured. "Rest. You know that you can always depend on me, as I have depended on you ever since I took my first breath on this earth."

"Go, my son, enjoy the sunshine before old man winter robs it from us," Red Thunder said, giving Panther a soft smile.

"*Nyoh*, I *will* enjoy my day today on my steed," Panther said, then left the lodge. He stopped when he heard a familiar voice behind him.

He turned a quick look over his shoulder and frowned when he saw Cloud running toward him. He knew what Cloud would want, and it pained Panther that he would have to refuse Cloud's company again today. He had vowed long ago to care for his friend, to be there always for him.

But he must search for the woman alone. If he did not find her, he would not want to look foolish in the eyes of his best friend at having wasted valuable time over a woman . . . and not only a woman, an *Iroquois*.

"Panther," Cloud said, breathless from his brisk run. "Where are you going? Can I come with you? I have missed your company of late. Life is boring without you."

"There is much you can do to pass the day away," Panther said, gesturing toward the people who were bringing in wood for fires and for building new lodges. This morning he had finally given them word that they would stay the winter in Illinois country. Other warriors were leaving with their firearms to hunt for fresh meat for the cook fires.

"Cloud, join the others," Panther said. "Give help where help is needed. I have my own chores. I wish to do them alone."

"Yesterday you shunned me and today you do the same," Cloud said, his eyes showing a keen hurt. "Why is that, Panther? What, or should I say who, have you found that takes the place of your best friend? Is it that woman you saw in Harrisburg? Have you found her again? Is she filling your hours when those hours used to be spent with Cloud?"

Panther's insides tightened. He did not want to tell anyone about his search for Rain Singing, not even his best friend in whom he had confided everything as a child. But this was now. They were no longer children. What Panther was dealing with inside his heart were the feelings of an adult . . . of a man hungry for a woman!

These were secret thoughts, to be shared with no one!

"Cloud, today, as yesterday, what I do is a private thing," Panther said thickly, avoiding any mention of Rain Singing. "It is not something I can share even with my best friend. Please understand, Cloud. And please know that I will make it up to you. We will soon hunt together again. We will play cards. We will laugh."

"But not now," Cloud said sullenly.

"*Neh*, not now," Panther said, flinching when Cloud gave him a heated look, then swung around and stamped away. Panther watched Cloud until he went inside his small dwelling, hoping with all his heart that he had not sent his friend to the jug of whiskey again.

But now wasn't the time to worry about such things. He had more on his mind than the problem of his friend downing great gulps of firewater. Panther had explained the evils of drink over and over. It was up to Cloud now to make things right for himself. Then he would find that there were many friends who would willingly invite him on the hunt.

It was certain that none of the warriors wanted him along on the hunt now, fearing *they* might lose an eye due to his carelessness.

Panther put Cloud from his mind and went to his *wegiwa*. There he slid several coins into his buckskin parfleche bag. He rushed to his horse, saddled it, then hung the parfleche bag of coins from the pommel of the saddle and rode off.

No matter how hard he tried as he rode beneath the brilliant autumn leaves, he could not get Cloud off his mind. He felt guilty about not allowing his friend to ride with him. He hoped that the answers he sought would be found today, and that they would be good enough answers to share with Cloud on his return to the encampment, or he might lose his friend's loyalty forever.

But he kept telling himself that he had no choice but to go alone. He had to see the woman again, and to make sure that those she made camp with were not a vast number of Iroquois who might be planning a surprise attack on Panther's people.

He hated thinking that he had brought his people this far from trouble, only to step right into the midst of it again!

Jealous and hurt by his friend's continued rejection of him, Cloud leaned from the opening of his small lodge and watched Panther ride away.

Deep inside his heart Cloud knew that Panther's rejection stemmed from Cloud's addiction to alcohol. He realized that soon he would have to make a choice. His friend, or his hunger for alcohol?

For now, it was firewater.

He crawled to the back of his *wegiwa* and grabbed up a heavy jug of whiskey. After uncorking it, he lifted it to his lips and guzzled down several swallows, shivering when its sting burned all the way down to his belly.

After watching the men make cigars for some time, and seeing no one being lax in his duties, Shanndel decided that it was all right to leave them to their jobs without a woman breathing down their necks; their resentment of her presence was plain to see in their eyes.

Knowing that her father was elsewhere, and would not see her leave, Shanndel ran to the stable and saddled her horse.

Just as she was ready to walk her steed from the stable, she looked over her shoulder at the scattering of straw beneath which lay the bag of Indian attire.

"Should I?" she whispered, stopping to stare at it. What if Panther hadn't known it was she standing at the window? Perhaps he had just happened on the house while out horseback riding and saw a silhouette in the window; which he had not recognized.

If so, she could still wear the Indian attire today and hope that she would run across him. Maybe she would still be able to talk with him, one on one, Indian to Indian, without his knowing that she was part white.

The truth would come later when she felt it was safe

enough to tell him. For now she wanted him to like her; to trust her.

She was ready to confide in him something that she had never told anyone. It was something she had already lied about to him because she felt the lie was necessary.

But now? She would test the waters with this truth.

Impulsively, she reached down and grabbed the travel bag from hiding.

As she rode off into the autumn day, Shanndel recalled that day long ago when her mother had told her about her past, when she had lived among the Iroquois. She had been married to an abusive man. His name was Iron Nose!

Oh, how she dreaded telling Panther that fact, but she knew that she must to gain his trust.

And she must tell him to test whether or not he could live with that truth. If not, it was best they go their separate ways now, rather than later, when she would only love him so much she would never be able to forget him.

"If I can forget him even now," she whispered, her pulse racing at the mere thought of being with him again.

Chapter Ten

She had not seen Panther at his village as she watched from behind a cluster of bushes, so Shanndel had decided to try the trading post.

She was there now, trying to stay hidden in the shadows. She didn't want Al, the trading post clerk, to recognize her, and then confront her about how she was dressed.

She felt lucky that the post was crowded, which made her presence less noticeable. Some of the people were buying supplies for the winter; prices at the trading post were sometimes half what they would be in Harrisburg.

Some trappers were there with their thick pelts. The stench of the freshly taken hides was repulsive to Shanndel.

But there was one thing that was missing, at least

from her point of view. There were no Indians at the trading post.

She would never forget the first time she came to the post with her father. She had been ten and was impressed by the wonderful variety of things for sale.

She had been enveloped by many wondrous fragrances—perfume, ground coffee, rich hot chocolate, fabrics, fresh fruit, breads, and smoked hams.

The pelts she saw that day were thick and rich and beautiful.

But the people there had gaped openly at her, causing her father to quickly sweep her outside, where he told her to remain until he was through with his transactions.

It was no different today. The white people at the trading post shunned her as though she were a skunk ready to spray its offensive odor on them.

Beginning to believe that Panther was not going to show up after all, Shanndel began to leave, but stopped abruptly when he suddenly entered. His presence caused a hush to descend on the crowd, and everyone gaped openly at him.

Her heart pounding, Shanndel wondered how to make her presence known to him without also revealing herself to Al, who knew both her and her father. Panther was just standing inside the door, his eyes slowly moving through the crowded room, as though he were looking for someone.

Shanndel's breath caught in her throat when it occurred to her that he might be looking for her. Yet why would he search for her at the trading post? He had never seen her there before.

When Panther did not notice her standing in the shadows, Shanndel was even more frustrated about how to approach him without Al seeing her.

Why hadn't she thought of that earlier? she despaired. She couldn't let Al see her in the Indian attire. The next time her father came to the trading post, Al would question him about Shanndel's strange behavior.

She now felt trapped. Surely it would have been better to have worn her usual attire. Then she would not have drawn undue attention at the trading post. She was going to explain her true identity to Panther anyhow.

She set her jaw as she realized that the only way to get this thing settled between herself and Panther was to approach him and forget Al. She had come here today with a purpose.

And since Panther had arrived there, as she had hoped, she would not let him leave without explaining things to him. She wanted him to understand her, for she doubted that she would ever find another man who touched her heart as Panther did. It was surely destiny that had brought them together.

She stood still in the shadows, scarcely breathing, while Panther gathered his supplies and placed them on the counter. She waited for the right moment. . . .

Panther turned and gazed slowly along the shelves to see if he had forgotten anything. He felt discouraged that Rain Singing wasn't at the trading post, as he had hoped.

Of course he had known it was a long shot that she would be there. But he had hoped that her curiosity about him matched his about her. He had hoped that she, too, would be looking for him.

He wanted the fact that she was Iroquois to mean

nothing to him. But because Rain Singing was not willing to tell him where she made her camp, he could not trust her.

Trust had to be earned.

She had not yet earned his.

His eyes stopped on a tin of hot chocolate powder. Afraid that the one tin he had bought for his father might not be enough, Panther decided to add one more to his supply. He went to the shelf and raised a hand for it, stopping when he looked across the shelf and saw the woman he'd been seeking step out of the shadows into full view. Their eyes met and held.

"Rain Singing?" Panther said, unknowingly grabbing the tin of hot chocolate powder and holding it tightly to his side.

Feeling awkward now in his presence, Shanndel searched her mind for something to say to get a conversation started.

She glanced down at the tin of hot chocolate powder that he held at his side, then looked up at him and smiled. "I, too, enjoy hot chocolate," she murmured, her heart pounding. He gazed intensely at her as though he were looking deeply into her soul, perhaps for answers he needed to know about her.

"It is for my father," Panther blurted out. He smiled slowly. "But I also enjoy a cup now and then."

He looked down at her empty arms, and then at the lovely beaded purse that hung from her shoulder. "You have come for supplies for, perhaps, your father?" he asked guardedly. He looked over his shoulder at the counter where he had left his supplies, seeing no other piles that might be hers. He then questioned her with his eyes. "Have you just arrived? Have you many supplies to buy?"

"I did not come for supplies," Shanndel found herself saying. She swallowed hard, and her face grew hot with a blush. "I . . . I . . ."

"You came because you thought I would be here," Panther said thickly, finishing her words for her. He stepped closer and gazed down at her, his dark eyes filling her with a pleasant warmth she had never known before. "I, too, came because I thought you might be here."

"You . . . did . . . ?" Shanndel said, eyes wide, her throat suddenly strangely dry.

"One meeting with you was not enough," Panther said, longing to touch her lovely copper cheek, knowing that it must be as beautifully soft as his wife's had been. Oh, how he had enjoyed brushing kisses across Little Sun's petal-soft cheeks, and then her rich red lips.

He hungered to do the same now with Rain Singing, for she had helped get him past that hurtful longing for a wife he would never see again until he reached the high road that lay ahead of him when his life was over.

But he had much to get sorted out about Rain Singing before he could make his fantasies come to life. He must have answers.

"I wish to talk with you away from all of these people," Shanndel said, looking over her shoulder at the other shoppers.

She blinked her eyes nervously as she looked up at Panther again. "Can we go someplace where we can have privacy?" she murmured. "There are things I must say to you."

"I must first pay for my supplies and then load them on my horse," Panther said, his heart pounding to know that she had sought him out to speak to him. Surely she would give him the answers he needed before pursuing a true, meaningful relationship with her.

"I shall go outside and wait for you," Shanndel said, feeling euphoric that she would have a second chance with him. She had thought she would never see him again, much less be able to talk with him about the things that had to be said.

"I will join you soon," Panther said, unable to resist the temptation of touching her.

He saw her catch her breath when he reached a gentle hand to her cheek.

He saw a look of utter joy in her eyes when his flesh met hers. He felt the same joy to know that she cared so much for him.

Nyoh, they must clear things up between them, for he knew that he had found the one woman who could fill his heart, which had been empty and alone ever since his wife died.

He so longed to tell Rain Singing that she was a *u-le-thi-e-qui-wa*, a beautiful woman . . . that she was *ke-sath-wa-a-lag-wa*, the sun and stars. And in time he *would*. Today had proven they had a second chance with one another.

But for now, he slowly took his hand away.

Their eyes held for a moment longer, then the spell was broken when Shanndel forced herself to turn and walk away from him.

His loins on fire, his pulse racing, Panther went to the counter and placed the tin of hot chocolate powder among his other supplies. Just as he untied the buckskin bag from his waistband to get his coins, he saw the store clerk's eyes look quickly past him. The man seemed to be looking at someone with keen puzzlement in his eyes. When the clerk spoke the name Shanndel, Panther turned to see whom he was addressing.

When no one answered to that name and Panther saw Rain Singing stop stiffly for a moment before leaving through the door, he wondered why, then shrugged off his curiosity when she hurriedly went on outside.

"Damned if that don't beat all," Al said, idly scratching his narrow brow. Then he went to Panther and began counting up what he owed.

Being of a curious nature, Panther wanted to question the man about the woman named Shanndel, yet he did not know this man well enough for such small talk. He let the question leave his mind as quickly as it had entered.

"More powder for hot chocolate, I see," Al said, remembering Panther from the day before. "Well, as I see it, it's best that you're hooked on something like that instead of firewater. Cain't do you no harm. I kind'a like a cup occasionally myself."

Rarely indulging in conversation with a white man unless it was necessary, Panther only nodded, then paid the man the number of coins required to get him quickly out of the trading post and in the company of the lady who awaited him.

Still pale from being recognized by Al, Shanndel unswirled her horse's reins from the hitching rail with trembling fingers. When Al had called out her name, everything within her had gone cold.

Had he spoken it again before she got out of the building, she would have had no choice but to answer him.

Since she hadn't, surely Al would think that he had been wrong and forget the "mistaken identity" by the time he saw her father again.

This time she had lucked out. But she had learned a valuable lesson. She must never wear the Indian attire again. It could raise too many questions among those who knew her, questions that might reach her father's ears. If he knew about her involvement with Panther, he would become furious and refuse to allow her to see him again.

When Shanndel heard footsteps coming up behind her, she stiffened, praying it was not Al.

Slowly she turned, then smiled with relief when she found Panther coming toward her, his horse already loaded down with his supplies.

"I know of a place where we can talk in private," Shanndel said as he stopped only a few inches from her.

She still could hardly believe that she was being so matter-of-fact with him, a total stranger and an Indian chief.

"You lead, I will follow," Panther said. Their eyes momentarily locked, causing his heart to pound.

As though she were in a dream, Shanndel mounted Blue Smoke and rode off with Panther until she came to a secluded place where a shallow brook rippled and sang over rocks.

It was a peaceful and romantic place. Among the widely separated oaks and elms and hickories, flickers were singing, with a background chorus of trilling and whistling from thrushes.

Shanndel avoided Panther's eyes. Her pulse was racing so fast she felt dizzy. She would soon reveal truths about herself that no one but her mother knew. The closer she came to this moment of truth, the more she wished not to tell Panther.

But she must, and *now*. His mention of Iron Nose and his obvious hatred of the man was something she could not ignore, for Iron Nose was a part of her past. He had been her mother's husband all those long years ago.

Feeling Panther's eyes watching her every move, Shanndel swung herself out of her saddle.

When she felt Panther next to her, she wished that what she had to say was already said and that he had accepted it without hating her.

She knew that in a matter of moments he could be gone from her life forever.

"Shall we sit?" Shanndel said, gesturing toward the soft grass on the riverbank.

His heart thumping wildly now that he was finally alone with Rain Singing, Panther nodded. He took her horse's reins and led both her steed and his beneath a birch tree and tethered them side by side, then went back to Shanndel and sat down beside her.

"I haven't been altogether truthful with you," Shanndel said, avoiding looking at him as he sat there so quietly.

"I know that," Panther said, his voice drawn. He dreaded hearing which nontruth of all those she had said to him she had chosen to admit. If she spoke Iron Nose's name. . . . !

"It is because I am Iroquois that things are so awkward between us, isn't it?" Shanndel asked, looking quickly at him.

"The Iroquois are the longtime enemy of the Shawnee, so you can see why it would be hard for me to accept that you, a woman I am attracted to, are of Iroquois descent," Panther said, watching her reaction to his admission of being attracted to her.

His insides melted when he saw her eyes soften. Suddenly they were sweet and beautiful, whereas only a moment ago they'd been filled with wariness.

"You . . . are . . . attracted to me?" Shanndel said, her voice almost a whisper. "Truly? You are?"

"You knew that or you would not be here with me now," Panther said hoarsely. "Nor would I if I did not know that you felt something special for me. We are of two worlds. That alone should keep us apart. Yet here we are, wanting to make things right between us."

"I so badly want to," Shanndel said. She swallowed hard when she looked away from him, for the moment of truth was so near. As each moment passed, she felt less sure about telling him what must be said.

"Rain Singing, do you have something to confess to me?" Panther asked softly. "You have led me to this place of seclusion to tell me *what*?"

The sound of her Indian name on his tongue made Shanndel's heart melt, for it sounded so right coming from him, as though she had been given her Indian name just for him to speak it.

Oh, Lord, what if the secret she was about to tell him

stilled that name on his lips forever and ever?

Yet . . . she . . . *must*! And *now*!

"You mentioned an Iroquois chief's name to me before," Shanndel said, her heart thudding wildly inside her chest, her breathing shallow. "You called him by the name Iron Nose."

"*Nyoh*, I asked if you knew him and you said that you did not," Panther said guardedly.

Shanndel's eyes were wide as she glanced quickly at him. "I *don't* know him," she said, her voice breaking.

She humbly lowered her eyes. She swallowed hard again. When she spoke, the words seemed wrenched from the very depths of her being. "But my mother knew him," she said softly.

She flinched when she heard Panther's quick intake of breath. She could almost feel his rage as his breathing quickened.

"Your mother knew him?" Panther said in a low, questioning voice.

He paused, then said, "How? In what capacity?"

"Let me first explain something about my mother to you," Shanndel said, pleading with him with her eyes to understand. "Long ago she lived among her Iroquois people. She was married to a man who was abusive to her, both mentally and physically. She fled him and the pain he gave her. This man, Panther, was . . . was . . . Iron Nose."

Shanndel flinched, and she wanted to die when Panther leapt to his feet, his full shadow falling over her, his eyes filled with rage and warning.

She wished that she could read his mind and know what he was thinking, but seeing the hatred was enough.

As she had expected, the fact that Shanndel had any relationship at all with the evil Iroquois was too much for Panther to accept.

Panther's heart pounded wildly inside his chest. Shanndel's confession had placed a barrier between them that could never be breached.

He couldn't accept the fact that Rain Singing was Iron Nose's daughter.

He could not allow himself to have a relationship with the daughter of the man he hated with all of his being.

As far as this woman was concerned, he was cursed.

He walked abruptly away from her toward his horse.

Unable to bear the thought that she had ruined things between herself and Panther, Shanndel rushed to her feet and went to him.

She stepped around him and stopped in his path. She then did something very out of character for her—she boldly flung herself into his arms.

"Please don't let what I said upset you so," she murmured, gazing pleadingly up at him.

She winced when she saw that his eyes were like hot coals as he gazed down at her unfeelingly.

"Didn't you hear me?" she said, her voice breaking. "My mother fled from Iron Nose's tyranny long ago. He is nothing to her, *nor* me."

Panther placed his hands on her shoulders and shoved her away from him. "Iron Nose is my worst enemy. He may be stalking my people even now. I cannot allow myself to feel anything for anyone who is kin to this man, especially his daughter," he hissed.

"His . . . daughter . . . ?" Shanndel gasped. "I didn't

say that Iron Nose was my father. Panther, he *isn't*. Believe me when I say that he isn't.''

"Of course you would say that," Panther said stiffly. He laughed mockingly. "But I will play the game with you for a while longer." His eyes glittered down at her. "If Iron Nose is not your father, who is? Where is he? Where is your camp? Take me to it. Take me to your father."

Feeling trapped again, Shanndel went quiet, for to tell him the full truth might be worse than his thinking that she had an Iroquois father. She could not tell him that her father was white; probably white people were as much an enemy to him as the Iroquois. The whites had taken from the Shawnee more than the Iroquois ever could!

Her breath was stolen away when he yanked her into his arms and kissed her, then went to his horse and swung himself into the saddle and rode away at a hard gallop.

Shanndel was as stunned by his sudden departure as by the kiss, which left her knees weak.

Panther's moods were so changeable, she never knew what to expect of him next. Shanndel could not find the courage to go after him.

By the way he had kissed her, though, she knew he had feelings for her that he could not deny. Yet she knew he was fighting those feelings with all the will-power that Indians were taught as children.

Dispirited, Shanndel went to her horse, removed the clothes from her travel bag, and changed into her normal riding clothes. She had botched this meeting; surely it was the last she would ever have with Panther.

*   *   *

Iron Nose was now riding through southern Illinois. He had seen an Indian encampment not far ahead through a break in the trees. Then he had spotted a woman on horseback who resembled his long-lost wife so much, he could not help following her to her home.

As he hid in the shadow of many cottonwood trees, he watched Shanndel go inside the two-storied pillared mansion, puzzled as to why a red woman would go there as though she belonged.

Also, why was she dressed as a white woman?

Could that mean that his wife, Princess Dancing Sky of the Iroquois nation, had married a white man after she had fled the life of an Iroquois wife?

His jaw tightened, for finding and killing Panther now came second to finding and reclaiming his long-lost wife.

He watched the house with narrowed, angry, yet anxious eyes. He was certain that if he waited long enough he would finally see Dancing Sky!

Having decided to place her mother's clothes back inside the trunk where she had found them—for she would never wear them again—Shanndel laid the travel bag on her bed and slowly slid the lovely dress from inside it.

Tears came to her eyes as she held it to her cheek and enjoyed the softness of the doeskin against her skin. She wished she was wearing it now; she wished she was in Panther's arms, his lips searching hers with a passionate kiss. . . .

"Shanndel, why do you have my dress? Why did you take it from the trunk?"

Guilt heavy in her eyes and heart, Shanndel dropped the dress and turned sharply to look at her mother. She watched her mother go to the travel bag and remove the moccasins and purse.

"Shanndel, not only have you taken my dress from the trunk, but also these?" Grace said as she held them out toward Shanndel. "Why, Shanndel? And why were they in a travel bag? Where did you take them?"

Shanndel lowered her eyes, then gave her mother an apologetic look. She had no choice but to make a complete confession . . . why she stole the dress, how she wore it to make the Shawnee warrior think that she was a full-blooded Indian, and how her plan had sorely failed!

Chapter Eleven

In his excitement at seeing Shanndel at the trading post, Panther had forgotten to purchase tobacco for his father, but Red Thunder had not questioned him about it. He and all of his people were excited about having found a salt lick in the Saline River close to their camp.

As Panther watched his people eagerly place salt from the river into their large parfleche bags, he did not feel the same excitement as everyone else. He knew that in 1803 the United States Congress had authorized the Secretary of State to lease all salt springs and licks for the benefit of the Government. As a result of those leases it was against the white man's law to remove the salt, as his people were doing today.

But salt was a necessity of life for all people. If Panther's people could extract much of it now without being caught by the whites, it could last them even until they reached Oklahoma. If they did not have to trade for salt, they could keep their money and trading objects to use for other necessities.

"My son, you are so quiet," Red Thunder said, reaching over to place a hand on his arm. "You fear what we are doing, do you not?"

"Father, we risk so much by even staying among whites who resent our presence, much less removing salt that they say belongs to them," Panther said. "Do you not recall the sheriff's warning? Did he not say that if he was given cause, he would hang any red man who was caught participating in wrong against the white community? What we do today is wrong in their eyes. I hesitated before giving permission to take the salt. I only did so because our people have already lost so much at the hands of whites. Taking their salt is at least a small way to get payment from them for our losses."

"I see it that way also, my son. Do not fret so much over what you have given permission to do," Red Thunder said, patting Panther's arm reassuringly. "I agreed with your decision. I urged you to make it. Should harm come to our people, I will take full blame."

"I would never allow you to take blame for anything," Panther said softly. "I would never allow you to be taken by the whites to be punished. If it comes to anyone being accused and punished, it will be me."

"You are our acting chief," Red Thunder said thickly. "You must never be taken from our people for any reason. Without you they might never reach Oklahoma."

"I sometimes doubt that we will, anyhow," Panther

said, his voice breaking. "It is one obstacle after another, Father. The prejudice seems worse with each
white man we meet. We have a long journey ahead of
us, Father. There are many white men still to contend
with."

"You are a strong, wise leader, one who will get us
to our new home without harm," Red Thunder said,
easing his hand from Panther's. He gripped his cane
with both hands as a cough tore at his insides.

"Father, you should not be out here in the wind,"
Panther said as he watched the morning breeze blowing
briskly through the leaves overhead.

"Is not the sun bright?" Red Thunder said when the
cough finally subsided. "Although I cannot see the sun,
I feel it."

"*Nyoh*, but still the wind is your enemy today, Father," Panther said. He placed a hand under his father's
elbow and led him to his horse. "Father, I will see that
you get safely back to camp and then I will return and
hurry along this harvest of salt. I will breathe much
more easily once it is hidden in brass pots among our
people's dwellings."

"The more substantial dwellings must be built
soon," Red Thunder said as Panther helped him into
his saddle. "Is there not enough lumber ready now to
build them?"

"*Nyoh*, there is enough lumber," Panther said as he
watched his father slide his cane into the sheath at the
side of his horse.

"Tomorrow, my son," Red Thunder said. "Tomorrow the building of homes must begin. The salt can be
hidden in holes dug in the ground beneath the cabins.

No white man will ever think to look there for the stolen salt."

"I will not wait until tomorrow," Panther said, swinging himself into his own saddle. "After you are safely in your lodge, I will return to the salt lick and appoint several of our more sturdy warriors to start building our new homes today. Your plan is good, and it is best that we get the salt hidden as soon as possible from any white man who might happen along."

"And the tobacco?" Red Thunder said as he rode back toward their camp with Panther at his side on his own magnificent black steed. "When will you go and purchase tobacco? That, too, we must have in abundant supply before the cold winter winds begin to blow. Many a night will be spent in smoking pipes as the winds howl outside our people's lodges. The smoke will help warm the hearts and souls of those who enjoy the pipe."

"Tomorrow, Father, after I see that the building is under way, I will then purchase tobacco from the man who owns the vast tobacco fields," Panther said, his thoughts straying to the night when he had seen the woman standing at the window.

He could not help wondering if it had been Rain Singing.

But that was foolish.

Rain Singing was Indian.

The woman in the house must be white to live in such a massive mansion. It was just a coincidence that she was as tall and as shapely as Rain Singing.

But he hoped that tomorrow when he went to the

tobacco grower's house he would see the woman who had stood in the window.

He wondered if she might recall that night, also, for he believed that she had seen him on his steed in the moonlight.

Would she recognize him?

If so, would she tell those who lived in the house with her that he had trespassed?

He *had* taken a chance going so close to a white man's mansion!

"Your mind is straying, my son," Red Thunder said. "It strays often of late. Where do your thoughts take you? Is it worry that makes you become so quiet and full of thought? Does what our people do today weigh too heavily on your shoulders? If so, we can reverse our decision to take the salt."

"*Nyoh*, I do worry," Panther said, riding into their camp and making a sharp turn right as he went toward his father's small lodge with him. "But, *neh*, I do not wish to take from my people today that which makes their eyes light up with excitement. We will take the chance of being discovered. Seeing our people with something special in their lives once again is worth the risk."

"Panther, Cloud is elusive these days," Red Thunder said, drawing his reins tight and stopping his horse. "Was he at the salt lick? Does he share the same excitement as his Shawnee brothers and sisters? I did not hear him join the laughter and joking as the salt was being extracted."

"Cloud is an unhappy man right now," Panther said sadly. "I am the cause."

"You?" Red Thunder said as he carefully slid from his saddle. "How can you blame yourself for anything Cloud does or feels? You are a devoted friend. I have heard you talking with him and trying to lead him on the right road of life. He does not listen. He still drinks the firewater no matter what you do or say."

"*Nyoh*, that is so, yet I feel that, of late, I have let him down," Panther said, taking his father's horse's reins as his father took his cane from the sheath. "There has been much on my mind that does not include him. I have not asked him to join me when I have the need to ride alone with my thoughts."

"I, also, find that strange," Red Thunder said, taking the cane and leaning heavily on it. "Scarcely have you ever forbid your friend to share things with you, especially when you ride your horse. Is there something you are not telling me, my son, that should be said? Are you harboring too much fear of being stalked by Iron Nose? Is that why you leave alone on your horse? To patrol the area?"

Panther felt trapped, for never had he lied to his father. If he did not admit to having a woman on his mind, he *would* be lying. Yet it was certainly true that he was worried about Iron Nose.

That was why he had hidden sentries around the camp just last night. If Iron Nose did arrive, he would be the one to be surprised!

"Iron Nose has been on my mind ever since the slaughter he left in our village," Panther said finally. "Then later, on that night when I led our warriors back to his camp to retaliate, Iron Nose was not there to receive one of my arrows. That he still lives has haunted me both day and night, Father. As long as he lives, our people will not be safe.''

"We are now far from Iron Nose's home and I doubt he would take time from his duties as chief to seek us out, for we are a mere few Shawnee for him to concern himself about,'' Red Thunder said. ''You are doing what you can to assure a good life for our people, and Iron Nose has the same duties. My son, leave the sentries hidden near our camp each night, but otherwise forget Iron Nose and get on about your business as chief. To allow Iron Nose to take away from your leadership is granting him victory, just as surely as if he had downed you with his arrow.''

"Even though what you say is true, I can never let down my guard,'' Panther said, his voice drawn. ''And, Father, although I am bothered by worries about Iron Nose, you can depend on me to be the best chief I can be for our people.''

"I know that, Panther,'' Red Thunder said, nodding. ''I did not mean to belittle you with my advice.''

"I did not take it as belittling,'' Panther said. He reached down and placed a gentle hand on his father's shoulder. ''Go inside your lodge and rest. Be assured that soon you will have a more substantial dwelling that will give you much comfort on the long winter days ahead.''

Panther smiled. ''And I *will* get you the tobacco you desire,'' he said. ''But for now I must return and pick the warriors who will start building our lodges. The sooner the salt is hidden, the less concern you will hear in this son's voice.''

"Go and *Moneto* be with you, my son,'' Red Thunder said, turning toward his dwelling. His hands feeling for the opening, he bent and entered.

Panther took his father's steed and placed it with the others in the corral.

Then, with a frown creasing his brow, he rode back to the salt lick and watched awhile before dismounting, his mind again filled with worries that he could not shake. He was on land that was the property of the United States Government. He dared not think what the punishment would be should his people be caught taking what belonged to the rulers of this land.

Chapter Twelve

Shanndel stood at a podium before a crowd of men in her father's huge tobacco auditorium. She faced many tobacco buyers who had traveled for miles to hear her speech about tobacco. She waited patiently as the rest of the men filed in and sat down.

She glanced over at her father, who stood at the far side of the room watching and counting how many had arrived, smiling at those he knew.

Shanndel then glanced at the open windows along the sides of the building, and at the open door at the back of the auditorium. The day was warmer than usual. The windows and the door had been opened to let in the gentle autumn breeze. A faint aroma of leaves burning wafted through the windows as did the song of birds that had not yet flown south for the winter.

Dressed in a floor-length, lovely blue silk dress, with

a matching blue satin ribbon holding her hair back from her face, and with delicate leather slippers and sheer black stockings, she felt quite feminine among the gathering crowd of men.

But she recalled having felt even more feminine in her mother's doeskin attire and regretted that she would never wear it again. Her mother had taken it back to the trunk along with the lovely beaded purse and moccasins.

Shanndel would feel as though she were trespassing on her mother's intimate past life should she go to the trunk again.

She felt ashamed that she already had, although her mother, in her sweet, soft way, had not made her feel that shame.

It was the fact that Shanndel had done something behind her mother's back for the first time in her life that made her feel small and cheap.

The reason for her secretiveness came to Shanndel's mind. When she saw Panther in her mind's eye and remembered how angry he had been after she had confessed the connection between her and Iron Nose, she felt empty inside.

And then, though, there was that sudden kiss that had come out of nowhere, and the wonderful passion it had awakened inside Shanndel.

That kiss was something she would never forget, for she doubted that any other man could ever again awaken such feelings within her.

"Shanndel, it's time," Edward said, coming to sit down close to the podium behind her. "Everyone who matters is here. Begin the lecture, Shanndel. Begin it now.''

Shanndel was shaken from her thoughts by her father's voice. She gazed at him and smiled weakly, then spread the notes she had prepared before her on the podium. The light from the window was enough by which to read them should it become necessary for her to check one fact or another.

As she began to talk, her mind was momentarily distracted from thoughts about Panther. She was well versed in the history of tobacco, and although she did believe and regret that people could become addicted to it, she knew that it made her father proud for her to teach its history to interested persons.

There was an instant hush in the auditorium when Shanndel began talking in a quiet, yet knowledgeable tone. She spoke with pride, the focus of all eyes.

''Because of its delicate nature, very careful work is involved in tobacco planting,'' she said. ''And the planter must always be aware of the dangers of insects and certain types of fungus that could quickly destroy the crop.''

She paused and gave her father a quick glance, then centered her attention on the listeners again. ''Cigar tobacco is subjected to a heavy fermentation, which results in one-half or more of the nicotine disappearing during the production of cigars,'' she said. ''All of the cigars here at my father's factory are made by hand. A tender, binder leaf is wrapped around a bunch of cut filler leaf. This is then overwrapped with a fine wrapper leaf.''

She continued with her lecture, yet wished that she could be elsewhere.

Panther!

Oh, Lord, she wished that she could be with Panther and that he would greet her appearance with a smile instead of his usual suspicious scowl.

But she knew that was wishful thinking. She would probably never see him again, much less be the recipient of his smile . . . or kiss.

She absently touched her lips with a forefinger, where his mouth had left that brief yet wondrously beautiful kiss.

Once the salt was gathered and safely hidden back at the camp where some log dwellings were quickly taking shape, Panther left camp long enough to go and bargain for tobacco. He would buy not only for himself, but also for others whose supply was running low.

On the rear of his horse hung many empty parfleche bags, which he hoped would be heavy with tobacco on his return home.

He inhaled a deep breath, enjoying the pleasant smells that wafted through the forest. He enjoyed riding through the forest today. Summer seemed to have arrived again, perhaps for its last demonstration of warm, balmy breezes and sunshine before old man winter came with his harsher icy winds and blowing snows. Here and there apple trees were so loaded with the weight of their fruit, the boughs gracefully bent down to the ground.

Glistening among thorns, full of dark red juice, wild blackberries were like manna in the wilderness.

Panther smiled when he thought about the times he had found blackberries that were so ripe they would almost hop from the bush into his hand. If a person had to tug at the fruit, it was not yet sweet.

He always enjoyed a supper of fine, fat berries.

He smiled when he thought of times when he had inched his hand through the ferocious brambles to reach those fattest, farthest berries. The inevitable scratch was forgotten when the black suns burst on his tongue.

Wearing only a breechclout and moccasins, Panther rode onward, enjoying the warmth against his bare chest, back, and legs. Before long he would be burdened with heavy buckskins and blankets. He did not feel as free in the winter as he did when he could wear so little.

But the more he thought about the clothes he wore today, the more he doubted that he had made a wise choice. To arrive at the white man's dwelling so scantily dressed might make him look more the "savage."

And just as he was thinking that and realizing that it was too late to turn back, he came to a break in the trees and saw the rich tobacco owner's land stretched out far and wide ahead of him. At the far side stood the huge house where he had seen the silhouette of the woman in the window.

But seeing that house again was not what made him stiffen. Outside the other large dwelling, which he assumed was some sort of white man's council house, were many horses and buggies. That had to mean that many white people had come there.

Panther brought his horse to a stop and gazed at length at the large building where the door and windows were open to the breeze. He wondered what sort of council was being held there.

His heart skipped a beat when he thought that the

.meeting might concern Panther's people having made camp on land that belonged to white-eyes. Were they assembled there to make plans about how to rid their land of the Shawnee?

His eyes narrowed and his jaw tightened at that thought. He had to find out if that were true. With so many white people assembling for a raid against the Shawnee, he must prepare his people to either fight the white man's decision, or leave and seek shelter elsewhere.

He, himself, preferred to fight, for he was sorely tired of being subjected to the greediness and selfishness and lies of whites.

But his people were few now, and too many were old and weak. He knew that if they were asked to leave, they had no choice but to go. And the fight was almost gone in the mightiest of his warriors, for fighting had gained them naught! They argued among themselves now, saying why fight when it gained them nothing but lost lives of their brethren?

"I will not let this go that far," Panther whispered to himself. "I shall go and listen to the white people's plan."

Nyoh, if the men were plotting against Panther's people, he would return quickly to his beloved Shawnee and uproot them. They would be gone when the whites arrived with their insults and hatred.

His back stiff, Panther rode onward. When he came within a few feet of the building where the meeting was being held, he inched his horse closer.

He was taken aback when a woman's voice wafted

143

toward him from the open windows and he recognized it.

It was the voice of Rain Singing!

She was inside the building, talking to those who had congregated there!

Why? he puzzled to himself.

And what was she saying?

Was she among those who would come to order his people away?

If so, how could that be?

Her skin was not white! She was Iroquois! Why would whites join with her to do anything?

And why wasn't she with her Iroquois people instead of here among so many whites?

Or . . . were her people there to join the whites against the Shawnee?

That thought sent Panther quickly out of his saddle. He tied his horse among the others.

His heart pounding, he followed the sound of Rain Singing's voice and walked stealthily toward the door, stopping just outside to listen to what Rain Singing was saying.

His eyebrows arched when he realized that what she was saying had nothing to do with his people. Her words were about tobacco. She seemed to be teaching the people who were congregated inside this council house . . . about . . . tobacco.

His puzzlement mounted, for why would an Iroquois maiden be asked to teach whites about tobacco when surely those who owned this land knew all they needed to know to make it profitable for them?

It was certain that the owner of the huge tobacco field

had received much wealth from it or he would not own so much land covered with huge tobacco plants.

Nor would he and his family make their residence in such a plush, grand home.

Nyoh, there was much about Rain Singing that Panther still did not understand, but her being here today was the most puzzling discovery of all.

Unaware of Panther lurking outside the door, Shanndel continued her lecture.

"If leaf-stemmed tobacco is not bought in ready-stemmed form, the first step in turning it into a product that the consumer can smoke, chew, or take as snuff, is to remove the *midribs*, which are the central veins," she said. "For most products, manufacturers blend leaves of various types, origins, grades, and crop years to obtain the qualities they require and assure uniformity over the years."

Wanting to see Rain Singing and also observe how the white people were receiving the teachings of someone whose skin was not the same color as theirs, Panther stepped just inside the door.

He stopped and stared when he saw Rain Singing standing at the far end of the room behind a podium. He was stunned to see her wearing a silk dress such as rich white women wore. And seeing her there as though she belonged, seeing the white men so attentive to her teachings, truly mystified him.

Yet he quickly recalled the other time when he had seen her in Harrisburg dressed in white woman's attire and moving among the white people as though she belonged.

Was she a lying, conniving trickster who only dressed

as an Indian when she saw that it benefited her? Did she live among whites instead of her Iroquois people?

Everything about her was a lie!

He had to get away from there . . . away from *her*. He never wanted to see or hear her voice again. She had made a complete fool of him by tricking him into caring for her, when she was not worthy of any man's love!

Just as he turned on a heel to leave, Panther heard Shanndel abruptly stop speaking.

He swung around again and saw by the startled look in her eyes that she had seen him standing there.

As everyone's head turned to see what or who had interrupted her lecture, gasps spread through the crowd.

Panther's and Shanndel's eyes met and held. Everything within Panther wished he could trust this woman whom he might have loved with all his heart and soul. But, realizing that she was someone he no longer wanted anything to do with, he turned and rushed from the building and to his horse.

Blinded with rage, he swung himself into his saddle and rode off in a hard gallop.

Shanndel had been frozen with surprise at seeing Panther standing there gazing at her with utter contempt in his eyes. But she was galvanized into action when she heard him ride away. Although her father was now on his feet crying out her name, and everyone else was watching her with astonishment, Shanndel lifted the skirt of her dress and ran from the building.

When she got outside, she placed a hand over her eyes to shield them from the brightness of the sun and looked into the distance, where she could still see Panther riding away at an angry gallop.

"No," she cried, tears rushing to her eyes.

She placed a hand over her mouth to stifle a sob. "Oh, Lord, *now* what does he think of me?" she whispered to herself. "Why . . . was . . . he . . . here? Oh, Lord, why did he have to see me in this setting?"

"Shanndel Lynn, what's got into you?"

Her father's voice startled Shanndel. She turned and gave him an uncertain look, then forgot everything but the need to go after Panther. She couldn't let their relationship end like this. It was time for her to come clean and tell him everything.

Then if he still hated her, she would have done everything humanly possible to make things right between them.

Not caring that she was wearing one of her most delicate dresses, nor that her father was rushing down the steps to come after her, Shanndel ran to the nearest saddled horse and swung herself into the saddle. She raced off after Panther.

Realizing that she now not only had explanations to make to the man she loved, but also to her parents, she rode onward.

Pounding her heels into the flanks of the brown mustang, Shanndel finally caught up with Panther and sidled the steed she rode closer to his.

"Please stop!" she cried. "Let me explain!"

Panther glared at her. "Woman, nothing you say would be believed by this Shawnee chief!" he cried back.

He sank his heels into the flanks of his black steed and left her behind in a faster gallop.

Skilled with horses, Shanndel rode harder and again

came up next to Panther. "Please, Panther?" she cried, tears flooding her eyes. "Please listen?"

The pleading in her voice grabbed at Panther's heart. He pulled on his reins and came to a shuddering stop.

Sighing with relief, Shanndel stopped beside him.

"Speak quickly, for my patience runs thin with you," Panther said, fighting an urge to reach over and grab her from the horse and onto his lap to comfort her when he saw tears rushing down her copper cheeks.

Shanndel wiped her face dry with the back of a hand, then searched through her mind for what she truly *could* say.

"Panther . . ." she began, swallowing hard.

Iron Nose was lurking in the forest near the tobacco fields and saw all that had happened between Panther and the Indian woman. He felt that this might be a good opportunity to find out who she was. This woman could not resemble Dancing Sky so closely unless there were blood ties between them. With everyone so involved in what was happening in the large council house, surely no one would notice if something happened to Dancing Sky.

Iron Nose knew that Dancing Sky was not among those who were in the large council house. He had been watching long enough to know that she was still inside her two-storied dwelling.

The woman speaking to Panther looked so much like his first wife that she must be her daughter. At last he had found Dancing Sky! As he had suspected so long ago, she had run away with a white-skinned man! He had searched for her until he had become exhausted and had finally given up.

A thought came to him that made his heart skip a beat. If that was Dancing Sky's daughter, she must have been born not long after her mother had left him. This daughter might also be *his*.

That thought almost sent him after the young woman, yet his need to be with Dancing Sky, to make her pay for having embarrassed him by disappearing all those years ago, was stronger than his desire to seek out a woman who might be his daughter. He had no feelings for a daughter he had not raised. Never would he!

He tethered his horse to a low tree limb and ran stealthily through the trees until he was closer to the back of the mansion, yet positioned so that he could see who came and went from all doors. He anxiously awaited the moment Dancing Sky would come from that house, alone.

He smiled when he thought of the fear that would leap into the dark eyes of his wife when she saw him standing there, a threat to everything she had become since she had abandoned her life as an Iroquois princess and wife.

Chapter Thirteen

"Panther, first I want to tell you that I'm sorry for having not been altogether truthful with you," Shanndel said, growing uneasy under his steady, cold stare. "But . . . but . . . after you mentioned Iron Nose to me, and I heard how you felt about him, I was afraid to tell you the truth. I so . . . so . . . badly hoped that we could become friends. Even . . . more . . . than that . . ."

Her voice drifted off and her face grew hot with a blush, for again she was being forward with this man, and no other man had ever brought out that trait in her.

"Trust is the foundation for friendship," Panther said, trying to ignore that she had said she wanted more than friendship from him.

She was Iroquois.

He was Shawnee.

And she not only knew Iron Nose, she was his daughter.

"Yes, I know," Shanndel said, lowering her eyes.

She then looked up at Panther, her eyes wavering when she still saw distrust and anger in his. "Can we go and sit by the stream as we talk?" she asked.

Panther said nothing, but he did slide from his saddle as she dismounted, then walked along with her to the stream, where his steed bent low and began drinking from it, as did Shanndel's.

Leaving the horses to their pleasure, Shanndel sat down beneath a towering elm tree, disappointed when Panther stood stiffly over her, his eyes never leaving her.

Feeling uncomfortable with his superior position, Shanndel pushed herself up from the ground and stood before Panther. She nervously clasped her hands behind her as the gentle breeze fluttered her skirt around her legs.

"Panther, Iron Nose is *not* my father," Shanndel insisted. "Yes, my mother was married to him. As I said before, my mother's marriage was not a good one and when she got the opportunity to flee Iron Nose, she did so. She left her Iroquois life behind to . . . to . . . marry a white man. She then had a daughter nine months later born of her love for this white man. Panther, that daughter is *me*."

Shanndel tried to read Panther's feelings in his eyes but it was too hard. He stood perfectly still, showing no emotion of any kind. It was as though she were talking to the wind.

151

Yet she continued. . . .

"Yes, Panther, I am a half-breed," Shanndel said softly. "My father is white. My mother is Iroquois. I am known as Shanndel in the white community. No one but my mother knows that I have an Indian name. That is because Mother secretly named me out of the presence of my father. She named me Rain Singing, Panther. It is a name I love, one that I cannot speak in the presence of those I have been raised among. It was so wonderful to . . . to . . . share it with *you*, for you see, Panther, I am so proud of that part of me that is Indian. I just have never been allowed to outwardly claim it. It is hard enough for me to live in the white community with the brand of a 'breed,' much less try to make others accept that I have a name so different from theirs."

As Panther listened, he took her words into his heart, overjoyed that she was not related to Iron Nose.

And it was good that she was opening her heart to him and telling him things she would tell no one else.

Yet there was the fact that she had lied to him so easily, and that she was, in part, white.

Although it made his heart ache to think it, being part white was almost as bad as if she had been born Iron Nose's daughter.

It was taboo for the Shawnee to marry whites. In the past, white men had mated with Indian women as a means of destroying pure strains of Indian blood among the tribes. Long ago, the Shawnee had decreed that the blood of an Indian woman and white man must never be allowed to mix, under threat of most severe penalty. In the same sense, no Indian male should marry a white woman!

"I'm so glad you have listened to me," Shanndel said, though she felt unnerved that he still had not responded.

She wondered how he was taking her confession.

Did he hate her even more than before?

Did he even *believe* her?

Did any of this truly matter to him?

Had she been wrong to think there was something special between them that first time they met and talked? It seemed to her that something unseen was trying to draw them together.

Yet it seemed as though something else more powerful stood between them, not allowing it.

Despite all that, she knew now that she had fallen in love with this man. Her love for him came from somewhere deep inside her, as though it had been there long ago in another time.

And she would die if he did not return her love.

"Panther, my mother told me that it was taboo for Shawnee people to marry whites," Shanndel said, again feeling brazen, yet needing to find a way to break through his silence.

In a flash she recalled the kiss he'd given her and the wonder of it! "Is that true?" she murmured. "Would it matter if a woman had white blood flowing through her veins as well as Indian? Should any of that come between us? If you truly feel something for me, why would you want to fight it?"

She took a step toward him. She fought the urge to reach up and touch Panther's sculpted face. "Panther, it is known that love can happen quickly between two people," she murmured. "It happened that way between my mother and father. It has happened for *me*. I love you, Panther. And, oh, Lord, I know that, if you could get past those things that hold you there like a stone pillar, you could love me as much. The way you kissed me. The way you looked at me before you had cause to be angry and mistrustful of me, and told me that your feelings for me match mine for you. And, Panther, the way you became so angry when you suspected that I had duped you. You would not have become this angry if you did not care about me.''

Panther's eyes softened momentarily. ''*Nyoh*, it is true I have feelings for you that I am fighting. But you *did* trick me,'' he said tightly. ''It is wrong to play games with a man's heart!''

His confession that he cared for her, made tears of joy rush to Shanndel's eyes, yet she still held herself back. She would not fling herself into his arms as she had the other time. This time if he wanted her in his arms, he would have to be the one to place her there.

''Then . . . you . . . *do* care,'' she said, a glorious smile quivering across her lips.

''I care, but too much still stands in the way of the caring,'' Panther said, wanting so badly to claim her lips again.

''Only because you allow it to be there,'' Shanndel said, sliding her hands apart, reaching out to touch him, then yanking her hand back when she saw him flinch.

''I can look past most of the obstacles, even the fact that you lied, but there is your white father,'' Panther said thickly. ''There are my people who still shun anyone who is in any way related to whites. The whites have taken too much from my people.''

"Yes, I lied," Shanndel said softly. "But you surely know that I had no choice but to pretend that there was no white blood running through my veins, at least until I knew you loved me. Then I hoped that your love for me would be so strong it would not matter."

She sighed. "And, Panther, if you are really afraid your people wouldn't accept that part of me that is white, they need never know," she murmured. "When you first saw me you thought I was a full-blooded Indian. Why wouldn't your people think the same?"

"Because I would never allow such a game to be played on them," Panther said tightly. "And that you would even suggest it makes me think that I should still not trust you. How would I know when or if you were deceiving me again in our relationship?"

The blood rushed from Shanndel's face. How stupid it had been to suggest playing such a ruse on his people when only moments ago she had finally convinced him that she was trustworthy!

She turned away from him and lowered her eyes with shame, for she now doubted that he would ever trust her. She wished she could take back those words, but knew that they were engraved on his mind like leaves fossilized in stone.

"I'll leave now," she said, still not looking at him. "I have . . . I . . . have taken up enough of your time. And . . . and . . . what must father think of me? I'd best return home where I belong and say a few apologies. I hope they will be received there better than they were here."

She started walking away, but her breath was stolen when she felt a sudden hand on her wrist, stopping her.

Her heart racing, she turned and gazed into the deep, dark eyes of the man she would love forever. "Why did you stop me?" she dared to ask, her knees weak from the overwhelming passionate need that assailed her.

"To hold you," Panther said huskily. Slowly he drew her to him. "I have wanted to hold you from the moment I saw you. And that first kiss was not enough. I want more, Rain Singing. I want everything from you."

He yanked her against his hard body. Her lips were warm and wonderful against his as he kissed Shanndel with a deep longing that had been born within him on the day of their first eye contact.

And not because she resembled his wife.

It was something more!

It was like an awakening inside him, as though he had never loved before until . . . until . . . now!

Then the reality of who her mother was came to him again. His jaw tight, his eyes filled with fire, he released Shanndel and again looked questioningly down at her. "As much as I want and need you, I find it hard to accept that your mother was married to my worst enemy," he said hoarsely. "How can I know for certain that Iron Nose is not your father? How can *you* be certain? You were not aware of anything on the day you were conceived. Has *she* been truthful to you, Rain Singing? Has she told you who your true father is?"

Shanndel's face drained of color. "My mother has never lied to me," she said, her spine stiffening. "My father is white and he is a decent, God-fearing man, nothing like the dreaded Iroquois chief Iron Nose. My mother has told me everything about Iron Nose. It was a blessed day when my mother met my father at a trading post where he had gone to sell his tobacco. I told you theirs was an instant love. She sneaked away with him and has never regretted it.''

Shanndel looked warily into the darker depths of the forest at her left side, then gazed up at Panther again. "I imagine my mother is worried now about the Shawnee camping so close to her home," she said softly. "If Iron Nose has followed you and your people, then might not Iron Nose also find his Dancing Sky?''

"Dancing Sky?''

"My mother's Iroquois name.''

He took Shanndel's hand, led her down to the ground, and sat down beside her. "I do not wish to put fear in your heart, but I must tell you something,'' he said thickly. "Your mother might have cause to worry about Iron Nose. He might be searching for me and my people. It is because of vengeance that he would travel so far from his people.''

"What happened to cause him to hate your people so much?'' Shanndel asked, feeling suddenly close to him.

He explained how he had led his people from his home in Upper New York, then how he and his warriors had backtracked and attacked Iron Nose's village to avenge the havoc Iron Nose had wreaked on Panther's village.

"My wife and unborn child and my beloved mother were killed on the day of Iron Nose's raid on our village,'' Panther said, shuddering visibly. "And not only them, but oh, so many more of my beloved people died at the hands of Iron Nose and his warriors. And . . . my . . .

father was blinded that same day when a blow to his head came suddenly from an Iroquois war club.''

''Your father was blinded?'' Shanndel murmured, paling. ''And your wife and unborn child, and even your mother, were killed?''

He turned to her and placed a gentle hand on her cheek and raked his eyes over her face, taking in features so much like his late wife's. ''*Nyoh*, everything dear to me,'' he said thickly. ''My wife was only one month with child. Both were taken away from me that day. And . . . and . . . you resemble her so much you could be her sister.''

''Is that what attracts you to me?'' Shanndel asked, her voice breaking. ''Do you feel while you are with me that you have her back again?''

''At first it was the resemblance that stopped me to stare at you,'' Panther said, his voice drawn. ''But it was for only that instant. I then saw you as someone I desired because *you* stole my heart away, not the memory of my wife. Rain Singing, I have not looked at women since my wife's passing. Now . . . now . . . I cannot get you off my mind.''

''Nor I you,'' Shanndel said, disappointed when he drew his hand away. He stared ahead of him and winced as though he was recalling something horrible.

''That day when so many beloved ones died, I thought I would never feel alive inside again. But you have brought life into my heart,'' he said, his voice breaking.

He looked over at her again and took one of her hands. ''I want to believe everything you have told me,'' he said. ''I want to feel free to love you. But there is so much between us that stands in the way."

"Your people?" Shanndel murmured.

"Your mother," Panther said, his voice tight. "You see, Rain Singing, I am not certain I should be seen with you, for even though I did avenge the deaths of my beloved people, Iron Nose still lives. If he has followed me and discovers that your mother is in the area, do you not see the danger she would be in? I would not want to be the cause of anything happening to your mother."

"Do you truly believe Iron Nose might be near?" Shanndel asked, chills riding her spine at the thought of her mother being in danger.

"I hope not," he said. "My warriors spilled much blood at the Iroquois village. When Iron Nose returned from wherever he was that day, he must have found that he had many burial rites to tend to in his village. That should keep him from seeking vengeance at this time. Then once he gets past his mourning period, I hope he will realize that my people are so far away he cannot find them."

Hearing him speak of "spilling blood" made Shanndel uneasy. She tried not to envision that savage side of this man she adored. She didn't want to think about his killing anyone, even if it was because so many of his people had died.

She tried not to think about his having been married or having lost his wife and unborn child.

This was now.

This was *their* lives, *their* time to be together.

"You have not said yet whether you have forgiven me for not having been altogether honest with you," she murmured. "Can't you please forget that part of me that is white? Can't you forget Iron Nose while with me? As for my mother, my father adores her and would protect her with his life. Panther, if you truly love me, allow yourself to act out this love by holding me again and kissing me. Let me prove my love for you. I want to make love with you."

Finding it hard to believe that she had actually offered herself to a man for the first time in her life, she scarcely breathed as she awaited his response.

She wanted him with every fiber of her being.

While with him she felt things that she had never felt before. The strange, new burning ache between her thighs was surely a woman's response to loving a man. She hungered for his hands to caress her there!

Panther's body was instantly filled with flame as he yanked Shanndel against him. He kissed her fiercely as she strained hungrily against him. And although he knew that he could have her, and his body ached for her, he felt this was not right. This was not the proper setting, the proper time to make love with this woman he wanted for eternity. He wanted their moment of coming together to be magical, not something that she might be doing to satisfy him.

He wanted the satisfaction to be *hers*, so that she would know that he made love to her because he truly loved her. He did not want their union to come about because she thought it was the only way to make him love her.

Sharing in such a way must be done with tenderness, with endearing love, not only with the heat born of passion, though he wanted her so much that his loins ached unmercifully.

Shanndel was stunned when he broke away from her. When she gazed questioningly into his eyes, she knew that his longing matched hers, yet still he hesitated.

She felt a sudden shame for having offered herself to him like some loose hussy.

A sob lodged in her throat to think that again she might have done something wrong—something that had made him turn away from her.

"This is not the time," Panther said huskily. His hands gently framed her face. "When we come together as man and woman, it must be a time when there is less stress and tension between us. I do want you and I understand your want. It will be fed soon, Rain Singing. It must be done when the moment is more magical." He searched her eyes. "Do you understand?"

After he had explained it to her in that way, she *did* understand, and her shame melted away into a loving appreciation of him. He had not taken advantage of the moment as most men would have when they were with a woman who was ready to give up her virginity for them.

She paled at the thought of his thinking that she would behave like this with any man.

Perhaps he did not think her a virgin at all.

"I have never offered myself to a man before," she blurted out, her eyes again searching his. "I . . . have . . . never been with a man in that way. Never have I wanted to be. I only . . . offered . . . myself because I truly, sincerely love you, Panther."

She smiled weakly up at him. "Please tell me that you believe me," she murmured.

"If I did not believe you and I saw you as the sort of woman who bedded men easily, I would have not hesitated to seduce you," Panther said. He drew her gently into his arms. "As it is, I do want to come together with you, but only when the time is more appropriate."

He held her away from him and smiled at her. "And know that a man can tell when a woman is virginal," he said. "It is evident in the woman's eyes and body language."

Shanndel didn't have the chance to tell him how glad she was that he believed her. The sound of a horse approaching at a hard gallop forced them quickly apart.

The blood drained from Shanndel's face when she saw that it was her father. Her heart leapt to think that had Panther not stopped what she had started, she could have been making love with him when her father found them together! She wasn't certain what such a scene as that might have caused her father to do.

Even so, the sight of her alone with an Indian might be enough to make her father's wrath spill over. She held herself tight and tense as she awaited the moment of discovery.

She looked over at Panther. He was as apprehensive as she. He held himself rigidly, yet there was such pride and nobleness about him that she was certain he would get through this confrontation with her father far better than she.

Chapter Fourteen

Shanndel's father wheeled his horse to a stop a few feet away from Shanndel and Panther. She flinched when she saw the contempt in his eyes as he gazed at Panther, then looked at her in a quiet, yet accusing manner.

She had no idea what to expect next. She had never done anything that displeased her father so deeply. She wondered what he was thinking about having seen her brazenly chase after a man, and not any man . . . an Indian.

He had to be wondering how she and Panther had met and why she would throw herself at him like this. She had always been the sort of young lady who carefully chose who would escort her, whether it was to a formal reception, or just a simple dinner at Barger's Restaurant in Harrisburg.

And to have done it so openly, so that the whole

surrounding community of tobacco growers could see it, had surely embarrassed her father terribly.

"Daughter, get your horse," Edward said flatly, his eyes sparking angrily. "Shandell, you're coming with me. *Now*. And by damn, you have some explaining to do."

Edward's jaw tightened and his blue eyes narrowed. "And, Indian, whoever you are, stay the hell out of my daughter's life," he ordered in a cold and measured tone. His chest heaved as he wheezed. "And, damn it, don't let me ever catch you on my property again. Do you understand? There's laws against trespassing."

Edward shivered with disgust as his gaze raked over Panther's brief attire. "Especially savages who run around half naked," he said coldly.

The word "savage" grabbed at Panther's heart like someone's fingers suddenly squeezing it. He clenched his hands into tight fists at his sides. His throat became dry with a sudden hatred for this man who he now knew was Rain Singing's father.

It took all of the restraint that he had been taught by his father when he was a young brave not to lash out at this white man.

Were this man not Rain Singing's father, Panther would do worse than just give him a tongue-lashing. He was bone tired of being treated like a savage when, in truth, he saw all white men as savages in the way they behaved toward the red man. The Indians were the true first occupants of this land . . . land that had been taken not only by force, but also by the trickery of treaties.

"Father, please don't," Shanndel softly pleaded,

ashamed that her father would treat Panther in such a way.

How could her father forget that her skin was the same color as Panther's?

How could he forget that his wife had been born and raised among the Iroquois people?

Shanndel would have thought that fact alone would make her father less prejudiced, especially since he had found an Indian who was as gentle as a spring breeze, the woman whom he was proud to call his wife.

"Just come along with me, Shanndel Lynn," Edward said, nodding toward her horse. He sucked in a wheezing breath, then slowly exhaled. "And, savage, you'd best ride away while you can, for it wouldn't take much for me to draw my pistol and gun you down. I'd not be condemned for it, either. You've been caught with my daughter. I'd say you forced her and that I found you in the act of raping her."

Shanndel gasped and stared at her father disbelievingly. "Father, you wouldn't," she said, her voice breaking. Yet she saw that nothing she said would change the way her father felt about having found her with Panther.

She was just glad that he hadn't openly shamed her in front of the man she would love forever . . . a man she would not be denied, not even by an angry father.

She *would* make things right between herself and Panther.

But first she had to convince her father that nothing he could say or do would keep them apart. She had to make it clear that if he harmed Panther, or any of his people, he would lose her forever, just as though he had

downed her with a bullet the same day he downed the
Shawnee.

"Go with your father," Panther urged, turning to
Shanndel. He placed a gentle, warm hand on her cheek,
ignoring how that simple gesture drew a gasp of horror
from Edward Burton. "We will meet again soon. I vow
to you, Rain Singing, nothing he says or does will keep
us apart."

"Rain . . . Singing . . . ?" Edward gasped out, paling.
"You have even given my daughter an Indian name?"

Shanndel turned quick eyes her father's way. "No,
Father, Panther didn't make up this name and give it to
me," she said, realizing the implications of telling such
a truth . . . that it would bring her mother into the conversation. But it had to be said, and should have been
said long ago. She knew now that it was wrong to have
kept so much from her father.

"Mother gave me that name," she blurted out. "It
was something we felt we must keep from you." She
lifted her chin proudly. "And, Father, it is a name I
have carried proudly inside my heart. It was wonderful
to share it with Panther."

"Your mother named you Rain Singing?" Edward
said, his voice drawn. He began wheezing again. "You
both kept such a thing as that from me? I trust you both
so much. How could you . . . ?"

"It was something that had to be done, Father, and
we both knew you would speak against it," Shanndel
said.

She turned and gave Panther one last smile, then went
to her horse and grabbed its reins.

Again it flashed in her mind's eye what she might

have been doing when her father had arrived. She could have been making love with Panther out in the open for him to see.

During those magical moments with Panther, she had forgotten that her father would ride after her to see what had prompted her to follow the Indian.

Everything but her love for Panther, and her need to prove it, had been swept from her consciousness.

If her father had caught her making love, she doubted he would have ever forgiven her.

And she expected that he would have jerked his pistol from his holster and shot Panther before Panther had the chance to defend himself. Her father would see this man, this wonderful Shawnee chief, as a threat to the future he had long ago planned for her.

Panther went to his own steed. He swung himself into his saddle as Shanndel swung into hers.

Panther's eyes met and held Shanndel's. He resisted a strong urge to kiss her. That would come later, for nothing would keep him away from her now that he knew her feelings for him were true. Now he understood why she had been forced to tell him so many lies. Meeting her father was explanation enough.

He glanced angrily over at Edward, then rode off, his waist-length black hair lifting from his shoulders, the flaps of his breechclout flipping against his muscled legs. He fought against looking back at his woman, for he did not want to see her riding away with her father. He had no idea what her father would say or do to her.

Panther vowed to himself that should the yellow-haired man harm her, he would pay dearly for the crime.

As Shanndel rode off with her father, she dared one

last look at Panther, who rode so tall and straight in his saddle. She prayed to herself that her love for him would not end in tragedy for the Shawnee.

Her father was the richest man in Saline County. Because of what his money brought to the community, he could get anyone to do anything for him.

Even murder! Should he ask someone to rid the land of the Shawnee, it would be done.

"Father, I'm in love with Panther," Shanndel stated flatly, thinking it was best to meet this problem head-on. "It just happened. Our love for one another was instantaneous. Please do nothing to harm him or his people. They have already suffered too much injustice and disgrace at the hands of whites. Should you cause any more—"

"I don't plan to harm anyone," Edward said, glowering at her. He wheezed and coughed, his face an angry purple. "But I want you to forget that you ever met him and this foolish notion of being in love with him. I want more for you than marriage to a red-skin. You will one day inherit the family business. Don't throw it all away over an infatuation. Surely it is the novelty of having met a man whose skin color matches yours that drew you to him. It can't be anything else. You are an educated woman. Life has much in store for you."

"Father, it's far more than an infatuation and you know it," Shanndel said softly. "You know that I never enter lightly into anything I do, especially a relationship with a man."

"You've never allowed yourself to become involved with men before," Edward snapped back. "All of the men who've tried to court you have been given their walking papers. And now? You choose an Indian?'' He looked quickly away from her. ''No, Shanndel Lynn. I just can't have it.''

''You don't have a say in the matter,'' Shanndel blurted, trembling inside at showing her father such disrespect. She tried to ignore his wheezing and his pallor. What had to be said must be said now. He would react no differently later.

''I am a grown woman,'' she murmured. ''I will marry the man of *my* choice. Not yours.''

''Marry?'' Edward gasped out. ''You are truly considering marrying that savage?''

''Father, if you call that man a savage only because his skin differs from yours, then you may as well call me by the same disrespectful name, because my skin color is the same as his,'' Shanndel said, sighing heavily.

''This is all too much for me to take in,'' Edward growled, his chest heaving. ''First I see you go after an Indian while those who came to hear your lecture look on, then I hear that damn Indian calling you by an Indian name your mother gave you. Too much has been done behind my back for me to understand, especially about your mother. I thought she kept nothing from me.''

''She only kept our secret talks from you because she knew you would disapprove of her telling me things she felt I should know,'' Shanndel said. She gave him a soft, accusing look. ''Father, you know that you wouldn't have wanted Mother telling me about our Iroquois heritage. You sure wouldn't have approved of her giving me an Indian name.''

169

"She left that life behind her the day she chose to marry me," Edward said tightly. "I thought it had been left behind a long time ago. Lord, she dresses like a white woman. I give her everything. Diamonds, silks, satins, everything any woman's heart could desire. And now I know that she has harbored so much inside her that she did not feel free to share with me? It hurts, Shanndel Lynn. It hurts."

"Father, no one has meant to hurt you," Shanndel said. She sidled her horse closer to his. She reached over and gently touched his arm. "Mother and I adore you. But there was a part of both of us that had to be dealt with out of your presence because we both knew you wouldn't accept it."

"When I look at you both, I don't see Indians," Edward said, his voice breaking. "I see a lovely daughter and wife. That's all."

"That's only because you wish to deny that we are of Indian descent," Shanndel said softly. "And it is that Indian side of me that has fallen in love with Panther."

"Panther," Edward said, as though testing the name on his lips. He gave Shanndel a quick look. "If he is in the area, then there must be more like him. Shanndel Lynn, are they making camp near here? Is that how you met him?"

"Yes, they are near," Shanndel said, hating to tell him where, but knowing she had no choice. He would not have far to go to find them, himself.

She started explaining things, and he listened. She told him how far the Indians had traveled to get there. She explained why they were so close to Harrisburg.

"They plan to leave in the spring," she concluded.

"Father, I hope to be among them, for I *do* love Panther and will marry him if I am honored enough to be asked."

"I could stop it, you know," Edward growled out.

"Yes, I know, but if you did, you would alienate me from you forever," Shanndel said tightly. "I am no longer a little girl you can dictate to. I am my own person. And this is the first time, ever, for me to be in love. I don't want anything or anyone to interfere."

"You are blinded by some foolish attraction only because a part of you is Indian," Edward said, swinging his horse to the right to ride toward home. "Your mother mistakenly married an Indian when she was young. If not for me, I doubt she would be alive today. Her first husband was abusive to her. How do you know all Indian warriors aren't as abusive to their wives?"

"I just know, that's all," Shanndel said, shivering sensually when she recalled the gentleness of Panther's kisses and embraces. "Panther is nothing like Iron Nose, Father."

Edward gasped. "How do you know about Iron Nose?" he asked, giving her a startled stare.

"He, too, was a part of my mother's teachings when we talked of her past and the life she had with the Iroquois before she met and married you," Shanndel said. "Father, Mother told me everything about her past life long ago when I began questioning why my skin color differed from yours."

"I doubt she told you everything," he said, looking quickly away from her. No, he doubted that his wife would tell their daughter something that might turn Shanndel against her mother. And he would not be the one to break the news to her. In time, perhaps. But . . . not . . . now.

"What do you mean?" Shanndel asked, raising an eyebrow. "What do you think Mother left out about her past?"

"Nothing, Shanndel," Edward said sullenly. He gave her an assessing look. "Daughter, let's let it drop. Okay? I've so much to think about. I've got to have time to think over what I've discovered today about you . . . your mother . . . and the Indian."

"No matter how hard or long you think about me and Panther, nothing will change," Shanndel said, stubbornly lifting her chin. "I am in love, Father. And he loves me as much."

"Oh, daughter, how do you know what true love is?" Edward said, his voice drawn. "I still say it's an infatuation."

"Mother's feelings for you weren't born of an infatuation," Shanndel replied quietly. "Nor are mine for Panther."

She shuddered when he gave her a look she didn't understand. She was afraid to think what that look might mean. She was afraid that because of her, Panther and his people's lives might now lie in balance.

"Rain Singing," Edward said, arching his eyebrows as he stared at Shanndel. "Your mother named you Rain Singing?"

"She told me that the name came to her one day when I was a baby and she was holding and rocking me," Shanndel said, smiling softly at her father. "It was spring. It was raining. To her, it seemed more like singing than rain. She felt the loveliness of that moment deep inside her heart and allowed me to share it with her forever by giving me that beautiful name."

Everything within her grew warm with love for her father when he suddenly gave her a soft, wondrous smile. She knew that things would be all right between them. She wasn't sure how long it would take, though, for him to give in and give her his blessings.

I hope soon, she thought to herself, for she could not stay away from Panther for long. A sensual union born of love and dedication to one another awaited them. Ah, but it would be such a savage joy to make love with him.

"Daughter, get those stars out of your eyes. I am not going to give up this fight all that easily," Edward said, frowning again, as though he had read her thoughts.

Her smile faded and a wariness set in that she did not want to feel about her father. He was the only man she had loved devotedly until the day she set eyes on Panther.

Grace was standing at her upstairs bedroom window watching the tobacco buyers leave, some on horseback and others by horse and carriage. She had heard the commotion outside earlier and had gotten up from her knitting just in time to see Shanndel ride out after the Indian.

She had known that Edward would want to follow her, to stop her, but he had been forced to stay behind to apologize to those who had traveled far to hear Shanndel's lecture.

Grace knew from the short time Shanndel had been in the auditorium that she had not had time to give her full lecture. She knew that many people would be disappointed.

But most of all they would wonder about Shanndel's chasing after the Indian warrior. Some might be so stunned by her behavior they would not return for future lectures.

"Oh, Rain Singing, why did you not think of the consequences of acting before thinking?" Grace whispered to herself. "And why did he come here? Panther. That surely was Panther."

She wasn't sure how Shanndel had noticed Panther on their property. Surely she had seen him through the opened windows.

Surely he had seen her and knew that she was more white in her behavior than Indian!

Grace had seen Panther ride away in a hard gallop, anger etched on his handsome face.

"He surely feels as betrayed as my Edward now feels," Grace whispered. She stifled a sob behind her hand. "Oh, Shanndel, when your father caught up with you, what did you tell him? How much of it was about you and me and our secret talks?"

Not seeing as much as she would like from her window, and wanting to be outside when her daughter and husband arrived back home, Grace lifted the skirt of her red velveteen dress and left the room. She took the steps down the staircase gingerly, so as not to fall in her long dress and pretty leather shoes.

When she got outside, she saw that all of those who had come to hear the lecture were gone. There was a strained silence as the wind whispered through the brilliant autumn leaves in the nearby trees.

A sudden chill raced up and down Grace's spine as she looked into the distance and still didn't see any signs of her daughter and husband.

But she did feel a presence.

Her brown eyes wary, she looked toward the darkness of the forest. She knew that anyone could be lurking there, watching her.

Suddenly she felt vulnerable. Yet she did not want to flee back inside to the safety of the house. She had to be there for Rain Singing and Edward when they returned. She had much to explain to her husband. And she must again warn Shanndel of the hardship of loving a man with red skin.

When he saw his first wife step out of the house, alone, Iron Nose's heart pounded. Finally she was at his mercy.

He would see to it that she would never enter that two-storied mansion again. She would never again share a bed with that yellow-haired white man.

And tomorrow, when the songbirds awakened to a new morning, Dancing Sky would not hear them. She would be dead, but first she would die in the worst way for having dishonored her Iroquois husband those long years ago.

He would first rape her, then enjoy watching her die after he sank a knife deep into her belly!

Almost giddy from the thought of finally being able to avenge himself on her, Iron Nose yanked his long, razor-sharp knife from its belt and started to go for her. He stopped suddenly and rushed back into the darker shadows of the forest when he heard horses approaching.

His eyes narrowed angrily when Shanndel and Edward rode past so close he could reach out and touch them. His plan to steal Dancing Sky away had been foiled.

"I . . . will . . . still have her!" he whispered harshly to himself, still lurking, watching, leering.

Chapter Fifteen

Bathed and dressed in a soft, comfortable gingham dress, Shanndel had suffered through the dinner hour with her parents. Shanndel now only had coffee and dessert in the parlor to struggle through before she could escape her father's glowering glances and her mother's worried eyes.

Sitting in a plush chair opposite the settee on which her mother and father sat in front of the massive stone fireplace, Shanndel was too nervous to eat dessert.

Her father had been uncharacteristically quiet since they had arrived home. She glanced over at her mother. Even she was quiet, as though if she avoided talking about her daughter's involvement with Panther, it might magically go away.

Finally having had enough of this strained silence, Shanndel set her plate of untouched cake on the table beside her. She wanted to clear the air so that she could retire to her room. It had been a long day. She had never had such a day as this, in which she discovered that the man she loved now trusted her, allowing himself to love her.

The wonders of being in his arms, his kisses passionately sweet, lived inside her heart. They were so real now it seemed as though he were there, his hands on her cheeks, his midnight dark eyes branding her as his.

She wished to be alone in the privacy of her bedroom so that she could live all over again those precious moments in her lover's arms. She had never known that loving a man could be this wonderful . . . this fulfilling.

Ah, yes, what a savage joy they would share when they finally made love.

"Father, you have something to say. Say it," Shanndel blurted out, her spine stiffening when her words brought his cold blue gaze her way again, in his expression an anger she had rarely seen.

"Yes, I have much to say to you, daughter, but I'm not sure if now is the time," Edward said, his voice becoming a wheeze.

"Father, I'm sure there is never going to be a good time for me to hear what you have to say," Shanndel said, sighing hard. "So just say it and get it over with. I . . . I . . . am sorely tired. I would like to retire to my room and go to bed early tonight."

"But would you truly go to bed? Or sneak out after your mother and I are in the privacy of our own rooms? Would you go and be with the savage again?" he grumbled, the word "savage" drawing a quick intake of shocked breath from his wife.

He gave her an apologetic look. "All right, Grace, I know how you abhor that word and I promise not to use it again in your presence," he said.

"Nor mine, I hope," Shanndel said, again drawing her father's eyes her way.

"Shanndel, what you did today was not only embarrassing to me, but reckless," Edward said, his chest heaving as he wheezed. He plucked a cigar from a gold-engraved case on the table beside him. He bit off the end and spat it into the fire, then placed the cigar between his teeth and wetted the tip as he slowly rolled it around the inside of his mouth.

"I'm sorry for having embarrassed you," Shanndel apologized. "But I'm not sorry for having gone after Panther. I could not allow him to think the worst of me, which he did when he saw me addressing that huge throng of men. I had earlier led him to believe that I was a full-blooded Indian who lived with her tribe. I'm not good at lying. I regret that I lied to him."

"And to us?" Edward said, leaning down and lighting his cigar at the edge of the fire.

"I never lied to you," Shanndel said. "I just didn't tell you what I was doing."

"That's the same thing," Edward said between wheezes as he tried to relax again against the back of the settee. He crossed his legs and puffed at his cigar as great balls of smoke billowed from the corners of his mouth.

"Again, I'm sorry," Shanndel said, nervously shifting her weight in the chair. "Now may I be excused?

179

I *do* plan to go to bed. Today's activities have drained me.''

"I would think so," Edward said. He took the cigar from his mouth and held it between his fingers as he rested the palm of that hand on his knee. "Listen to what I have to say, and then, daughter, you can go to your room. Listen well, for this will be the last time I will talk about this to you. You are your own person. You will suffer the consequences of whatever you choose to do with your life. Your mother's life and mine will go on without you, if we must.''

"Edward," Grace gasped, paling.

"Grace, let me say what needs saying," Edward said, giving his wife a soft, apologetic look. "It might not be what you want to hear. Nevertheless, it must be said. You have to realize, Grace, that our daughter is no longer a little girl.''

Shanndel's eyes lit up with hope. She never would have thought that her father would give in this easily. Surely she was hearing wrong.

Her pulse raced as he gave her an unsteady stare, then began speaking again.

"Shanndel Lynn, I have tried to make you understand, more than once, that those feelings you have for that Indian are pure infatuation. You are attracted to him, because you are part Indian, yourself," he said. "Let me remind you again that your future is here, as are the riches you will receive if you keep the tobacco fields healthy and productive after your mother and I have passed away.''

When he went on and on about the same things, merely saying them differently, Shanndel's hopes sank.

He would never understand that nothing could sway her from loving Panther.

When her father's words finally died away and the room became quiet except for his dreadful wheezing, Shanndel rose from her chair and stood with her back to the fire. She looked slowly from her mother to her father.

"Again I apologize for having caused you distress," she murmured, nervously clasping her hands behind her. "I apologize for doing something that you will never understand. But, Father, no matter how many times you say my feelings for Panther are mere infatuation, there is no way you can convince me. I love Panther. I love him more than I knew a woman could ever love a man."

"I hear you," Edward said, interrupting her. He rested his cigar on an ashtray, then pushed himself up from the chair.

He covered his mouth with a hand and coughed into it, then sucked in a deep breath. When that spell was behind him, Edward faced Shanndel and took her hands in his, his eyes softly imploring her.

"But, Shanndel, for me, for your *mother*, don't see Panther for several days so that you can have a clear head to think all of this through," he said hoarsely. "Both your mother and I want more for you than what an Indian can give you. Isn't it true that the Shawnee are nomadic . . . a tribe that never plants roots for any length of time anywhere? Isn't it true that they are always on the move?"

"As far as I know, yes, that is true," Shanndel said, gently sliding her hands from his. She placed them behind her and tightly clasped them together. "But, father, if that is so, it is only because white people have always forced them to move on."

"They blame whites, yet is it not true that all Indians have enemies among opposing tribes who also force things upon them?" Edward said softly.

"Father, this is getting us nowhere," Shanndel said, wincing when she saw how those words made a quick anger leap into his eyes.

"Shanndel Lynn, not only have you foolishly become involved with an Indian, you've become insolent," Edward said, stamping from the room.

"Shanndel, you should be more patient with your father," Grace said, rising from the settee. She went to Shanndel and drew her gently into her arms. "You know that your father only wants what is best for you. Otherwise he wouldn't bother lecturing you."

"Mother, I hate getting lectures as well as giving them," Shanndel said, easing from her mother's arms.

She bent over and smashed the foul-smelling, smoking cigar out in the ashtray, then plopped down in her chair again and stared into the fire. "Seems no matter what I say or do, I can't make father understand."

Shanndel looked quickly at her mother, who was sitting again on the settee, her hands clasped together on her lap. "Nor do you understand, and you, of all people, should sympathize with me," she said. "Mother, didn't you fall instantly in love with father? Didn't you go against everything you were taught by your Iroquois people to be with him? Must I be forced to go totally against my own family to be with Panther? Oh, Mother, I don't want that. Surely you don't either."

"It's your unhappiness that I don't want," Grace said, her voice drawn. "You have so much, Shanndel. With Panther you will have so little. Can you truly adjust from one sort of life to another?"

"Didn't you, and do very well at it, Mother?" Shanndel asked softly.

"Yes, but there is quite a difference in our situations, Shanndel," Grace said, reaching over to take her daughter's hand. "I went from poverty to riches. Who could not adjust to such a life as this?"

"But the Indian in you?" Shanndel persisted. "How could you deny that part of yourself? Don't you ever crave to see your people?"

"So much it hurts," Grace said, lowering her eyes. But then she looked at Shanndel again. "But, Shanndel, remember that I left a life of abuse behind and started life anew with the most gentle man on earth," she said, her voice breaking. "He helped me forget my longing for the other side of my life. He filled my heart and soul with love and understanding. His touch has never been anything but gentle. How could I not want the life he has given me?"

"And so would *I* if I had the chance to live with Panther as his wife," Shanndel argued back. "Mother, I want him. He wants me. I *will* go to him. I *will* be his wife should he ask me."

Shanndel lowered her eyes, then told her mother about Iron Nose's recent atrocities against the Shawnee, and what Panther had lost due to the attack on his people's village.

"Mother, I won't forsake him and make his life as empty as it was before we met," Shanndel murmured.

"He lost a wife and unborn child. I offer him myself and eventually that child he craves."

Shanndel noticed that a strange sort of fear had come into her mother's eyes. "Mother, what's wrong?" she asked, leaning over, touching her mother gently on the arm.

"Shanndel, I implore you to reconsider your decision to marry Panther," Grace said, her voice breaking. "There is more here than your love for that man. There is *me*, Shanndel. There is your *mother*."

"Mother, please don't ask me to choose," Shanndel said, swallowing hard.

"Shanndel, I fear not only for your safety, but also mine," Grace said, her voice now low and fearful. "You now know everything Iron Nose is capable of. He was abusive to me. He killed and maimed at Panther's village. Panther, in turn, went and killed and maimed at Iron Nose's village. If Iron Nose is still alive, he will pursue Panther until the end of his days to achieve vengeance. His fury over what Panther did must be eating away at his heart." She stifled a sob behind a hand to think that among those who had died were relatives and friends she had turned away from so long ago. "I know the depths of Iron Nose's hate when he has cause to hate. He won't rest until he finds Panther, and if he comes this far to find him, he most certainly will not only find Panther, but also the woman that wronged him. That woman is me, Shanndel. Me."

Seeing the fear in her mother's eyes and hearing it in her voice, Shanndel made a quick decision that broke her heart. She decided to stay away from Panther, for if what her mother said was true about Iron Nose, he *would* find Panther, and more than likely it would be before Panther moved on next spring for Oklahoma.

If Shanndel was not seen with Panther, then Iron Nose would have no cause to know that her mother was anywhere near.

Yes, although it would break her heart to turn her back on Panther, for now she must make the sacrifice for her beloved mother, and give up the man who meant the world to her. She hoped that in time, she could move on with her own life and be free to love Panther.

Shanndel went and bent to her knees before her mother. She reached out and hugged her. "Mother, for now I won't go to Panther," she murmured. "I'll stay away long enough to see if Iron Nose is a problem. If I see that he isn't, though, nothing will stop me from going to the man I love."

"Darling, darling," Grace said, sobbing. "Thank you. Thank you."

As Shanndel still hugged her mother, tears splashed from her eyes. She knew that if she didn't go to Panther soon, he would think that she had forsaken him. He might never give her another chance.

Trying to block out the thought of losing him forever, she closed her eyes tightly.

Chapter Sixteen

His face set in harsh lines, Panther sat quietly before his lodge fire carving a figure of a wolf from wood. He was still disturbed by what had happened the day before, especially about Rain Singing having been forced to leave with her father in such a way.

He was at least happy about one thing. When he returned to camp, he had joined the other warriors who were busy building log cabins and had gotten several finished, including his. He had worked at an incredible pace, his anger firing his energy to twice what it normally was.

When his father had wondered about the rage in his son's voice when he returned without the tobacco, Panther had only touched upon why he did not have it. He had not mentioned Rain Singing, but he *had* told his father that the white man who owned the tobacco was not one easily dealt with.

Although Panther knew that his father wished to know more about the encounter with the tobacco owner, Panther's rage had caused his father not to delve more deeply into the matter. His father had left it alone, to discuss later when Panther was more ready to talk about it.

Today, as Panther sat on his thick pallet of furs before the roaring fire, the figure of a wolf taking shape in the piece of oak, he thought of Rain Singing's lies. Now he understood why they had been necessary. Her father was surely not an easy man to live with. Surely she had not wanted Panther ever to meet him face to face. He was obviously a prejudiced man, even though his daughter was, in part, Indian. She had not wanted to be embarrassed by his blatant show of prejudice. She had not wanted her father to know that Panther made camp close by her father's home, surely afraid of how he would react to that news.

But in her surprise at seeing Panther standing in the door of the huge council house, she had forgotten caution. By chasing after him, she had brought Panther and her father together in the worst way possible.

"Will he retaliate?" he whispered to himself, that fear just now entering his heart. He hoped he had not brought undue problems to his people by wrongly making his presence known at the council house.

If he had just gone there and purchased tobacco, there would be no reason for the white man to hate him.

"Panther, you are in such deep thought you did not

hear me enter,'' Cloud said as he sat down beside him on the spread pelts.

Shaken from his thoughts, Panther looked with a start at Cloud. ''*Neh*, my friend, I did not hear you enter,'' he said thickly. He laid his carving aside. ''And, *nyoh*, I *am* deep in thought.''

''Something is bothering you,'' Cloud said, his eyes seeing the anger in Panther's. ''Yesterday when you returned without tobacco and you threw yourself angrily into building lodges, I wanted to ask you what had happened to cause such anger, but thought better of it.''

''It is as it always is,'' Panther said, sighing heavily. ''My meeting with the white man was not a pleasant one.''

He refused to speak about Rain Singing to Cloud, for he was not certain whether she would dare see him again. Surely her father would guard her well to keep her away from him.

Years ago when warring was profitable for his people, he would have gone to war with this white man over the woman.

But as it was, his warriors were few and he had many elderly people and children's lives to protect from such skirmishes with the whites. He had to settle things as peacefully as possible.

Yet if this woman was denied him, how could he go about getting her without clashing with her white father?

''Panther, your lodge is built very well and will now hold out the cold, howling winds of winter,'' Cloud said, sensing that his friend did not wish to speak further about his problems.

Cloud smiled. His reason for being there was a good one, something that would bring a happy gleam into his friend's eyes. At least for the moment he could bring some sunshine into his friend's heart, whereas too often of late he brought nothing but frustration and disappointment to his friend's life by refusing to give up the firewater.

"*Nyoh*, the lodges we have built are fine," Panther said, looking over his shoulder at the large room that now held his personal belongings.

His gaze lingered on a large rug that had been thrown over the part of the wooden floor that had been cleverly built to hide the salt from the spring.

He smiled as he thought of the other lodges that hid salt from the prying eyes of the white men. The salt was now the Shawnee's. The white men would never find it.

"Panther, I did not come today to speak of lodges and weather," Cloud said. "Panther, I have news that will gladden your heart."

Panther looked quickly at Cloud. "What is it, Cloud?" Panther asked, thinking that nothing today except having Rain Singing with him would gladden his heart. It ached so for her.

"What I have to tell you comes from deep within my heart," Cloud said, then rose to his feet. He gestured toward the cabin door. "Come outside with me, Panther. I have something to show you."

"Something to show me?" Panther asked, arching an eyebrow. He rose to his feet and walked toward the door with Cloud. "You have been on the hunt? You have perhaps brought back a fat buck that you are proud of?"

"*Neh*, I have not been on the hunt, but I will join the warriors soon to hunt. Soon they will want me there instead of shunning me because they see me as too dangerous to be around while weapons are being used," Cloud said. He stepped aside so that Panther could go outside.

He followed him and smiled as he saw Panther staring questioningly down at the jug of firewater that sat on the ground before him.

Panther stared at the jug for a moment longer, then frowned at Cloud. "Again you bring firewater to my lodge, hoping I will drink it with you?" he said vehemently. "Is this what you have to offer that you feel will bring laughter and sunshine into my life?"

He glared at the jug and kicked it, causing it to fall to one side.

"You will never give up, will you, Cloud?" he growled. "Leave. Take the firewater with you. Do not return again to my lodge until you come to tell me that you will never touch the stuff again. I tire of worrying about you. I am especially tired of lecturing you when you are too stubborn to listen."

"I *have* listened and listened well," Cloud said. He bent to a knee and picked the jug up. He yanked the cork from it, then smiled up at Panther as he tipped it upside down and allowed the liquor to flow in a steady stream from it.

"Have you ever seen me throw away liquor before?" Cloud asked, anxiously awaiting Panther's response.

"*Neh*, and I do not find it amusing that you are doing so now as a way to trick me into thinking you do not wish to drink it," Panther said, angrily placing his fists on his hips. "Take the empty jug away, Cloud, for I know there is more in your lodge awaiting you. I have not time for this today."

Cloud still held the jug upside down, some liquor still dripping from it. "This is the last of my firewater," he said proudly. "I will drink no more, ever."

"And you think I will believe you?" Panther said, raking his fingers through his long, jet-black hair in frustration. "Please go away, Cloud. I tire of you."

Not to be dissuaded, Cloud stood his ground. He bent over and placed the empty jug on the ground, then clasped his hands on Panther's shoulders. "My dear friend, I have come today to tell you about *go-na-pa-di-a-so-ka*, three visions that came to me in one night," he said hoarsely. "Panther, in these visions I, your friend *Cloud*, was a spiritual leader for our Shawnee people. I will make the visions come true. I will become that spiritual leader. I will drink no more. You and our people will be proud of a man you all lost faith in long ago. I truly understand that drinking firewater is wrong. I truly know that it is a fatal poison to our people. From here on out I will lecture against firewater to those who will listen!"

Stunned by the change in Cloud, Panther was momentarily left speechless. He couldn't find words enough to tell his friend how happy he was to hear him speak with such strong conviction.

Was it true? Could Cloud stay with this decision and be the person Panther had known him to be long ago?

"Panther, you are not happy for your friend Cloud?" Cloud asked, his voice drawn. "Or is your silence because you still doubt me?"

Panther suddenly wrapped his arms around Cloud and gave him a fierce hug. "What you say has touched my soul," he said, his voice breaking. "I do believe in you. And the knowledge that you have put your drinking days behind you is something that makes my heart sing."

"I vow to you that I shall never again take another drink of the fiery liquid," Cloud said, returning the hug.

Then they separated and smiled at one another, pride showing in both of their smiles.

"Cloud, you know as well as I that a Shawnee Medicine Man Prophet must act as the conscience of the tribe and guide the people's morals," Panther said thickly.

"I, above all others, would be the best teacher of those morals, for it is I who have failed and then come back again a stronger person," Cloud said, his voice steady and strong.

"But what if you fail and give in to your hunger for firewater again?" Panther asked. "What sort of teacher would you be then?"

"My life has been changed by my visions, and my need to spread the word about right and wrong is strong," Cloud said. "I vow to be the best man I can be. Believe in me, Panther, and I will never let you down."

"I will believe in you with all of my heart," Panther said, now convinced that Cloud was dedicated enough to this new ideal to make it true and forever.

"Thank you, friend," Cloud said, swallowing back a sob of joy. "Your trust and faith in me will guide my every movement toward becoming the best medicine man prophet I can be.''

''Cloud, you know, as do I, that Two Spirits, our people's medicine man prophet, is old and frail and needs to be replaced with someone younger and more vital,'' Panther said, his eyes eager. ''If you prove to everyone that you are worthy of being our people's prophet, then I will see that you are taught all you need to know. The position of medicine man is awarded by the Shawnee council. The selection is made from someone tutored by the Medicine Man Prophet who is to be replaced.''

''You are saying that I, Cloud, could be next in line when Two Spirits retires from his duties to our people?'' Cloud said, his voice filled with awe. ''You will make it so, Panther? You . . . will . . . make it so?''

''*Nyoh*, if you are as sincere as I believe you are, you could make a great medicine man prophet, for everyone who has ever known you, and who has looked past your weakness for firewater, knows that you are a man of kind heart and gentleness,'' Panther said, filled with admiration for a friend who was so determined to put his life back on the right road. ''Cloud, from this day forth I shall do everything within my power to see that you are our next medicine man prophet.''

Cloud flung himself into Panther's arms. ''Thank you, my friend,'' he said, his voice full of emotion. ''Thank you for not giving up on me . . . for having faith that I will make a worthy Medicine Man Prophet.''

They parted quickly when they became aware of the arrival of horses in their camp.

Growing cold inside, Panther stood next to Cloud and

watched Sheriff Braddock and several of his deputies gallop closer.

Panther's first thought was of Rain Singing. Had her father's rage been so great that he'd sent the sheriff to arrest Panther for having been with his daughter? Had her father lied and told the sheriff that Panther was guilty of rape?

Panther knew the penalty for raping a white woman. He would be hanged from the neck until he was dead. His people would also suffer in ways he did not wish to think about.

His hands balled into tight fists at his sides, his jaw tight, his teeth grinding together angrily, he waited for Sheriff Braddock, for there was nothing he could do now, to prepare for this visit. Whatever the white people chose to do to his small group of Shawnee, they would do. Again, they were at the mercy of whites.

Sheriff Braddock's eyes locked with Panther's as he swung himself out of his saddle. He stood glaring and quiet as the other dozen or so white men dismounted with rifles in hand, awaiting the short, squat, red-faced sheriff's orders.

"Why are you here in my people's camp in such great numbers and with the threat of weapons?" Panther asked. Out of the corner of his eye he saw his people move into small clusters, their eyes filled with alarm.

"A farmer came with a complaint that an Indian shot and stole his prized cow," Sheriff Braddock said, sneering. "Have you Indians taken to shooting deer with bells on their necks?"

"None of my people are guilty of killing any white man's cow," Panther said, fighting to hold his anger at bay. "They have been busy building their lodges. What meat they have on hand they hunted as our warriors have hunted since the beginning of time. They would not take a white man's animal, for it would not be a part of the proper way to hunt. They are proud warriors. They never forget the importance of the hunt."

"That's a lot of hogwash," Sheriff Braddock growled. "If your warriors saw a cow grazing where they could steal it without being seen, they would take it and save themselves the trouble of hunting for their meat."

"The Shawnee are hunters by tradition," Panther said tightly. "They would not lower themselves to steal an animal that is owned by someone else, especially a cow. Cows' meat is repulsive to the Shawnee. It has the taste of skunk." He swung his hand in a wide gesture toward the lodges. "Search our camp. See if you can find any signs of any cow having been slaughtered here. When your men do not find such, I will expect you all to leave us in peace."

Deep inside Panther's heart he felt blessed by *Moneto*, that the sheriff's visit had nothing to do with Rain Singing or her angry father. Today's visit would bring no harm to his people, although he hated the fact that the white men could enter his camp with weapons drawn and get away with it. He wished he could show them how he would have received them long ago when his people were triple in number what they were today.

"All right, I'll take you up on that offer to search your lodges," Sheriff Braddock said. He gave the order to his deputies to begin the search.

As Panther watched the men marching in and out of

his people's lodges, dirtying the floors and air with the filth of their boots and breaths, he was enraged, but kept his anger to himself, for he had learned through the years to tolerate such insults and interferences.

He waited patiently until the men went back to their horses after having found no beef in the camp.

"I'll leave you be now," Sheriff Braddock said, swinging himself into his saddle. "I guess someone else stole that cow." He laughed throatily. "You'd better thank your lucky stars that none of your people were guilty of the crime, for I'd love to have an excuse to use the noose on one of your warriors to teach you all that you'd best keep your noses clean."

Still laughing, Sheriff Braddock rode away with the deputies, leaving a strained silence behind him. The Shawnee watched the sheriff's departure, their eyes filled with a loathing they had not been able to show while the whites were among them.

"It goes on and on," Panther said as he watched the sheriff ride out of view. "It will never end. Not in *my* lifetime, that is."

"The news about your friend Cloud should help ease the stress of what you have just gone through with the whites, should it not?" Cloud said, placing an arm around Panther's shoulders and drawing Panther's eyes his way.

Panther's lips curved into a proud smile. "*Nyoh*, let us go and share the news with my father," he said. "He must be alarmed about the white men's presence in our camp. His sightless eyes did not see them, but his ears heard them as they went into his lodge searching his belongings. Let us go and help calm his anger and embarrassment.''

''*Nyoh*, let us go and tell him about how I will one day be our people's Medicine Man Prophet,'' Cloud said proudly. He stepped away from Panther and walked with him to Red Thunder's newly built cabin. He sat with him beside the warm fire.

First Panther explained about the white men's wrongful accusations, and then proudly told his father about Cloud.

''It makes my heart swell to know that you will no longer poison your body with firewater,'' Red Thunder said, reaching out and placing a hand on Cloud's cheek. His fingers slowly wandered over his features. ''You are the same as a son to me, Cloud. You have been in my life as long as Panther. And today you make me as proud as a father is proud for his son.''

''Our people will be proud of Cloud, too,'' Panther said, patting Cloud's bare knee. ''If Cloud learns everything required, I personally will encourage those in council to allow him to take Two Spirits' place soon.''

''That is good,'' Red Thunder said. ''For too long now I have worried about my old friend's deteriorating condition. It is time for Two Spirits to step down from his duties and rest.''

Cloud hugged Red Thunder and left the lodge, beaming, while Panther stayed behind and prepared his father a cup of hot chocolate. Panther wanted nothing more than to sit and talk with his father about Rain Singing. He wanted to share his feelings about Rain Singing being a part of his future, about his hopes of having her as his wife.

But there were many reasons why Panther wouldn't tell his father any of those things. He now realized that it might be impossible for him and Rain Singing to have a future together. If her father had anything to do with it, it would never happen. . . .

Chapter Seventeen

As Shanndel slipped her boots on, she felt a slight quivering beneath the floorboards of her bedroom. Panic seized her, for she had felt this before. The New Madris Fault ran close enough to Harrisburg for the area to be affected by an earthquake.

Awaiting another tremor, she held her breath. When nothing happened and the room was as usual, she exhaled a nervous breath and went on about her business. She had promised her father to check the laborers as they collected the huge tobacco leaves from the fields, to make sure they removed the whole leaf instead of only portions. This was one of the best harvests her father could boast of in years. She could almost see the dollar signs multiplying inside her mind when she thought of the profit her father would make just this one growing season.

But it would only be something else for him to use to try to encourage her to forget Panther, for most women would gladly accept such an inheritance.

"I wish I could make him understand that all I want is the man I love," she whispered as she began brushing her thick, black hair in long strokes.

Yes, she would give up the wealth, the luxuries of the mansion, and all of the finery that went with it if she could have Panther as her husband.

"I've got to make Mother and Father understand," she whispered, fear grabbing her heart when she felt another tremor in the floor, this one twice as strong as the last.

She placed her brush on the dressing table and went to the window. She gazed across the vast stretch of land, then gasped and went pale when shock waves began to spread in all directions, causing the house to sway dangerously from side to side.

When the floor buckled beneath her, Shanndel screamed and grabbed the sheer curtain at the window as she lost her footing. The curtain came down in a shroud of white over her.

"Shanndel Lynn!" Grace cried as she struggled to enter the room, the floor rippling like waves beneath her feet. "Daughter! We must leave the house! Father is already outside. Hurry! We must find him."

Shanndel's breath caught in her throat and terror leaped into her heart when her mother lost her footing and sailed across the room as though she had wings and had taken flight.

"Mother!" Shanndel cried as she crawled over, grabbed her mother, and held her close at her side.

"We must get to safety, Shanndel," Grace said, sobbing. "I'm afraid. Never have we had an earthquake like this. Everything will be ruined. The house is already so damaged it might take weeks to get it back to normal."

"The house should be the least of your worries, Mother," Shanndel said, placing an arm around her mother's waist and helping her up from the floor. "Lean against me. I'll get you down the stairs."

Although Shanndel was concerned about herself and her parents, her thoughts went quickly to Panther and his people. Out in the open, living in mere cabins, his people were so vulnerable. If the earthquake worsened, the whole earth could open up and swallow the Shawnee.

As soon as she saw to her mother's safety, she must go and see if Panther was all right. Even if she had to go against everything her father had told her, she *would* go to Panther today. Nothing would keep her away. Surely he had no idea what was happening. Where he came from, she doubted they ever had earthquakes. They were rare in this area; she could remember only one other time it had happened.

That time only a few things had been destroyed. Today it seemed as though all hell had broken loose and was releasing its furious wrath on everyone.

The house cracked and popped as the earthquake aftershocks continued. She could hear trees snapping and falling outside. She could hear the mortar in the fireplace crumbling, the stones popping away from the wall like popcorn over a hot fire.

"It's a nightmare!" Grace cried as she watched her

expensive crystal chandelier, which hung over the entrance foyer, crash to the floor, the splintered glass spreading in all directions.

"It soon will be over," Shanndel reassured her as she held onto her mother's waist and led her around the pieces of glass. "It can't go on forever."

Just as they rushed through the front door, things became calm. The sound of creaking, swaying broken limbs on trees that had not been totally uprooted was eerie to hear.

Shanndel gasped when she saw the devastation to the tobacco crop. Where there weren't large, gaping wide cracks in the land, huge ridges of earth had formed across the field. The tobacco leaves curled down into the open gaps.

Shanndel saw her father staring blankly at the crumpled tobacco leaves. This year's crop, which had been so promising, was now a total loss.

She looked further and saw the auditorium where she gave her speeches downed amidst a rubble of trees that had crashed over it.

Horses whinnied in the stable, the walls of which were half down, some of the wood sticking up into the air like giant, sharp toothpicks.

"I've never seen anything like it," Grace said, tears streaming from her eyes. She turned and stared with relief at the house. It had miraculously come through the earthquake with only minor damage.

Although Shanndel was feeling the despair her parents felt over what had been destroyed, she knew that, except for the destroyed tobacco crop, everything else could be repaired and life could be normal again.

But it was the thought of what might have happened to the Shawnee people that was uppermost in her mind. Had they survived the ravages of the earthquake? And what of the aftershocks? Were they truly over?

Edward came to Grace and drew her into his arms and comforted her. "Darling, at least we are alive," he said thickly. "Nothing else matters, now does it?"

"But the tobacco you were so proud of," Grace sobbed as she clung to him.

"There is next year for the tobacco crop, Grace," he said, gently stroking her back through her delicate silk dress. "And soon the house will be repaired and as good as new."

"My chandelier, Edward," Grace said, her voice filled with despair. "It's broken."

"I shall send to St. Louis for another one even prettier than that one," Edward reassured her.

Shanndel was moved almost to tears at the love her father had for her mother. That affection was so wonderful and intense she could not help thinking of her brief, precious moments with Panther. Although new, an enduring love was also shared between them.

Again she looked across the land, at the devastation. In her mind's eye she could see Panther's people in despair over their own losses. She couldn't stand not knowing if Panther was all right. She *must* go to him.

Without further thought, or considering what her father would do, Shanndel broke into a mad run toward the stable.

"Shanndel!" Edward cried, yanking himself away from his wife. "Where are you going?"

"Father, please understand!" Shanndel shouted back,

rushing through the debris at the door of the stable.

She breathed a sigh of relief when she found that Blue Smoke was unharmed. Although a part of the wall had fallen in beside Blue Smoke, none of the sharp pieces of wood had stabbed him.

"Thank God you are all right," she whispered as she hurriedly saddled him. "We've someone to check on, Blue Smoke, to see if he has survived this terrible ordeal."

Wheezing, his face red, Edward ran into the stable. His blue eyes pleaded with Shanndel. "Don't do this," he said. "Shanndel, don't leave. Things aren't safe. There might be more aftershocks."

"Father, the Shawnee are vulnerable out there all alone," Shanndel said, swinging herself up into the saddle. Her eyes wavered as she gazed down at her father. "Please don't hate me, Father, for going against your wishes. I love Panther. I *must* see if he is all right."

"Shanndel, you're old enough to know your own mind, and too old for me to punish you when you do something I don't want you to do," Edward said hoarsely. "I can't stop you. I won't even try anymore. Just be careful. Devastation lies all around you. Anything can happen."

"I'll be all right," Shanndel said, tears flooding her eyes. She reached down and gently touched her father's cheek. "Thank you, Father, for not forbidding me to do this."

"Have I ever downright forbade you anything?" Edward said, taking her hand and affectionately squeezing it.

Shanndel smiled down at him, then when he released

her hand, she rode on out of the stable. She drew her reins tightly only long enough to give her mother a soft look of apology, then rode away across the ravaged land, avoiding the fallen, broken trees and the long, crooked gaps in the ground.

When she got halfway between her home and the Shawnee camp, there was a fierce, shuddering aftershock. The shock waves spread out in all directions, causing the river along which she was riding to swirl and hiss strangely.

Shanndel screamed and held tightly to her reins when a crack opened up in the earth, enough for Blue Smoke's front hooves to stumble over.

Shanndel was thrown from Blue Smoke and hit her head when her body made contact with the ground. The dreadful pain momentarily disoriented her.

Through the haze of pain she saw Blue Smoke riding away. She shouted at the animal, but to no avail. He was soon lost to her sight.

Once the land and river were calm again, and the trees overhead were no longer swaying, Shanndel pushed herself up from the ground. She fell again when pain stabbed at her head.

Moaning, she held her face in her hands.

Panther was walking from one cabin to the other, checking on his people's welfare. He was relieved that only a few minor repairs would have to be done to their lodges. Although the ground had rocked and swayed, and trees had snapped in two all around them, not much damage had been done to his people's things.

The worst, it seemed, was the horses' fright. When

the trees snapped where the makeshift corral had been made with ropes strung from tree to tree, several horses had run off.

But most of them had been rounded up and were now in a newly made corral.

The children who had cried with fright during the worst of the quake, were now calm.

The elderly were no longer chanting and praying to *Moneto* to spare the Shawnee's lives.

"We came through the earthquake very well," Cloud said, rushing up to Panther. "But it was unlike those we have seen before. In Upper New York, where earthquakes are rare, there was only a slight shifting and rippling of the land."

He looked toward the river. "Did you see how the water seemed to turn backwards on itself?" he said, glad to see that it was its normal, quiet self again. "It was as though a demon had been released in it."

"*Nyoh*, but all is calm now," Panther said, sighing.

His heart leapt into his throat when he saw a horse approaching, its saddle empty. He knew the horse. It was Shanndel's. And if she was not in the saddle, it had to mean that something had happened to her. Perhaps the earthquake had claimed a victim after all! His Rain Singing!

Filled with panic, he ran to the corral, grabbed the reins of his black steed, and vaulted onto its back.

"Where are you going?" Cloud shouted after him, grabbing the reins to Shanndel's horse and stopping it. He gazed at the horse at length, then looked at Panther again. "Whose horse is this that has come to our camp without a rider?"

Panther did not respond to his friend's question. His heart was too filled with concern for his woman. She could be lying somewhere terribly injured. Worse yet, she might be dead!

As he rode farther away from his camp, he looked desperately from side to side for signs of Shanndel. He began shouting her name, his voice echoing back at him from the depths of the forest.

When he saw Shanndel sitting beneath a tree, her face held in her hands, relief flooded Panther to know that she was alive.

But when she did not respond to his calling her name, he was afraid to know the extent of her injuries.

He drew a tight rein and came to a halt beside her.

Her head throbbing, Shanndel looked slowly up at Panther; then she rose to her feet and fell into his arms as he held them out for her.

"I was thrown," she murmured. "My head. It aches so."

She looked wild-eyed up at him. "Panther, I was coming to see if your people came through the earth-quake safely," she said, desperately searching his eyes. "Are they all right? Was anyone hurt?"

"*Moneto* protected us," Panther said, relieved to see that the only thing wrong with her was a headache from being thrown from her horse. "All of our newly built homes are intact. My people are unharmed."

He framed her face between his hands and gazed into her eyes. "Are you all right?" he asked thickly. "Is your family?"

"My family has suffered many losses today, but they, themselves, are unharmed," Shanndel said softly. She reached up and touched a bump on the side of her head. "And if all that I suffer is a bump on my head, I feel lucky."

"The pain is great?" Panther asked as he reached a hand around and gently touched the lump.

"It was until you arrived," Shanndel said, leaning into his embrace, relishing his arms around her. "Now I feel wonderful."

"I will take you to my home," he said hoarsely. He swept her into his powerful arms. His dark eyes smoldered into hers. "I vow never to allow anything to happen to you again. I will always be near to protect you."

"I want nothing more than to be with you," Shanndel murmured, her pulse racing as he brushed a sweet kiss across her lips. She clung to him as he carried her toward his horse. "But I must return home. There is much to—"

"First you come with me to my lodge and then you return home," Panther said softly. "I will make your wound better."

"I'm fine," Shanndel said softly. "I don't need doctoring."

He stopped and gazed intensely into her eyes. "There is more than doctoring on my mind today," he said huskily. "Before, when we were together, did we not discover the depths of our feelings for one another? Today I wish to prove the true depths of my feelings for you. Do you wish to prove yours for me?"

"Yes, but . . ." Shanndel stammered out, her face hot with a blush from knowing just what he was referring to. They had come so close to making love the last time they were together.

She wanted it now the same as then.

But was it the right time?

Should she chance losing him forever by saying no to what he asked of her?

Shouldn't she rush back home now that she knew he and his people were all right?

What was behind his desperate need to make love at this time?

Was it a way to pull her away from her old life because he knew that she was torn between two loyalties—to him, and to her parents?

Once they made love, he knew that she would be his, heart and soul, forever, and that she could never deny him anything again.

Instead of taking her onto his horse, Panther took Shanndel into a grove of cottonwood trees where there was a private glen beside a slowly flowing stream. Gently he placed her on the ground where the grass was thick and soft, and wildflowers grew thickly.

"I want you now," Panther said, his hand trembling as he slowly traced her facial features with a forefinger. "Say you want me. Say you love me."

Trembling, caught by a sudden sweet desire, Shanndel looked into his smoldering dark eyes. "I want you desperately," she whispered, her heart thudding so hard she was breathless.

He reached for her hand. He drew her fingers to his lips and kissed them lightly, his tongue flicking.

"There is only now," Panther said huskily. "There is only us."

"Yes, yes—" Shanndel said, closing her eyes in ecstasy when his hand slid slowly down the front of her toward her breast, soon cupping it through her dress.

Her body incandescent with sensation, she hardly dared breathe when he slowly unbuttoned her blouse, soon freeing both of her breasts from her blouse and chemise.

Never having experienced such desire before, or allowed any man such liberties with her body, she felt her nipples pucker to hardness as he cupped the orbs within both of his hands.

"Your breasts are so firm, high and lovely," Panther said thickly, his thumbs slowly swirling around the nipples. "Your body is perfect."

He bent low and flicked his tongue over one and then the other nipple, causing the blood to pulse wildly through Shanndel's body. She was floating; being with him in this way seemed natural, not forbidden.

And as he slid a hand up inside her skirt and touched her where no man's hands had been before, slowly caressing her where she seemed suddenly warm and alive, that alone obliterated all thought and reason.

"Are you certain you are ready for this?" Panther whispered into her ear, his body on fire with need.

"I want you so much it hurts," Shanndel whispered back, her heart leaping with rapture when his mouth covered hers in a wild, hot kiss.

Everything seemed to progress magically when suddenly his breechclout was removed and her skirt was raised and her body was arching toward his.

She bit back a moan when he placed his thick, hard shaft against her pulsing entrance.

As he slowly shoved into her, he continued to kiss

her, his mouth wet and hungry, his tongue sliding and darting between her lips with a rhythm that matched Shanndel's heartbeats.

For Shanndel there was a faint tinge of pain. Then the pleasure came and spread through her as Panther pushed and pushed, her tightness yielding with a slow, delicious ease.

As his hands lifted her hips, in one more, deep, smooth push, he was finally fully inside her. He made a low, throaty sound as he held her closer to his heat and began his rhythmic thrusts.

Shanndel sighed contentedly. Never had she felt such pleasure. Nor had she ever felt as cherished or needed. She clung around his neck as she moved with him, his thick shaft stabbing more deeply into the white-burning heat of her that until now had lain dormant. Each of his short, hard thrusts brought her an awakening of more and more splendid sensations.

Panther's body was fluid with fire. As his lips left Shanndel's and he gazed at her, he felt a bonding between them he had never had with any woman before her.

And it was not because he had denied himself such pleasures for so long.

This woman had awakened pleasures he had never known before. He realized they were kindred spirits, that *Maneto* had brought them together for a purpose.

Theirs was a special love that would bring many children into the world.

That she was part white no longer mattered.

That she was there with him, sharing the ecstasies men and women in love shared, was all that mattered.

"My love for you is everlasting," he said thickly, then again became lost in a wondrous kiss.

Their thighs pressed together, their bodies moved, their souls were on fire as they fell into the deep, wonderful chasm of fulfillment.

Chapter Eighteen

Relieved that his people had fared well during the earthquake and had resumed normal life, Red Thunder had decided to go and commune with *Maneto*, to give thanks for his protection of the Shawnee people. He knew that Panther was with Cloud in Two Spirits' lodge where the Medicine Man Prophet was teaching Cloud the art of his craft.

When Red Thunder had sat in a private council with Two Spirits, to get his feelings about stepping down from his duties and living out the rest of his life with the other elderly warriors, relaxing, talking of old times, and smoking their pipes, Two Spirits had eagerly accepted the idea. He had said he would teach Cloud everything he knew before he handed those duties over to him.

The only thing that Two Spirits had worried about was Cloud's love of white man's firewater.

Red Thunder had explained to Two Spirits about Cloud's visions and that firewater was no longer a part of his life.

That Red Thunder had faith in Cloud was enough for Two Spirits. He had agreed to be Cloud's teacher.

Leaning on his cane, Red Thunder left his lodge. Stopping, he smiled as he listened to the children at play.

Looking forward to the evening meal, he inhaled the aroma of meat cooking over the many outdoor fires.

The whinnying of the horses made a melancholia grab at his heart. His time of training them and riding them with abandon had been robbed from him the day his eyesight had been taken from him.

Nyoh, he could still ride, but no longer as a free spirit with the wind whistling through his thick, black hair.

"That day is gone forever," Red Thunder whispered to himself, sighing. "As is so much of my life that is now spent in darkness."

Feeling shame for pitying himself even for that brief moment, Red Thunder proceeded to feel his way along the ground with his cane until he found the back of his cabin. Then he turned toward the dense forest where squirrels were scampering overhead, their bushy tails swishing.

"Little creatures, I hear you," Red Thunder said, laughing when the playfulness of the squirrels knocked an acorn down onto his head.

Then he heard a blue jay squawking in the distance, its mate returning the call in a farther part of the forest.

Red Thunder's heart melted when a cardinal began

singing its lovely song. The cardinal had always been his favorite bird; he had loved to watch them at play on the snowiest days of winter. He would never forget how their bright feathers so resembled the color of wild, bright red roses in the spring.

"Were I to see them again, I would cherish the moment even more," he whispered, walking onward and leaving the cardinal's song behind.

Then he heard the sounds of other birds and remembered that soon most of them would fly south, leaving the air quiet except for the blue jays, which stayed the winter with their loud, sometimes aggravating squawking.

"But, blue jay, I love you as much as the others," Red Thunder said, hearing a quick rush of wings overhead. He wondered if it was the blue jay flying away.

Still reaching out around him with his cane, Red Thunder finally found a cushion of moss beneath a tall oak tree.

His body tired and worn out, he groaned as he sat down and laid his cane beside him.

"I wonder just how much longer this old blind chief has on this earth," he said softly, chuckling at the sudden morbid direction of his thoughts. "I shall be here to hold grandchildren in my arms!"

Grandchildren, he thought to himself. The one grandchild he could have held by now had been silenced inside its mother's womb before having the chance to take that first cry of life.

"Iron Nose, how could you have done it?" he said, tears flooding his eyes. "How could you take so much from my people?"

His head bowed, he grew quiet except for the silent movement of his lips as he began his heartfelt prayers to *Moneto*.

He prayed for his people's safe journey to Oklahoma in the spring.

He prayed that his son would find happiness with a woman again.

He prayed for many grandchildren.

But most of all, he thanked *Moneto* for having saved his people from harm during the frightening earthquake. He had felt the wide cracks in the ground as he had come to this place of prayer. He had found many fallen trees.

Yet none of this had happened where his people had made camp.

Nyoh, Moneto, in his goodness, knew of Red Thunder's people's recent losses and saved them from having to suffer again so soon.

"Please make it so forevermore," Red Thunder whispered aloud. "We have suffered enough!"

Suddenly he was aware of the silence around him whereas only moments ago the birds chattered overhead. Even the squirrels no longer romped and played.

But now it was as though time itself had become stilled.

Such silence always meant one thing to the red man . . . that danger was stalking near!

"Who is there?" Red Thunder asked, his hand scrambling at his side for his cane.

When he heard the soft whinny of a horse, he knew for certain that he was no longer alone.

Then he smiled. Surely it was Panther coming to make sure he was safe.

"Panther?" he said, reaching a hand out before him. "Speak up, son, if it is you, for your silence unnerves this old chief."

When no one responded, Red Thunder's spine stiffened, for he knew that if the one approaching on horseback was Panther, or anyone from his village, he would speak up.

Feeling trapped in his blindness, Red Thunder tightened his hand around his cane. His breath caught in his throat when he heard the creak of leather and knew it was the sound of a man dismounting his horse.

"Whoever is there, speak up," Red Thunder said, his knees too weak from fright to rise from the ground.

And even if he did get to his feet, he knew that if this was an enemy playing silent games with him, he would not get far before being downed by the enemy's weapon.

Iron Nose, he thought, his heart skipping a beat. What . . . if . . . it . . . was Iron Nose?

"And so, old enemy, you were foolish enough to go into the forest alone," Iron Nose said. He sneered down at Red Thunder as he slowly slid his razor-sharp knife from the leather sheath at his side.

The familiar voice came to Red Thunder like ice water splashed onto his face. It *was* his dreaded, worst enemy, Iron Nose, who·had come upon him alone in the forest.

Without a doubt, Red Thunder knew that he was taking his last breaths of life and he was glad that he had spent them in prayer to *Moneto*. His path to the hereafter was paved with goodness.

And when he began to ride down that path on his favorite steed, which had been shot from beneath him during Iron Nose's attack on his village, Red Thunder would no longer be sightless!

He would see again, and he would join those of his family who had gone on before him.

He smiled and was not afraid of impending death when he thought of joining his beloved wife. Their meeting in the clouds would be a joyous one. He would sweep her up on his mighty steed with him and hold her tenderly as they rode off into the wonders of a glorious sunset.

Laughing wickedly, an evil sneer on his face, Iron Nose stood over Red Thunder. "You are the first to die." Then I will kill my wife Dancing Sky, and . . . then . . . Panther, he thought, savoring the words that delighted his heart.

Yet he could not understand why hearing this did not put a grimace on his enemy's face.

Instead, there seemed to be a look of total serenity.

There even seemed to be a savage joy in his smile.

Too dignified to plead for his life, and truly ready to die, Red Thunder waited for his death with a proud, lifted chin.

His body flinched, but he emitted no sound of pain when Iron Nose's knife entered his chest.

It was at that moment when Red Thunder saw his wife's smiling face and her hand reaching out for him.

He saw his horse awaiting him, as white as the

clouds; it shook its mighty mane and whinnied a welcome to its old friend.

Watching Red Thunder inhale his last breath and his head slowly lower so that his chin gently touched his chest, Iron Nose chuckled and bent to a knee. He wiped Red Thunder's blood off his knife on the bed of moss that spread out on both sides of the dead Shawnee chief.

"At long last, he is no longer a thorn in this Iroquois chief's side," Iron Nose said, sliding his knife back inside his leather sheath as he stood and glared down at Red Thunder's lifeless form. "For too long you have been my enemy. It is good to see your body so still. Blinding you was not enough. It is your utter silence that pleases me."

He stared a moment longer at Red Thunder, then swung himself back into his saddle. "One down . . . two to go," he whispered, his eyes narrowed with venomous hate.

As he rode off, his thoughts went to Dancing Sky. Every time he thought he'd been given an opportunity to abduct her, it was foiled by the sudden presence of her husband or daughter.

"I *will* find you alone," he snarled, leaning low as he worked his horse through the thick grove of trees. "And when I do—"

He laughed throatily. "It has been a long time, wife, since you warmed my blankets," he said. In his mind's eye he was recalling how his very presence had always repulsed her.

Their marriage had been an arranged one between two proud Iroquois chiefs.

He had not been able to forgo bargaining for her when he had seen her loveliness.

He had hoped to make her love him, and when she hadn't, he could not help being abusive to her, for his pride had been injured those times she spat at his feet after he had forced himself upon her.

"One more time, Dancing Sky," he whispered harshly. "I will take you one more time and then no man will ever have you again. You will die!"

Today, as he had been riding through the forest to get to Dancing Sky's tall mansion again, he had just happened to find Red Thunder alone.

He hoped he would have the same luck soon with Dancing Sky.

His time away from his people had already stretched out into too many months!

Chapter Nineteen

Proud that Cloud was learning everything so quickly, Panther could hardly wait to tell his father this wonderful news. As he entered his father's lodge and found Red Thunder gone, he was at first puzzled.

Then he smiled when he thought of his father's craving for silent, solitary moments with *Moneto*.

Yet would he not have been certain to come home for the evening meal? A large pot of newly cooked stew hung now over his father's fire, waiting to be eaten.

Panther had even planned to eat with his father. They were going to share many things tonight in a celebration of their people having come through this latest ordeal without much mishap.

They were going to eat, talk, and leisurely smoke their pipes.

Cloud was going to come soon to join them in all of these things.

"Father, where are you?" Panther whispered, scowling as once again he slowly searched the interior of his father's lodge.

He saw everything that was dear to his father—his cache of old weapons, which had been used during his youth while warring with his enemies; his carved wood figures; his strings and belts of precious wampum.

He gazed with sad eyes at a parfleche bag in which Panther's beloved mother's dresses were stored. He knew that if he went and took them from the bag he would still smell her familiar, beautiful scent on them.

He had seen his father take the clothes from the bag more than once to inhale her scent and dream of what once had been.

Panther looked away from the bag, and then at the doorway. Still his father was not home and it would soon be dark; shadows were already deepening in the forest.

With hurried steps, Panther left the lodge and walked from lodge to lodge to see if his father was visiting one of their people.

He soon discovered that no one had seen him since earlier in the afternoon.

Panther went back to his father's lodge and still found only silence there.

Then alarm grabbed at his heart when he thought of Iron Nose and the threat he posed to the Shawnee.

Neh. Surely Iron Nose hadn't left his duties as chief behind him to venture so far away from his people. Panther truly doubted that Iron Nose had anything to do with his father's strange disappearance.

But something else frightened him as much. What if his father had gotten lost in the forest on land that he was not familiar with? What if he had fallen in one of the open veins left from the earthquake?

This thought spurred Panther onward.

He ran from the cabin and rushed into the forest, the shadows growing darker by the minute.

Frantic now, truly afraid that his father was in trouble, Panther ran in one direction, then backtracked and ran in another until his head was spinning.

He felt as though he were going in circles.

He would arrive at one spot, and soon discover, by the crushed grass, that he had been there already.

The shadows growing longer, the darkness edging in more closely around him, Panther cupped his hands over his mouth and shouted his father's name over and over again, his voice echoing back at him as though dozens of people were out there also crying his father's name.

Dispirited, heartsick, Panther began his search anew, but the growing darkness disoriented him so much he was not sure if he could find his way back to the camp.

He turned and gazed through a break in the trees. He was relieved when he saw the glow from his people's outdoor fires. Somehow he had managed to move in a wide circle and was now almost back to where he had begun the search for his father.

The squawk of a blue jay in the forest caused Panther to flinch and look quickly to his right.

Again the blue jay squawked, then took flight, its rush of wings alarmingly close.

Feeling as though the bird had been sent there from *Moneto* as a sign, that perhaps it was a way to lead him to his father, Panther broke into a run through the thick grass.

Panting, he wove in and around groves of tall trees.

Although he surely had been there already, searching, he nonetheless hurried onward. It would be easy to overlook something in this thick forest.

He swallowed hard. "Especially someone who might have come to harm," he whispered to himself, praying to *Moneto* that was not the case.

He hoped to find his father waiting for him, perhaps too tired to find his way back home.

Yet if that were so, why wouldn't he have answered Panther when he had called his name?

That fact alone made Panther's heart ache, for now he was almost certain that something had happened to his father.

Iron Nose leapt into his mind again, sending chills through him. If Iron Nose had found his father alone in the forest, would he have taken advantage of the moment and killed him?

Suddenly Panther stopped. There was just enough light left for him to see his father slumped against a tree.

Having found his father this way before, when sleep had come to him in the peaceful forest at the end of his prayers, Panther smiled with relief. It seemed it had happened again.

And he knew how soundly his father slept.

Even the sound of Panther shouting his name might not have awakened him.

Panther ran onward. He didn't shout his father's name now for he didn't want to startle him awake. He was sleeping so soundly, he hadn't stirred at all while Panther was watching him.

When Panther grew close enough to see his father more clearly, he stopped again. He muffled a cry of agony behind a hand when he saw the bloodstains on his father's buckskin shirt. It was as though Panther's feet were frozen to the ground; he died a slow death inside, realizing that his father was more than likely dead.

Finally able to shake himself out of the trance, Panther hurried to his father and knelt down before him. His eyes filled with tears when he saw the chest wound.

"Iron Nose!" he cried, his eyes narrowing in fury as he looked into the darker depths of the forest. "Was it you? Are . . . you . . . the one?"

Too filled with despair even to think further about the murderer, Panther gathered Red Thunder up into his arms. His father's kind words and laughter had been stilled forever.

Holding him close and wailing, Panther began carrying his father's lifeless body through the darkness that now hung around them like a black shroud.

Through his tears, he could just make out the fires at his camp, leading him to his people.

As he entered their camp, and everyone saw him carrying their beloved Red Thunder, a general mourning and wailing began. It reached up into the heavens, a part of the universe, forever.

Chapter Twenty

Unable to sleep because she had made a promise to her mother that she doubted she could keep, Shanndel slipped from her bed.

Yawning, her silk gown clinging to her tall, slim body, she went to the window and slid it open to get a breath of fresh air. Soon she wouldn't be able to enjoy the fragrant night breezes. The temperatures would be too cold.

This year she dreaded winter more than ever before. She would be worrying about Panther and his people out there with only drafty cabins and fireplaces to keep them warm. When the winds came howling across the land, and snow blew in high drifts, anyone who did not have adequate protection against the weather might not make it until spring.

But she reminded herself that since the beginning of

time Indians had known how to survive the long, cold winters. Long ago most of them only lived in tepees.

Her thoughts were interrupted when she leaned closer to the open window and heard something strange wafting to her on the night breeze. Her heart skipped a beat when she listened more intently and realized that what she was hearing were wails coming from the direction of Panther's camp.

She looked quickly into the sky and saw the reflection of a huge fire in the dark heavens.

"Fire!" she gasped, fear seizing her heart. "The people are wailing because the lodges at their camp are on fire!"

Having read articles in newspapers about white men going to any length to rid the land of red-skins, often burning their lodges to the ground, she thought of Sheriff Braddock and his deputies and their hatred of Indians.

"Lord, no," she whispered, paling. "Please don't let it have happened!"

No longer considering the promise that she had made her mother, Shanndel yanked her gown over her head and quickly dressed in a riding skirt and blouse, cursing beneath her breath when she had to struggle to get her feet into her boots.

Leaving, her hair long and free down her back, she rushed from her room. She didn't even take one look at her parents' closed door. At this moment her only concern was Panther and his people.

But when her father let out a loud, hacking cough, her spine stiffened and she stopped to look at his door. Of late the wheezing had worsened. And not only that, he was troubled by a strange cough. He had begun to look gaunt. His face had a strange gray pallor to it.

Shanndel felt guilty to be sneaking out in the middle of the night. She loved both of her parents dearly and hated to disappoint them, yet her love for Panther was so intense she couldn't bear to think that he might at this very moment be in jeopardy.

Her jaw tight, her chin firm, Shanndel focused only on her concern for Panther and left the house in a mad rush. She went to the rebuilt stable and quickly saddled Blue Smoke, then rode off into the dark night.

Shivers ran up and down her spine when the wailing became more pronounced and the reflection of the fire seemed to leap higher into the dark heavens.

"Oh, please let Panther be all right," she prayed. It made her insides grow cold to think that she might be hearing wails brought on by the death of a chief.

That thought sent shivers of dread through her. What if Sheriff Braddock and his men had gone to the Indian camp and not only set the lodges on fire, but also killed Panther? Surely that would frighten the Shawnee so much they would leave the Illinois country.

As Shanndel grew closer to the camp and saw that the fire was not the cabins burning after all, but instead a huge outdoor fire sending flames high into the sky, dread almost overwhelmed her. The wails must mean that someone of importance had died. She closed her eyes, trying not to hear the rhythmic moaning that rose into the heavens.

"Please, oh, God, please don't let it be Panther," she prayed again.

Her breath caught and her eyes opened quickly when

she heard a sound of rushing feet and soon found herself surrounded by several Shawnee warriors on foot. They held drawn bows aimed directly at her heart.

"Stop!" Cloud shouted at her, causing her to pull hard on her reins to halt Blue Smoke.

Just as her horse came to a shuddering halt, Cloud reached up and dragged her from her steed. He held her steady against his hard body, her back to him.

"What are you doing?" Shanndel cried as his arm tightened around her waist. "Let me go! I've come to see Panther!"

She tried to pry Cloud's arm from around her. "Let . . . me . . . go!" she cried, not able to budge his hold on her. "Please release me. I'm a friend."

"Quiet, woman," Cloud growled as he forced her to walk ahead of him.

Knowing that nothing she said would convince this Shawnee warrior to release her, Shanndel grew quiet and walked along with him to Panther's cabin.

When she was shoved inside, her heart warmed to see Panther sitting there beside his fireplace on a thick pallet of furs. At least she knew that he was alive!

As for being manhandled, she couldn't imagine why she was being treated so callously.

"Panther?" she said as Cloud released her and left her alone in his chief's lodge.

Panther turned with a start and gasped when he found her standing there. He rose quickly to his feet and gazed speechlessly at her. Surely she didn't know. How . . . could . . . she have known about his father?

"Panther, why am I being treated like a prisoner?" Shanndel blurted out. "I was surrounded. I was grabbed from my horse by one of your warriors. I was brought to you as if I . . . I . . . were an enemy. I came to see what was wrong at your camp. I heard the wails. I saw the reflection of a large fire in the sky. Panther, you know that I am no threat to anyone. I came because I was worried.''

Panther rushed to Shanndel and drew her into his arms. His eyes filling with tears, he hugged her desperately.

''I am sorry that you were mistaken for a possible enemy,'' he said thickly. ''You see, my father was slain today. Now my warriors see everyone but the Shawnee as an enemy, for it is not known yet who sank the knife into my father's body.''

Shanndel's heart skipped a beat. She looked quickly up at him and saw the despair and tears in his eyes. ''Someone killed your father?'' she gasped out. ''Oh, Panther, I'm so sorry.''

''Can you understand why you were manhandled?'' Panther said, placing a gentle hand on her cheek. ''My Shawnee now trust no one. Even Cloud, my best friend, thought you were no different from others because I have not shared with him news of our meeting and our love for one another.''

''Who do you suspect?'' Shanndel asked softly, his pain now hers, for she could feel his anguish in her heart.

''Anyone who has ever spoken against the Shawnee is seen as the possible criminal in the eyes of my people,'' Panther said, his voice drawn.

He framed her face between his hands. ''Stay with me, Rain Singing?'' he asked, his voice breaking.

"Help ease the pain of having lost my father?"

Shanndel refrained from asking if he thought that Iron Nose had killed his father. Because of her mother, she was afraid to know. If it *was* Iron Nose, would her mother be the next to die?

Shanndel wanted to go and warn her mother, to stay with her as she had earlier vowed to do, yet she couldn't. Not now, when Panther had asked her to stay with him during his time of grief.

Yes, Panther needed her. And her mother had her husband to protect her.

And if Iron Nose had not committed the murder, it wouldn't be fair to go and startle her mother for nothing.

No. She wouldn't worry about such a farfetched thing as Iron Nose having come this far to kill his wife and his worst enemy. As Panther had said, surely Iron Nose had other things on his mind than vengeance. His people's welfare surely came first.

"Rain Singing, you will stay?" Panther asked, his voice drawn, his eyes searching hers. "Will you help ease the pain in my heart?"

"Yes, I will stay," Shanndel said, flinging herself into his arms. Overjoyed that Panther's life had been spared, she held him tenderly against her.

As she sorted through her mind for who might have killed Red Thunder, she thought again of Sheriff Braddock. She could not help thinking that he might have done this vicious deed against the Shawnee. She wondered if anyone would ever truly know if he was this heartless . . . this prejudiced against Indians.

Or was it Iron Nose, who had finally succeeded in

destroying his old enemy? If so, who would be his next victim?

She shivered at that thought, knowing that she, too, was vulnerable.

"You shivered," Panther said, holding her away from him so he could look into her face. "You are cold?"

Shanndel hugged herself with her arms. "Yes, inside my heart I am suddenly very cold," she murmured. "Panther, I . . . I . . . am suddenly afraid."

She was glad when he took her again in his arms and hugged her protectively against him. For the moment she felt safe, but what about those times when she would be alone?

She doubted that she could ever ride her horse again with the same abandon that she had always ridden him in the past.

She cursed whoever had taken that carefree existence away from her!

Chapter Twenty-one

Though she knew her father would start searching for her the moment he discovered that she had fled sometime in the night, Shanndel had spent the entire night at the Shawnee camp.

And she hadn't slept one wink. She had remained at Panther's side as a comfort to him while he mourned his father's passing and prepared the old chief for burial.

Shanndel had been there as the Shawnee people filed into Red Thunder's lodge, each showing their mourning for their fallen chief in his or her own different way.

With a warm blanket wrapped around her shoulders, Shanndel stood back from Panther as he now spent his last moments with his father before Red Thunder was taken to his grave for burial.

Tears came to Shanndel's eyes as she looked at Red Thunder's cold, still form. The body lay cleansed and groomed and wrapped in a fine new scarlet blanket on a wooden bier at the far side of the lodge.

On the floor around the platform and body, and in the available spaces on the top of the platform, were a large number of items that the mourners had brought as a tribute to their fallen friend and chief.

Shanndel gazed through misty eyes at small belts of wampum, colorful ribbons, swaths of calico, wooden bowls, small brass pans, fine new moccasins, vests and leggings, and a variety of food in small wooden boxes, and various drinks in flasks.

Lying at his side, closest to his wrapped body on the bier, lay various items that had been the most important to him in life. On one side lay his knife in its sheath and his tomahawk, as well as his flintlock rifle, and a lovely carved bow and huge quiver of otter skin filled with his finest arrows. On his other side was the beautiful headdress of feathers that he had worn in council when he had been chief. Lying beside the headdress was his long-stemmed calumet pipe.

The item that brought the most emotion from Panther was one of his mother's dresses, which he had draped lovingly across his father's wrapped body, its beads and fringes so fine against the white doeskin fabric. It was Panther's way to help his mother's and father's joining together before his father's spirit entirely left the earth. His true journey would begin after he was resting peacefully in the ground.

Shanndel smiled at Panther as he came back and stood beside her. She proudly stood with him while his people filed into the lodge to say their final goodbyes to their fallen chief. Then his body would be taken to the grave that had been prepared sometime during the night when the moon was high and bright, and when loons were crying to one another across the cool, calm waters of the river.

Shanndel was surprised at the ease with which Panther's people had accepted her presence at his side. It was without question that they walked past her, gazing at her with kindness, as though she truly belonged there.

Shanndel's gaze swept over the people and saw that they wore what seemed to be the simplest of clothes, void of ornamentation. Their hair was loose. Their faces were colored with lines and curves of indigo, ocher, and vermilion. Even Shanndel had stood quietly as Panther painted her face for mourning.

All males above ten years of age were smoking *kinnikinnick* in small pipes. From the stems hung teal feathers or ermine tails.

After entering the cabin, the Shawnee took turns stepping up to the bier to gaze at the blanket-swathed, lifeless form of their onetime loyal leader.

They then moved on so that the next person could have a moment with Red Thunder.

Outside, the meat of deer, ducks, and geese was roasted and ready to be eaten once the burial was behind them.

On a broad, fresh cloth were flat loaves of hard bread and a score of jugs. The jugs were filled with rusty-colored apple juice and also *melassanepe*, a nectar of water and maple sugar, both of which would be served in strips of smooth thin bark cut into sections and rolled into cone-shaped cups.

As the sun neared the top of the trees to the west,

seven warriors came to the bier and, along with Panther, stood four to a side. They passed four broad rawhide straps under the blanket-wrapped body. Each gripped one end of a strap, and together they lifted the body and carried it, along with the dress still draped over it, out of the lodge.

Shanndel walked behind Panther and the other warriors who were carrying their fallen leader, joining the Shawnee as the slow procession headed toward the burial place. A spot had been prepared for Red Thunder beneath tall, beautiful birch trees, and far enough back from the river that, should it flood, his grave would not be disturbed by the water.

When the grave was reached, Shanndel stood back with the others as Panther and the warriors lowered Red Thunder into the ground with the aid of the straps.

With no weapons, food, or earthly possessions in the ground with him other than his wife's dress, Red Thunder now lay peacefully in his grave as everyone formed a single line and passed by to gaze down at him.

Shanndel moved to Panther's side. Chills ran up and down her spine as she listened to the death chant the people began. It was a melancholy, fluctuating tone, embodying grief and despair. And as the throbbing chant filled the air, the mourners sprinkled *milu-famu*, sacred tobacco, over Red Thunder's wrapped body.

After everyone had had a final look at the fallen leader, three warriors came forth and began scooping dirt with their hands onto the grave.

When the grave was filled with fresh earth, Panther himself rolled a smooth boulder onto it to protect his father's body from animals that might come to disturb the remains of the dead.

Then, as the chanting continued, the Shawnee turned from the grave and made their way slowly back to the camp.

Shanndel was surprised that no words had been spoken over the grave. Until the chanting had begun, the burial had been conducted in silence.

And even now, as they reached the camp and settled onto blankets around the huge fire where the food awaited them, no one spoke of the dead. As their voices became still and food was passed around the wide circle of mourners, the Shawnee ate mechanically.

The delicious taste of the food caused no looks of pleasure on their faces. They were solemn, as though their hearts had been left back at the grave.

Finally Panther rose, standing tall and noble over his people, and broke the silence. "My father's spirit rises even now into the heavens to join those who have gone there before him," he said, looking heavenward. "We must rejoice, my people. Do you not know the happiness my father is finding on his road to the hereafter? He is soon to join hands with my mother! He will even look upon the face of my unborn child. He so mourned the death of his grandchild. Now he will see the young brave who would have made a powerful Shawnee warrior. He would have one day been a *k-tch-o-ke-ma*, a great chief."

Tears filling his eyes, Panther reached his hands heavenward. "Father, your eyes can now see!" he cried. "Your arms can now hold those you have mourned while on this earth. I shall no longer mourn for you, Father. I shall be happy!''

His cry to his father, his effort to try to convince everyone that he was accepting his father's death without too much pain, was interrupted by a loud commotion at the far end of the camp.

When Shanndel heard her father's voice as he cursed those who manhandled him, she paled, gasped, and looked quickly over her shoulder. Her father was being half-dragged into the camp, his face red with rage.

''No,'' Shanndel whispered, covering her mouth with a hand. ''Oh, Father, why did you have to come *now*?''

She was torn by conflicting feelings as she watched him being forced toward the wide circle of Shawnee. The warriors who had been left to guard their people had obviously caught her father approaching their camp.

Panther quickly recognized Shanndel's father. He gave her a swift questioning look, then swept an arm protectively around her waist.

His jaw tight, he vowed to himself that he would not allow this white man to take his woman away from him a second time.

She was there.

She had told him last night that she would stay!

She had promised to be his wife when despite his grief, he had found the words to ask her if she would marry him.

''Shanndel, damn it, I was afraid this was where I would find you when I discovered your bed empty this morning,'' Edward said as he was shoved directly in front of Shanndel and Panther. His eyes narrowed angrily at her as his gaze swept over her painted face.

Edward then glowered at Panther. "What kind of hocus pocus magic have you used on my daughter to cause her to behave so irrationally?" he shouted. "She must have spent the night with you."

He jerked away from the warriors, his hands knotted into tight fists at his sides. "I swear, Shawnee, if you so much as—"

"Father, please don't say anything else," Shanndel said, grabbing his hands. "Only moments ago Panther buried his father. You have interrupted a . . . a . . . time of mourning."

Edward gazed at length into Shanndel's eyes, then turned an apologetic look Panther's way. "I'm sorry about your father," he said thickly. He glared at the warriors who had dragged him from his horse, then looked again at Panther. "I guess that was why I was manhandled."

"You were brought here because my warriors are protecting my people from whoever sank the knife into my father's body," Panther said, his voice tight. "In my people's eyes, any stranger is an enemy."

"Your father was murdered?" Edward said, paling. He frowned at Shanndel. "And you are gallivanting around footloose and carefree while a murderer is out there killing innocent people?"

"Father, I had to come to be with Panther," Shanndel murmured. "Please understand. He . . . he . . . needed me."

Edward yanked his hands from hers. He grabbed Shanndel by an arm. "Well, he might as well get used to *not* needing you, Shanndel Lynn, for you are returning home with me, and if I have to post a guard at your bedroom door to keep you from coming to this Indian, damn it all to hell, I will.''

When a bout of coughing incapacitated him, Edward released his hand from Shanndel's arm and covered his mouth. He was wheezing so much, he could hardly breathe.

Shanndel went ashen to see him suffering so much; his wheezing had grown worse because he was so angry. ''Father, please go on home,'' she pleaded. ''I'm staying with Panther and there's nothing you can say or do to persuade me otherwise. He needs me, Father. He needs me.''

She watched him grimace at those words; his coughing and wheezing had subsided. She watched him look over his shoulder at the threat of the warriors, whose arrows were nocked onto their bows.

He then frowned and looked into Panther's eyes. ''My daughter never behaved in such a way until she met you,'' he said dryly. ''And by damn, red-skin, I'll have her back with me before you can say 'scat.' ''

With that, he turned and stamped away. The warriors stepped aside so that he could return to his horse and leave.

Shanndel felt afraid of what he might do to get her behavior under control, yet she would not go back on her word to Panther. She was there to stay, and she *would* marry him. As soon as she dared, she would tell her father those truths.

She only hoped that he wouldn't do anything foolish like asking the sheriff to come here and force her to leave at gunpoint.

Then a sudden realization came to her that made her

grow cold inside. She recalled her vow to her mother that she would stay with her to protect her against Iron Nose. What if he *had* killed Red Thunder? What if he was in the area, a true threat to her mother? Her father wasn't there to protect her. She was vulnerable. She could be abducted and killed.

That possibility made Shanndel break into a run after her father. When she caught up with him at the edge of the camp, where his horse was only a few feet away, its reins being held by a Shawnee warrior, she grabbed her father's hand and stopped him.

When he whirled around and looked at her with hope in his eyes, and she knew that he thought she had changed her mind about staying with Panther, guilt flooded her. Now she realized just how much her decision to stay with Panther was going to hurt not only her father, but her beloved mother, as well.

But still she had her life to live and she would live it as *she* wished to. She would no longer live it for someone else, no matter how much she loved her parents or felt she owed them for having been so good to her all of her life.

"Daughter, you are going home with me after all?" Edward asked, his eyes showing his relief. "You've come to your senses? You know where you truly belong?"

"No, Father, I'm not going home with you," she said sadly. "But, Father, please listen to what I have to say. For mother's sake, listen and take it seriously, for she might be in danger. Iron Nose might have killed Red Thunder. He might even now be planning to kill

Mother. Go to her. Protect her. Make sure she's all right.''

Remembering that his wife was alone at the house, her father gasped, rushed to his horse, and swung himself into his saddle. He didn't stop to look back at Shanndel. He rode off in a panic.

This was Sunday, he thought in despair. No one worked at his plantation on Sunday!

His wife was totally alone, vulnerable to the madman Iroquois should he be near their house, awaiting the opportunity to grab her!

He looked heavenward and prayed.

Chapter Twenty-two

Eager to complete his vengeance, Iron Nose watched the two-storied dwelling that housed his first wife.

He had watched with a thudding heart as Dancing Sky's white husband rode away at a hard gallop not long ago.

Iron Nose had surveyed the land around him, where workers usually came and went doing their daily chores, and had found it curiously deserted today.

Then he smiled cunningly when he recalled how he had learned long ago that white people took one day a week to worship their God. He had found that a most peculiar habit of white people; the Iroquois worshipped their Great Spirit with every sun's rising and setting.

After he had learned of this strange custom of white people, he had understood how many white men could be so evil. Any man who worshipped his God only one day a week could not have a good heart, for one day's teaching was not enough to keep a man walking the straight path of righteousness.

Placing himself above those he considered heathens, he snickered when he thought of how Dancing Sky had forgotten her early teachings.

It appeared as though she didn't even follow the white man's teachings, for he had not seen her leave today for the white people's place of worship. Perhaps she understood that going to their place of worship would not gain her anything in her afterlife, and so she did not practice a custom that she knew was worthless.

He was yanked from his deep thoughts when he saw the front door of the massive house open. He sucked in an anxious breath when he saw Dancing Sky step from the house carrying a small wicker basket. He watched her with a racing pulse as she stopped to inhale a deep breath of the sun-drenched air.

His gaze moved slowly over her. Even though she was dressed as fancy white women dressed, in a silk dress with a low, revealing neckline, she was no less lovely than the day he had taken her as a wife in the Iroquois fashion.

In a white doeskin dress embellished with bright, shiny beads, she had been something to behold that day.

He had been so proud for his people to watch him take her as his wife, for they had witnessed her unique loveliness.

But when he had been alone that first night with Dancing Sky and he had taken her to his bed, she had spat in his face for having forced himself on her so quickly and painfully.

He had taken her again just as quickly to prove to her that he would take her whenever and however he wished, for she was now his wife.

He had looked past her hatred of him and had enjoyed her body the short time she was with him. He remembered how soft and beautiful her skin was when he ran his hands over her flesh.

His loins ached even now from wanting her when he thought of how her breasts were so heavy when he held them in his hands.

Everything about her heated his blood with a desire long denied him.

And without hesitating any longer, his need as strong as it had been on their wedding night, he took one last look around. She was bending low to pluck flowers from her vast garden.

When he found no one anywhere near her, he yanked his knife from its sheath and ran stealthily to the back of the house.

His heart pounding, he crept up behind her.

In a flash of movement he had his sharp blade at her throat, his free arm around her waist, yanking her close to his hard body.

"No!" Grace cried, but she kept her body perfectly still. She could feel the cold steel of the knife blade at her throat and knew that she could die instantly.

"My princess, I have come to claim you once again," Iron Nose growled out, the wondrous scent of her making him almost blind with sexual need.

"Iron Nose, please do not do this," Grace said, her voice pleading. "You will be caught. You will be killed. Why would you risk this? Do your people mean so little to you that you would chance everything to carry out whatever you plan to do to me?''

"You are not the reason I have traveled so far from my people. I came for vengeance, to kill an enemy. I did not even know you were here until I happened to see your daughter, who is the mirror image of you. Then I knew that you must be near," Iron Nose said, tightening his hold on her waist. "Now walk, Dancing Sky. I must get you into hiding before your white man returns on his horse.''

Grace knew that she had no choice but to do as he said. She walked with Iron Nose as he shoved her toward the shadowed forest. She was angry at herself for being careless today. She never should have gone outside, realizing that everyone, even those who had guarded her since word had come to her that Iron Nose might be in the area, was gone this morning to attend church. To keep herself out of harm's way, Grace had purposely not gone to church. And then she had been reckless enough to put herself at this madman's mercy!

"You came this far to kill Panther?" Grace dared to ask as he released his hold on her when they reached the protective covering of the trees.

She turned and glared at him. "Vengeance is just an excuse to kill again, is it not?" she hissed. "You, who could have been a wonderful chief had you not loved spilling other men's blood so much, are wrong to leave your people to pursue vengeance."

She lifted her chin boldly and placed her hands on her hips. "My husband is a gentle, God-fearing man, but, Iron Nose, when he discovers me gone, he will search for me until he finds me. I pity you when he does, for he will take pleasure in taking you to the sheriff and putting you behind bars until the day they place a noose around your neck," she said icily. "You won't get the chance to kill anyone on this expedition of hate, Iron Nose. You will be the hunted and then the one who dies."

"I have already killed," Iron Nose said, grabbing her wrist, forcing her toward his horse. "And *I* am your husband, *not* the golden-haired white man."

Grace paled. Scarcely breathing, she looked guardedly at him. "Who . . . did . . . you . . . kill?" she asked, her voice breaking as she thought of her beautiful daughter somewhere out there, perhaps the victim.

"The Shawnee chief who was once my worst enemy now lies in the ground, his life's blood drained from him," Iron Nose said, nodding toward the horse. "Get on the horse. If you do not do it by yourself, I shall do it for you."

"You killed a Shawnee chief?" Grace asked, inching away from him instead of mounting the horse as he had ordered. "Oh, please do not tell me that you killed Panther."

"No, not Panther. I killed his father," Iron Nose grumbled.

He thrust his knife back into its sheath and grabbed Grace by the waist. He bodily heaved her into the saddle, then swung himself up behind her and held her tightly against him as he took the reins in his free hand and rode deeper into the forest.

"You are evil through and through," Grace said, shoving at his arm but finding that his muscles were like steel as he held her firmly against him.

"You are the evil one," Iron Nose said, his voice thick with hate. "When a woman leaves the bed of her husband and sneaks away with another man and becomes his wife, that makes her the most evil of all."

"You know that our marriage was forced on me by my father after you paid him a hefty sum in pelts for me," Grace said, her voice breaking. "That alone made our marriage a mockery and, in my eyes, illegitimate."

Tears came to her eyes when she recalled the very moment Iron Nose had come to claim her from her father.

She had begged her father not to force such a man on her but he had made a promise that he could not break, or her father's whole people would suffer as a result.

Iron Nose would have returned with his warriors and attacked her village with a vengeance. He would not have left until all women and children were dead.

"You were my wife," Iron Nose said. "You still are. You are my princess. I had hoped that you would give me children. Were that so, surely you would not have left me so eagerly. You would not have separated a child from its true father."

He suddenly grabbed her hair and forced her face around. "This daughter of yours," he said, glaring at her. "Is . . . she . . . mine?"

Grace's face drained of color.

"Never!" she hissed out. "Had I borne your child, I never would have claimed it as mine." She swallowed hard. "A child born with your traits would be a child I could *never* mother."

She scarcely breathed as she awaited his reaction to

what she'd said, relieved when he said nothing but instead removed his hands from her hair, drew a tight rein, and stopped.

But then a coldness rushed through her when she suddenly thought that he was stopping to throw her from the horse and beat her because of the venomous way she'd denied his parternity.

Then she saw that he was staring at something. She turned her eyes to see what he was looking at and found that he had brought her to some sort of a cave nestled deep in the forest, with a stream trickling beside it.

Her spirits fell, for if he hid her there, surely her husband would never find her. Edward had never spoken of a cave in the forest. Surely he knew nothing of it.

Her breath was knocked out of her when Iron Nose suddenly shoved her from the horse and she fell on her back on a slab of rock.

As she regained her breath she looked up at Iron Nose, who now stood over her, his eyes narrowed, his lips formed into a mocking smile.

"Woman who is still my wife, I hope you will enjoy your new home, yet it truly does not matter, for you will not be alive for much longer to enjoy much of anything," he said, kicking her toward the cave. "Now get up. Go inside while I hide my horse in the brush."

Trembling, Grace did as he said. The coldness of the cave struck her face as she stepped slowly into the entrance.

She immediately saw that he had been staying there, for in the middle of the small cave she saw the smoldering coals of a campfire, whose smoke filtered upward and escaped through small cracks in the cave ceiling.

She winced when Iron Nose came up behind her and grabbed her by one arm. He forced her farther inside the cave, to where he had made camp.

The bones of eaten animals lay at one side of the fire.

A dead rabbit lay, unskinned, waiting to be cooked for Iron Nose's next meal.

"Sit down and skin the rabbit," Iron Nose said. Then on second thought, he decided not to give her his knife. He opened a parfleche bag and took out two ropes. With one he tied Grace's wrists behind her back. With the other he tied her ankles together.

Chuckling, he shoved her away from him and grabbed the rabbit. He began skinning it himself, all the while giving her quick glances as she settled down on a blanket close beside the hot coals of the campfire.

"First I killed Chief Red Thunder; next I will kill Panther," Iron Nose said, chuckling. "And then, before I kill you, I will kill your daughter."

"No, please do not kill my daughter," Grace pleaded, tears rushing from her eyes. "She has done nothing to you. Why do you want to kill her? Kill me. Let that appease the hate you have held in your heart for me since the day I left you. But do not kill my innocent, sweet daughter. She is all that is good on this earth."

"She must die," Iron Nose hissed, resuming his task. "She looks too much like you to be allowed to live. She must be erased from the earth and therefore my mind. But it will not be today or tomorrow that I will kill her *or* you. I am going to toy with you, my beautiful wife, to make you beg for mercy."

Grace saw no use in arguing with him. She sat and stared at the man she had loathed since the first night she was forced to sleep with him as his bride.

"How could you have left me?" Iron Nose suddenly asked, his voice breaking.

Grace thought that she actually saw the shine of tears in his eyes as he looked pleadingly at her.

"Did you not know how your leaving humiliated me?" he asked sullenly. "Did I not give you everything a woman would want? You . . . were . . . my *princess*."

"I was never your princess," Grace said icily. "I was never anything to you. You were and still are a madman . . . a man who enjoys killing too much. I take much savage joy in telling you that I never, ever loved you. You sickened me then. You sicken me now."

Iron Nose dropped the knife and bloody rabbit carcass to the cave floor.

He reached over, grabbed Grace's hair, and yanked her face close. Then he spat on her.

Gagging, choking, trembling, Grace turned her face away from him, thankful when he grabbed his knife, jumped to his feet, and suddenly left the cave.

Wiping the slimy, cold spit from her face on the shoulder of her dress, she thought of something that made her smile in her moment of despair and fear.

That day she had left Iron Nose she had had other motives besides just wanting to be away from him for her sake alone.

She had carried a secret with her since the day she had fled from him, a secret she had shared with no one except Edward and her beloved friend Bright Star.

That secret, and knowing that she had at least this

power over the man she hated, would give her the strength to get through the next moments with him.

And that cherished secret, as well as her beloved white husband, was the very reason she would find a way to flee this man again. She would watch and wait for that moment when he would be off guard.

Then she would make her move.

She would make him wish he had never taken her liberty from her a second time!

She winced when she heard the screeching of bats at the far end of the cave. No doubt they had been disturbed by the argument.

Holding her breath, she watched as several bats began flying around her head.

Having heard tales of bats lodging themselves in the hair of women, she ducked as low as she could, praying to her Great Spirit that she would find a way to escape soon.

She prayed, too, that her daughter would be safe from the maniac who killed for pleasure!

Chapter Twenty-three

Shanndel sat beside Panther with his people on blankets around the huge, roaring fire. Everyone had resumed eating after her father had left, but with one difference. Not wanting any other visitor to know about the burial, they had all washed the paint from their faces.

Shanndel, herself, didn't want to eat. She had never thought the practice of eating immediately after someone was buried was decent, so she declined the offer of food even as a sweet young Shawnee woman offered her a platter piled high with delicious-smelling morsels.

And anyway, something else was nagging at her consciousness that made hunger the last thing on her mind. She was being torn between her loyalty to her mother, whose life might be endangered due to Shanndel's decision to be with Panther, and to Panther, who had never needed anyone as badly as he did now that the death of his father was so heavy on his heart.

And her father, Shanndel thought to herself. . . . Oh, how her decision to stay with Panther had hurt her father.

And then there was the way her father had suddenly ridden off after she had told him that Iron Nose could have been the killer, and her mother was now alone at the mansion.

If Iron Nose was in the area, and he realized his wife was near, oh, Lord, what would he do? Shanndel despaired.

"Food is good for the soul," Panther said, holding out a piece of meat toward Shanndel. "Eat, Rain Singing. My people are excellent food makers."

Shanndel's eyes wavered as she saw the food and then looked up at Panther and took in the soft pleading in his eyes.

Smiling softly, she accepted the piece of meat. Just as she started to bite into it, the sound of approaching horses made her lower it.

She dropped it to the ground and rose quickly with Panther. Pin-pricks of fear raced up and down her spine when she quickly recognized Sheriff Braddock and three of his deputies at the far side of the camp. She could not help believing that her father was responsible for the arrival of the sheriff. No doubt it was his way of retaliating at Panther for having stolen his daughter away.

But her father had not had time to ride into Harrisburg to seek the sheriff's help. It hadn't been that long since he was at the Shawnee camp. Surely the first place he would have gone was to see if his wife was safe.

Then why would the sheriff come at a hard gallop into the Shawnee camp? she wondered. The United States Government had given the Shawnee permission to stay there. Could it be that he had heard about a Shawnee chief being buried on land that was not Shawnee? Would he be so rude and unfeeling as to order them to open the grave and take the body far from Harrisburg?

She inhaled a deep, unsteady breath when the sheriff drew a tight rein a few feet from where Shanndel stood with Panther.

Panther's people were now on their feet. Their eyes were filled with searing hatred. Shanndel understood that they wanted to be left undisturbed at such a time as this. Their moments of grief should be private, free of the presence of all white-eyes.

Shanndel's presence had been accepted, but once the people had realized her father was white, their attitude had changed subtly. She had seen in the eyes of many that her being there was resented.

Especially after word spread among them that she was of Iroquois descent . . . and Panther's intended.

"What brings you into the Shawnee camp again?" Panther asked flatly. It seemed to him that the presence of the sheriff and his men was unholy since Panther had only moments ago buried his beloved father.

Yet he would make sure not to mention his father's passing to the sheriff. He did not think the white man would approve of an Indian being buried on land that belonged to the white man. He knew from past experience that white men saw Indian burial grounds as something frightening, as though the dead might reach up from their graves and pull the living into the earth with them.

His jaw tightened and his temper flared at the possibility that the sheriff had received word of the burial.

He would never disturb his father's final resting place, even if it meant having to fight until his own death to protect it.

Sheriff Braddock dismounted. Placing his fists on his thick hips, he glared at Panther, then slid a slow, wondering gaze Shanndel's way. Finally he centered his attention once again on Panther.

"Word has come to me that your people found a salt lick and illegally took salt from it for your own purposes," Sheriff Braddock said in a low, accusing growl. "Moccasined footprints were left on the banks of the creek where salt was removed. You know all salt licks belong to the United States Government, so I order you now, Chief Panther, to hand over the stolen salt."

Panther smiled cunningly. "Search my village, and if you find stolen salt you are free to take it," he said. He gestured with a wide sweep of a hand toward the people's lodges where he knew the salt was hidden so well beneath the floorboards that no one would find it. "As you see, my people are having a feast. No one is in the lodges. Go. Search. And when you find nothing, leave us in peace."

Sheriff Braddock stared questioningly at Panther for a moment, then gave his deputies a look over his shoulder. "You heard the chief," he shouted. "Get off your damn horses and search the lodges. When you find the salt, bring it to me. I think we'll have a chief's neck to place in a noose.''

The Shawnee people drew closer together, their eyes warily watching the deputies with their heavy guns holstered at their hips go from lodge to lodge.

They breathed sighs of relief when the men finally returned to their horses and mounted them.

''You found no salt?'' Sheriff Braddock asked as he looked from deputy to deputy, his frustration showing that he had not been able to best the Shawnee.

''Each lodge is as clean as a whistle,'' his main deputy said, slouching in the saddle, his beady eyes glaring from one Shawnee to the other.

Sheriff Braddock stamped over to the food that lay in piles on platters beside the outdoor fire. Grumbling to himself, he yanked up a leg from a cooked rabbit and bit off a big bite and chewed it.

His eyes gleaming, he went back to Panther. He held the rabbit leg out for Panther. ''I dare you to tell me that you used no salt in your preparation of this rabbit,'' he growled out. ''Taste it, Panther. Tell me there was no salt used on it.''

''I need not taste it,'' Panther said, his voice tight and cold. ''If you know anything about hunting and animals, you should know that, when cooked, rabbit has its own natural salty flavor.''

Sheriff Braddock turned and questioned his deputies with his eyes.

When they nodded an affirmative answer, agreeing with Panther, the sheriff threw the rabbit leg down on the ground and hurriedly swung himself into his saddle.

''If I can ever prove that you stole salt from the

United States Government, it will be my pleasure to place the noose around your neck myself, Chief Panther,'' he growled, then wheeled his horse around and started to ride away. He stopped abruptly when Shanndel's father rode hard into the camp, his face drained of color.

''Thank God you're here,'' Edward said, drawing a tight rein beside the sheriff's steed.

''Good Lord, man, you look as though you've seen a ghost,'' Sheriff Braddock said, his eyes wide.

Shanndel's heart skipped a beat to see her father so pale, his wheezing far worse than usual. She ran to him. ''Father, what's wrong?'' she asked, afraid to hear the answer.

''I . . . went home and . . . and . . . found flowers spilled all over the place where your mother had been cutting them,'' he blurted out, his voice frantic. He wheezed. ''I also saw signs of a scuffle. Shanndel, your mother is gone, and she did not leave on her own. I hurried to the sheriff's office for help. I was told he was here.''

''Your wife is missing?'' Sheriff Braddock said, sidling his horse closer to Edward's.

''I'm almost certain she's been abducted,'' Edward said, wiping the back of a hand over his dry mouth.

''Whom do you suspect?'' Sheriff Braddock asked, raising an eyebrow.

''An Iroquois chief who was once my wife's husband,'' Edward blurted out. This news caused the sheriff's eyes to widen. His gasp of disbelief filled the still air.

''This isn't the time to question who my mother was

258

or wasn't married to before she married my father,"
Shanndel said, glaring at the sheriff. "Sheriff, your
business here at the Shawnee camp is over. And if you
want to have your fun hanging an Indian, Iron Nose is
the only one in this area that deserves hanging."

She stopped short of telling him that Iron Nose had
already killed one person. She didn't think it wise to
bring up Red Thunder's death. She didn't want the sheriff to ask where he was buried.

"Iron Nose," Sheriff Braddock said, thoughtfully
kneading his chin. "I've never heard of an Iron Nose."

"Well, you have now," Shanndel said, placing her
hands on her hips. "My mother is gone." She swallowed hard. "I hate to think of her being at the mercy
of a man who has cause to hate her."

"And why is that?" Sheriff Braddock asked.

"There's no time to get into that," Edward said, im-
patience setting in. "We're wasting time. Let's go find
my wife."

"I will join the hunt," Panther said, nodding toward
the boy who always tended to his steed. "Get my horse
and my bow and quiver of arrows. Be quick, young
brave."

As the sheriff, his deputies, and Shanndel's father
rode away, Shanndel mounted her own steed.

She and Panther rode off and soon caught up with
her father and the others, riding somewhat behind them.

Shanndel broke away from Panther momentarily and
brought her horse closer to her father's. "Please don't
blame me," she said, tears flooding her eyes.

When her father said nothing to her, but instead
looked at her with his blue eyes, all icy and accusing,

she knew that he did see her as the cause of her mother's disappearance.

Guilt-ridden, she looked away from him, then fell back and rode at Panther's side.

They were far enough back from the sheriff for her to speak freely to Panther about things she would not want the sheriff to hear.

And it was good to have something besides her agonizing worry over her mother to speak of.

"Panther, do you know anything about the salt lick?" she asked softly, realizing that Panther had never outright said that he didn't.

His slow, pleased, cunning smile was all that she needed to see to know that he had cleverly bested the sheriff.

Chapter Twenty-four

Grace couldn't believe her luck that Iron Nose would actually take the time to cook and eat the rabbit before raping her.

With an anxious heartbeat she watched him even now as he sat beside the fire with his back to her, tearing the meat off the bones with his teeth and eagerly chewing.

She wasn't sure if Iron Nose was taking the time to eat only to torment her by making her wait for the moment he would rape her, or if he was truly hungry. It was obvious that he had made the rabbit kill just before he abducted her.

She wondered what had made him decide to come to her house and spy on her instead of eating first.

Had he just arrived at the cave with the freshly killed rabbit when he saw her husband ride through the forest toward the Shawnee camp?

Had her husband ridden so close to the cave on his way there? Was the Shawnee camp near this cave?

If so, if she could get herself free, she could hurry to the Shawnee camp and seek their protection against this madman.

She doubted Edward would still be at the Shawnee camp, for he would be quick about his business with Panther. If Shanndel had been there, he would surely have her with him now and be already on his way home.

Should he arrive home and discover that his wife was gone, he would realize that she'd been abducted. She had told him she would not leave the premises.

Yes, hell would break loose in the community, for her husband would go immediately to Sheriff Braddock. A posse would be formed. Iron Nose would soon pay for all of his dirty deeds. If he wasn't gunned down, he would die by hanging!

"I offer you no food," Iron Nose grumbled as he looked over his shoulder and glared at Grace. He tossed a bone onto the pile of already discarded, rotting bones. He wiped grease from his mouth with the back of a hand. "You will soon be dead. Why waste rabbit meat on you?"

Laughing, he turned away from her again, picked up another piece of cooked meat, and resumed eating.

Grace smiled at his stupidity in placing his back to her. Of course he thought she was helpless.

Ah, how wrong he was. He had forgotten that she had been raised among the Iroquois people and had been taught many ways of survival.

She worked diligently with a sharp rock behind her as she began cutting into the ropes at her wrists.

As she continued to rub the rope back and forth across the sharp rock, she watched Iron Nose guardedly. At any moment he could quit eating and proceed with his plan to rape and kill her.

If she could only get the ropes at her wrists off, she could reach up inside her dress and grab the knife that she had wisely placed at her upper right thigh when she had first realized Iron Nose might be in the area.

Her sheathed knife was the one article of her precious Iroquois belongings that she had always kept hidden in her dresser drawer for times like this.

Edward had not known that she had placed it there. He had thought for many years now that she had left all of her Iroquois ways behind her.

But survival in the Iroquois fashion could never be wiped from her consciousness. She had been taught by her mother long ago that a woman was never safe without a knife sheathed beneath her dress. Too often white men were lurking in the brush near Indian encampments. They would look for a squaw, as white men called Indian women, to rape, just to have something to brag about to their white friends.

In her younger days, when she had been known only as Dancing Sky, she had frightened off more than one white man with the viciousness of her sharp knife.

Now it was one of her own people whom she would use it on, for if she did get the chance, she would sink the knife deep into Iron Nose's back and finally rid the world of his evil, filthy ways.

It saddened her to know that such a man existed among her people. It surely made everyone think that all Iroquois people were the same as he: vicious and bloodthirsty.

It was sad for her to realize that because of Iron Nose, many of her Iroquois people had died. Iron Nose's bloodletting among the whites had often led white men to massacre the Iroquois.

Those thoughts were brought to a halt when the ropes suddenly fell away from Grace's wrists and she knew that she was that much closer to being free.

Her pulse raced as she slowly slid her hands around. The flesh ached where the ropes had dug into her wrists.

Her eyes wide, her breathing shallow, she watched Iron Nose as she slid her hand down the side of her right leg and inside her dress.

Her fingers trembled as she unsnapped the sheath, afraid that even that slight sound might alert Iron Nose to what she was doing.

But he was still too absorbed in eating to hear her do anything, even when she sliced the ropes at her ankles in two and she was totally free of her bondage.

Her heart pounding, her insides quivering with fear, Grace moved slowly to her knees.

Watching Iron Nose, whose back was still to her, she crawled slowly toward him.

She winced when rocks scattered beneath her, making a sound he could not fail to hear.

Knowing that she must make her move now, Grace raised the knife into the air. Just as she started to plunge it into his back, Iron Nose turned around. When he saw the knife, he leaned quickly to one side. The knife missed his back, but not his right arm.

As it slashed through the buckskin of his shirt, and

then his flesh, Iron Nose let out a yelp and grabbed at the knife. Blood spurted through his fingers.

Grace rushed to her feet, and just as she started to run away from Iron Nose, he reached out and shoved her with his other hand.

Screaming, Grace lost her balance.

As she fell to one side she managed to slash Iron Nose's leg. His screams of pain echoed to the far end of the cave, again awakening bats and causing them to fly around the cave in a blind frenzy.

Leaning low to escape the wrath of the bats, and thinking that she had wounded Iron Nose enough to disable him until she could bring the sheriff back with her to take Iron Nose into custody, Grace scurried from the cave.

Suddenly she felt a blow to her head as Iron Nose came up behind her and slammed a rock down hard on it.

She fell to the ground, unconscious.

With blood pouring from both of his wounds, Iron Nose stood over Grace. When he saw blood seeping from her head wound, he decided that she would soon die.

He gazed at his own wounds. He must see to them soon or he, himself, would die from loss of blood.

He looked toward the darker depths of the forest. In there he would find the herbs he needed to medicate himself. Then he would return and hide Dancing Sky's body in the cave. Although he had not achieved his vengeance against her as he would have liked, at least she would cause him no more embarrassment or grief.

She would soon be dead. He would leave her body for wolves or bears to feast upon.

Groaning with pain, he struggled until he finally managed to get to his horse.

Sweat beading his brow, he moaned as he pulled himself up into his saddle.

Without looking back at the wife he had hated for so many years, he rode off. His head bobbed as the loss of blood started taking its toll on him.

Grace moaned as she slowly awakened. The throbbing of her head was so intense she was dizzy from it. With trembling fingers she reached up and touched the wound, wincing when she felt the stickiness of blood.

Then she fell away again into the darkness of unconsciousness.

Chapter Twenty-five

No matter how hard he tried, Panther could not feel comfortable joining the white men on the search for Shanndel's mother. He had never aligned himself with whites before; his resentment toward them was too strong for him to have such dealings with them.

It was no different now. The longer he was with the sheriff who had spoken so insultingly to him, the more he resented the need to be anywhere near him.

Yet there was his Rain Singing. He glanced over at her and saw her worried expression. He knew how concerned she was about her mother's disappearance. He had to continue the search for her sake, but it could be done without the white men. He and Rain Singing could break away and search for her mother separately. If she did not agree to this, he would go alone. He just couldn't stay with the white men any longer, no matter the reason. He had only done so because of the woman he loved. He would do anything for her . . . except this.

He felt as though he looked like a fool falling in with the white sheriff so quickly when Braddock had so recently come into his camp and insulted his people.

Shanndel could feel Panther's eyes on her. She looked quickly over at him and saw something in his eyes she did not understand. It was a kind of hidden pain that he seemed to be feeling.

But of course, she thought to herself, it was because of his father. A sudden guilt overwhelmed her now that she thought of his being there with her to help search for her mother when he should be with his people mourning the loss of his own loved one.

"Oh, Panther, I'm so sorry," she said, guiding her horse closer to his. "I shouldn't have expected you to come with me to search for Mother. Please return to your people. I understand. When . . . when . . . I find Mother and know that she is all right I shall come to you. Truly I will."

"*Nyoh*, I *should* be with my people, but I also should be with you," Panther said, repositioning his bow more comfortably across his left shoulder. "But not in this way. I can no longer ride with those I consider my enemy. The sheriff has insulted my people. It is wrong that I ride with him now."

Shanndel's eyes wavered. "Then you are returning to your camp?" she said regretfully. While he was at her side she felt his strength and courage. She needed that to be able to cope with the possibility that her mother had been harmed. If she had been, then Shanndel would feel to blame for it, for she had broken her word to her mother and had gone to Panther, even knowing that her relationship with him could lead Iron Nose to her mother.

"I will return to my camp when I know that your mother is alive and well," Panther said.

"Then I don't understand," Shanndel murmured. "You just said it is wrong for you to ally yourself with those you consider your enemy, yet you are still going to ride with them?"

"*Neh*, I will no longer ride with them," Panther said thickly. "I hope you will not, either."

"What are you asking of me?" Shanndel said, her eyes searching his for answers. "You know that I must help find my mother."

"I would not ask you not to search for her," Panther said, slowing his horse.

She followed his lead and dropped farther back from the others with Panther. "Then what do you mean?" she asked.

"Let us break away from the white men and search alone for your mother," Panther suggested. "I am one with the earth. I am astute on the hunt. I know hidden places white men can never find. Come with me, Rain Singing. Join me on the hunt today for your mother. We will find her."

"You truly believe so?" Shanndel asked, her heart racing as she gazed ahead at her father and how stiff and worried he looked sitting in his saddle.

What would he think if she chose Panther's way over his?

Would he hate her for making such a choice, even if she and Panther did, in the end, find her mother?

In the eyes of his friends, how would her father look if his daughter aligned herself with a red-skin instead of him, a man who had given her everything a daughter would ever want?

But, as before, she had to put that concern behind her, for she did believe that Panther had more knowledge of the forest than any white man. He had been born and raised amidst wide stretches of forest and surely *did* know all of its haunts, even in this land that was not familiar to him.

"Yes, let's separate ourselves from the others and look for my mother without them," Shanndel blurted out, convinced that she was doing the right thing, even though her father would not think so. If she and Panther did manage to find her mother, surely her father would forget his resentment of Panther.

"Come then," Panther said, guiding his horse to the left.

Shanndel looked up again at her father where he rode so stiffly in his saddle, unaware of what was happening behind him.

She looked at the sheriff, who rode at her father's side, and then at the deputies. They were far enough ahead of her and Panther that they were not aware of what was happening behind them. Their horses' hooves were making such a loud sound, the noise of two horses going in another direction would be drowned out.

She turned and caught up with Panther so she could ride proudly at his side.

As they both peered around on all sides of them continuing their search, they spoke no words. They had a purpose, one they shared now, and it was wonderful to be with him, alone, on this heartfelt search.

Deep down inside herself, Shanndel had a deep trust in Panther's ability to find her mother. Each time she glanced over at him she would see his eyes intent on the forest around them.

It touched her deeply that he placed her needs above his people and their mourning, yet it troubled her at the same time. She was afraid that resentment was building against her back at the Shawnee camp. She hoped that she would be welcome there when all of this was behind her.

"I see something up ahead on the ground," Panther said, shielding his eyes from the sun.

Shanndel's heart skipped a beat when she, too, saw something . . . no, not something . . . some*one* lying on the ground beneath a canopy of cottonwood trees.

As she grew closer she saw that it was her mother, and she saw a pool of blood beside her. Shanndel's heart sank and everything in her became weak with the fear that her mother had been murdered and left for the animals to feast upon.

Tears flooding her eyes, Shanndel sank her heels into the flanks of her horse and left Panther behind in a hard gallop.

When she reached her mother she slid out of the saddle, deep sobs lodging in her throat when she saw the dried blood on her mother's beautiful hair.

Panther rode up and quickly dismounted. He swept an arm around Shanndel and steadied her when he saw her swaying as though she might faint. He held her as they both bent to their knees. Shanndel's hand trembled as she reached out and touched her mother's throat for a pulsebeat.

A deep, trembling sigh came from within her when she felt the steady rhythm of the pulse and the warmth of her mother's skin. "She's alive," she said, almost choking on a sob. She gave Panther a relieved smile. "Thank God, Panther, she is alive."

With his fingers, he separated Grace's hair and saw the huge lump and the break in her skin at the base of her skull. "She has been downed by a hard blow," he said, looking beside her and seeing the bloody rock that had been used to knock her out.

Shanndel shivered as she looked at the amount of blood on the ground beside her mother. "She . . . has . . . lost so much blood," she cried. "Surely she has lost too much to survive."

"I doubt all of that blood came from your mother's scalp," Panther said, studying it at length. "I would think that someone else has lost blood, too." His eyes followed a trail of blood to a tree where he saw signs of a horse having grazed recently. "Whoever inflicted this wound on your mother was wounded himself, somehow. It is that person's blood you see. Not your mother's."

"Iron . . . Nose . . . ?" Shanndel whispered, paling at the thought of her mother having been accosted by the evil Iroquois chief.

"If it was, his wound might eventually kill him," Panther said, his eyes narrowing. "If it does not, he will be found by my warriors and killed by an arrow."

"Do you think my mother wounded the man before he . . . before . . . he harmed her?" Shanndel asked, cradling her mother's head on her lap. "She has always been such a gentle person, I can't imagine her harming even a fly, much less a man."

"She was born among people who taught her the art of survival," Panther said. "So she would have carried her knowledge of that with her into the white world."

"Mother, oh, Mother, please wake up," Shanndel murmured, caressing her mother's cheek. "Please, Mother. Please be all right."

"We must get her where her wound can be treated," Panther said, hopping up. He gathered long branches with which to make a travois. "I shall make her journey to my camp a comfortable one. I will put together a travois for her."

Shanndel looked all around her. "I'm so disoriented," she said, swallowing hard. "Is your camp closer, or is my home? Which would be the better place to take her?"

"My camp is closer," Panther said, gazing through the trees at the shine of the Maple Fork River. "You see the river? It will lead us quickly to my camp. Once there, my Medicine Man Prophet will medicate her wounds and pray over her."

As Shanndel held her mother's head on her lap, she continued to caress her cheek. "Mother, please hang on," she whispered, not at all hesitant about an Indian medicine man seeing to her mother's wound. Something deep inside her told her that her mother would want it that way, for way back, when she was living among her people, she had been taught to trust the teachings of medicine men. And although she had only been around white doctors for many years, when she awakened and found a medicine man at her side, surely she would smile and welcome him there.

After the travois was ready and attached to Panther's horse by long poles, he placed Grace gently on it.

They then headed toward his camp.

Shanndel's mind was splintered with a million thoughts. She wished that she could tell her father at this moment that his wife was all right, but she had no idea where he was, or how far away.

Also, she wondered about who had injured her mother. Was it Iron Nose? If so, she wondered how far he had gotten after losing so much blood.

If it was Iron Nose, and he survived, he would have twice as much reason to find and kill her.

Shanndel sighed. When was this nightmare going to end? And when it did, how much of it would be blamed on her? Would her mother ever truly trust and love her again?

Would her mother be her sweet self and understand what had prompted Shanndel to go against her word to her? Her mother had deep feelings for people. Surely she would understand Shanndel's need to be with Panther in his time of sorrow.

Finally at the outskirts of the Shawnee camp, Shanndel rode onward with Panther. When the people saw the woman on the travois, an Indian woman dressed like a white woman, they stood quietly by as Panther and Shanndel went to Two Spirits' lodge.

Shanndel watched Panther carry her mother inside the lodge. She followed and stood back in the shadows as Two Spirits washed the head wound and then treated it with what appeared to be some sort of herbal mixture.

While doing this, he was chanting something soft and low over Shanndel's mother. His chant seemed magically to reach deep inside her consciousness, for soon her eyelids began to flutter open.

Panther reached back and took Shanndel by the hand. He gently pulled her to her knees beside her mother, who was resting on thick pelts and blankets.

"Mother, it is I, it is Shanndel," she said softly, reaching a gentle hand to her mother's cheek. "Mother, you are safe now."

Grace's eyes slowly opened. She reached up and took Shanndel's hand, a quiet desperation in her eyes. "Iron . . . Nose . . ." she gasped out, then fell back into the dark realm of unconsciousness.

Shanndel and Panther gave each other startled looks, the worst of their suspicions confirmed. Iron Nose was near. But was he alone? Or was he with other warriors who could attack the Shawnee at any moment?

Panther couldn't help fearing the nearness of his people's worst enemy. He was also filled with rage that this Iroquois chief was again interfering in the Shawnee's lives. Panther knew now that Iron Nose's reign of tyranny would not end until Iron Nose was dead.

"I vow to find Iron Nose and kill him before he wreaks any more havoc on anyone else," he said. He moved quickly to his feet. "I must go now and find him."

Shanndel rushed to her feet. She clung to Panther's arm. "I'm so afraid," she said, her voice breaking. "If his wounds haven't killed him, he's as dangerous now as ever."

"What makes him so dangerous is his mastery of

hiding, or I would have killed him long ago,'' Panther growled out.

Shanndel looked down at her mother. Tears flooded her eyes once again. ''What about her?'' she murmured. She stifled a sob with her hand. ''Is she going to be all right? And if so, will he eventually return to kill her?''

''I have sent warriors to find your father,'' Panther said, drawing her gently into his arms. ''He will come soon to take your mother home. This time he will keep her well guarded.''

He placed a finger beneath Shanndel's chin and lifted her eyes to his. ''And trust me, Rain Singing,'' he said throatily. ''Two Spirits' magic is strong. Your mother will be well soon.''

''How can I thank you for everything you've done?'' Shanndel said, fitting herself more tightly against him. ''My darling Panther, oh, how I love you. Should anything happen to you . . .''

Her words trailed off when she heard a horse approaching outside the cabin. She leaned away from Panther and gazed up at him. ''It's probably my father,'' she said, swallowing hard. ''He . . . he . . . will want me to return home with him.''

''You do what your heart tells you to do,'' he said, reaching up to smooth a lock of hair back from her eyes.

''You are certain mother will be all right?'' she asked, searching his eyes for reassurance.

''As certain as the stars are wed to the evening sky on a beautiful spring night,'' he said, smiling down at her.

''Then, Panther, my place is here with you,'' Shanndel said, again hugging him.

When her father was directed inside the lodge, Shanndel gazed at him uncertainly.

Then she went and hugged him. "Father, Mother is going to be all right," she murmured, then told him everything . . . who had done this, and how Panther and his warriors were going to find him.

"And, Father, I am going to ride with Panther on the search," she said, stepping away from her father when she felt his muscles tense.

"Your place is home with me and your mother," Edward said as he looked down at his wife.

"My place is with Panther," Shanndel said, hating to hurt her father, yet knowing she could not desert Panther.

Edward looked at her again.

Their eyes locked.

She held hers steady.

His wavered.

Then he knelt down beside Grace and stroked her brow with his hand. "I've come to take you home," he whispered.

"A travois awaits her," Panther said. "It will make her journey to your home more comfortable." He stepped to the lodge door. "I will appoint several warriors to make sure you arrive home safely."

Edward frowned up at Panther. "That won't be necessary," he said tightly. "The sheriff and his men are waiting for me outside the camp. They will accompany me and Grace to our home."

Edward looked over at Shanndel again. "You are certain of what you have decided to do?" he asked thickly. "Your loyalties are not misplaced?"

"You know that I shall always feel loyal to you and Mother, yet the man I love needs my loyalty just as much, Father," Shanndel said, her eyes locking with Panther's.

"Where is that travois?" Edward growled, gently sweeping Grace up into his arms.

"Outside," Shanndel said, stepping aside as her father walked past her.

She followed him outside. She stood beside Panther as Grace was placed on the travois. Her heart warmed when a Shawnee maiden came and draped a blanket over Grace. That gesture proved that Panther's people's resentment toward Shanndel and her family did not run as deeply as she feared.

Everyone was quiet and stood aside as the travois was tied to Edward's horse.

Shanndel then went to her father. She gave him a fierce hug, glad when he returned the gesture of love with a hug as warm and gratifying as hers.

"Daughter, stay safe," Edward said. He slowly stepped away from her. He placed a gentle hand on her cheek, then bent low and brushed a kiss across her lips.

Choked with emotion, Shanndel watched her father mount his horse and then ride slowly away with her mother safely wrapped and covered on the travois.

After he was out of sight and on his way home with the sheriff and his deputies, Panther told his people about Iron Nose's presence in the area. He instructed his warriors. Some were to stay and guard the camp. The others were to go with Panther to search for their longtime enemy.

Shanndel rode proudly beside Panther as they left the

camp. The sound of the many hoofbeats was like thunder reverberating through the dense forest, matching the wild thundering of Shanndel's heart. Strange how she felt as though she belonged among the Shawnee. She was one with them on this search for a man who left death and destruction wherever he went. It would please her to be present when he was finally downed, for this man had almost robbed Shanndel of her precious mother!

"Let us find him soon," she murmured to herself.

Chapter Twenty-six

The moon was high in the sky and still Panther and Shanndel hadn't found Iron Nose. Shanndel was witnessing firsthand Iron Nose's skill at eluding people. She and Panther found a trail of blood more than once, but they would just as quickly lose it, for the trail would suddenly disappear. The last trail of blood had led into the river. No blood had been found since.

The cry of a loon echoed eerily across the river, startling Shanndel.

Thinking the bird's cry might have been caused by someone's presence other then hers and Panther's, she eased her horse closer to Panther's, her eyes roaming slowly from side to side. She was always afraid that Iron Nose might be so skillfully hidden they would not find him until one of them was attacked.

When she saw no one, she sighed and slumped her shoulders. Never had she been so weary.

And worry about her mother's welfare lay heavy on her mind. The fact that her mother had awakened at least long enough to speak Iron Nose's name made Shanndel believe that her head wound was not a fatal one. It had not robbed her of her ability to remember.

And now that her mother was home with Shanndel's father, she believed that her mother would soon be out of bed and smiling her sweet smile.

"You are lost deep in thought. Is it about your mother?" Panther asked, reaching over to take Shanndel's hand. When she looked at him and nodded, he gently squeezed her hand. "Your mother will be all right. Time will heal her wound."

"But what if Iron Nose is still able to return to finish what he started?" Shanndel asked, swallowing hard at the thought of her mother having been at that man's mercy for even one second.

"He will make a wrong move soon and his mistake will cost him his life," Panther said, his jaw tight. "And his loss of blood will have weakened him enough to keep him from doing much more harm to anyone."

"I'm so tired," Shanndel said, sighing deeply. "It's been such a long, arduous day."

"We shall return to my camp," Panther said, drawing her hand to his lips and gently kissing it. "There I will hold you in my arms until you sleep."

"I should go home to see how my mother—" Shanndel began, but was interrupted by Panther.

"Your mother has your father," Panther said thickly.

281

"And you have this Shawnee chief. Stay the night and then tomorrow I will accompany you to your home so that you can see for yourself that your mother is faring well enough."

"That sounds good to me," Shanndel said, smiling softly at him. "My wonderful Shawnee chief, I welcome your arms. I shall sleep, oh, so wonderfully in them."

"I will not sleep," Panther said, riding along the Maple Fork River, where the moon was reflected in the water.

"You won't?" Shanndel asked, her eyebrows lifting. "Why not?"

"I will be looking at you," Panther said, a slow grin on his lips as she gave him another of her wondrous, heart-warming smiles.

"I wish we were there now," Shanndel said, breathless at the thought of staying the night with him. She wished there could be more than just sleep to look forward to.

But she doubted that he would want to make love after having just buried his father.

Casting him a shy glance, she felt shameful for thinking about it herself, with her mother lying in bed with a head wound.

Suddenly Panther edged his horse closer.

Shanndel was swept quickly into paradise when Panther reached over, put an arm around her waist, and whisked her over onto his lap.

Sitting sideways against him, she gazed up at him and saw the hungry need in his eyes. They were on fire with longing. He lowered his lips and took her mouth savagely in his, igniting a hot, pulsing desire between them.

Her body a tempest of desire, Shanndel wrapped her arms around Panther's neck and strained her breasts against his chest.

She moaned throatily when his free hand slid between them and unbuttoned her blouse. Her breasts throbbed when they sprang free and his hand cupped one of them, his thumb tweaking the nipple.

Weakened by passion, Panther swept his hand even lower and reached around to unbutton her skirt. He could feel the hammering of her heart against his chest as he slid his hand down the front of her skirt and found her wet and ready for his fingers as he began caressing her swollen nub.

Dizzy with pleasure, feeling his fingers warm and trembling against that part of her that seemed to have a life of its own, Shanndel drew her lips from his and let her head fall back with a deep, throaty sigh.

When he slid a finger up inside her, she felt herself at the brink of total rapture.

Not wanting to go on that flight of wonder without him, she reached down and removed his hand.

Their eyes met in a silent understanding as Panther drew a tight rein and stopped his horse.

Filling his arms with Shanndel, he slid from the saddle, laid her quickly on the ground, and blanketed her with his body.

''My need for you is endless,'' he whispered huskily as he lifted her skirt up past her thighs.

He bent low and brushed a soft kiss across her woman's center; the pleasure was so keen, Shanndel cried out. She writhed as his lips and tongue continued to pleasure her in this way. Unable to ask him to stop, to join her in the ultimate ecstasy, she arched her body closer to his lips.

Closing her eyes, she bit her lower lip and trembled as she was gripped with intense, savage joy.

She clung to Panther's shoulders as his tongue continued to sweep slowly over her, swirling, his teeth sometimes nibbling on the soft flesh that surrounded that part of her that had been awakened to such heights of pleasure.

"I must have you now," Panther whispered huskily as he rose over her. His hands trembled as he unfastened his buckskin breeches, then slid them down.

He took one moment to gaze down at her, his pulse racing as he saw her loveliness beneath the shine of the moon. Her dark hair, which was the same color and texture of his, was flowing softly around her shoulders. Her breasts were high and full, her lips parted in breathless wonder.

"I love you so," he whispered in a husky groan.

"As I love you," Shanndel whispered back.

"You are not too tired to do what we are about to do?" Panther asked, brushing a hand over her breasts, feeling her nipples responding and tightening against his flesh.

"Tired?" Shanndel murmured, not recognizing her own voice in its huskiness. "At this moment I don't even know the meaning of the word."

He smiled at her, stroked her cheeks lovingly with his thumbs, then in one eager thrust he plunged deep within her. Their lips met in a torrid kiss as his mouth closed over hers.

His hands went to her breasts and kneaded them. Shanndel grew languorous at his touch, the stormy passion causing her to forget the trauma of the day, and the dangers of being alone, mindless, in such a way, when there was a murderer lurking somewhere in the dark.

All she could think about was now . . . was *them* . . . and their intense love and need for one another. Everything else seemed far away, perhaps belonging to another time, another place.

She was bubbling, ready to burst. His rhythmic thrusts were almost torture. Bright threads of bliss were beginning to weave through her heart. She clung to him. She arched herself higher so that he could penetrate her more deeply.

Unable to hold back much longer, the pleasure mounting within him, his body yearning, Panther swept his arms around her and crushed her to him so hard she gasped.

Feverish with desire, his lips slid from her mouth.

His pulse racing, their bodies straining together hungrily, he flicked his tongue around one of her nipples, then sucked it until she moaned and thrashed her head from side to side.

His hand slid again down to that part of her that ached. As he continued thrusting himself into her, his fingers caressed her tight, throbbing nub.

Again he kissed her and darted his tongue into her mouth, her tongue moist and hot against his.

Shanndel drew her lips quickly from his. ''I am so

near—'' she cried, all warm and wonderful inside as the pleasure spread. It seemed incredible that she was about to experience such wonder again. She had never truly lived until she had met Panther and found paradise within his arms. Nothing could be more wonderful, or more satisfying.

"My body is on fire," Panther whispered huskily into her ear. "You are what ignited it."

It was at that moment that Shanndel gave herself over to total rapture. She clung to him as her body quaked and spasmed. He soon followed, gripping her hard against his body, his wild thrusts deep and long, his moans throaty.

Afterward, he rolled away from her and lay on his back, his manhood still hard and throbbing from pleasure.

Shanndel turned to him. She looked at him blissfully. "I wish we could spend the night here," she murmured.

She ran her hand down his lean, tight belly.

She smiled when her touch caused his flesh to quiver sensually.

When he reached for her hand and led it down to his manhood, she questioned him with her eyes, then knew what he wanted when he placed her fingers around him.

She watched his eyes close in pleasure as she began moving her fingers slowly over his hardness, somehow knowing to move them in an up-and-down fashion.

She felt a renewal of her own arousal as she pleasured him in this way. Her own body grew warm with needs that had been foreign to her before she met him.

He opened his eyes and looked down at her, his gaze slumbrous. When he placed his hands gently behind her head, twining his fingers through her hair, and pressed her lips close to his throbbing member, she wondered what he was doing.

"Taste me," he whispered huskily, his eyes flaring with building passion.

Stunned by the suggestion, she hesitated.

But then she recalled how he had pleasured her there, where her senses now seemed to be centered.

Wanting to give him equal pleasure, she bent low, and as he held her hair out of the way, she slowly flicked her tongue out and touched the tip, then sank her mouth down over him. She knew by his deep groans that she was doing everything he wanted of her at this moment.

When she felt a shuddering begin in his loins, and saw how he arched his hips higher so that she could take him deeper, she continued, then stopped when he gently held her face between his hands and urged her away from him.

"I would not ask *that* of you," he said huskily, smiling at her almost wickedly. "Mount me, woman. Sit atop me. Take your pleasure along with me."

Shanndal moved over him and inhaled a quick, wondrous breath as he thrust himself up inside her. She had discovered so many ways to make love tonight, and had found each lesson in love as wonderful as the last.

This time the ultimate ecstasy was quickly found.

And when again they were snuggling beside one another on the ground, fulfilled and wondrously in love, they lay and stared together at the stars.

"My father is up among the stars," Panther said,

drawing Shanndel closer to his side. "He has his place there now until the end of time."

"It's good that you can look at your father's death in such a way," Shanndel murmured. "It makes his dying less sorrowful."

"Everyone dies," Panther said thickly. "It is something one knows and accepts." He leaned on an elbow and turned toward her. "Of course, dying hurts those who are left behind. But there is something deep within all of us that makes losing our loved ones something we can live through."

"I hope Mother is all right," Shanndel said somberly. "I feel so responsible for what happened to her."

"And you would, because you are a woman with such a caring heart," Panther said. He reached up and placed a gentle hand on her cheek. "But had you chosen not to come to me because of your concern for your mother, do you not see that moments like these would have been robbed from us? You cannot live your life for your parents. You are a grown woman with needs and passions of your own. You deserve to love as your parents have loved. For them to ask you not to is the height of selfishness."

"Yes, I know that you are right, but still—"

"Say no more," Panther said, placing a gentle hand over her mouth, sealing her words behind it. "Just think of us and what the future holds for us. Our love is forever, my woman. Nothing should be allowed to take that from us."

"Nothing and no one," Shanndel murmured, placing

an arm around his neck and drawing his lips to hers. Their kiss was a soft and gentle one that turned quickly into raging heat.

Again they made fiery love.

Chapter Twenty-seven

The night had been beautiful for Shanndel. After she and Panther had made love again and again beneath the blanket of stars, they had gone to his lodge and spent the night in his bed, his arms holding her close. She regretted leaving him, but she had no choice. She had to see if her mother was all right. She *had* to show her mother that she cared.

She rode beside Panther until her house came into view through a break in the trees. Shanndel gave Panther a wistful glance. Just looking at him made her heart race and the pit of her stomach feel deliciously warm. She had never known that anyone could love as intensely as she loved Panther. She didn't even see how she had lived without him.

She now knew that if she lost him, life would be unbearably empty.

"Panther, I hope you understand why I have to return home this morning," she said, breaking the silence between them.

When he looked her way, she saw in his eyes a quiet understanding that comes between people who love each other. She saw such wondrous love, she wished she could fling herself into his arms and stay there forever.

One day soon, she hoped to make that wish come true!

"I understand the love between daughter and mother, yet I still feel that your place is with me," Panther said, his voice drawn. "Rain Singing, I am your best protection against the madman Iroquois chief. Iron Nose might abduct *you* to get back at your mother since he did not succeed in killing her yesterday."

"I'm sure he thinks she's dead or he wouldn't have left her lying there," Shanndel said, shuddering to think again of how she and Panther had found her beloved mother. At that first sight, Shanndel had truly thought her mother was dead. Surely Iron Nose had thought the same when he left her lying there so coldheartedly.

"If Iron Nose has survived his wounds, he will return to hide her body so that proof of her murder is kept from the white man sheriff," Panther said. "The only reason he did not take the time to hide her body was because he was injured. No doubt he went to search for herbs in the forest to stop the bleeding. Once that was done, I do believe he would have returned to your mother. I am certain that by now he knows she is either alive, or that someone has found her body and returned it to her family. Either way, he is still a threat, especially to you, Rain Singing."

"Even if what you say is true, Panther, I must check on my mother," Shanndel murmured. She reached over and gently touched his arm. "And, darling, I can't expect you to watch over me every minute of my life." She gazed ahead. They were on the edge of the tobacco field, where a few workers were harvesting those leaves that hadn't been destroyed by the earthquake.

She drew a tight rein and stopped, then looked over at Panther again. "You need not go any farther with me," she said. "As you see, there are workers in the field. I am safe enough to travel onward by myself. I think it's best that you and my father aren't brought face to face again so soon. He holds deep resentment, I am sure, over how you have taken his daughter from him, as he sees it."

"He *will* come face to face with me *soon*," Panther said throatily. "I will return for you, Rain Singing, to escort you safely back to my village. You are mine now, heart and soul. I will not rest easy until you are with me again."

"That will be soon," Shanndel said, guiding her horse closer to his. "I love you, Panther. I already miss you with every beat of my heart."

He twined his fingers through her hair and drew her mouth to his. Their lips trembled with passion as they kissed, and then too soon he was gone from Shanndel, with her wishing she could follow, yet knowing that she couldn't. Her mother was her first priority at the moment.

When she was finally free to go back to Panther, he

would forevermore be first to her in everything.

She watched him until the dark shadows of the forest gulped him up, then she rode onward to the house.

After dismounting she handed her reins to Danny. "Blue Smoke needs a brisk rub-down and brushing," she said, glancing at the stable, which had been quickly repaired.

She then went to the house and carefully walked up the loose boards of the front steps, then opened the door, which was still loose on its hinges from the earthquake.

What she found inside the house made her heart leap with happiness. It was nothing like she had expected. Her mother, dressed in a beautiful, flowing green silk dress, greeted Shanndel with open arms. Only a bandage around her head gave proof of the traumatic experience she had gone through while with Iron Nose.

And the house! Except for the hole left in the ceiling where the lovely chandelier had once hung, everything seemed back in its proper place.

Then Shanndel became aware of something else. There was no exuberance in the way her mother embraced her. There was a strange sort of desperation.

Shanndel supposed that was because her mother had worried so much about her and was glad that she was home again.

"Mother, you don't have to hug me so tightly," Shanndel murmured, yet she didn't draw away from her. She returned the hug, enjoying her mother's wonderful fragrance, her nearness. She didn't want to think again of how she had almost lost her mother in the forest.

"Shanndel, oh, Shanndel, I'm so glad you are all

right,'' Grace said, then stepped away from her, tears rushing from her eyes. "Oh, Shanndel, I don't know how to tell you. I ... I'm so afraid you are going to blame yourself.''

"Blame myself for what?" Shanndel asked, sudden fear gripping her heart when she saw how distraught her mother was. Why wasn't she happy? They were both safe.

Shanndel glanced around her, then up the wide spiral staircase. Coldness spread through her when she suddenly realized that her father wasn't there also to greet her. She knew that no matter how disappointed he was in her, he would never hold such a grudge that he wouldn't speak with her.

Shanndel gripped her mother's arms. "Mother, where ... where ... is father?" she asked guardedly, flinching when she saw how her mother cried harder upon hearing the question.

"Shanndel Lynn, come with me," Grace said, taking Shanndel by the hand.

"Mother, for goodness sake, tell me what's wrong," Shanndel said, following her mother up the stairs. "Where is Father, Mother? Is this strange mood of yours because of Father?"

Grace's deep sobs kept her from answering.

Knowing that something was terribly wrong, Shanndel broke away from her and ran on up the stairs.

When she came to her parents' bedroom door, she stopped and sucked in a deep breath. She was almost afraid to knock on the door. If her father didn't respond right away ...

Grace stepped up to her side. Her hand trembled as

she placed it on the doorknob and slowly turned it.

When the door opened enough for Shanndel to see inside, her heart sank and tears rushed to her eyes. Her father was lying so lifelessly on the bed.

She turned to her mother. "Mother, what's wrong with him?" she asked, a sob lodging in her throat. "Why . . . why . . . is he so still? Please tell me it's only because he's asleep."

"It's more than that," Grace said, taking Shanndel's hand again. "Come to the bed with me. Let's see if he will respond to you when you speak his name."

"What do you mean . . . *if?*" Shanndel murmured, her whole body quaking with fear as they approached the bed and her father did not respond to their presence.

Her mother's words—"Don't blame yourself"— kept running through Shanndel's mind.

Blame myself for what? she thought desperately. But when she stepped up to the bed and got a full view of her father's face, she knew.

She could hardly bear seeing the drool rolling from the corners of her father's mouth and the pleading in his blue eyes as he opened them and looked up at her.

She covered her mouth with a hand to stifle a scream when she saw that her father saw her, yet did not.

There was no recognition in his eyes, only blankness.

"Father, Father," Shanndel cried, bending over him to hug him. It felt as though her heart was splintering into a million pieces when even then he did not respond except to wheeze against her cheek something unrecognizable.

"He's had a stroke," Grace said, dabbing at her eyes with a handkerchief. "He is paralyzed from his neck down and . . . and . . . he knows no one. Not even me, Shanndel. And apparently . . . not even you.''

Feeling drained, Shanndel moved from her father and fell to her knees beside him. "A stroke," she said, the word like poison as it crossed her trembling lips. "Oh, Lord, it's totally incapacitated him."

She gave her mother a quick look. "Mother, what caused it?" she asked, afraid to hear the answer. "Did Doc Adams say . . . what . . . caused it?"

Grace sat down in her rocking chair beside the bed. She picked up her knitting and began rhythmically clacking the needles together. What had been a labor of love yesterday was now only something to keep her hands busy.

When her mother didn't answer her, Shanndel went and knelt down before her on the floor and gazed up at her. "Mother, I am at fault here, aren't I?" she asked, tears flowing from her eyes. "This happened because of me and my relationship with Panther."

"Darling daughter, my beautiful Rain Singing," Grace said, laying her knitting aside. She stroked her fingers through Shanndel's thick black hair. "I told you not to blame yourself. He was devastated over the loss of the tobacco fields. And his bad lungs have weakened his entire body. I . . . I . . . tried to get him to stop smoking so many cigars each day. You also begged him to take better care of himself. As you know, all our pleadings fell on deaf ears."

"But he had the stroke *now*, and I can't help thinking that I am the sole cause," Shanndel said, crying as she laid her head on her mother's lap. "I love Panther so, Mother. How could I have turned my back on him? But because I went to him, you were abducted and left for dead and . . . and . . . Father now lies like a strange sort of vegetable on his bed.''

"Darling Rain Singing, do you not know that your destiny, as well as your father's, was planned when you were but a tiny seed in your mother's womb?'' Grace said quietly as she caressed Shanndel's tear-soaked cheek. "What happened to me, to your father, to our land and tobacco field, and between you and Panther, was planned from the beginning of time. No matter how much you believe you are the cause of what has happened, it is not so.''

She placed gentle hands on Shanndel's face, framing it. She drew Shanndel's face up so that their gazes met. "Rain Singing, your destiny was to meet and love Panther, as mine was to meet and love your father,'' she murmured. "Never regret loving Panther, for it is a great gift given to you by God. Such gifts are to be cherished, Rain Singing.''

Grace glanced over at her husband, then looked quickly down at Shanndel once again. "Time passes quickly,'' she said, her voice breaking. "Do not waste a moment of it in regrets. Go to Panther. Love him. Cherish him.''

"But Father . . . ?'' Shanndel said, her eyes searching her mother's.

"There is nothing you can do for him,'' Grace said solemnly. "Nor can I. All I can do now, Shanndel, is sit vigil at my husband's bedside. If he worsens, I shall send Danny to the Shawnee camp for you.''

"You truly think I should leave?'' Shanndel asked, her voice breaking again.

"I think you should go to Panther," Grace said. "He will comfort you."

Sobbing, Shanndel reached up and hugged her mother, then rushed from the room.

Blinded by tears, she left the house and ran toward the stable.

"Panther," she cried. "I need you so much, Panther. My heart is breaking!"

The wounds inflicted on him by Shanndel's mother had been treated with herbs he had gathered in the forest, and now Iron Nose was lurking on his horse just beyond the large tobacco field. Making sure to keep out of sight of those who were laboring there, he watched the mansion. His eyebrows arched and he smiled when he saw Shanndel run from the house, crying.

He was glad to see her distraught, for that might mean that her mother had died. When he had returned to the spot where he had left Dancing Sky and found her gone, he wasn't sure if she had been found alive or dead.

Now he guessed that she had more than likely died, just now. Why else would the daughter be reacting in such a way now, instead of earlier when they had found her mother?

He had been watching the house since dawn. He had seen Panther escort Dancing Sky's daughter here. He had been tempted to go after Panther then and kill him, but being too curious about the welfare of his first wife, he had stayed in hiding and waited.

And the waiting had been worth it. With Dancing Sky's daughter so off guard in her grief, Iron Nose had the perfect opportunity to grab her. He would abduct her, get answers from her about Dancing Sky, and then he would kill the daughter. If Dancing Sky was still alive, he would watch and wait for his next opportunity to abduct her and finish the job he had started.

If Dancing Sky was dead, he would continue his vengeful acts until Panther was destroyed.

Iron Nose's heart pounded with excitement when he saw Dancing Sky's daughter riding in his direction. He would wait for her to get farther away from the laborers, so that they could not hear her scream when he grabbed her off her horse.

He watched with narrowed eyes as Shanndel grew closer and closer. He edged his horse back into the thicker brush so that she would not see him.

He snarled when she rode past him into the darker shadows of the forest. He proceeded after her, then when he felt it was safe enough, he overtook her. When she saw him, her eyes went wide with fear. But just as he reached out a hand to snatch her from her horse, he felt the pain of an arrow entering his back and then coming out his chest.

His eyes wild from the severe pain, Iron Nose grabbed at the arrow that was dripping with his life's-blood.

Losing his balance, he fell from his horse, yelping with pain when falling on the ground on his back broke the shaft of the arrow, leaving only the piece that penetrated through his chest.

Stunned speechless, Shanndel stared down at the evil man as he writhed on the ground, groaning, gripping the arrow with both hands, trying to dislodge it.

Just as his body spasmed in a death dance, Panther rode up next to Shanndel and grabbed her from her horse onto his lap. He held her tightly against him when he felt how she was shivering from the shock of what she had just witnessed.

"I did not get far when my concern for you made me turn back," Panther said softly. "I saw Iron Nose. It only took a moment to nock an arrow to my bowstring to kill the evil creature. Finally, Rain Singing, Iron Nose's days of tyranny are over."

"Panther, oh, Panther, so much has happened because of that wicked man," Shanndel cried. She proceeded to tell him about her father, then said something to him that she had only moments ago decided she must do. "I was coming to you to stay with you, but I've changed my mind. I must stay with Mother and help her through this ordeal. She needs me, Panther. Please understand."

"Now that Iron Nose is dead, I feel comfortable saying that your place, for now, is with your mother," Panther said as Shanndel leaned away from him and gazed adoringly into his eyes. "Go to her. When you feel it is right, come to me. I will be awaiting you with open arms."

"You are so wonderful," Shanndel said, hugging him. "And I shall come to you soon. I promise. But for now, I truly believe my place is with my mother."

He lifted her over onto her saddle.

Shanndel took her reins and gazed down at Iron Nose, the very sight of him making her shiver uncontrollably.

"What of him?" she asked, looking quickly at Panther.

"I will see to him in the proper way," Panther said, dismounting. "I know and understand the importance of all men having a proper burial so that their spirits can enter the other life."

Amazed that Panther would show such kindness to a man who had done nothing but evil to him, Shanndel watched Panther lift his saddle from his horse and remove the blanket that lay beneath it. He wrapped Iron Nose within this blanket, then tied it securely around him.

Her eyes widened when Panther took this wrapped body and placed it high in a tree, on limbs that reached out on both sides of the body like arms.

Before Panther went back to his horse, he went to Shanndel. Reaching a hand up and twining his fingers through her hair, he drew her lips down to his. "Go now," he whispered, then gently kissed her.

He watched her ride away, then mounted his own steed and headed back toward his camp.

His heart was light and filled with love toward *Moneto* for having blessed him this day. He inhaled a deep sigh of relief to know that finally it was over, this thing between his people and the Iroquois. With Iron Nose's death, surely a long-sought-for peace would be possible between the two tribes! It was Iron Nose who had always created the tension between his people and Panther's.

"*Nyoh*, thank you, *Moneto*," he cried to the heavens, a radiance in his dark eyes.

Chapter Twenty-eight

When Panther came within view of his camp he grew cold inside. His eyes narrowed angrily as he stared at Sheriff Braddock, who was just riding into the camp. That man's presence never meant anything good. Panther knew that if the sheriff had any idea that Panther had killed a man—no matter that it was done in defense of his woman, or that the man who died was a deceitful, lying, heartless Iroquois—that fact alone would prompt the sheriff to order Panther away from this land.

Expecting the worst, Panther rode on into camp and went to his lodge, where the sheriff had dismounted and was waiting outside for him.

When Panther's and Sheriff Braddock's eyes met, a silent battle occurred.

Yet there was a smugness today about the sheriff especially evident as his lips curled into a victorious smile. Panther dismounted and stood stiffly before him.

Panther was certain now that the sheriff's coming would bring no good to the Shawnee.

"Why are you here?" Panther demanded, folding his arms across his muscled chest. He glanced around himself and saw his people standing warily in a half circle behind him.

He glared at the sheriff again. "Why have you come again into my village?" he asked, trying to keep his voice steady and devoid of rage.

"Word was brought to me about Edward Burton," Sheriff Braddock said, resting his hands on his holstered pistols, which hung heavy at each of his hips. He took a step closer to Panther, his eyes squinting angrily. "It's being said around the town of Harrisburg that Edward's stroke was caused because this renegade Iroquois chief who was only in the vicinity because of his hatred for the Shawnee. Edward's wife was involved with this Iroquois chief. This was the chief who abducted her. The strain of that event triggered the stroke."

Panther stood quietly listening, not ready to offer any explanation to the sheriff. His eyes glittered as he waited for the sheriff to continue.

He was almost certain that his people would not be on this land for long. It was there in the way the sheriff continued to smile, as though he was dragging this out purposely so that he could taunt the Shawnee, who were still awaiting his true reason for being there.

Panther knew better than to try to explain to this white man that Iron Nose was dead and with his death came peace for everyone, for he knew that the white sheriff would not listen or believe him.

He knew that if the sheriff realized who had killed the Iroquois chief, he would seize that opportunity to arrest Panther for murder, even though it would have pleased the sheriff to have been able to have done the deed himself. His hate for all red-skins was evident in everything he said and did.

Neh, Panther would offer nothing to this conversation. He had no choice but to stand there and listen as the sheriff made a mockery of him and everything that being a chief stood for. To Panther, dignity and respect meant everything.

"It's just what I've always said about Indians," Sheriff Braddock grumbled, pausing to spit on the ground between himself and Panther. He smiled crookedly as he slowly ground the heel of his boot into the spit.

He gazed intently again at Panther. "Yep, it's just like Indians to bring trouble with them everywhere they go," he growled out. "I warned you about trouble, Panther. You and your people pack up your things. I'll return soon with many men who will escort you savages far away from here. This land belongs solely to whites."

Hate for this white sheriff boiled like molten lava within Panther, yet he knew that anything he might say at this time would be words wasted and would only humiliate him more.

Nyoh, he would leave. He never should have thought he could stay here with his people after having met the sheriff that first time and realizing that he was a man of deep prejudices.

His thoughts went quickly to Rain Singing. Theirs

was a love so wonderful, so unique and beautiful, yet he knew that he must give her up. This sheriff had proved that nothing would ever be different for the red man. Everywhere that Panther might roam, possibly even where his people were headed, there would be no stability, no permanent home.

Nyoh, it seemed that planting permanent roots was as unlikely as getting this white sheriff to change his mind about the red man. Once Panther and his people *did* reach Oklahoma, would it be their final home, a place that could be called home forever?

Or in time would they be forced from there to continue wandering, with no one welcoming them anywhere?

"Well?" Sheriff Braddock said, placing his doubled fists on his hips. "What's it to be, Chief? Cooperation with me? Or must I send my deputies back to make you leave by force?"

"My people will move onward," Panther said, seeing out of the corner of his eye that many of the women grabbed up their children and hugged them desperately to their chests, and many of the elderly hung their heads, hopelessness in their eyes.

But he knew they understood that what he had chosen to do was the only way it could be. They were too few in number to force anything on this white man of authority.

And when the sheriff found the dead Iroquois chief on his resting place in the trees, would the sheriff not have another reason to come down with a vengeance on the Shawnee?

"*Nyoh*, we will leave, but we do not need to be escorted from this area," Panther said, clenching his fists tightly at his sides. "By sunrise tomorrow we will be gone."

"Leave the cabins intact," Sheriff Braddock said, gazing from one lodge to the other. "The white people who are steadily moving into our territory can make good use of them."

Panther smiled slowly as he thought of the salt that was hidden beneath the floorboards of each building. When the whites moved into these lodges and discovered the storage area, they would wonder what had been stored there, but would never know.

"The lodges will be left behind but not without a curse for those who will make their homes within them," Panther said in a hiss. "At night, when their lanterns are dim inside their lodges, they will see shadows they do not understand. I tell you now that it will be the spirits of those who were forced to leave. The curse will remain always as a reminder to the whites that once again the red man was wronged."

"Spirits?" Sheriff Braddock said, chuckling. "Hogwash. Now get on with you, Panther. Get things ready. And don't think I'll not keep watch to make sure you aren't gone by sunrise."

"We will be long gone by then," Panther said, his voice smooth and even.

Sheriff Braddock nodded, swung himself into his saddle, then after taking a slow, cautionary look around him, rode off with his right hand resting on the rifle sheathed at the side of his horse.

Cloud came to Panther's side. "Winter will soon be

upon us," he said, his eyes worried. "Where can we make winter camp now, Panther, without meeting the same prejudices as here?"

"I doubt there is such a place," Panther said. He turned and stepped into the privacy of his lodge, where he could meditate for a while alone before giving the command for his people to start packing their belongings for the long journey ahead.

Tears sparkled in his eyes as he thought of Rain Singing. He knew from what had just happened that he could never offer her any stability in her life if she were to marry him and live the life of an Indian. Since she had been raised in the white world with its comforts, he doubted that she could live under the strain of his life without in the end hating everything about it, including Panther.

"*Neh*, I will not ask her to go with me," Panther said, dying inside at the thought of never holding her again in his arms. No one could love anyone as fiercely as he loved this woman.

And he had looked forward to a future of children with her!

How sweet and pretty a daughter would be born of such a woman as his Rain Singing!

Ah, what sons they would have made together! Future chiefs! That's what their sons would have been!

And a daughter? *Nyoh*, she would have been raised in the tradition of a Shawnee princess.

"Aieee!" he cried, his voice filled with agony. "To never touch my Rain Singing again? To never hold her? To never taste her lips again? How can I leave her? How?"

But he knew that he must.

He had never felt as defeated or alone as now.

Feeling nothing like a powerful chief, Panther hung his head and let tears stream from his eyes.

Chapter Twenty-nine

Shanndel had gone to sleep after telling her mother about Iron Nose's death. Finally she could relax, especially after seeing the joy in her mother's eyes at hearing of the evil Iroquois man's demise.

Shanndel stirred on her bed, waking slowly, then jumped when she heard a mournful wailing coming from somewhere in the house. As the morning sun shone through the window onto her bed, Shanndel's mind went back to another time recently when she had heard such wails.

It had come from the Shawnee Indian camp when Panther's father had died.

She had discovered that wailing was how all Indians mourned the death of a loved one.

Knowing that the mournful sound was now coming from her mother, Shanndel covered her mouth with her hand as a shiver of dread raced up and down her spine.

Her mother's wails could only mean one thing. Oh, Lord, surely Shanndel's father had died sometime during the night.

Tears falling from her eyes, Shanndel rushed from the bed and ran barefoot down the long corridor, her long silk gown wrapping around her legs. The mournful cries grew louder as Shanndel drew closer to her father's room.

When she came to the closed door, Shanndel sought for the courage to turn the knob and take that first look at her dead father.

Was it only a few days ago that he had been riding his horse, a vital person with hopes and dreams of the promising future that his successful tobacco plantation afforded him?

Was it only a few days ago that Shanndel had seen her father take her mother into his arms and hold her as if she were some precious jewel he guarded with his life?

Oh, was it only a few days ago that Shanndel had disappointed her father for the first time in her life?

She lowered her eyes and wept, for she could not help blaming herself for all that had happened wrong these past several days.

But her mother's words came to her like a soft, sweet balm to her senses, telling her not to blame herself. Her mother had told her that love such as she felt for Panther came only once in a lifetime and that she should let nothing keep her from being with Panther.

Shanndel's mother had given Shanndel her blessings.

Shanndel swallowed hard and wiped the tears from

her eyes. She was thinking clearly enough now to know
that if anyone were to blame, it was Iron Nose! Had he
not come to this area, driven by his deep-seated lust for
vengeance, Shanndel's mother would not have been abducted, Red Thunder would not have died needlessly,
nor would her father have been downed by a stroke.

But, no, she could not blame herself, for if she did,
she would never be able to go to Panther. Every time
she looked into his eyes she would see her father and
feel guilty for having fallen in love with the wonderful
Shawnee chief.

Her hand trembling, Shanndel turned the knob.

First she gazed with an aching heart at her father,
who lay lifelessly on the bed, his eyes closed forever.

She stifled a sob behind her hand when she saw how
her mother had dressed him. He wore the buckskin
clothes that he had surely worn on the day he met this
Indian maiden who mourned his passing so sorrowfully.

Not only was he dressed in buckskin, beside him on
the bed were his favorite rifle, his Bowie knife in its
leather sheath, and a bundle of his favorite cigars.

Also there were parfleche bags, which Shanndel assumed were filled with food for his journey to the
hereafter.

No. There were no signs whatsoever of her father
being a rich man; his diamond rings and ascot diamonds
had been left in the wall safe of his office on the first
floor of the mansion.

His wife was going to bury him in the Indian tradition, not white!

If so, there would be no large assemblage of important, rich people coming to view a casket in which lay

the richest, most prominent man in Saline County.

Her father's ceremony would happen today more than likely, and it would be private.

Shanndel's eyes shifted to her mother, who was kneeling beside her dead husband's bed.

Shanndel's breath caught when she saw that she was dressed in full Indian attire as she continued her wailing, her eyes lifted as though in prayer.

Not only had she prepared her white husband for an Indian burial, Shanndel's mother was reaching out to the Indian side of her character for the comfort she needed to get her through the death of her beloved.

Her mother's thick black hair hung long and loose down her back. She wore the lovely doeskin dress and moccasins that Shanndel had worn when she was first trying to meet Panther.

Shanndel tiptoed up beside her mother. Her eyes widened when she saw that her mother had painted her face black with ash from the fireplace.

For some reason Shanndel felt gratified to see her mother's Indian side. She looked more natural in doeskin than silks and satins!

Having heard Shanndel, Grace turned tearful eyes to her. She reached out a hand for her. "Come," she said, a sob lodging in her throat. "Sit with me. Pray with me to the Great Spirit. Only he can get us through our grieving."

A fresh rush of tears flowing from her eyes, Shanndel nodded silently and knelt down beside her mother. She could feel the trembling of her mother's hand as she reached over and took one of Shanndel's. She gently squeezed her fingers around her mother's, then closed her eyes and listened as her mother's wails began again.

As though by magic, as though she had done this sort of mourning ritual many times before, Shanndel began wailing.

It seemed so natural, so heartfelt, so right.

When her mother became quiet, Shanndel opened her eyes and ceased wailing herself.

"Your father showed me long ago his choice of burial spots," Grace said, reaching over to place a comforting hand on Shanndel's tear-soaked cheek. "It is on the far side of Harrisburg in a cemetery named Sunset Hills. It is a beautiful place of trees and flowers. There is a lot that lies next to where we will bury your father that will be mine when it is time for me to go over to the other side to join your father."

"I wasn't aware that you and Father had chosen your resting places," Shanndel murmured. "But I am familiar with the cemetery. It is a lovely place. I have passed by it on Blue Smoke at sunset. The cemetery is such a beautiful place in the evening."

"Your father also chose gravestones for our final resting places," Grace said as she dropped her hand away from Shanndel. She pushed herself up from the floor and stood over her husband to look adoringly down at him. "He even saw that our names were engraved in the stones." She swallowed hard. "Now I must see that today's date is engraved beneath your father's name."

"Mother, are you going to be all right?" Shanndel asked quietly, realizing the pain her mother was feeling at this time. Shanndel's own pain was intense. So she

313

knew that her mother, who loved her husband in such a special way, must be hurting twofold.

"Once the burial is behind us, yes, I shall be all right," Grace said. She bent to her knees again and slowly and meditatingly wrapped her husband's body in a blanket. Ropes dangled at the sides of the bed, ready to be tied around his body.

"Mother, so many people will want to mourn with us," Shanndel said, recalling how funerals were arranged in the white world. She had been forced to go and view the dead more than once in the homes of the departed.

"I know that most will feel that my way of burying your father is wrong," Grace said, tying the ropes to secure her husband's body within the blankets. "But I care nothing for what they think or do. They were mostly your father's friends, not mine. Too many saw me as a savage pretending to be white."

Grace looked over her shoulder at Shanndel. "I only wore those fancy dresses and jewelry because it pleased your father," she murmured. "Shanndel, I vow to you that I shall never wear them again. You see me today as you will see me tomorrow and all days before me. And your father would approve. When he bought me those fancy dresses he told me that he would not expect me to continue to wear them if he died before me. I knew he wanted me to wear them while he was alive. I pretended to love them."

She smiled, her dark eyes twinkling. "And when I looked into a mirror I saw what he saw and understood," she murmured. "I saw a pretty lady."

"Yes, you are so pretty," Shanndel said, welcoming

her mother's arms as she embraced her. But Shanndel doubted that her father would approve of her mother changing into the Indian attire today. He would probably deplore it. And surely her mother knew that but tried hard to believe otherwise because she felt more comfortable now being Indian instead of white.

Her father would not have wanted to be buried in the Indian tradition, but Shanndel would not persuade her mother to bury him in any other way. Again, she knew that her mother's sorrow would be eased by burying him in the way she thought was right.

"Shanndel, your father and I talked at length one evening not so long ago about how we would choose to be buried when we passed away," Grace murmured as she slowly and gently stroked her daughter's back. "He said that if he died before me, I should bury him in the tradition that would make me more comfortable. But he didn't ask how it would be. I guess he was afraid to know, afraid he would not agree. He loved me that much, Shanndel, that even in death he wanted what was best for me."

Grace looked down at her attire, then smiled at Shanndel. "I also told him that I would prefer the same sort of burial . . . in my doeskin dress, and private," she murmured.

Shanndel's thoughts went quickly to Panther. She drew away from her mother and went to the window to gaze out in the direction of his camp. "I would like for us to include at least one person at father's burial rites," she said quietly.

Grace went to her and slid an arm around her waist. Her eyes followed the path of Shanndel's. "I have already sent Danny for Panther," she murmured. "I knew that you would want him to accompany you to the cemetery. And I have already sent word ahead to the caretaker of Sunset Hills. A grave has been dug. A proper casket awaits us there, Shanndel. Go quickly. See if Danny has returned yet. I want to get your father in his grave where he can truly rest for eternity."

"Thank you, Mother," Shanndel said, flinging herself into her mother's arms. "Thank you for understanding my need to be with Panther at such a time as this."

She gave her mother one last hug, took a heart-wrenching look at the wrapped body, then ran from the room and hurried to the stable. Danny's horse was gone, which meant that he had not returned yet.

She then turned and watched as her mother directed several men to go up to the bedroom to get her husband's body while another man went into the stable and took from it the buckboard wagon that Shanndel had used that day for supplies when the wheel had fallen off, and when she had seen Panther up close for the first time.

So much had happened since!

Everything in Shanndel's world had changed!

Tears rolling from her eyes, Shanndel watched her father's wrapped body being brought from the house to the wagon. She watched as his special belongings were placed in the wagon with him; they would join him in the grave.

She glanced down at the wagon wheels, smiling when she saw that all four had been replaced with new. Had her father known that he had been preparing this wagon for his last journey in it?

When she heard a horse's hoofbeats approaching, she turned and began to run to meet Panther, but her mouth parted with wonder when she found only Danny coming toward her. She strained her neck to see behind him, for surely Panther would soon follow.

But her heart sank when Danny came up beside her and gave her a strange look, but said nothing.

"Well?" Shanndel asked, her eyes imploring him. "Where is he? Isn't he coming?"

Danny slid out of his saddle. He fidgeted with the reins, twirling them around a finger as he gazed at Shanndel with a quiet, questioning stare.

Unnerved by his silence and by his strange attitude, Shanndel grabbed him by the shoulders. "What's happened?" she cried, afraid to hear the answer. "Why are you looking at me so . . . so . . . strangely?"

"Panther is gone," Danny said, his voice drawn. "Shanndel, all of the Shawnee are gone. The cabins are empty, their belongings gone. That means they are gone for good, Shanndel."

Shanndel felt suddenly dizzy. She reached out for Danny just as she blacked out into a fuzzy unconsciousness.

Chapter Thirty

Dressed in one of her mother's beautiful doeskin dresses, which Grace had wanted her to wear to her father's burial rites, Shanndel was numb as she rode beside her mother on the buckboard wagon away from the cemetery. Her world had crumbled around her. She had not only lost her beloved father, but now also Panther.

She still couldn't believe that he had left the area without telling her he was leaving, or why.

She couldn't believe that he could vow to love her forever and then leave her behind as though she were some sort of baggage he would not want to be bothered with.

When she noticed that her mother had turned away from the road that led to their home, and was instead headed up Sloan Street toward town, Shanndel gave her a quick questioning look.

"Mother, where are you going?" she asked, gripping the seat with tight fingers as her mother sent the horse into a brisk trot down the dirt road that caused dust to roll behind them.

When her mother didn't respond, instead kept flicking the reins against the horse's back to make him go at a gallop, Shanndel saw people scurrying out of the way.

Shanndel knew that their questioning, shocked stares were caused by more than the speed at which Shanndel's mother chose to go down the narrow street that was lined on each side with neat white clapboard houses.

Surely they were wondering about the way Shanndel and Grace Burton were dressed, when no one had ever seen either of them in doeskin. Today they did not represent the white people of the community. They were Indians!

When Grace made a quick turn onto Main Street and headed north, directly toward the town's square, Shanndel gave her mother another questioning gaze.

"Mother, where are you going?" she cried. "Why are you doing this? Mother, I wish to go home. I . . . want . . . to be alone, Mother. I feel totally empty."

"You are not going to go to your room and drown yourself in pity," Grace said as she looked quickly over at Shanndel. "And, Shanndel, I will not allow you to lose the man you love as I have just lost mine. There is no sense in allowing it to happen. I am forced to live alone now without my man. I am going to do everything in my power to make sure that does not happen to you."

"But, Mother, how can you change things?" Shanndel said, sighing. She reached up and smoothed her hair back from her eyes, glad that her mother had slowed down the horse as it trotted up a slight incline in a street lined by more expensive, two-storied homes, some with grand pillars at the front.

"We will find Panther," Grace said, snapping the reins when the street smoothed out as they reached Harrisburg's downtown section.

"What do you mean . . . we . . . will find Panther?" Shanndel asked, touched deeply by her mother's determination to help her find Panther. She had been momentarily afraid that her mother might resent her for being partially to blame for her husband's death.

"Just you watch me," Grace said, giving Shanndel a slow smile. "I will show you spunk you have never seen before in your mother."

"Mother, I don't know what to say," Shanndel said softly, eyeing her mother speculatively. She could not help being worried about her. Was she in shock over the loss of her husband? She did seem to be acting irrationally.

She was nothing like the mother Shanndel was familiar with. Her mother had always been soft-spoken and had let her husband lead the way when decisions had to be made.

Her mother was taking charge today as though she was practiced at it.

"Shanndel, things have happened that must be corrected," Grace said, drawing a tight rein directly in front of the courthouse on the square. "And I plan to do just that." She reached over and took Shanndel's hand in hers. "Shanndel, Panther did me . . . he did *us* a favor . . . by killing Iron Nose. Today I plan to return that favor.''

"How?" Shanndel asked as her mother slid her hand away. "Mother, I don't understand at all what you have in mind, or what you are talking about. Please explain it to me."

"Shanndel, I've already told you," Grace murmured. "I am going to help you find Panther."

Shanndel glanced at the huge courthouse, where people were coming and going through the wide, spacious door, then gazed at her mother questioningly. "What does being here have to do with finding Panther?" she asked, flinching when the grand old clock at the top of the courthouse began chiming the Westminster Chimes; it was exactly noon.

"Just come with me," Grace said, sliding her hand from Shanndel's. "You will see exactly why I am here and what it *does* have to do with finding Panther."

"Mother, I'm not sure that what you have in mind is the best way to go about this," Shanndel said, stepping from the wagon, ignoring the people who stopped and gaped openly at her attire.

She shuddered as she gazed at the courthouse, now almost certain whom her mother was going to question about Panther's whereabouts.

Sheriff Braddock!

Who else would she be stopping there to see? He was the only one who had the power to order Panther away from the area.

Or had Panther decided to leave of his own volition because he had gotten involved too deeply with a woman whose kin were his enemy?

After thinking things over, had he regretted ever taking her into his confidence . . . his arms . . . his *bed*?

No, she did not believe that Panther could have decided to leave because of her. When they had made love and he had vowed to love and protect her forever, he had been sincere.

No, he *loved* her. They had vowed to love one another for eternity. That meant being together to share that love.

"Come, daughter," Grace said, reaching a hand out for Shanndel. "We shall go and face Sheriff Braddock together. I know that he has something to do with Panther's departure. I am here to get answers from the sheriff."

As she took Shanndel's hand and they walked determinedly toward the stone steps that led into the courthouse, Grace gazed straight ahead, ignoring those who still stopped and stared.

"My husband was the richest and most influential man in Saline County," she said to Shanndel. "What was his has been passed on to me, which includes the power that goes with it. The sheriff will have no choice but to acknowledge that I am now the one in charge of so much of this community's destiny, for it is my money that could be taken elsewhere."

Stunned by her mother's shrewdness, but enjoying this courageous, spirited side of her mother, Shanndel went inside the huge building. Her chin held high, she stepped into the sheriff's office with her mother. She smiled to herself when she saw Sheriff Braddock's reaction to the way they were dressed. As his mouth gaped open, the cigar he was smoking dropped from between his lips. His eyes wide, he rose from his desk so quickly that his chair toppled over backwards.

"I demand to know what you said to the Shawnee chief to make him and his people leave this area," Grace said firmly as she placed her hands on her hips. "I know you are responsible for sending them away. I demand an explanation."

"What do you think you are doing coming here dressed like a savage squaw demanding anything of me?" Sheriff Braddock said, gaining control of himself. As he sat back down in his chair behind his cluttered desk and retrieved his smoking cigar from where it had fallen on a journal, he glowered from Shanndel to her mother.

He smiled smugly. "But I'm not at all surprised to see you dressed in that savage garb," the sheriff said, nodding. "I always knew you were no better than the color of your skin."

Seeing how those words made her mother's eyes widen with shock, Shanndel stepped closer to the desk and leaned down into the sheriff's face.

"You are an insulting sonofabitch," she hissed out. "How dare you speak to my mother in such a way! Especially so soon after the burial of her beloved husband. Don't you know how vulnerable she is? She only came here on my behalf to ask about Panther. You owe her an apology, *sir*."

The sheriff's eyes wavered. He rested his cigar in an ashtray and gazed questioningly at Grace. "You... you... just buried your husband?" he said, paling. "Edward Burton is dead?"

"Yes, he's dead," Shanndel said, taking charge since

she saw that her mother had run out of steam emotionally. "We just buried him at Sunset Hills Cemetery."

"Without telling anyone?" Sheriff Braddock said, raising an eyebrow. "Without allowing anyone to come and pay respects? Without having a viewing at his house?"

"Yes, without all of those things," Shanndel said, sighing heavily.

"Why, that's the way a heathen would be buried, and your father was anything but a heathen," Sheriff Braddock gasped out.

Grace's eyes narrowed as she regained courage enough to continue. "We didn't come here to discuss my husband's passing or burial," she said, her voice breaking. "We have come here for answers about Panther and his people."

"Well then, by damn, you'll get them," Sheriff Braddock said. "Yes, I sent them packing, all right." His voice softened as he gazed at Grace. "And, Grace, of all people, you should be glad. If that damn savage hadn't arrived here, I bet my bottom dollar your husband would still be alive."

"My name is Dancing Sky," Grace said, boldly lifting her chin. "Never address me as Grace again. From this day forth I will distance myself as best I can from people such as you. Taking my Iroquois name back is the first step."

She reached over and took Shanndel's hand. "And Shanndel's true name is Rain Singing," she said proudly.

"Whatever you say," Sheriff Braddock said, shrugging nonchalantly and smirking as he glanced from Grace to Shanndel.

"You will pay for having sent Panther away," Dancing Sky said, her eyes flashing angrily, her hands again on her hips. "With my husband's passing comes my control of all he possessed. If I wanted to, I could take all of my money out of Harrisburg's bank, and then where would this town be?"

"And so now you are threatening me?" Sheriff Braddock growled.

"No, I am not threatening you, I am telling you how it could be if that is how I wish it to be," Dancing Sky said. "And, listen well, Sheriff, to what I have planned." She smiled smugly. "My daughter and I are going to find Panther and his people. We are going to invite them to return with us. I am going to offer them land on which to stay the winter. *My* land. *Rain Singing's* land. I would not interfere if I were you."

"You wouldn't," Sheriff Braddock said, paling. "You will make me look like a fool, for everyone knows I sent the Shawnee away from Harrisburg."

"You were a fool for having done it," Dancing Sky said stiffly. "You know that they should not have been forced to travel at this time of year. I shall offer my land to Panther, not just for the winter, but for as long as his people wish. Even *forever*, if that is their desire. You would not dare try to force them off land that belongs to me and my daughter."

Shanndel stood beside her mother, in awe of her strength and courage to stand up against the sheriff in such a way.

But she was even more thrilled with what her mother

was going to offer Panther. A place to stay forever with his people.

When her and Panther's children were born, it would be on land her father was so proud of.

Also, they would continue her father's legacy by bringing life back to his tobacco fields!

But most of all, Shanndel was so happy to know that she had nothing to do with Panther's decision to travel onward. He did not leave her because he wanted to be rid of her. He loved her, oh, Lord, he still loved her.

But thinking now of how he must be feeling made a deep sadness overwhelm her.

"Daughter?" Dancing Sky said, breaking through Shanndel's deep thoughts. "Come, Rain Singing. I know how to find Panther."

Shanndel's eyes widened. "You do?" she said softly. "The sheriff told you?"

"No," Dancing Sky said, sliding an arm around Shanndel's waist. "I don't need him to tell me anything. I am knowledgeable about tracking. My father taught me those skills long ago so that I would never get lost in the forest."

Shanndel went with her mother back to the wagon. They hurried home and exchanged the wagon for two horses.

Surprised at the skills her mother knew—she had never even seen her ride horseback before—Shanndel rode away from their property and led the way to the abandoned Shawnee camp.

Dancing Sky drew a tight rein and began studying the land, smiling when she found many signs of travois marks where they had left the camp loaded with supplies. "We will find Panther and his people soon," she assured Shanndel, now slowly following the hoofprints and travois trails.

They traveled until the sun began lowering in the sky. Shanndel's hopes of ever finding Panther had sunk, because she could now see the shine of the Maple Fork River. If Panther and his people had already crossed the river, chances were that she and her mother would never find them.

Then her heart leapt into her throat when she saw something ahead through a break in the trees. It was the Shawnee people walking in a slow procession several yards from the riverbank.

Without taking the time to tell her mother, Shanndel slapped her reins hard against her horse and rode off at a hard gallop, shouting Panther's name.

When she saw him at the head of his people, she cried his name even more loudly, smiling when he turned and saw her racing toward him.

But when she rode up to him and he looked away, his expression cold and unfeeling, Shandell's heart sank.

Chapter Thirty-one

Panther's heart was pounding hard at seeing Shanndel. His gaze swept over the woman that was with her. She looked different than she had lying unconscious in Two Spirits' lodge.

He was amazed at the resemblance of his departed wife not only to Rain Singing, but also to Rain Singing's mother. How was this possible when there could be no connection between them?

But this was not the time for such wonder. Rain Singing's sudden appearance caused tumultuous feelings within him. He wanted nothing more than to be with Rain Singing, yet he still did not believe it was right for her.

Yet there she was. He was not only surprised to see them there and dressed in Indian attire, but also curious as to how Rain Singing and her mother had followed and found him. He wondered how they had managed to do that when Shanndel's father, although ill, would have done everything he could to stop them.

And he could hardly believe that Shanndel's mother would go against her husband in such a way or wear Indian clothes when it was obvious that he had tried to turn her into a white woman.

But even though they had surely defied the white man to find him, Panther still thought that it was best to deny himself the woman he loved. He could never offer her any stability. If she joined his people, all that he could give her was misery forced on her by whites wherever they might travel.

"Panther, please look at me," Shanndel said, a sob catching in her throat when she saw how he looked away from her. It was as though she weren't even there. "Why are you treating me like this? Why didn't you come and tell me that the sheriff had forced you to leave? Don't my feelings mean anything to you? Were your words of love to me all . . . a . . . lie?"

Panther's eyes wavered. The hurt in his woman's voice, and the realization that she would think he didn't love her, cut deeply into the core of his heart.

Yet would he not have felt the same had she been the one to leave in such a way?

But even so, he still felt that it was best to let her feel disillusioned. It would be easier for her if she rode away from him and forgot him forever.

"Panther, I know you are just pretending not to love me," Shanndel said, edging her horse closer to his. She reached a hand over and gently touched his arm. "Oh, darling, such pretenses aren't necessary. You don't even have to continue your desperate flight. Mother and I talked to the sheriff. We persuaded him that you should be allowed to return with me and my mother and stay as long as you wish.''

Panther's breath caught in his throat as he listened to what she was saying, yet he found it hard to believe. How could they have gone against Shanndel's father in such a way? Where was he now?

He turned his gaze to Dancing Sky, arching an eyebrow as he once again studied her attire. The fact that she wore doeskin still puzzled him. It could only mean that she had turned her back on her husband and was going to live her life as an Indian.

Yet if that were true, surely her husband would not welcome her or Shanndel back home, and especially not with the Shawnee.

"I do not understand any of this," he finally said, his eyes slowly raking over Shanndel, finding her exquisitely beautiful in the white doeskin dress. Nothing about her showed that she had ever lived in the white world. There was no evidence of her having a white father.

And perhaps that was so. Surely her father had disowned her!

"Much has happened since I last saw you," Shanndel said, easing her hand from him. She gave her mother a soft look, then gazed again at Panther. "Panther, this is my mother. In the white world she has always been called Grace. Her Indian name is Dancing Sky." She swallowed hard. "My mother wore black ashes from our fireplace on her face until only a short while ago."

"She . . . wore . . . ashes?" Panther gasped out,

knowing why Indians wore black. Either for mourning or for warring.

Suddenly he understood why her mother was with Shanndel today to seek him out, and why they both wore Indian attire.

Surely a burial had occurred only a short while ago and they had buried her father in the traditional way of the red man.

"Father had a stroke and has joined his ancestors in the sky," Shanndel said, swallowing hard. "Though Mother just buried her husband, she has left her mourning behind her long enough to come and offer you land for the winter. Or longer, if you choose to stay."

He looked quickly at Dancing Sky. "Your . . . land?" he said, stunned that she would be so kind, especially when she might have blamed him for the loss of her husband. If Panther had not made camp close to their land, and if Panther had not fallen in love with the white man's daughter, perhaps he would not have died.

"You would do this for me and my people?" he asked softly.

"You should not have been forced to leave," Dancing Sky said. "Please return with me and Rain Singing. My land, which I share equally with Rain Singing, is yours. Come with us. Stay as long as you wish."

Panther smiled warmly at her, then frowned at Shanndel. "It is not wise for me and my people to return," he said thickly. "It would only bring you and your mother problems. The sheriff and his deputies . . . the white community as a whole . . . would find ways to make us leave, and you as well."

"The sheriff has no rights to my mother's land, nor

does he have the right to order her or me around,'' Shanndel said tightly. "My father's vast land is now solely my mother's.''

Shanndel gave her mother a soft smile, touched deeply that her mother had referred to her land as Shanndel's also. Yes, her mother would be generous to her, for their bond was strong.

She turned to Panther again. "Mother has the right to invite anyone she pleases to stay on her land,'' she said.

When Panther looked away, silent again, Shanndel reached over and took his hand. "Panther, this isn't the time to be stubborn,'' she said. "Please don't refuse my mother's offer. Can't you see how it would make her feel? By rights she should be home mourning the loss of her husband. Instead she came here to make things right in your life.''

"I am sorry about your father,'' Panther said, reaching up to run a hand caressingly down the side of her face. He then lowered his hand and gave Dancing Sky a wavering look. "As I am sorry about your husband. I wish it could be different, but things happen that we have no control over.''

"But, Panther, we *do* have control over some things,'' Dancing Sky said, smiling at him. "I am offering you and your people a safe haven for the winter. You know that the winter will be harsh. Your people need permanent shelters from the cold winds and snows. Come with me and Rain Singing. I have many men in my employ. They will help build quick dwellings for your people. By tomorrow night your people should be sitting before their warm lodge fires with food cooking over the flames.''

Panther listened with an open heart and with much love for this woman who was his woman's mother. He gazed up at the trees and saw how one by one the leaves were falling. Soon the limbs would be bare. Soon they would be heavy with ice and snow.

He swallowed hard when in his mind's eye he saw his people dropping one by one on the trail from exhaustion and the cold. It pained him to envision such awful happenings among his people.

But he knew that was the chance he would take if he refused this kind woman's offer.

And knowing that he and his people would meet with resistance wherever they tried to build their lodges, even for one night, he turned his eyes to Shanndel and then her mother.

''*Nyoh*, I will lead my people back to your land and stay there during the long months of winter,'' he said huskily. He reached over and took Shanndel's mother's hand. ''Thank you for your kindness during a time that should be spent only in mourning.''

He eased his hand down and placed it on Shanndel's cheek. ''Thank you, my woman, for believing in me and knowing I loved you although I, for a while, pretended not to,'' he said thickly.

''I knew you could not lie about something as special as what we share between us,'' Shanndel murmured. She smiled. ''But for a moment there I have to admit you did give me a fright.''

''It hurt me so to leave without explaining why,'' he said, edging his horse even closer to hers. He reached for her and grabbed her around the waist, then pulled her over onto his lap. "I thought you would be better off without me."

Hardly aware of the many eyes on her, especially her mother's, Shanndel twined her arms around Panther's neck. "My life would be worthless without you," she whispered, then kissed him, her heart thumping wildly in her excitement at having her man with her again.

And should any man try to separate them, she would get her father's shotgun. She knew enough about firearms to send a load of buckshot into the seat of any man's breeches who interfered in their lives again.

She smiled when she envisioned how it would be to use the shotgun on the sheriff. She enjoyed the thought of seeing him running away from her, yelping as he clutched at his raw behind.

Panther eased his lips from hers. He gazed down at her and smiled. "I could feel your lips curve into a smile while we kissed," he said, his eyes dancing into hers. "It is because you are so happy?"

"Immensely," Shanndel said, giggling, keeping her thoughts about the sheriff to herself. She didn't want to shock her future husband with her unfeminine thoughts.

Yes, soon they would be married, she thought excitedly. Soon she would be married to a proud, handsome, virile Shawnee chief.

"I have duties to attend to," Panther said. He brushed a soft kiss across her lips, then placed her back in her saddle.

She watched proudly as he rode over and gathered his people around him.

His chin held high, his heart filled with much love

for his woman, Panther told his people about the change in plans, that they would stay in Illinois country for the whole winter after all.

It warmed Shanndel's heart when she saw Panther's people smile. Relief showed in their eyes as they cheered and whooped and hollered.

She thanked the good Lord above that she and her beloved mother had been able to make all this possible for the Shawnee.

Panther rode up next to Shanndel. He reached over and took her hand. He lifted it to his lips and kissed it.

Then he rode up to Dancing Sky's steed and leaned over and gave her a warm, gentle hug.

Then they all rode away together, back across the land they'd already traveled.

"Life sometimes is good . . . sometimes bad," Panther said as he smiled over at Shanndel. "Right now it is very *good*."

She returned his smile, choked by emotion at seeing how happy he was when only moments ago he had been tormented. Oh, Lord, she felt so good inside to be a big part of his refound happiness!

Chapter Thirty-two

The cool winds were howling. Autumn leaves were blowing crisp and beautiful from the trees. Food was cooking over the flames of the fireplace in Panther's newly constructed lodge. It had taken only a full day and night to build enough lodges for the Shawnee people.

Shanndel's mother's men had joined in and worked tirelessly until the last slab of mortar was in place in the many chimneys.

Tonight, the Shawnee people were celebrating their new homes with games, singing, and dancing.

Snuggled close, Shanndel was lying with Panther on warm, thick pelts before his lodge fire instead of being outside with the others just yet. Being with him alone was helping momentarily to erase the sadness that was eating away at her heart over her father's death. With her mother's blessing, Shanndel and Panther would be married tomorrow.

"Do you think it will seem disrespectful of me to marry so soon after my father's burial?" Shanndel murmured, breaking the silence between her and Panther.

She turned on her side and faced him. His nude body had a copper sheen beneath the light of the fire.

She shivered with pleasure when he slowly ran a hand over her naked breasts, then lower. Her belly rippled sensually as his fingers danced lightly over her flesh.

She sucked in a wild breath of rapture and closed her eyes when his hand went to the feathering of hair between her thighs, separating the fronds with his fingertips, slowly caressing her woman's center.

In the privacy of Panther's new lodge, they had already made love once this evening. She knew that it would not be the last time before they left the lodge and joined the celebration outside with Panther's people.

"Anyone who knows you would not think of you as disrespectful," Panther said, placing his hands at her waist, positioning her above him.

His pulse raced with the fire building within him when her breasts lay against his chest, her nipples pressed into his flesh.

"You are a kind, warm, thoughtful woman," he said huskily. "Everyone who knows you knows of your love for your father."

"I . . . I . . . did things that displeased him at the end," Shanndel said, tears blurring her eyes. "But, Panther, were I given the chance to change that, I could

337

not." She gazed lovingly down into his eyes. She reached down and slid his dark hair farther back from his face. "He asked the impossible of me. He asked me to forget you. My love, how could he ask that of me, knowing how much I love you?"

"Men who hold prejudice against the Indians of our country cannot look past that prejudice," Panther said softly. He reached up and framed her face between his hands. "Not even for a daughter I know he must have cherished."

"He did love me so," Shanndel said, sniffling as tears slowly trickled from her eyes.

"And he knew that you loved him," Panther said, placing his hands at her waist, sliding her slowly beneath him. His eyes were smoky with need. "Let us not dwell on things that are sad, Rain Singing. Let us enjoy this moment, for who is to say what will happen next? Live for the moment, Rain Singing. Live for now. Not yesterday. Not even tomorrow. Who is to say if there will be a tomorrow?"

"There *are* too many uncertainties in life," Shanndel said, twining her arms around his neck. "But with us and our feelings for one another, we can feel secure."

"Tomorrow we will be joined together as one being," Panther whispered against her lips as he lowered his mouth to hers.

"We are as one soul and heartbeat already," Shanndel whispered back, inhaling a deep breath when she felt his throbbing shaft probing where she was wet, hot, and ready for him. "Love me, darling. Oh, Panther, make love to me again. I need you so."

His loins aflame, Panther took Shanndel's lips in an

all-consuming kiss. With a slow, delicious ease he filled her waiting heat with his stiff, hard shaft.

Quietly groaning with intense pleasure, he moved rhythmically in her tightness, sliding, withdrawing, then thrusting into her again.

Shanndel's hands were all over his body, touching, clutching, caressing. When he withdrew from within her and reached for her hand to place it on his manhood, she gripped him within her fingers, then stroked his silky stiffness.

Her very touch, the way she stroked him, seemed to shoot pure lightning through Panther. He closed his eyes and gritted his teeth as his pleasure mounted; her hands were oh, so cool against his heat as she continued pleasuring him in this sensual way.

Gently taking her hand away, he plunged himself deeply into her again and resumed his thrusts, his senses reeling in drunken pleasure.

Again he took her mouth by storm, his hands worshipping her flesh, touching her, stroking her, her breasts pushing into his chest as he reached around and gathered her fully into his hard, strong arms, pressing her more closely and tightly to his aroused body.

Imprisoned against Panther, and adoring it, Shanndel quivered with a wondrous desire, her body yearning for that moment of ultimate pleasure.

She wrapped her legs around his waist and arched herself closer to him, crying out when doing so sent him even farther into her. His throbbing hardness touched something inside her that had not been touched before, sending shivers of rapture throughout her.

Hungering for his kiss, for his lips, frantic with passion, Shanndel twined her fingers through Panther's hair and sought his mouth with wild desperation.

They kissed, their tongues touching, and Shanndel clung to him as she felt the urgency building within her. Her head began to reel and her body tingled. With a sob she shuddered, arched, and cried out as the climax came, shattering and violent. His body answered in kind as he held her close to him while he reached his own release within her yielding silk.

Just as he came down from his cloud of ecstasy, Panther realized that Shanndel was sobbing against his shoulder. With dark, imploring eyes he placed a finger under her chin and lifted her eyes to meet his.

"Did I hurt you this time?" he asked huskily, his eyes searching hers. "Was I not gentle enough?"

"You could never hurt me," Shanndel whispered, wiping tears from her face with the back of her hand. "My darling Shawnee chief, don't you know that my tears are from pure joy? You have brought such happiness into my life. Before I knew you, my life was meaningless. Now every moment amounts to something, for I am living it for you."

Smiling, he kissed her tear-soaked cheek, and then brushed soft kisses across her wet lashes. "I never knew love could be so powerful," he said, his voice breaking. "My first love was one of deep emotion. But my love for you surpasses everything I could ever feel, or felt, for any other woman."

"When we first met and you looked at me as though you had seen a ghost, I never thought it possible for you to see past those feelings you had for the woman in your life before me," Shanndel said, shivering with ecstasy when he gently cupped her breasts in his warm hands. "I thank God every day for the chance to love you and for the love you have returned, and not only because I resemble someone else, but because you love me, because I am me."

"*Nyoh*, you are you, and you are the one I love now and forevermore," Panther murmured. His departed wife's resemblance to Rain Singing and her mother was something he would never understand nor ever question aloud. All that mattered was that Rain Singing was with him, forevermore. His love for her was greater than he could ever feel for any other woman.

He looked toward the lodge door when laughter came to him from the celebration. "The people are enjoying games," he said. "Would you like to see the games of our people?"

"Yes, very much," Shanndel said, easing away from him. "I want to know everything about your people. I want your people to see that I truly am interested, and that I do wish to be one with them."

"They already know that," Panther said, rising to his feet. He went to a washbasin on a stand along the far wall. Lifting his softened member in his hands, he splashed water over it, then patted it dry with a towel as Shanndel came and also washed herself.

After they were refreshed and dressed, their long hair brushed and falling thick and black down their backs, they left the cabin.

Hand in hand, they went and sat beside Shanndel's mother on a blanket before the great, roaring fire in the center of the Shawnee encampment, which had been built a short distance from the vast, empty tobacco fields.

Reaching over to her mother, Shanndel took her hand and clung to it. Shanndel's eyes misted with tears, for her mother looked so content and radiant among Panther's people. It was as though she belonged there, even though they were Shawnee and she was Iroquois.

Dancing Sky smiled at Shanndel. "Rain Singing, your eyes show a radiance I have never seen before," she murmured, then looked past Shanndel and caught Panther gazing with adoration at Shanndel. "I do not have to ask why."

Panther felt Dancing Sky's eyes on him. He looked at her and smiled, then looked at Cloud as he directed some small braves in the game of mumblety-peg. He first showed them how to play the game with a knife, and then *shequkonurah*, stones.

Elsewhere the elderly men were gambling with dice, or playing cards procured from traders long ago.

"Tonight the games are not strenuous ones," Panther said, casting Shanndel a quick look and chuckling. "Sometime I will show you some games that are more challenging."

"Everyone seems so content." Shanndel sighed, turning to watch her mother as she went inside Panther's lodge. "That's all that matters."

When her mother came out of the lodge carrying a tray with three mugs of hot chocolate, Shanndel giggled. "Seems my mother knows how to please you," she murmured, smiling a thank you to her mother as she handed her one of the mugs, and then Panther.

They drank the hot chocolate as other women began

taking food from the many cook fires and readying it to eat on platters.

It was hard for Shanndel to think back to a time when life had been so different for her. Being among the Shawnee people seemed so natural. And once she exchanged vows with Panther, it *would* be right.

There was one thing that chilled her heart like a cold wind whenever she thought of it. She hated to think that Sheriff Braddock might find a way to interfere again.

No.

She would not allow herself to dwell on such thoughts.

She would think positively!

She was to become a wife to a wonderful man tomorrow!

Chapter Thirty-three

With Cloud officiating because Two Spirits was ill in bed, Panther and Shanndel were in the midst of their wedding celebration. The Shawnee people, as well as Shanndel's mother, sat on the ground on blankets in a broad oval before the great outdoor fire.

Panther's buckskin blouse and leggings were flamboyantly decorated with painted porcupine quills in geometric designs. Dangling from his ears were huge silver earrings. Tied snugly around his neck was a hiplength cape of ermine. A thick braid of his hair hung behind his left ear and was held together at the end by a cylinder of silver.

Having never felt as beautiful, Shanndel wore her mother's favorite dress, the one her mother had worn when she married Shanndel's father. It was snow white and decorated with intricate pink beadwork interwoven

with feathers and tiny shells. The hem of the dress was
heavy with thick fringe.

In her hair, hanging down the left side behind her
ear, were the same delicate white swan feathers that her
mother had worn on her wedding day. They had been
stored carefully in her trunk with her dresses and were
only slightly yellowed with age.

Around her wrists and the long column of her throat
were soft, white fluffs of rabbit fur. Around her ankles
were strands of painted shells, which tinkled, like music, when she walked. On her feet were moccasins made
of the same white rabbit fur, and when she walked she
felt weightless, as though she were floating on air.

The main part of the ceremony was now over and
only a dance and words at the end of that dance remained to complete their union.

Feeling blessed to be there with the man she loved,
her smile radiant, her eyes beaming, Shanndel clung to
Panther's arm as the dance music began. She was surprised at how many sorts of instruments were being
played. There were drums, panpipes, willow flutes,
gravel-filled gourd rattles, a lute, harmonicas, and fid-
dles obtained by trade.

Shanndel's attention was drawn to a small number of
women her age who were taking their places before the
people some yards back from the great fire. They stood
in a straight line across from the same amount of men,
each woman having positioned herself opposite the man
of her choice. The women wore lovely buckskin dresses
adorned with beadwork, and some of them had hair
reaching their ankles.

Shanndel took her place among the women as Panther did with the men, his eyes glittering as he gazed passionately at Shanndel. She had been instructed about the dance, and the words she would speak in Shawnee at the end, which would bring the wedding to a close.

Shanndel glanced quickly at the musicians as they began playing discordant and unconnected music, which soon moved into a more rhythmic pattern that became pleasant and melodious to her.

Her gaze turned back to Panther when he began a chant to the accompaniment of the music . . .

"*Ya-ne-no-hoo-wa-no, ya-ne-no-hoo-wa-no, ya-ne-no-hoo-wa-no,*" Panther chanted as his eyes locked and held with Shanndel's.

Remembering her instructions, Shanndel began swaying along with the other women in time with Panther's chanting. She gradually inched toward him, as the other women inched toward their own chosen men.

When the women and men were close enough to touch, the women began chanting the same phrase, alternating with the men, who had now joined in Panther's song.

While chanting, the women moved forward toward their chosen ones until they were separated only an inch or so, their hands clasped behind them.

Now they had reached the point of the ceremony that meant the most to Shanndel and Panther. Trying hard to remember the Shawnee words he had taught her that morning before the sun rose in the sky, Shanndel leaned forward so that her breasts were pressed against his broad chest and her face was close to his. She wasn't even aware that the other dancers had left and that she and Panther now stood alone before his people, with everyone's eyes on them.

"*Psai-wi-ne-noth-tu*," Shanndel sang in time with the music, calling him a great warrior.

Panther then pressed himself against her, and their eyes met, expressing a love so dear they felt as though they were in their bed making love. "*U-le-thi-e-qui-wa*, beautiful woman," he said huskily.

They continued swaying together, their bodies moving sensually against each other, their flesh growing hot.

"*U-le-thi-ski-she-quih*, pretty eyes," Panther sang huskily. "*Cat-tu-oui-ni-i-yah*, your body is perfect. Like mine, *ps'-qui-ah-quoi-te-ti*, your blood runs hot."

"*Oui-sha-t-kar-chi*, your face is filled with strength," Shanndel sang back to him. "Ah, but you are a *k-tch-o-ke-man*, a great chief. You are my man."

The tempo of the dance slowed. Panther and Shanndel's hands came together. "*Ni-haw-ku-nah-ga*," Panther said throatily as he pressed himself more intimately against her, grinding his loins into her special place, which she arched toward him. "Rain Singing, I take you now as my wife."

"*Ni-wy-she-an-a*," Shanndel murmured softly in his ear. "And you are now my beloved husband."

The onlookers rose to their feet and cheered, bringing Shanndel out of her trance. She blushed and gazed at Panther, who still held her close to his body.

Then her breath was stolen away when he swept her fully into his arms and carried her away from the crowd, brushing her cheeks and brow with soft kisses as he headed toward their lodge.

Once inside, with the door locked behind them, Panther trembled as he undressed Shanndel.

Her heart was pounding inside her chest, her knees weakened by passion, as she in turn undressed him.

Finally nude, feeling the warmth of the lodge fire on his back, Panther twined his arms around Shanndel's waist and led her down onto the soft pelts that he had readied for them before they had left for the ceremony.

"My love, finally we are together for always," Panther said huskily, his hands moving over her, touching her pleasure points knowingly. "*Ni-haw-ku-nha-ga*, my wife. I can now say you are my wife!"

"*Ni-wy-she-an-a*, my husband," Shanndel breathed out, sighing sensually when he leaned down and swept his tongue over one nipple and then the other. She strained forward so that his whole mouth covered the nipple, his tongue flicking.

She swallowed hard with a building pleasure as he swept his hands down to where she pounded unmercifully with need of him. Her breath came in slow, deep gasps as he caressed her swollen nub, then dipped a finger into the moist, wet place that throbbed with need.

And when he moved down and settled himself between her legs, gently parting them with his hands, and she felt the tip of his tongue where his fingers had just been, she closed her eyes in ecstasy. She would have thought the way he pleasured her was forbidden until she knew him and his wondrous ways of making love to her. Nothing so wonderful could be wrong, she kept telling herself, for it was causing sensations unfamiliar, yet sweet to her. She felt as though she would burst with ecstasy as his tongue delved deeply into her, and then flicked the tender spot again until she felt even closer to exploding.

"My love," she murmured, placing her hands on his cheeks, bringing him away from her.

As he kissed her and she tasted the strange taste on his lips that she knew had come from her body, she reached down and twined her fingers around his throbbing heat and slowly caressed him in an up-and-down fashion until he moaned and groaned against her lips for her to stop.

Following his bidding, she led his velvety member to where she awaited his entrance. She shuddered with ecstasy when the glossy tip touched her swollen nub, then slid on past and inside her, magnificently filling her.

As they clung and rocked, and as he thrust deeply into her and they kissed and licked, they once again found the ultimate of rapture.

"Tonight perhaps a seed planted in your womb will bring children into our lives," Panther whispered into her ear. He still held her close against him. "One child was denied me. *Ni-haw-ku-nah-ga*, my wife, give me another."

"I shall give you many, *Ni-wy-she-an-a*," Shanndel whispered back, reveling in his embrace as once again he filled her.

"Once is not enough tonight, my love," Panther whispered again against her ear. "I want you again and again."

"As I do you," Shanndel whispered back, her body moving with his, floating on clouds of rapture.

Again they soared and soared, as everyone outside sang and danced and ate. For the moment the Shawnee were content and feeling as though they had a place where they could belong, at least for a little while.

For the moment at least, they felt threatened by no one. Their longtime enemy was dead and the white man sheriff had been put in his place.

Dancing Sky sat among the Shawnee, sad that none of them were Iroquois, for being among people of her own color, and dressing as she had dressed before her marriage to the white man made her hunger for those times in her past when she had been content among her people.

She looked toward the lodge where her daughter was perhaps planning children with her husband. She placed a hand on her abdomen and recalled the time when she gave birth.

She bit her lower lip in remembrance of a decision she had made on that day . . . a remembrance that cut deeply into her heart.

And she knew that one day she would tell Shanndel the secret that she had carried with her all the days of her life.

It only seemed fair that she should tell Shanndel the truth, even though she had vowed to Edward never to tell anyone.

But Edward was now dead and telling Shanndel would not take away anything that Edward had wanted to protect while he was alive . . . the fact that he was sterile. He had wanted no one to see him as anything less than virile. Having a daughter to show off was his way of proving it!

Yes, she would tell Shanndel one day. But not now. Once Shanndel knew the truth, the *full* truth, there was the chance that Shanndel would hate her.

Chapter Thirty-four

In a great grove of maple trees just beyond Shanndel's mother's land, the Shawnee were busy tapping the trees. Plumes of smoke rose from the large vats where sap was boiling and being rendered down to maple sugar.

In the past, when the Shawnee were on their own land, maple sugar was a valuable item for trade as well as a luxury for their own consumption.

But now, since they were on land that did not belong to them, they were taking only enough sap this spring for their own use. They were certain if they took it for trading, the white sheriff would interfere.

Thus far through the whole winter he had kept his distance.

But now, with the arrival of warmer weather, when the sheriff would be out on his horse more than not, the

Shawnee had to be extra careful not to be caught defying his orders.

Dressed warmly in a long, heavy bearskin robe, Shanndel looked over at Panther. "Now aren't you glad that I came with you for the maple harvest?" she asked, beaming as she walked alongside Panther as he carried another bucket of maple sap to one of the vats. "If not to join the actual harvest, since you are afraid it might threaten the child I carry within my womb, at least to be with you?"

Dressed in a buckskin coat and leggings, his hair drawn back from his face and tied like a pony's tail with a leather thong at the back, Panther smiled down at Shanndel. His eyes went to her stomach, which had not yet started to swell with her pregnancy.

"The child within your womb is but a tiny seed growing arms and legs," he said. He looked into Shanndel's eyes, his expression serious. "I will watch over you during your pregnancy and see that nothing happens to you or our child."

Then his lips quivered into another soft smile. "But, *nyoh*, my wife, I am glad that you are here walking at my side," he said softly. "I would be lonely without you."

"I'm going to make sure you are never lonely again," Shanndel said, reaching over to take his free hand in hers.

She glanced at her mother who was walking with an elder of the tribe. He was a handsome, stout man in his early fifties. He had been widowed on the long journey from the Upper New York area.

Her mother and Standing Horse had found something

special between them. Shanndel expected their relationship to carry them into marriage, which pleased her
more than anyone would know.

This spring Shanndel had talked Panther into staying
another year on her mother's land, because Shanndel
didn't want to leave her mother.

She doubted that argument would be needed the next
time Panther talked of moving onward. Her mother
would want to go with them so that she could be with
Standing Horse.

But there was something about her mother that
Shanndel didn't understand. Her mother had placed her
mourning behind her and was in love again, yet there
were times when Shanndel felt as though her mother
wanted to confide something in her. Yet just when she
seemed ready to speak, she would walk away, leaving
the words unsaid and Shanndel frustrated.

Shanndel had learned to place her concern about her
mother's strange behavior behind her. She hadn't even
prodded her for answers. When the time was right, her
mother would tell her.

As for now, Shanndel was too content to wonder
much about it. She had never been so happy. Everyone
seemed to be happy and content to stay where they
were. There was the fear of losing such contentment
once they moved on.

The smell in the air, a mixture of burning wood,
spring breezes, and sweet, boiling sap, made Shanndel
inhale deeply. "I have always loved spring better than
any other season in Illinois," she said. She watched
squirrels scampering and birds busy making their nests
overhead. "Isn't it just too beautiful, Panther? Soon we

can put aside our coats and robes. The air will be deliciously warm and smelling of spring flowers.''

Her words faded and she went tight inside when the magical morning was interrupted by the sound of many horses approaching through the forest.

When she saw the man in the lead, she groaned out Sheriff Braddock's name.

She looked quickly up at Panther. "What are we going to do?" she said, her voice breaking. "What if he arrests us for trespassing on land that is not my mother's? We are taking sap from the maple trees."

"The man surely will not refuse us the small amount of maple sap my people are taking this morning," Panther said, setting his bucket down on the ground beside him. "Surely the white man cannot be that selfish."

"Selfish has nothing to do with it," Shanndel said, her pulse racing as the sheriff rode closer.

She glanced around at the Shawnee people, whose faces showed panic.

Even her mother, who was beside Standing Horse, seemed to have lost the color in her face.

Yes, her mother knew that Sheriff Braddock had the right to do anything he pleased to the Shawnee. She knew he would enjoy seeing them grovel.

When Sheriff Braddock drew his horse to a halt a few feet away from Panther and Shanndel, Panther crossed his arms defiantly over his chest and proudly lifted his chin.

He forced himself not to flinch when Sheriff Braddock suddenly yanked his pistol from its holster and aimed it at Panther.

Shanndel felt faint at the sight of the pistol aimed at

her husband. She had never thought the sheriff would actually go this far to get back at the Shawnee . . . to get back at her and her mother!

"Shawnee chief, you thought you were so smart getting Grace Burton on your side so that you could stay the winter on land that belonged to her, but, Chief, the last laugh is on you," he snarled.

He nodded toward his deputies. "Go and pour out all of that sap," he said, smirking. "Make sure none is left in the vats or buckets. Go and take all of the apparatus they are using to get the sap from the trees. Throw it all in the river!"

"You are despicable," Shanndel hissed out, her hands doubled into tight fists at her sides as one of the men came and took Panther's bucket of sap and poured it out close to his feet. "What can it hurt for the Shawnee to have some of the sap from these trees? You know that no one has ever used them for the maple harvest before."

"It don't belong to the savages, that's why," Sheriff Braddock said, narrowing his eyes as he glared at Shanndel. "It don't belong to you or your mother, either."

He smiled crookedly as he gazed at Panther again. "What's the matter?" he said, chuckling. "Cat got your tongue? Or do you know that I have the right to keep your people from the sap and realize you would be wasting words by arguing with me?"

Panther still said nothing. He knew his words *would* be wasted on this evil man. He would not lower himself to the sheriff's level by arguing with him. Everyone here knew the wrong that was being done the Shawnee. It need not be spoken aloud.

And Panther would never beg. Maple sugar was an article of luxury for the Shawnee. They had learned long ago to live without things of luxury!

Sheriff Braddock glanced around him at the Shawnee and how quiet they were and realized that none of them had weapons. Trusting souls, they had come to property that was not theirs without means of protection. If he wanted to, he could shoot them one at a time and be rid of them for good, and none of them could fight back.

He smiled to himself at how easy it would be. And most of the white community would not deplore such an action. He might even be considered a hero!

But there would be those who might condemn him enough to hang him. The people who had established the many churches in the area, especially the Baptists, would not stand for out-and-out murder, not even of savages. The church-going people were ruled by the teachings of their Bible. They would make him pay for his sin.

He looked around again at the Shawnee people until he found Grace, who now went by the strange name Dancing Sky. Flipping his pistol into its holster, he went to stand before her. His fists on his hips, he glared at her, and then at the tall, hefty Shawnee standing at her side. He had heard reports that she had fallen in love, this time with a man of her own skin color.

Clearing his throat nervously, Sheriff Braddock glared at Grace. "You were wrong to allow these Indians to stay on land that belonged to Edward Burton," he said thickly. "You know Edward wouldn't have allowed it."

"The land is mine," Dancing Sky said, lifting her

chin proudly. "I say who does and who does not set foot on it." A smile flickered across her lips. "I dare say, Sheriff, *you* had best have second thoughts before coming on my land, for you are never welcome."

She looked around her, her eyes wavering as she watched the precious maple sap being poured out onto the ground; then she looked angrily up at the sheriff again. "How dare you come today and take something that means nothing to you," she hissed. "It is everything to the Shawnee."

"Exactly," Sheriff Braddock said, chuckling. He rested his hands on his holstered pistols. "And now they don't have any, do they?"

"Some day you will pay for the evil you do," Dancing Sky said, walking away from him. She went to Panther. "Son-in-law, please instruct your people to return to their camp. Today's harvest is no more."

"Now you're talking sense," Sheriff Braddock said. "Now listen good to what I say, Injuns. I'm not going to arrest you today for trespassing, but I'd better not see any Shawnee taking anything else from land that is not the property of Grace Burton. Even when you hunt, it must be only on Burton land. If you do not heed my warning, you and your people will pay dearly."

Panther fought hard to hold down his rage.

So did Shanndel and her mother.

Chapter Thirty-five

The planting moon was high, reflecting its silver sheen over trees whose limbs showed fresh green sprouts blowing gently in the breeze, and over land planted with new tobacco plants.

The moon's glow also swept down over another stretch of land that lay just behind the Shawnee's lodges. There the fertile, dark earth lay in long, furrowed mounds, beneath which lay seeds for the food that would feed their people.

Panther had made certain his people dug no farther than land allotted them by Shanndel's mother. He was determined to keep the white sheriff from coming and saying once again that the Shawnee were trespassing on land that was not theirs. He did not want the sheriff to order them to dig up the seeds.

As Panther and Shanndel lay asleep on their bed,

which Shanndel's mother had sent from Shanndel's bedroom for their comfort, men in dark clothing slipped stealthily through the night across the Shawnee's planted field of crops. They went from row to row, up-turning the earth, exposing the seeds.

When their chore was done they left as silently as they had arrived, the sheriff's badge picking up the shine of the moon as he leapt onto his horse and rode away.

Panther stirred in his sleep. He tossed from side to side, then woke up with a start. Having been awakened by what he had thought were horses' hooves, he was careful not to disturb Shanndel when he left the bed.

Throwing a blanket around his shoulders, he went to the door and pushed it quietly open, then stood at the doorway and surveyed the night with narrowed, suspicious eyes.

When he saw no movement, he inhaled nervously, then went back to stand over the bed.

His eyes softened as he gazed down at his Rain Singing and how peacefully she slept. The silk gown brought from the large, white house was sheer and revealing as the moon swept over her through the window.

Through the fabric he could see the gentle swell of her breasts, their nipples dark and pointed, and then lower, the slight swell of her stomach beneath which lay their first child.

Filled with emotions brought on by his deep love for this woman, Panther shrugged the blanket from his shoulders and crawled in next to Shanndel. He smiled as in her sleep she found comfort again against his body, her backside snuggling up against the front of him.

Panther slid his arm around her and held her, his hand cupping one of her breasts, gently kneading it. Never had he been as content as now. This woman had brought an intense peace inside his heart that he had not felt for too long before having met her. Without her he would be nothing. He would be only half a leader to his people, for so much of him had died when he had lost his wife and unborn child, and precious mother.

And then to lose his father!

Life had not been fair to him in so many ways, nor to his people. But now, for at least a little while, there seemed to be some promise to their future. He had the deep love of a woman. He was going to be a father. And his people were safe. The Shawnee were going to stay here as long as it took to build the strength of their elderly, and then they would continue their journey to their new homeland.

"Home," he whispered, his eyes slowly closing, sleep again claiming him, his wife's body warm against his.

The cries of his people and their mournful wails awakened Panther again, this time into full daylight.

Shanndel also awakened, alarm in her eyes as she watched Panther leap from the bed and hurry into a pair of buckskin breeches.

"What is it?" she cried, shivering uncontrollably when she, too, heard the Shawnee people crying and wailing. "Oh, Lord, what has happened now?" She slipped quickly from the bed. "Oh, Panther, who could have died?"

He cast her a troubled glance, then left the lodge while she changed into a buckskin dress.

When he got outside his eyes followed the sound of the wails and his heart went cold when he saw what had caused his people's grief. No one had died. The crops that his people had toiled over and planted so carefully in the ground were ruined! Now with the sun casting its morning light over the land, the destruction of their garden could be seen, whereas last night it was invisible.

He doubled his hands into tight fists at his sides, knowing now that horses' hooves *had* awakened him. The horses ridden by those who had brought destruction to his people's crops.

"Panther, oh, Lord, who could have done this?" Shanndel gasped out, paling when she saw the total destruction of the Shawnee's garden.

She covered her mouth with a hand and stared. For as far as she could see, the dirt was upturned and the seeds lay dried and scattered across the land.

"Who could have done this?" Panther hissed, frowning at Shanndel. "There is only one man I can think of who would do such a thing to our people. If he cannot run us out of Illinois country, he will deprive us of our crops. Did he not already deprive us of the privilege of hunting on land not owned by your mother? Did he not deprive us of the maple sap? Do you not see his plan to starve our people? If not in one way, another?"

"But if Sheriff Braddock is responsible for this, he is the one who trespassed *this* time," Shanndel said, glancing quickly over at her mother as she came running toward her in a buckskin robe, her long, black hair flowing in the wind behind her.

"*Nyoh*, he is responsible and, *nyoh*, he trespassed," Panther said, bending to a knee to run the earth through his fingers. He glowered at Shanndel. "But he will not admit to anything. He will lie!"

"I'll go with you, Panther, to demand the truth from him," Shanndel said, taking her mother's hand as she came up beside her, her eyes wide and disbelieving.

"He will never stop," Dancing Sky said, her voice breaking. "Even though I own the land and gave permission for you to have your garden, this man will not allow it."

"I will go to him and get answers from him," Panther said, rising.

"But he will never, ever admit to having done this," Dancing Sky said, her eyes sad. "Let's just replant and then make sure the garden is well guarded at night."

"All of our seeds were used for *this* garden," Panther said thickly. "There are no more."

"Then I shall go into town and purchase more seeds myself," Dancing Sky said tightly.

Panther's gaze swept slowly over her. "And you think you will get whites to sell you anything now that you are no longer part of their world?" he asked, his voice drawn.

"They will sell me anything I ask to buy," Dancing Sky said, stubbornly lifting her chin. "I am still the richest landowner in Saline County, even though I now wear the clothes of my true people."

"Mother, please don't do anything that might place you in danger," Shanndel pleaded, truly afraid for her mother. If she began pushing her weight around, the true prejudices of the people would surface. Shanndel was not sure how far the people would go to stop her.

"I have stayed like a church mouse in my home all these years and let your father run everything," Dancing Sky said. She turned to Shanndel. "I can no longer be only an observer. I must be a doer. What is right is right. I will not allow your husband's people to be pushed around. They are on my land. They have the right to do anything they wish." She swallowed hard. "Especially plant seeds for food for their children."

"I urge you to stay here while I ride alone into Harrisburg to question the sheriff about this latest outrage against my people," Panther said, placing a gentle hand on Dancing Sky's shoulder and slowly turning her to face him. "Then later, if you desire, ride into town with Shanndel to buy needed supplies."

"But, Panther, surely word will have spread and no one will willingly sell seeds to us," Shanndel said, her voice breaking. "I'm afraid we are now standing up against a whole community of people, not only the sheriff."

"Rain Singing, when *I* ride into town with Panther, no one will dare deny me anything," her mother said, sighing heavily. She looked up at Panther. "And I can bring many of my workers with us. Those men are loyal to me, not the people of Harrisburg. For too many years Edward and I paid them decent wages. They know where their loyalties lie."

"I need no one but myself to do this for my people," Panther said, spinning away from her and taking the reins of his horse as a young brave handed them to him.

"Let me go with you," Shanndel pleaded.

"For our child's sake, *and* yours, I prefer you to stay here," Panther said, glancing down at her abdomen, then swinging himself into his saddle.

Cloud stepped up next to his horse. "I will go with you," he said, his voice tight.

Panther paused and weighed this decision in his mind, then nodded. "*Nyoh*, ride with me, my friend," he said. "I welcome you at my side."

Smiling, his shoulders squared proudly, Cloud mounted his horse when it was brought to him.

Shanndel slid an arm around her mother's waist as she watched her husband and Cloud ride away.

"They will be all right," Dancing Sky said reassuringly. "No one would dare harm your people's chief and Medicine Man Prophet. Surely they would expect retaliation."

"But my husband's people are so few in number," Shanndel murmured.

"The white men know, though, that there are enough Shawnee warriors to kill many whites before the Shawnee are downed by white men's bullets," Dancing Sky said, her eyes troubled at the mere thought of warring on her land. "And . . . no one wants to die."

With so many things to worry Dancing Sky, she looked at her daughter as Shanndel silently watched her husband riding toward Harrisburg. Dancing Sky had yet to say anything to Shanndel about the secret that had been locked within her heart for so long.

But now that Shanndel's husband was going to be gone for a while, leaving mother and daughter alone, this would be the ideal time to tell Shanndel everything and finally be freed of that burden forever.

But would her confession only create another burden that could eat away at her heart for eternity? If she told Shanndel the truth, oh, Lord, the *full* truth about that day, would Shanndel hate her mother and see her as heartless?

No, Dancing Sky didn't think she could take that chance. And she didn't want to place an unneeded burden on her daughter's shoulders at this time, when she already had so much to worry about.

And then there was the child. Dancing Sky didn't want to do anything that might threaten her daughter's unborn child, which upsetting Shanndel might do.

Yes, she must remain silent awhile longer.

Panther stood over the sheriff, seething at the man's indifference to what Panther had disclosed to him about the seeds being destroyed.

"You've wasted your time by coming to me with tales of someone trespassing on Grace Burton's property in the darkness of night," Sheriff Braddock said. He laughed sarcastically. "I'm not responsible for anyone but myself, and I swear to you that I had nothing to do with what happened last night."

"You know that you are responsible," Panther said, his voice tight and drawn. "Even if you did not dig up our seeds, you . . . are . . . responsible for it being done, for you spread your hatred for the Shawnee everywhere you go."

"I'd watch what I was saying if I were you," Sheriff Braddock said, pushing himself up from his chair. He stood behind the desk and glared at Panther. "Threats don't get anyone anywhere."

Then Sheriff Braddock stepped from around the desk and smiled mockingly at Panther. "But now that you see what the community will do to rid itself of the likes of you, don't you think it's best that you and your people move on?" he said. "Can't you see that you aren't wanted here? It's spring, Panther. Travel for your people is safe. It's time for you to move on."

Panther leaned into the sheriff's face. "*Neh*, we are going nowhere," he said tightly. "My people will replant. We will have a good harvest!"

As Panther turned on a heel and stalked from the office, he heard the sheriff utter something beneath his breath. Panther's spine stiffened when he heard himself being called a "sonofabitch."

He almost turned around and went back to the sheriff to grab him by the throat, to make him take back the insult to his dead mother, but thought better of it when his wife came into his mind's eye. She needed him now more than ever since she was carrying their child.

Bitter to the very core of himself, Panther hurried outside and swung himself into his saddle. His chest proud and bare, his long hair flying in the wind, he rode away from the courthouse as many white people stared slack-jawed at him.

Tired of being a person of ridicule, yet wanting to put fear in the hearts of those who gawked at him and who would call him a "savage" to his face, Panther let out a loud war cry.

He laughed when he saw people scurrying in all directions to find safe cover from the "heathen savage."

Chapter Thirty-six

It was autumn again. The crops had been cleared and packaged for storage at the Shawnee camp. Pumpkin, squash, and sunflower seeds had been ground into meal for bread and various dishes. Great strings of crabapple had been sun-dried. Pouches were filled with dried grains and vegetable seeds for next year's planting. These had been packed in well-greased skin bags wrapped in bark and buried in holes carefully disguised so that no one else could find them.

Shanndel's mother had seen to the tobacco harvest, which this year had netted her a great profit. She had taken that money and purchased a herd of cattle so that the Shawnee would have meat, since the hunt was still denied them by Sheriff Braddock. The Shawnee people had finally grown used to the red meat. They no longer described its taste as that of skunk. It was a taste they now enjoyed.

Much of the beef meat had been butchered and prepared to last the long winter months that lay ahead. The meat had been cut into strips and was now drying on racks over smoky fires.

Big with child, Shanndel moved more slowly these days, smiling often that secret smile that came to expectant mothers when the child within the womb gave a quick kick, or a nudge from a tiny elbow.

Breakfast was now over. Shanndel was washing dishes in a basin of water, glad that Panther had agreed to let her use a cook stove and eat off pretty china that she had grown accustomed to while growing up in a household of white customs.

But she didn't ask much more of Panther that might make him uncomfortable. She was fast learning the customs of the Shawnee, finding them similar to those her mother had taught her long ago about her Iroquois people.

There was sadness in watching the leaves falling from the trees outside the kitchen window. It was as though the trees were weeping, the leaves their tears. The trees seemed to know the hardships of the long months ahead when their limbs would be burdened with the heavy weight of snow and ice.

She started to think about the wonder of holding her child within her arms. The wind would sing and howl outside, but the cabin would be cozy inside. Her mother had sent her rocking chair from the house and it now sat beside Shanndel's fireplace, awaiting the time when she would rock her own child to sleep as her mother had rocked her to sleep those long years ago when she was a baby.

"It will be so wonderful," she whispered, a radiance in her eyes as she thought of Panther there, kneeling before her, his eyes proud as he gazed at his wife and child.

Her thoughts were cast aside and her heart skipped a beat when she saw movement in the forest, then heard the sound of horses approaching.

"Who?" she whispered. She laid her dishrag aside and was taken aback when she saw a beautiful Indian woman, perhaps the same age as her mother, leading the procession of warriors.

Panic seizing her, Shanndel rushed outside just as Panther and several of his warriors came running toward her. They ran on past the cabin and positioned themselves along the outer perimeters of the camp.

Breathless, Shanndel went to Panther. "Who are they?" she asked, her voice drawn with fear. She glanced quickly over at her mother, who came and stood beside her, her chin held high, in her eyes a strange excitement.

"It is my people, the Iroquois," Dancing Sky said, then gave Shanndel a reassuring look. "Do not fear them. Iron Nose is no longer the one who leads them. It is someone I know from long ago and she would never come with warring in mind. She has . . . come . . . to find her . . . brother."

"That is Iron Nose's sister?" Shanndel gasped out.

"Yes, that is Princess Bright Star," Dancing Sky said, now aware of Panther listening intently to her. She looked past Shanndel. "You remember her well, do you not, Panther? You know that she is not a woman who would choose warring over peace. She always tried to persuade her brother to become friends with the Shawnee.''

''*Nyoh*, I remember her well,'' Panther said, now gazing at length at the approaching woman, who sat tall and beautiful on the white steed. From afar he had always admired her gentleness and loveliness. But he had known that even if she was a person of peace, she was an enemy to the Shawnee because of the tyrannical ways of her brother.

As Princess Bright Star drew a tight rein a few yards from the waiting Shawnee, Panther slid a protective arm around Shandell's waist.

Everything was quiet as the Shawnee and Iroquois warriors stared at one another. And as the Shawnee people came to stand behind their warriors, their eyes filled with wariness, Princess Bright Star paid no heed to them. She was staring at Dancing Sky.

Her eyes then slid over to Shanndel and she gasped in amazement.

She dismounted and went to stand before Shanndel, then looked questioningly up at Panther. ''Word came to me that your wife Little Sun died during my brother's raid on your people,'' she murmured. ''Yet here she stands at your side. How can that be, Panther? Did she not die after all?''

''*Nyoh*, she died, as well as my unborn child that lay within her womb, as did my beloved mother,'' Panther said icily.

''Then this must be—'' Princess Bright Star began, then stopped and looked in wonder at Dancing Sky.

"Dancing Sky, this is the daughter you took with you that day you asked me to find a safe shelter for the baby girl who was too small and frail to travel with you?"

A hushed gasp washed through the crowd of Shawnee. Panther and Shanndel looked quickly at one another, then Shanndel gave her mother a questioning look.

"You . . . had . . . another . . . daughter?" Shanndel asked, her voice drawn. "I was not the only one? You left a daughter behind? I . . . had . . . a sister and never knew it?"

Dancing Sky's eyes filled with tears. She took Shanndel's hands, yet she couldn't speak. She was filled with sudden grief. She was cold inside, for she was just now realizing that the daughter she'd left behind was dead. Not only that. Her other daughter had been married to Panther!

For a moment longer Dancing Sky couldn't speak, but her remaining daughter was there and needing her. She needed answers.

Dancing Sky had waited too long. Now she was being forced to reveal everything to Shanndel in the presence of many. She wished now that she had done it all in private.

And now it was harder because she knew that her other child was dead! It sent an ache through her heart that she could hardly bear.

"Mother? Tell me what this is all about," Shanndel cried, drawing her mother out of her deep thoughts.

"You were a twin," Dancing Sky said, her voice catching when she saw the wonder and questioning in her daughter's eyes. "And there is much more to this than just that. Let us get Princess Bright Star's reason for being here behind us and then I shall tell you everything. I'm sorry I delayed this long telling you a truth you deserved to know.''

''A twin?'' Shanndel murmured, tears rushing to her eyes. ''Yes, I want to know everything, Mother.''

Shanndel's pulse raced as she cast a quick look at her husband. She now realized why she had looked so familiar to him. His wife had been Shanndel's twin sister!

She was filled with questions, stunned to know that her mother could have held such a truth from her all these years. A sister. She had had a sister. A sister . . . who was now dead and denied to Shanndel forever!

Then another realization hit her, as though someone had poured ice water through her veins. If Shanndel and her twin had been born only a short time after Shanndel's mother had met Edward Burton, oh, Lord, that had to mean that Edward Burton was not Shanndel's father!

She gave her mother another quick, questioning look. She wanted to demand that her mother speak aloud her true father's name!

But, Lord, she was afraid to know.

Oh, surely it was Iron Nose.

He had been her mother's husband when her mother had been pregnant with twins. Surely she had fled him the moment she had discovered that she was pregnant.

To have Iron Nose's blood running through her veins made Shanndel feel sick to her stomach. She swallowed hard and fought the nausea.

She forced herself to stand there attentive at her husband's side while inside she was filled with tumultuous feelings of wonder, of betrayal, and oh, so many other emotions she could not define.

Her father hadn't been her father?

Iron Nose was?

And, a twin?

She had been a twin?

"I have come searching for my brother," Princess Bright Star said, her voice breaking. "He came looking for you, Panther. Did he find you?"

Panther looked guardedly at the many Iroquois warriors and their weapons. If he told the truth about Iron Nose, that he was dead, would the Iroquois lift their weapons against the Shawnee?

Would there be much blood spilled today?

"Panther, your silence tells me what you do not say aloud," Princess Bright Star said, bringing Panther's eyes quickly back to her. "My brother came. My brother died?"

"Your brother came and killed my father," Panther said, his throat tight. "Your brother did even more, which I do not wish to discuss. But I will tell you, Princess Bright Star, since you and I never felt hatred for each other, that your brother is dead. He deserved to die. It was my arrow that downed him."

Panther saw sorrow enter Princess Bright Star's eyes.

Not knowing how else she would react, Panther held himself rigidly erect. He wanted to whisk Rain Singing away and hide her from the viciousness of the Iroquois, but he knew that wasn't possible.

"You have always been a man of good heart," Princess Bright Star said, tears streaming from her eyes.

"So I know that you would see to my brother's proper burial. Please take me to him, Panther. I will return him home so that my people can mourn him, then bury him among his ancestors."

Princess Bright Star swallowed hard. "And I am sorry that my brother came and brought more sadness into your life after having massacred so many of your people," she murmured. "I . . . I . . . do not hate you for returning the fight when you came and killed at my village. I understood too well what drove you to that moment of madness."

"I would have preferred never spilling anyone's blood," Panther said thickly. "It was your brother who could not let peace rest between us. It is good that he is finally dead, for have you not come in peace, Princess Bright Star? Would that have been possible were your brother still alive?"

"I hated that part of him that made him hunger for war," Princess Bright Star said, wiping tears from her eyes. "But I still loved him. He was my brother."

"I will take you to where I left him safely in a tree so that you can be on your way again and return your brother to his proper place among your people," Panther said, gesturing with a wide sweep of a hand for her to walk with him. "Come. Bring your warriors. They can retrieve his body from his resting place high in a tree. Also I will give you a travois for your brother's return home."

Panther waited for her to give her commands to the warriors, then, with Shanndel at his side, led the Iroquois to where he had left Iron Nose's wrapped body.

After Iron Nose's blanket-wrapped bones were resting on the travois, Princess Bright Star knelt down beside her brother's remains and began to wail.

"Let us leave her alone with her brother," Panther said, sliding an arm around Shanndel's waist. "Then the Iroquois will begin their long journey back to their people."

He could sense Shanndel's confusion about the things her mother had told her and knew that this was something they would have to work out between them. *He* was stunned to know that his first wife had been Rain Singing's twin, and that, as a child, she had been left behind.

But he knew that she had been a happy child who had grown into a happy woman and knew that being left by her mother had not harmed her in any way. She certainly had not known who her true father was. She had been raised by an Iroquois family of another band who had taken her in as their own.

When he and Shanndel reached his camp and found Dancing Sky waiting for them, Panther could feel the tension between his wife and her mother and understood. He himself was anxious, now, to know how it had happened that Dancing Sky had left her one daughter behind and had taken the other with her. He was happy about one thing. His wife was a full blood! She was not a breed!

"Come with us, Dancing Sky, to our cabin," Panther said, reaching a hand out for Shanndel's mother. "We will talk."

Dancing Sky nodded and went inside with them. She sat quiet in the rocker before the fireplace as she waited for Shanndel and Panther to sit down with her.

Dancing Sky was envisioning things she had pushed from her mind many years ago. She was recalling how she had dreaded learning that she was with child, for she had never wanted to bear Iron Nose any children. She had worried about his being abusive to them since he took such joy in causing *her* distress!

It had not been a hard decision to leave before he knew she was with child. What *had* been hard was to find a place to go where he would not find her.

Princess Bright Star had been the only one she could confide in. Bright Star was her trusted friend. And Bright Star loathed the way her brother treated his wife. She hated everything ugly about her brother!

"Bright Star and I traveled far from our village to find a place where I could spend my nine months of pregnancy without my husband finding me," Dancing Sky began as Panther and Shanndel sat down on a blanket on the floor. Shanndel rested within Panther's powerful, warm arms, her eyes wide as she gazed at her mother.

"You left Iron Nose when you were pregnant?" Shanndel gasped. "And he never found you? And . . . he . . . is my true father?"

"Yes, he is your father, but I never wanted you to know that," Dancing Sky said softly. "There were friends who took me in at an Iroquois camp you are familiar with, Panther. It was in that very village that your first wife was raised, but not with her true mother."

She gulped and swallowed hard. "Rain Singing, one day, just weeks after your birth, I met Edward Burton, and we fell instantly in love. I knew that I could not take both of my babies with me when he asked me to marry him," she murmured. "Little Sun was weak, sickly and tiny. She would have never lived through the long journey from Upper New York State to Illinois. I had to make a choice that day, one that I knew I would have to live with for the rest of my life. Princess Bright Star had come to help me during the birth. She found a family who promised to care for Little Sun as though she were their own. I now know that they did as promised, for Panther, Little Sun was the woman you married."

"*Nyoh*, she was my beloved wife," Panther said, his voice drawn. "And her very own father killed her on that day of the raid against my people."

"He never knew he had daughters," Dancing Sky said, staring into the dancing flames of the fire. "He only knew that he had lost a wife. He searched, I am certain, until he was exhausted. I was fortunate when he finally gave up that search and left me in peace."

"Did Father—I mean the man I always thought was my father—know about my sister?" Shanndel asked, stunned by all that she had learned today, and hating the knowledge of who her true father was. She had loved Edward Burton. She had always been proud to call *him* "father."

"No. When I met Edward at a trading post near the village, neither of you was with me. Later, I told him only of you and he welcomed you, oh, such a tiny, sweet thing, into his heart as though you were born of our special love," Dancing Sky said, her voice breaking. "It was a secret that I carried with me until today."

She reached over, took Shanndel's hands, and gazed at her with apology. "Darling daughter, of late I have come so close to telling you about your sister," she murmured. "Especially when you became heavy with child. When I see you, I see myself those long years ago when I was pregnant with my two daughters. I get to feeling so guilty over having left one behind. How . . . could . . . I have done it?"

Shanndel broke away from Panther. She went and hugged her mother. "Mother, don't feel guilty over something you did so long ago," she cried. "And you did it because you felt it was the only thing you could do. You said my sister was weak. She *wouldn't* have made the journey. As it was, she was raised to be a happy woman. She . . . even . . . had a chance to fall in love before she died."

She leaned away from her mother and gazed adoringly into her husband's eyes. "I love you so much for having loved and cared for my sister," she murmured. "Thank you for giving her those wonderful moments in your arms."

Amazed at how his wife had the courage and understanding to accept everything in such a wonderfully loving way, Panther drew her into his arms and hugged her. "How could I not have loved her?" he whispered in her ear. "She was an exact replica of you."

Tears flowing from her eyes, Shanndel clung to him. Knowing that her sister had been loved by Panther made her feel close to Little Sun, as though she were with her. She was glad that her mother had finally told her the truth. Shanndel didn't hold it against her that she had chosen to live with a secret that had surely lain heavy on her heart for far too long.

Shanndel leaned away from Panther. She held her

arms out for her mother. When Dancing Sky came to her, sobbing, Shanndel comforted her as her mother had comforted her through the years. "Mother, I love you so much," she murmured, stroking her mother's back. "And I understand. Oh, Mother, I do understand so much now."

Shanndel had never felt so at peace with herself as now when Panther slid his arms around her and her mother, embracing them both with his deep love and devotion.

Yes, things were going to be all right. Life was beautiful and her world would truly be complete when their child was born.

Shanndel smiled to herself when she felt another fluttering kick inside her womb.

Chapter Thirty-seven

"It is time for us to move on," Panther said as he gazed through the cabin window at the planting moon that was high and bright in the sky again.

He turned to Shanndel as she slowly rocked their tiny son in the rocking chair before a slow-burning fire in the fireplace. "My people are becoming too attached to this land and to the life your mother has given them," he said thickly. "It is not good for them to allow themselves to become so comfortable with a life they will not always have. Now is the time. No plants will be planted on your mother's soil this planting moon. The warmer winds are here now. No one will suffer because of the cold."

Shanndel's insides tightened at the thought of leaving this land that had always been her home. She gazed down at her little bundle of joy, who was completely wrapped in a soft blanket except for his face. The thought of such a long, grueling journey for a child this small made her apprehensive.

She thought of how her mother must have felt that day she had left her frail daughter behind to be raised by someone else.

A mother now herself, Shanndel understood to what length a mother would go to protect her young . . . even leave it behind if that assured its life. Shanndel dreaded taking *her* child on a long, difficult journey.

Yet she knew that Panther was right. She knew that it was wrong for his people to get any more used to this easy life when, in truth, a much harder life lay ahead of them.

And then there was her mother. Yes, her mother had adapted well to the change in her own life. She observed Iroquois customs, yet she still lived in the comforts of her large home. Would she be able to make the long journey and sacrifice everything that was now hers?

It would be a time of critical decision-making for her mother, for Shanndel knew how much she loved Standing Horse. Surely she would not want to part from him.

"Wife, you are so quiet," Panther said as he went and knelt down before her on his haunches. His eyes searched hers as she gazed at him.

When he saw how truly concerned she was, he reached up and laid a gentle hand on her cheek. "I know your thoughts," he said softly. "I know your worries. They match so many of my own, yet I cannot put off any longer what must be done."

"I know," Shanndel said. She smiled softly as he took the baby from her arms and unfolded the blanket so that he could have a full view of their son. "Hawke will make the trip just fine, Panther. So will I."

"We will take many long rests while on the journey," Panther said. He looked up at Shanndel. "I will protect you and Hawke with my life."

"And who would not know that?" Shanndel teased, trying to bring some lightheartedness into this serious talk.

"Your mother," Panther said, glancing toward the door, "has known for a long time that we would eventually move on. Do you think she will come with us, or stay?"

"I believe she will follow her heart," Shanndel said softly. "She will not want to say goodbye to Standing Horse."

Panther eased Hawke back into Shanndel's arms, then sat down on the floor before the fire and drew his knees up to hug them with his arms. He gazed into the flames, remembering many times in the past when he had sat beside the fire with his father, speaking of a new life . . . a new home.

It saddened Panther deeply that his father was not alive to see their dreams come to fruition. And it would be hard to leave his bones in earth that belonged to whites, not Shawnee.

But he would not disturb the grave. It was his father's spirit that mattered, and it would follow Panther wherever he would go until the end of time.

A knock on the door surprised both Panther and Shanndel. The hour was late, and everyone would either be already in bed or preparing themselves for their blankets. Panther and Shanndel had been drawn from their bed for Hawke's late feeding.

"Panther? Shanndel? It is I, Dancing Sky," Shanndel's mother said from outside the door. "I have come to tell you something. I would have come earlier but I was involved in council with someone."

"Who would she be meeting with this late?" Shanndel said, questioning Panther with her eyes.

Panther shrugged, then rose to his feet and went and opened the door for Dancing Sky.

Smiling, Dancing Sky stood on tiptoe and brushed a soft kiss across his cheek, then went on inside and sat down on spread blankets before the fire. She looked up at Shanndel with a sparkle in her eyes, yet said nothing.

"Mother, whom were you meeting with tonight so late?" Shanndel asked. Their cabin was on the far side of the camp, facing away from her mother's house, making it impossible for her to see or hear anyone coming or going.

"You know that I have been troubled over living in such grand style while you all are living in simple cabins," Dancing Sky said, looking at Panther as he sat down beside her. Then she looked at Shanndel again. "I sold the house, Rain Singing. Tonight I sold the house *and* land."

Shanndel's lips parted in a slight gasp. "Mother, you sold everything?" she asked.

"I signed an agreement that stated that as long as the Shawnee wish to remain on the land, the man who made the purchase would allow it," Dancing Sky said. "He will only take charge of the house and tobacco fields, as well as the tobacco business, as a whole. And when the Shawnee are ready to travel on to Oklahoma, the money I acquired from the sale of my house and land will be spent for the Shawnee people. Once they are in Oklahoma, they will be able to buy their own land ... not live on a reservation.''

She leaned over and took Shanndel's hand. ''Daughter, does that please you?'' she murmured, then smiled over at Panther. ''My son, does it please you?''

Both Panther and Shanndel were stunned to silence. They looked at each other, then both looked at Dancing Sky again.

''Mother, what you have done is ... is ... such a kind gesture I ... don't ... know what to say,'' Shanndel murmured, touched deeply by her mother's goodness. ''It is so wonderful that you are making provisions for the Shawnee in such a way.''

''Your heart is big and good toward my people,'' Panther said thickly, touched more deeply than he could say. He looked from Dancing Sky to his wife, and then to Dancing Sky again. ''It is with a humble heart that I accept your offer. My people will be forever grateful.''

He drew his hand away and sighed deeply. ''It *is* time for my Shawnee people to move on,'' Panther then said. ''The weather permits it now. And so does their health. There is not one among my people who is ailing now except the elderly who are weakened only naturally by age.''

''When did you make this decision to leave?'' Dancing Sky asked.

''Only a few moments ago, perhaps at the same time you put your name on the paper that sealed the deal with ... with whom, Dancing Sky?'' Panther asked, arching an eyebrow. "You did not say who purchased the land."

"Sheriff Braddock came to my house with an offer too large to refuse," Dancing Sky said, looking guardedly from Panther to Shanndel, tensing when she heard them gasp and saw how they looked at her in disbelief.

"But I turned my nose up at the deal," Dancing Sky blurted out, laughing softly when she saw the quick relief in both Shanndel's and Panther's eyes. "I would not sell that lowdown, heartless bastard anything of mine."

She giggled like a schoolgirl. "You should have seen the rage in his eyes when I gave him a flat 'no,' " she said. "You should have seen him stamp from the house."

She sighed. "Oh, how that pleased me," she said. "He so badly wanted my house and the tobacco fields. He talked often to Edward about wanting to buy it if ever he tired of the tobacco business. Edward only laughed at him, for as long as Edward was alive, he never would have parted with his tobacco fields, no matter how much he was offered for them."

"Then *who*?" Shanndel asked softly.

"Someone who will cherish the land as much as your father," Dancing Sky said softly. "Matt Harbison. Shanndel, you know his wife? She's an English teacher in Harrisburg. They are young. Their children are small. They will be happy with the house and land and will make good use of it."

"Mrs. Harbison," Shanndel said, sighing. "I loved her when she was my English teacher. She is such a sweet, caring person. Yes, Mother, I think it's wonderful that you sold your home to someone as nice as Mrs. Harbison and her family.''

''When are we going to leave for Oklahoma?'' Dancing Sky asked, her eyes dancing. ''Standing Horse and I wish to have a marriage ceremony before we head out on the long journey. I would love to be married here, on land that has been so good to me.''

Shanndel's eyes brightened. ''I think it's wonderful that you are going to marry Standing Horse,'' she murmured, tears shining in her eyes. ''He is such a good man.''

''I will then have had two good men as husbands,'' Dancing Sky said, tears shining in her eyes at the memory of the other man in her life who had meant the world to her.

Her eyes wavered. ''I never think of Iron Nose as having been my husband,'' she said, her voice catching. ''He is a part of my life that was ugly and sad.'' She gazed at the child in Shanndel's arms. ''Had my first husband been as kind and wonderful as my second, I . . . I . . . would have never been forced to leave a daughter behind for someone else to raise.'' She looked quickly up into Shanndel's eyes. ''You would have known your sister and loved her.''

''I think it is time for hot chocolate,'' Panther said, rising quickly from the floor. ''I shall fix us each a cup.''

Shanndel handed over her son to her mother. She joined Panther in the kitchen and helped him prepare the hot drinks.

''Panther, will you have council tomorrow and tell your people we are leaving soon for Oklahoma?''

Shanndelel asked as she took a hot cup of chocolate and set it down beside her mother.

"*Nyoh*, tomorrow," Panther said, taking Hawke from Dancing Sky's arms. He took him to his crib, which sat beside his and Shanndel's bed.

He went back and sat down on the blanket with Shanndel and Dancing Sky and sipped the chocolate, then he set his cup aside and gazed into the flames of the fire. "*Nyoh*, again my people will be on the move," he said. "As it was so long ago when whites came and took from the red man."

He gazed at Shanndel and then Dancing Sky. "There was once a Shawnee named Tecumseh," he said thickly. "When his name was spoken, it was in fearful whispers and bold cries. He brought with him hope *and* fright. Never before or since has an Indian of any tribe been as well known as Tecumseh, and he was not even a chief. He was a *psai-wi-ne-noth-tu*, a great warrior."

He picked up his cup and took another sip of hot chocolate, then set the cup down again and gazed into the fire as Shanndel and Dancing Sky listened, barely breathing. "Tecumseh was a man with a vision, a dream . . . a voice," he said proudly. "His was a voice that caused hearts to swell with pride. He was a phantom presence. Wherever he spoke, large crowds assembled and listened. He fought with all of his might with *words* in an attempt to drive back the white flood that he knew would forever drown the Indians if it was not stopped."

When Panther grew suddenly quiet, Shanndel slid closer to him and placed a hand on his arm. "What happened to him?" she murmured.

His frown and the dark glowering in his eyes was

answer enough for Shanndel. She knew that Tecumseh's words had been stilled, as well as his effort to save all red men.

She would not ask how.

"I must go to Standing Horse," Dancing Sky said, pushing herself up from the blanket. She smiled down at Panther and Shanndel. "I am so excited about everything. I feel like a young girl again who cannot wait for her marriage vows with the man she loves."

Panther and Shanndel smiled and watched her leave, then Shanndel went over to Panther and snuggled against him. "I, too, feel like a young girl with a schoolgirl's first crush," she said, giggling as he swept his arms around her and pressed her down on the blanket with his hard body. "Make love to me, Panther. There won't be many more moments of privacy like this for us. When we leave this cabin—"

He stopped her words as he took her mouth by storm with a fiery, hot kiss. He swept a hand up inside her skirt and caressed her satiny nub, lifting her up on a wave of desire. Then he plunged a finger deep inside her, causing her to arch toward him and moan against his lips.

Shanndel slid her mouth from his. She gazed into his passion-heated eyes. She reached down and caressed him through the buckskin of his breeches as he pressed a finger urgently inside her, making her heart leap with want.

"Take me now," Shanndel whispered, her cheeks hot with excitement. She slid her hand down the front of his breeches, feeling him flinch with pleasure when she wrapped his heat within her fingers. He closed his eyes and let his head fall back with a guttural sigh as her fingers moved seductively over him.

"I want you, Panther," Shanndel said in a husky voice she scarcely recognized. "Oh, how I want you."

He reached for her hand and slid it away from him. Then he shoved down his buckskin breeches and positioned himself fully over her. As he thrust his aching need deep inside her, his mouth covered hers again with sweet passion.

Wild, sensual pleasure leapt through Panther. He felt as though he were moving toward some bright light as he came closer to the ultimate pleasure. That light swam through him as he spent his seed deep inside Shanndel, his body plunging over and over within her as she clung and trembled in her own ecstasy.

Afterward, they sat beside the fire and drank another cup of hot chocolate as their baby slept soundly behind them in his crib.

"Tomorrow our lives will change drastically," Panther said thickly.

"And with your courage, and money to buy new land, we will manage just fine," Shanndel murmured, giving him a reassuring smile.

When the baby began to cry, they smiled at each other, then both went and stood beside the crib. They peered down and would not allow themselves to be afraid for their son.

"We will forever attend to the care of our son and all children who come later so that they may live in comfort and peace," Panther said thickly. "*Moneto* will make all good things happen for our children. When one listens to the teachings of the Great Spirit, one is happy . . . one is blessed! That is how it will be for our children and their children!''

Shanndel looked adoringly up at Panther. "I know that all you wish for our children will come to pass, for *you* are their father,'' she said, shivering sensually when he covered her mouth with a sweet, quivering kiss.

Dear Reader:

I hope you have enjoyed reading *Savage Joy*. The next book in my *Savage* series, which I write exclusively for Leisure Books, is *Savage Fires*. *Savage Fires* is an exciting book about the Ottawa Indians of Michigan. It will be in the stores six months from the release date of *Savage Joy*. This book is filled with much emotion, passion, and adventure. I hope you will read it and enjoy it.

For those of you who are collecting the books in my *Savage* Indian series, and want to read about the backlist and my future books, please send a legal-sized, self-addressed, stamped envelope to the following address for my latest newsletter and bookmark:

CASSIE EDWARDS
6709 North Country Club Road
Mattoon, IL 61938

Thank you for your support of my books. I truly appreciate it!

Always,
Cassie Edwards

"Lovers of Indian romance have a special place on their bookshelves for Madeline Baker!"
—*Romantic Times*

Ruthless and cunning, Ryder Fallon can deal cards and death in the same breath. Yet when the Indians take him prisoner, he is in danger of being sent to the devil—until a green-eyed angel saves his life.

For two long years, Jenny Braedon has prayed for someone to rescue her from the heathen savages who enslaved her. And even if Ryder is a half-breed, she'll help him in exchange for her freedom. But unknown perils and desires await the determined beauty in his strong arms, sweeping them both from a world of tortured agony to love's sweet paradise.

_3742-4 $5.99 US/$6.99 CAN

SAVAGE LONGINGS

CASSIE EDWARDS

"Cassie Edwards is a shining talent!"
—*Romantic Times*

Having been kidnapped by vicious trappers, Snow Deer despairs of ever seeing her people again. Then, from out of the Kansas wilderness comes Charles Cline to rescue the Indian maiden. Strong yet gentle, brave yet tenderhearted, the virile blacksmith is everything Snow Deer desires in a man. And beneath the fierce sun, she burns to succumb to the sweet temptation of his kiss. But the strong-willed Cheyenne princess is torn between the duty that demands she stay with her tribesmen and the passion that promises her unending happiness among white settlers. Only the love in her heart and the courage in her soul can convince Snow Deer that her destiny lies with Charles—and the blissful fulfillment of their savage longings.

_4176-6 $5.99 US/$6.99 CAN

CASSIE EDWARDS

TOUCH THE WILD WIND

Alone and penniless, Sasha Seymour has thrown in her lot with a rough bunch, and she is bound for an even rougher destination—the Australian Outback, where she and her jackaroos hope to carve a sheep station from the vast, untamed wilderness. All that stands between her and the primitive forces of man and nature is the raw strength and courage of her partner—Ashton York. In his tawny arms she finds a haven from the raging storm, and in the tender fury of his kisses, a paradise of love.

____52211-X $5.50 US/$6.50 CAN

SAVAGE SPIRIT

CASSIE EDWARDS

**Winner of the *Romantic Times*
Lifetime Achievement Award for Best Indian Series!**

Life in the Arizona Territory has prepared Alicia Cline to expect the unexpected. Brash and reckless, she dares to take on renegades and bandidos. But the warm caresses and soft words of an Apache chieftain threaten her vulnerable heart more than any burning lance.

Chief Cloud Eagle has tamed the wild beasts of his land, yet one glimpse of Alicia makes him a slave to desire. Her snow-white skin makes him tremble with longing; her flame-red hair sets his senses ablaze. Cloud Eagle wants nothing more than to lie with her in his tepee, nothing less than to lose himself in her unending beauty. But to claim Alicia, the mighty warrior will first have to capture her bold savage spirit.

_3639-8 $4.99 US/$5.99 CAN

SAVAGE TEARS

CASSIE EDWARDS

Bestselling author of *Savage Longings*

Long has Marjorie Zimmerman been fascinated by the Dakota Indians of the Minnesota Territory—especially their hot-blooded chieftain. With the merest glance from his smoldering eyes, Spotted Horse can spark a firestorm of desire in the spirited settler's heart. Then he steals like a shadow in the night to rescue Marjorie from her hated stepfather, and she aches to surrender to the proud warrior body and soul. But even as they ride to safety, enemies— both Indian and white—prepare to make their passion as fleeting as the moonlight shining down from the heavens. Soon Marjorie and Spotted Horse realize that they will have to fight with all their cunning, strength, and valor, or they will end up with nothing more than savage tears.

___4281-9 $5.99 US/$6.99 CAN